麥禾陽光 Sun&Wheat

一個溫暖、高質感、充滿趣味的閱讀環境,
帶給讀者一個全然不同的學習感受。

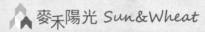

麥禾陽光 Sun&Wheat

一個溫暖、高質感、充滿趣味的閱讀環境，
帶給讀者一個全然不同的學習感受。

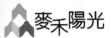
麥禾陽光

NEW TOEIC 黃金戰鬥力

一個月掌握商用必備單字及考試技巧，目標 990

附MP3

閱讀篇

Tactics for NEW TOEIC Reading Test

專為 **上班族、忙碌的你** 所設計的 **新多益考用書籍**

《 **必備商用單字30天 + Speed Reading** 》
+精選模擬試題兩回完整版大解析

黃金陣容帶你複習、教你解題，打造你的黃金戰鬥力！

徐維克 & 麥禾陽光編輯部 ◎著

如何利用每天只有一點點的時間來好好準備新多益考試？本書8大特色，教你輕鬆準備、開心應考去！

Feature-1 專業編寫團隊，全新試題、深入核心 　Feature-5 靈活運用瑣碎時間，掌握必備文法重點

Feature-2 必備300商用字彙，訓練耳力超easy 　Feature-6 模擬實戰warm-up，加強演練應考去

Feature-3 獨家Speed Reading，加深記憶100% 　Feature-7 聰明掌握學習進度，自主管理效率100%

Feature-4 試題難易分級，專家深入、詳盡的解題內容 　Feature-8 四國口音實錄MP3，聽力訓練一片搞定

作者序

　　目前，針對英文語言的測驗非常多，常見的有托福、雅思、多益、全民英撿等。托福和雅思屬於國外留學的認證，因此難度比較高，內容範圍較廣。而多益和全民英撿則是較生活化的內容，尤其是多益主要針對職場或商用的英文，意用性更高，而且也是全球性的測驗。

　　多益測驗的單字和文法都非常的意用及生活化，所以準備多益測驗，不僅僅是努力獲得一項認證而已，在準備的過程中，更是充意自己英文能力的好方法。透過準備多益測驗得到證書，除了提升自己在職場上的競爭力，還可以真正提高意用英文的能力，是不是一舉兩得呢！

　　雖然多益測驗的單字比較生活面，但是所有的語言測驗準備要領都不能忘記最重要的一點：多背單字。單字量愈多，在面對各種題目的時候，「猜測」的情況就會減低，如此更能提高答對的機率！

　　除此之外，多多練習模擬試題也非常重要，練習的過程中可以背更多單字以及複習文法，而且還能夠熟悉多益測驗的各種題型，知道自己哪些題型比較擅長、哪些題型的作答時間太長、還有各種題型的解題技巧。而且模擬試題可以幫助我們減低陌生感，到了真正的考場就不至於太緊張囉！

　　本書針對多益測驗的閱讀部分，仔細說明不同題型在作答時，應該掌握什麼原則，可以透過各種方式來解題。也附上一份完整的全真模擬試題，各位透過反覆練習，一定可以達到見題即答、百題百中的境界！

徐維克

編者序

　　相信大家對多益並不陌生，只要你擁有了多益證書（特別是金色的那張），不管是新鮮人求職或是社會人士面對轉職之際，都會發現有了這張英語認證，就像是為你的英語能力背書，拉抬你的競爭力，讓你在一堆求職者中脫穎而出。

　　多益考試是個全球性的考試，特別針對母語非英語的人士所設計，主要是在測試應試者在職場上的英語溝通能力，每個月都有多益測試，也就是說應試者可以依自己的工作安排、課業狀況來選擇比較適合自己的考試時間，應考後，可依自己所得到的分數獲得證書，對許多應試者來說真的很方便，所以目前考多益的人也就愈來愈多。

　　有鑑於此，我們特別設計了《NEW TOEIC 黃金戰鬥力—閱讀篇》與《NEW TOEIC 黃金戰鬥力—聽力篇》，希望能幫助有計畫參加多益考試的讀者，能夠在<u>最短的時間</u>、用<u>最有效率</u>的學習方式來準備考試。我們請到對多益考試相當熟悉且有研究的作者群，進行試題的編寫與分析，並加入必備高用300字，以每天學習10個單字與例句，搭配speed reading以加強

學習效果，在這個部份更附上MP3，讓讀者能挑選最方便的方式來學習與複習。

在試題解析的部份，利用題目當中所遇到的文法，加入「瑣碎時間看這裡」的單元，旨在幫助讀者能利用一兩分鐘的時間快速瀏覽文法重點，無需特意去背文法書的內容，積少成多，這就是滿分990的致勝關鍵！

當然，書中也提供多益相關的資訊及應考小物，像是學習進度表、單字確認單(word list)、單字小卡(word card)等等，讓讀者利用這一本書就能準備好多益測驗，並隨時記錄下屬於自己的應試重點辭彙，以從容、輕鬆的態度來面對多益測驗，相信這樣一定會在多益測驗中獲得好成績，祝福大家都能擁有黃金戰鬥力，信心滿滿應考去！

麥禾陽光　總編輯
Estelle Chen

目　錄

Chapter 1　　商用單字一把抓

使用說明

全書共分為 4 chapter，在最前面的部份有提供我的學習進度表以及NEW TOEIC 簡介，讀者可了解多益考試的題型及方向，並將每日的學習進度做記錄，讓學習成果能夠一目瞭然。

Chapter 1 總共包含 300 個實用的商用單字，總共分成 30 個小單元(Day 1~30)，每天都可以學習到 10 個單字與例句，附四國口音的錄音內容，不僅用看的，也可以用聽的和說的來學習，除了幫助單字記憶之外，也為聽力測驗打底。

在單字下方搭配一個段落短文，此部份內容也有附上錄音檔，建議可先試著填入空格的單字，再利用 MP3 及P107-112的Answer Key 來對答案，然後就可跟著 MP3 一起練習朗讀，段落下方有3個時鐘記錄小框框，這是讓讀者記錄下每一次念一整個段落短文的時間，當你愈來愈熟悉，你所花費的時間就會愈來愈短，這不但可以訓練你對單字的熟悉度，也能訓練你的口語及聽力哦！目標一分鐘，大家加油！！

Chapter 2 是一回完整的閱讀測驗內容，總共 100 題，依序為單句填空、短文填空以及文章理解（單篇&雙篇）。此章節重點在於熟悉各大題考試的題型，並跟著作者的講解，一步步征服多益考題。

每一題的後方都會以 * 號標示該題的難易度，接著在題目的下方會有題目中譯與解答提示，讀者可以先小試身手後，馬上做檢討。有些在題目中出現比較重要的文法重點，作者會在瑣碎時間看這裡多做補充，這樣可以馬上抓住重點，不需再另外去找文法書來補充文法概念，能充份利用瑣碎時間，不但提高學習效率，也方便在考前能夠翻閱文法重點作複習之用。

Chapter 3 是一回完整的模擬試題，讀者可以在此部份做練習，看看自己的實力，還有哪裡需要再做加強的，最重要的是，可以測驗看看自己是否能在限定的時間內完成閱讀測驗。

Chapter 4 是 Chapter 3 的模擬試題的解答與解析，在這裡同樣以 Chapter 2 的方式來做檢討，讀者不需前翻後翻，可以直接清楚看到自己錯在哪裡，立即看，立刻記，這樣才會有效率！

附錄一 有完整動詞時態表格，如果對英文時態還不熟悉的你，可以藉由這個表格來做個 quick review。

附錄二 將常用的動詞整理列表，附上動詞三態（原形 / 過去式 / 過去分詞）及中譯，另外針對不規則動詞變化的部份，也以套色的方式呈現，提醒讀者要多留意！

附錄三 將 Chapter 1 的單字以字母順序排列，除了當索引之外，在每個單字前面都有一個小方框，也可以當作是 checklist，如果背起來的單字，就可以開心的打個勾，一定超有成就感的！

附錄四 將 Day 1~30 的單字做成字卡的方式，方便讀者隨身攜帶，可以利用等車、等吃飯的幾分鐘背背單字，善用時間就是成功的最大關鍵。

 我的學習進度表

日期	複習進度	完成度	錯誤題數	備註
/				
/				
/				
/				
/				
/				
/				
/				
/				
/				

日期	複習進度	完成度	錯誤題數	備註
/				
/				
/				
/				
/				
/				
/				
/				
/				
/				
/				
/				
/				
/				

日期	複習進度	完成度	錯誤題數	備註
/				
/				
/				
/				
/				
/				
/				
/				
/				
/				
/				
/				
/				

新多益測驗是全球最大的職場與英語學習能力認證測驗，也是國際間認可的英語能力檢測，試題的設計以職場的需求為主要的考量，題材多元化，各個職場會發生的狀況，從一般商務內容（合約、行銷、會議）到人事、採購、旅遊、娛樂等等，通通都有，涵蓋種類繁多。

多益測驗包含聽力和閱讀兩大項，總共200題，皆為單選，不倒扣，兩項測驗分開計時：

	時間	45 分鐘		
聽力測驗	題型	第一大題：照片描述	10題	4選1
		第二大題：應答問題	30題	3選1
		第三大題：簡短對話	30題	4選1
		第四大題：簡短獨白	30題	4選1

	時間	75 分鐘		
閱讀測驗	題型	第五大題：單句填空	40題	4選1
		第六大題：短文填空	12題	4選1
		第七大題（1）：單篇文章理解	28題	4選1
		第七大題（2）：雙篇文章理解	20題	4選1

　　考生要留意的是，所有聽力的題目只會念一次，所以要盡可能在45分鐘的測驗時間內專心，有時間的話，不妨看看接下來的圖片或是選項，減短自己應答時的反應時間，這樣答題會更有效率。閱讀測驗的部份，總共有75分鐘，要記得掌握好答題的速度，如果真的遇到不會的，就先跳過，避免影響到後面題目的作答，盡量將時間留在雙篇文章理解的部份，因為這個部份需看完兩篇文章段落，才能回答接下來的5個閱讀理解題目，所以需要耗費比較多的時間。

　　考生利用鉛筆在電腦答案卷上作答。每一大類的答對題數會轉換成分數(5~495分)，聽力和閱讀的得分加總即為總分。考生在參加測驗日期的兩年內都可申請，證書上會列出聽力和閱讀的成績和總分，依成績可分成以下五個等級：

- 金色證書　　860~990　　分
- 藍色證書　　730~855　　分
- 綠色證書　　470~725　　分
- 咖啡色證書　220~465　　分
- 橘色證書　　20~215　　　分

Chapter 1
商用單字一把抓

Day 1 | conference ~ consider

Vocabulary 🎧 track 01

1. conference *n.[C]* 會議 📖 meeting, convention
   🔵 The conference was about the latest advances in nuclear medicine.
   這場會議是關於核醫學最新的進展。

2. agreement *n.[U]* 同意;一致 📕 disagreement, conflict
   🔵 We are in agreement to share our information, making it easier to get the project done.
   我們同意分享我們的資訊,使得完成此項專案更為容易。

3. arrangement *n.[C]* 安排
   🔵 We have an arrangement that is fair and takes into account everyone's viewpoint.
   我們有個公平的安排,而且把每個人的觀點都考量進來。

4. feedback *n.[U]* 回饋;反饋 📖 comment
   🔵 Can you give me some feedback on how I'm doing?
   你能夠給我一些回饋,看看我做得怎麼樣嗎?

5. assure *vt.* 保證;確保 📖 confirm, guarantee
   🔵 He assured me that I was doing fine and would need no further training.
   他向我保證我做得很好,而且不需要更多的訓練。

6. attend *vt.* 參加;出席 📖 be present 📕 be absent
   🔵 I want to attend your high school graduation, as you are one of my favorite cousins.
   我想要出席你的高中畢業典禮,因為你是我最喜歡的表哥之一。

7. **cancel** *vt.* 取消   回 repeal
    ● I have to cancel my doctor appointment because my car is broken.
    我必須取消醫生約診，因為我的車子壞掉了。

8. **competition** *n.[C,U]* 競爭   回 tourment
    ● The competition between the teams is very close, and we expect the results to demonstrate that.
    團體間的競爭非常接近，我們預料結果會這樣顯示。

9. **consequence** *n.[C]* 結果；後果   回 result, outcome   反 cause
    ● The consequence of cheating is a failing grade and shame for your family.
    作弊的後果是成績不及格，而且讓你的家人蒙羞。

10. **consider** *vt.* 考慮；考量   回 ponder, think, deliberate
                                   反 disregard, neglect
    ● I want you to consider me for the new position, as I have most of the skills you require.
    我想要您考慮我在這個新職位上，因為我擁有多數您要求的技能。

Paragraph 🎧 track 02

練習說明：

Step 1 下方有10個單字，請依文意將10個單字填入適當的空格中。

Step 2 播放MP3，確認填入答案是否正確，或可翻至P107-112對答案。

Step 3 請跟著MP3逐句練習，練習完畢，請自己將下列段落念出，並在段落下方的時鐘記錄下時間。

agreement arrangement consequence attend assure
conference cancel feedback competition consider

We had a 1 _____ in Taoyuan last weekend. It was an 2 _____ to enable us to focus on our company's 3 _____ . I was going to 4 _____ with my boss, but she had to 5 _____ . A client had to see her on short notice. We made an 6 _____ that I would keep careful notes for her. I 7 _____ her that I would give her 8 _____ afterwards, so she will know what we learned. As a 9 _____ , I will be in a position to help her greatly. I am going to have to carefully 10 _____ what I tell her, so that our company will benefit from this meeting.

我們上個週末在桃園有場會議。這個安排是讓我們能夠專注在公司的競爭。我要和我的老闆一起出席,但她必須要取消。忽然有一位客戶必須要見她。我們同意我會替她仔細地做筆記。我向她保證我之後會提供她回饋,所以她就會知道我們學習的內容。結果會是,我將處在對她幫助極大的位置上。我將必須仔細地考慮轉達她的內容,如此我們的公司將能夠從這場會議中獲益。

Speed Reading

1 　分　　秒

2 　分　　秒

3 　分　　秒

Day 2 　 convince ~ seminar

Vocabulary 🎧 track 03

1. **convince** *vt.* 說服　圓 persuade
   ● You must convince him to use us for his assembly needs.
   你必須說服他運用我們在他的組裝需求上。

2. **marketing** *n.[U]* 行銷
   ● The marketing department isn't doing its job on this product line.
   行銷部門在這條產品線上並沒有做好自己的工作。

3. **determine** *vt.* 決定　圓 decide
   ● We have to determine the best way to get them to see our side of the problem.
   我們必須決定出最好的方式，讓他們得以看到我們這邊的問題。

4. **opportunity** *n.[C]* 機會　圓 chance, occasion
   ● This is a golden opportunity to further my career, and I intend to jump on it.
   這是一個提昇我的職涯難得的機會，而我決意要把握它。

5. **improve** *vt.* 改進　圓 ameliorate, enhance　圖 decline
   ● We have to improve the on-time performance of that division.
   我們必須改進那個部門的準時表現。

6. **withhold** *vt.* 抑制；保留　圓 keep, reserve　圖 release
   ● The government will withhold that amount from your check.
   政府將從你的支票中扣留住那筆金額。

7. **negotiate** *vt.* 談判；協商　回 arrange, settle
   ◉ You can try to negotiate with them, but I don't think they will budge.
   你可以試著和他們協商，但我不認為他們會改變意見。

8. **notify** *vt.* 通知；報告　回 inform, report　反 conceal, hide
   ◉ You must notify the manager one month ahead of time for time off requests.
   針對於請假的請求，你必須在一個月前通知經理。

9. **assist** *vt.* 協助；幫助　回 support, cooperate
   ◉ This division will try to assist you in any way we can.
   這個部門將會盡力協助您，用任何我們可行的方式。

10. **seminar** *n.[C]* 專題討論會
    ◉ The seminar lasted well into the night, and we accomplished a lot.
    這場專題討論會持續到晚上，而我們達成了多項結論。

Paragraph 🎧 track 04

練習說明：

Step 1 下方有10個單字，請依文意將10個單字填入適當的空格中。
Step 2 播放MP3，確認填入答案是否正確，或可翻至P107-112對答案。
Step 3 請跟著MP3逐句練習，練習完畢，請自己將下列段落念出，並在段落下方的時鐘記錄下時間。

assist opportunity determine improve marketing
notify seminar withhold convince negotiate

_____1_____ is going to start the new campaign next week. We think this is a great _____2_____ to _____3_____ our sales. We must _____4_____ how many resources we will use to _____5_____ them in increasing profits. We will have a _____6_____ concerning this on Friday. Please _____7_____ me if you are unable to attend. Be ready to add your opinions, and don't _____8_____ any ideas you have that may help. We can _____9_____ time off for those who need it, but you will have to _____10_____ us that it is really necessary. We look forward to your attendance on Friday.

　　行銷在下個星期將開啟這場新的活動。我們認為這是個絕佳的機會來提升我們的銷售量。我們必須決定我們將要使用多少資源來協助他們，以增加獲利。關於這點，在星期五我們將舉行專題討論會。請通知我如果你無法出席。請準備加入你的意見，不要保留你任何可能有幫助的想法。我們可以協調出補休給需要的人，但你必須說服我們那是有必要的。我們期待星期五你的出席。

Speed Reading

1 　分　　秒
2 　分　　秒
3 　分　　秒

Day 3 | librarian ~ coordinate

Vocabulary track 05

1. **librarian** *n.[C]* 圖書館員
   - She is a reference librarian at the county library.
   她是縣立圖書館的諮詢圖書館員。

2. **pharmacist** *n.[C]* 藥師；藥商 圖 druggist
   - Our pharmacists work weekends and holidays on a rotating basis.
   我們的藥師在週末及假日輪值上班。

3. **profession** *n.[C]* 職業 圖 career, occupation
   - I don't enjoy my job, but finding a new profession would be tedious and expensive.
   我不喜歡我的工作，但是尋找一個新的職業很漫長，且代價很高。

4. **operator** *n.[C]* 接線生；操作者 圖 operant
   - You used to have to contact the operator to make a long-distance call.
   你以前必須聯繫接線人員來打長途電話。

5. **secretary** *n. [C]* 祕書
   - She is the executive secretary for our firm, accepting great responsibility for company operations.
   她是我們公司的執行祕書，承接公司執行的極大責任。

6. **factory** *n.[C]* 工廠 圖 plant
   - I worked in a factory when I was younger, but it closed and relocated to China.
   當我年輕時我在一間工廠工作，但後來它關掉並移到中國了。

7. **employment** *n.[U]* 僱用；受雇；職業；工作   圆 unemployment
    ● The employment rate for the country is at its highest level since the great recession.
    自從經濟大蕭條之後，目前這個國家的就業率是最高的。

8. **produce** *vt.* 生產   圖 make
    ● They can't produce parts quickly enough to satisfy our production demands.
    他們生產零件的速度無法滿足我們的生產需求。

9. **manufacture** *vt.* 製造
    ● We used to manufacture all the parts for our products, but we now rely on suppliers for some components.
    我們以前製造我們產品的所有零件，但我們現在某些零件依賴供應商。

10. **coordinate** *vt.* 協調
    ● He has to coordinate the efforts of several company divisions to finish this project.
    他必須協調數個公司部門的努力成果來完成這項專案。

Paragraph   🎧 track 06

練習說明：

Step 1 下方有10個單字，請依文意將10個單字填入適當的空格中。

Step 2 播放MP3，確認填入答案是否正確，或可翻至P107-112對答案。

Step 3 請跟著MP3逐句練習，練習完畢，請自己將下列段落念出，並在段落下方的時鐘記錄下時間。

> produce librarian factory profession manufacture
> pharmacist employment secretary operator coordinate

When I was young, I wanted to be either a 1 _____ or a 2 _____ . I grew up, though, and decided that neither one would make a good 3 _____ for me. I wanted to be in a company that 4 _____ things. I started in a 5 _____ that made typewriters, but we didn't 6 _____ any after everyone acquired a computer. My 7 _____ opportunities were better if I relocated, so I moved here. I have an excellent staff, including a 8 _____ who can 9 _____ the entire office staff. I'm now known as a smooth project 10 _____ , and this wouldn't have been possible if I hadn't moved out of Taiwan.

當我年輕時，我想要當一名藥師或圖書館員。然而，我長大後，決定兩者對我而言，都不是個合適的職業。我想要在一家製造產品的公司裡。我開始在一家製造打字機的工廠工作，但是在每個人都有電腦之後，我們再也不生產了。如果我換個地方的話，我的職業機遇會更好，所以我搬到這裡。我現在有優秀的員工，包括一位祕書，她能夠協調全辦公室的職員。現在大家都稱我是一名處事圓滑的專業執行者，而如果我沒有搬離台灣的話，這一切都不可能發生。

Speed Reading

1　分　　秒

2　分　　秒

3　分　　秒

Day 4 | transform ~ employee

Vocabulary 🎧 track 07

1. **transform** *vt.* 使改變；使轉變　回 change, convert　反 preserve
   ● He transformed his yard into a wonderful garden for outside living.
   為了室外生活景觀，他把他的院子改成一座美好的花園。

2. **attorney** *n.[C]* 律師　回 lawyer, counsel
   ● Not all attorneys are dishonest, as he showed when he sensitively handled our case.
   並不是所有的律師都不誠實，就像他細心地處理我們的案子時所表現的。

3. **manipulate** *vt.* 利用；操縱（市場的漲落等）　回 use, handle
   ● We have to manipulate the market to get our stock price higher than last year.
   我們必須利用市場來使我們的股票價格比去年更高。

4. **representative** *n.[C]* 代表　回 agent
   ● He is the leading representative of our company in Thailand.
   他是我們公司在泰國的主要代表。

5. **assistant** *n.[C]* 助理　回 helper
   ● She is more than an assistant, as she takes the lead on many projects.
   她不只是一名助理，因為她在許多專案都扮演帶頭的角色。

6. **architect** *n.[C]* 建築師；設計師　回 builder, designer
   ● We hired an architect for the new building, but we decided on our own in-house design instead.
   我們聘請了一名建築師來設計新大樓，但我們還是決定使用我們自己內部的設計。

Chapter 1 商用單字一把抓

7. **agricultural** *adj.* 農業的
   - This was an agricultural region before the farmers all sold out to manufacturing interests.
   在所有的農夫為了製造的利益賣光土地之前，這裡是農業地區。

8. **department** *n.[C]* 部門　▣ division, section
   - My department is the worst-organized in the company, and that's saying something.
   我的部門是全公司最沒有組織的，這說明了某些事。

9. **employer** *n.[C]* 僱主　▣ boss
   - He is not only the best employer in town, but his products are the most well-known.
   他不只是鎮上最好的僱主，他的產品也是最有名的。

10. **employee** *n.[C]* 員工　▣ worker, staff
    - This firm has 3,000 employees, so of course not all of them are going to be happy with their jobs.
    這間公司有三千名員工，所以當然不是所有人都對自己的工作感到滿意。

Paragraph 🎧 track 08

練習說明：

Step 1　下方有10個單字，請依文意將10個單字填入適當的空格中。

Step 2　播放MP3，確認填入答案是否正確，或可翻至P107-112對答案。

Step 3　請跟著MP3逐句練習，練習完畢，請自己將下列段落念出，並在段落下方的時鐘記錄下時間。

employer manipulate employee attorney architect representative agricultural department transform assistant

My 1 _____ was not being nice or fair to his 2 _____. He tried to 3 _____ us into doing unlawful things. We decided to hire an 4 _____ to further our legal claims against him. The attorney's 5 _____ was the 6 _____ of a plan to find a 7 _____ in each 8 _____ to testify against our boss. I think the boss thought this was still an 9 _____ economy, and that he could do anything he wanted as boss. We 10 _____ his thinking, and now it's a good place to work.

我的僱主對待員工不和善也不公平。他試著利用我們做違法的事。我們決定聘請一位律師來促成我們對他在法律上的請求權。律師的助理擔任設計師的角色，設計一個計畫，在各部門找一名代表，作證指控我們的老闆。我想老闆還以為現在仍然是農業經濟，他身為老闆能夠為所欲為。我們改變了他的想法，而現在這變成一個好的工作場所。

Speed Reading

1 分 秒

2 分 秒

3 分 秒

Day 5　capital ~ assume

Vocabulary 🎧 track 09

1. capital　*n.[U]* 資金；本錢　同 funds
   🔹 The initial capital raised to start the company was 230 billion dollars.
   一開始籌募設立這家公司的資金是兩兆三千億元。

2. risk　*n.[C]* 風險　*vt.* 冒險　同 chance, venture　反 safety
   🔹 You have to take risks if you are going to succeed in the marketplace.
   你必須冒險，如果你要在市場上成功的話。

3. confidence　*n.[U]* 信心　同 faith, trust　反 doubt
   🔹 We have every confidence that she will be a great leader as CEO.
   我們非常有信心她擔任執行長將成為一位傑出的領導者。

4. reduce　*vt.* 減少　同 decrease　反 increase
   🔹 In order to reduce waste, we are implementing new auditing procedures.
   為了減少浪費，我們正在實施新的審計程序。

5. audit　*n.[C]* 審計；查帳　同 examination, check
   🔹 During the tax department audit, I recommend you have your attorney present.
   在稅務部門的查帳當中，我建議你的律師在旁。

6. accounting　*n.[U]* 會計
   🔹 He is very good at creative accounting, making the profits seem less than they really are.
   他非常擅長於創造性會計，讓獲利看起來比實際的要少。

7. **accumulate** *vt.* 累積　同 increase, mass　反 spend
   - We are going to pay a dividend on our stocks, rather than accumulating cash.
   我們將發放股票股利，而非累積現金。

8. **aggressive** *adj.* 進取的；有幹勁的
   - She is an aggressive leader, the type that this company desires to bring us into the immediate future and beyond.
   她是一位非常有幹勁的領導者，這類型正好是這家公司希望，能帶領我們迎向近期的未來與更長遠的將來。

9. **asset** *n.[C]* 資產　同 property
   - We have many assets accumulated through the years, but our most precious one is our dedicated employees.
   這些年來，我們累積了許多資產，但我們最珍貴的資產是盡心盡力的員工。

10. **assume** *vt.* 假設；假定　同 suppose　反 conclude
    - You can't assume that the public will embrace our products simply because they have done so in the past.
    你不能假設說，大眾會樂於接受我們的產品，只因為他們以前都接受。

Paragraph 🎧 track 10

練習說明：

Step 1 下方有10個單字，請依文意將10個單字填入適當的空格中。

Step 2 播放MP3，確認填入答案是否正確，或可翻至P107-112對答案。

Step 3 請跟著MP3逐句練習，練習完畢，請自己將下列段落念出，並在段落下方的時鐘記錄下時間。

asset accounting accumulate risk assume
reduce aggressive audit confidence capital

Our 1   department is researching company 2   that have been 3   in recent years. This will allow us to see how we can spend 4   on new projects and acquisitions. We 5   that we are in a good financial position and do not need to 6   spending. This 7   will confirm our ability to be 8   in the purchase of new companies. We have 9   that we can be 10   -takers, so we can become the preeminent company in our field.

　　我們的會計部門正在研究公司近年來所累積的資產。這將使我們得以了解我們可以如何花費資金，在新的專案及支出上。我們想，我們的財務狀況很好，並不需要縮減支出。這次查帳將會證實我們的能力，是否可以積極地併購新的公司。我們有信心，我們能夠承擔風險，所以我們能成為這個領域卓越的公司。

Day 6 　revenue ~ mortgage

Vocabulary 🎧 track 11

1. **revenue** *n.[C]* 收入　📖 income, profit　🔄 debt, payment
   - Blue Jay Widgets, Inc. saw increased revenues of 14%, yet profits remained steady.
   Blue Jay Widgets公司的收入增加14%，而獲利維持穩定。

2. **balance** *n.[C], vt.* 平衡　📖 equivalence　🔄 unbalance
   - They have to learn to balance their work and domestic lives, for the good of their families.
   他們必須學會平衡工作和家居生活，為了他們的家庭而著想。

3. **invest** *vt.* 投資　📖 stake
   - If you invest those funds, you will most likely receive much greater income than if you leave them sitting in the bank.
   如果你投資那些資金，和你把它們放在銀行相比，將最可能獲得較大的收益。

4. **calculate** *vt.* 計算；估計　📖 compute
   - Please calculate the amount of overtime necessary to bring the project to fruition.
   請計算完成這項專案所需的加班時數。

5. **anticipate** *vt.* 預期；預測　📖 predict, foresee
   - We try to anticipate the trends of the market, but it's sometimes impossible to predict the impact of new products.
   我們試著預測市場的趨勢，但有時候預測新產品的影響是不太可能的。

6. **penalty** *n.[C]* 處罰；罰款　📖 fine, punishment　🔄 reward
   - They paid a penalty of 40 million dollars when found guilty of insider

trading.

當內線交易被判有罪時，他們付了四千萬元的罰款。

7. **foreign exchange** 外匯
   ◌ The foreign exchange market is a large part of the business community in Hong Kong.
   外匯市場是香港的商業界很大的一部分。

8. **dividend** *n.[C]* 股息；紅利　⬚ bonus
   ◌ They announced that, due to the decreased sales and profits in the recessionary economy, they would not pay a dividend this year.
   他們宣布，因為經濟衰退的銷量和獲利減少，他們今年將不發放股息。

9. **fluctuate** *vi.* 波動；變動　⬚ vacillate　⬚ remain
   ◌ The rate has fluctuated between 3.5 and 4 percent for most of the past three years, but is expected to rise in the coming year.
   利率在過去三年大多在3.5%到4%之間波動，但來年預計將會上揚。

10. **mortgage** *n.[C]* 抵押
    ◌ We have a mortgage against the house, but we have no other real family debt, so we are in a good position to invest our income.
    我們房子有抵押，但我們並沒有其他真正的家庭負債，所以我們很適合投資我們的收入。

Paragraph 🎧 track 12

練習說明：

Step 1 下方有10個單字，請依文意將10個單字填入適當的空格中。

Step 2 播放MP3，確認填入答案是否正確，或可翻至 P107-112對答案。

Step 3 請跟著MP3逐句練習，練習完畢，請自己將下列段落念出，並在段落下方的時鐘記錄下時間。

mortgage balance invest penalty fluctuate
revenue dividend anticipate foreign exchange

The 1 _____ market was hit hard by the recession. Many banks had 2 _____ heavily in real estate loans and hadn't 3 _____ their portfolios. Their incomes 4 _____ greatly because of this, and many are now paying the 5 _____ for this lack of diversity. Many banks have not paid 6 _____ for several years, and we don't anticipate good 7 _____ statements from them this year, either. Our 8 _____ 9 _____ market has taken a hit, too. There isn't as much money floating around as there was five years ago. We 10 _____ that our yearly income won't grow for another two years, at least.

抵押市場受到景氣蕭條嚴重的影響。許多銀行大量投資在房地產借貸，而沒有平衡投資組合。因此，他們的收入劇烈波動，而許多銀行現在正為了這種缺乏多元性而自食惡果。許多銀行已經數年未發放紅利，而我們今年也不預期他們會有良好的收入報表。我們的外匯市場也深受打擊。現在和五年前相比，已經沒有那麼多的金錢流動。我們估計年度收入至少還有兩年不會成長。

Speed Reading

1 分 秒

2 分 秒

3 分 秒

Day 7　establish ~ recognition

Vocabulary 🎧 track 13

1. **establish** *vt.* 建立　🔲 build, set　🔲 destory
   ● We are working to establish better relations with the marketing division.
   我們正努力與行銷部門建立更好的關係。

2. **evaluate** *vt.* 評估
   ● He evaluated the efficiency of each department, and these are his results.
   他評估每個部門的效率，而這些是他得到的結果。

3. **forecast** *n.[C], vt.* 預測　🔲 prediction
   ● The forecast for potential growth was very optimistic, and we did not achieve the expected results.
   對於潛在成長的預測非常樂觀，而我們沒有達成預期的結果。

4. **gather** *vt.* 蒐集　🔲 collect　🔲 divide
   ● We will gather data about our target consumers and report to the committee next month.
   我們將蒐集關於我們目標消費者的資料，並在下個月向委員會報告。

5. **joint venture** 合資
   ● It is a joint venture between Acme and United that we hope will lead to better results than each company could achieve on its own.
   這是Acme公司和United公司之間的合資，我們希望將能比各自公司所達成的結果更好。

6. **reputation** *n.[C]* 名聲；聲譽　回 fame　反 disgrace
   ● He had a reputation for being difficult to work with, but we cooperate very well.
   他不容易和人一起工作是出了名的，但我們合作得很愉快。

7. **resolve** *vt.* 解決；消除　回 solve, settle　反 question
   ● You must resolve your differences in order for everyone in the group to get along together.
   你們必須解決你們的歧見才能讓團隊中每個人都能好好相處。

8. **corporation** *n.[C]* 公司　回 company, firm, enterprise
   ● That corporation is the second-largest economic force in the county.
   那間公司是這個縣裡第二大的經濟實力。

9. **accomplishment** *n.[C]* 成就；成績　回 achievement　反 failure
   ● His accomplishments are legendary, and they show the benefit of working well with your fellow employees.
   他的成就非常的傳奇，顯示出和同事之間合作順利的好處。

10. **recognition** *n.[U]* 表彰；認同　回 acceptance
    ● He didn't want recognition for himself; he was content to see the results for the company.
    他自己不要表彰；他很滿足看到公司有這樣的成果。

Paragraph 🎧 track 14

練習說明：

Step 1　下方有10個單字，請依文意將10個單字填入適當的空格中。

Step 2　播放MP3，確認填入答案是否正確，或可翻至P107-112對答案。

Step 3　請跟著MP3逐句練習，練習完畢，請自己將下列段落念出，並在段落下方的時鐘記錄下時間。

Chapter 1 商用單字一把抓

corporation forecast joint venture establish resolve
reputation recognition gather accomplishment evaluate

The economic 1   for the immediate future is good. We think that this is the time for this 2   to embark upon a 3   with Consolidated Industries. The various departments must 4   any conflicts they may have, so they can 5   good relationships with their counterparts in Consolidated. We have a 6   for 7   data well, and those who help in this will get 8   for their 9   . In the coming weeks, we will 10   our needs and make decisions regarding personnel needed to carry out this project.

對於短期未來的經濟預測是良好的。我們認為現在是好時機，這間公司和Consolidated Industries開始著手合資計畫。不同的部門必須解決可能的任何衝突，這樣他們才能和Consolidated公司相對應的部門建立良好關係。我們因擅長蒐集資料而享有聲譽，從中協助的人都將會因為他們的成就而獲得表彰。在接下來幾個星期，關於執行此專案所需的人員，我們將評估需求並做出決定。

Day 8   franchise ~ prosperity

Vocabulary 🎧 track 15

1. **franchise** *n.[C]* 經銷權；加盟店
    - He bought the rights to open Subway franchises in two coastal towns.
      他買下在兩座海岸城鎮開立Subway的加盟店的權利。

2. **entrepreneur** *n.[C]* 企業家；創業者   回 founder
    - Many people want to become entrepreneurs, opening their own business and becoming their own boss.
      許多人想要成為創業者,開啟自己的事業、自己當老闆。

3. **merit** *n.[C]* 價值；長處；優點   回 value, good   反 fault
    - We judge people on their merits, not on which school they graduated from.
      我們以人們自身的價值來評斷他們,而不是以他們畢業的學校。

4. **achievement** *n.[C]* 成就；成績   回 accomplishment   反 failure
    - It was a great achievement, but he never lived up to that potential later in life.
      那是個了不起的成就,但他自此再也不曾達到那樣的潛能了。

5. **reinforce** *vt.* 加強；補充；補強   回 strengthen   反 undermine
    - Living that lifestyle only reinforces people's opinion that she is a spoiled child.
      過那樣的生活方式只是加強人們的評價——她是個被寵壞的小孩。

6. **revise** *vt.* 修改；修正   回 correct, edit
    - We have to revise our sales forecast in light of the latest productivity data.
      我們必須依據最新的產能資料來修正銷售預測。

7. **subsidiary** *n.[C]* 輔助者；子公司 ▣ branch, secondary
    ◉ That is a wholly-owned subsidiary of Acme Chemical, Inc.
    那是Acme化學公司獨資的子公司。

8. **adhere to** 堅持；堅守 ▣ keep to, hold on
    ◉ He always adheres to company policy, which sometimes means making unpopular decisions.
    他一直堅守公司政策，有時候那表示要做些不受歡迎的決策。

9. **enhance** *vt.* 提高；增加；提升 ▣ improve ▣ reduce
    ◉ We are going to enhance the customer experience, making it more personal for them.
    我們將要提升顧客經驗，讓他們感到更個人化。

10. **prosperity** *n.[U]* 繁榮 ▣ wealth, affluence ▣ proverty
    ◉ The current economy promises to give prosperity to the majority of people.
    現在的經濟有可能帶給多數人繁榮。

Paragraph 🎧 track 16

練習說明：

Step 1 下方有10個單字，請依文意將10個單字填入適當的空格中。

Step 2 播放MP3，確認填入答案是否正確，或可翻至P107-112對答案。

Step 3 請跟著MP3逐句練習，練習完畢，請自己將下列段落念出，並在段落下方的時鐘記錄下時間。

entrepreneur enhance prosperity merit subsidiary
revise adhere to achievement franchise reinforce

We grew up thinking that 1 _____ would never come to this island. Most people were not able to be 2 _____ . They had given up on the idea that they could 3 _____ their lives on their own 4 _____ . It felt like we would always be a 5 _____ of the mainland. The government 6 _____ a policy of maintaining tight control over everything. However, once the leaders 7 _____ their way of thinking, our lives became much better. That is 8 _____ by the fact that I can now have my own McDonald's 9 _____ . Opening up the country to a world viewpoint is our government's greatest 10 _____ .

　　我們成長時就想繁榮永遠不會來到這座島嶼。多數人無法成為創業家。他們已經放棄他們能夠靠著自己提升生活的想法。感覺我們永遠是本土大陸的附屬。政府堅守對凡事維持嚴密控制的政策。但是，一旦領導者修正他們的想法，我們的生活變得更好了，這點可以透過一個事實來加強驗證——我現在能夠擁有自己的麥當勞加盟店。開放國家迎向世界觀是我們政府最大的成績。

Speed Reading

1　分　　秒

2　分　　秒

3　分　　秒

Day 9 | accommodate ~ strike

Vocabulary 🎧 track 17

1. **accommodate** *vt.* 通融；給...方便；提供住宿　▣ board
   - We will accommodate their request, as it won't inconvenience us at all.
   我們將通融他們的請求，因為那完全不會對我們造成不便。

2. **situation** *n.[C]* 情況　▣ circumstances, status
   - This situation will require all our concentration to resolve.
   這個情況將需要我們全心全力來解決。

3. **appointment** *n.[C]* 任命；指派；約會；約定　▣ assignment
   - His appointment to the board of directors was a surprise to nearly everyone in the company.
   他受到指派進入董事會，全公司上下幾乎都很訝異。

4. **calendar** *n.[C]* 日曆；行事曆　▣ agenda
   - We will have to separate our calendar year from our fiscal one.
   我們必須把日曆年和財務年分開。

5. **directory** *n.[C]* 姓名住址簿；通訊錄
   - The directory of employee contact information has to be updated this month.
   員工聯絡資料的通訊錄這個月必須要更新。

6. **interrupt** *vt.* 打斷　▣ intrude, interfere
   - He constantly interrupts our conversation with mindless chatter.
   他時常用無意的嘮叨來打斷我們的對話。

7. **partition** *n.[C]* 隔板；分開　同 divider, separation　反 attachment
   - The partition between her office and mine is quite thin, so we have no secrets from each other.
   她的辦公室和我的辦公室中間的隔板相當薄，所以我們彼此沒有祕密。

8. **punctual** *adj.* 準時的　同 on time　反 late, tardy
   - She is a very punctual person, so I think her tardiness means something is wrong.
   她是個非常準時的人，所以我認為她會遲到表示有事發生了。

9. **prohibit** *vt.* 禁止　同 forbid　反 allow
   - The law prohibits us from selling stock immediately after our IPO.
   法律禁止我們在首次公開募股之後立刻出售股票。

10. **strike** *n.[C]* 罷工　同 quit
    - The workers of that food company had been out on strike for six months.
    那家食品工廠的員工已經罷工六個月了。

Paragraph 🎧 track 18

練習說明：

Step 1 下方有10個單字，請依文意將10個單字填入適當的空格中。

Step 2 播放MP3，確認填入答案是否正確，或可翻至P107-112對答案。

Step 3 請跟著MP3逐句練習，練習完畢，請自己將下列段落念出，並在段落下方的時鐘記錄下時間。

punctual accommodate interrupt strike prohibit
situation partition directory calendar appointment

This 1 ＿＿＿＿＿＿ forces us to 2 ＿＿＿＿＿＿ the wishes of our employees. We don't want them to go out on 3 ＿＿＿＿＿＿, as that would greatly 4 ＿＿＿＿＿＿ our business flow. We can't 5 ＿＿＿＿＿＿ them from striking; therefore, we have to respond 6 ＿＿＿＿＿＿. We don't want to create a 7 ＿＿＿＿＿＿ between employees and management. Take a look at the 8 ＿＿＿＿＿＿ and consult the 9 ＿＿＿＿＿＿ of middle management leaders. The 10 ＿＿＿＿＿＿ of a go-between must happen very soon.

這個情況迫使我們迎合員工的希望。我們不希望他們上演罷工，因為那會嚴重打斷我們的商業流程。我們不能禁止他們罷工，所以我們必須準時地回應。我們不想在員工和管理階層之間建立隔閡。看一下日曆，然後查詢中階管理主管的通訊錄。調停人的指派必須要快一點。

Speed Reading

1　分　　秒

2　分　　秒

3　分　　秒

Day 10 personalize ~ vacancy

Vocabulary 🎧 track 19

1. **personalize** *vt.* 使個人化
   - You are not allowed to personalize your workspace, as too many people have put up inappropriate decorations in the past.
   你不被允許把工作職場個人化，因為過去有太多人曾經放置一些不合宜的裝飾品了。

2. **assignment** *n.[C]* 任務；分配　🔲 task
   - This assignment will involve overseas relocation for you and your family.
   這項任務將包括你和家人派駐海外。

3. **remove** *vt.* 移除
   - If you don't remove that unsightly mess, you will receive a reprimand from management.
   如果你不清除那難看的一團混亂，你將會收到管理階層的責難。

4. **document** *n.[C]* 文件；證件　🔲 papers
   - It is a document of great historical importance and must be carefully preserved.
   這是一份極具歷史重要性的文件，必須小心保存。

5. **motivate** *vt.* 刺激；激發　🔲 stimulate, prompt
   - He tries to motivate through negativity and criticism, and then wonders why his employees are so negative.
   他試著在負面想法和批評之中產生激勵，想知道為什麼他的員工那麼的負面。

6. Xerox *n.[U], vt.* 影印　　🔲 copy
   🔹 The Xerox machine is not functioning properly and must be brought to the attention of the technician.
   影印機運作不順，必須讓技師注意一下。

7. headquarters *n.* 總部
   🔹 This is the former headquarters of National Widgets, and is being remodeled to fit his company's needs.
   這是National Widgets公司以前的總部，現在正在重新改建以符合他的公司需求。

8. memorandum *n.[C]* 備忘錄；章程　　🔲 reminder
   🔹 That memorandum became famous for its brevity and effectiveness.
   那份章程因為簡潔有力而出名。

9. workshop *n.[C]* 工場；專題討論會　　🔲 seminar
   🔹 Edison had a very busy workshop with many talented and creative assistants.
   愛迪生有一間非常忙碌的工場，那裡有很多有天份、有創造力的助手。

10. vacancy *n.[C]* 空缺
    🔹 There is now a vacancy in the department, since Marge decided to take time out of her career to raise her family.
    現在部門裡有一個空缺，因為Marge決定從職涯中撥出時間給家人。

Paragraph 🎧 track 20

練習說明：

Step 1 下方有10個單字，請依文意將10個單字填入適當的空格中。

Step 2 播放MP3，確認填入答案是否正確，或可翻至P107-112對答案。

Step 3 請跟著MP3逐句練習，練習完畢，請自己將下列段落念出，並在段落下方的時鐘記錄下時間。

headquarters remove vacancy workshop document
Xerox memorandum personalize motivate assignment

You may have seen the 1 _____ we put out today. Please do not 2 _____ the 3 _____ from the bulletin board. It tells of a 4 _____ in the design 5 _____ . We made 6 _____ copies of it and put them up all around 7 _____ . We hope this will 8 _____ some of our staff to show their creativity. If you are interested in the position, please send a 9 _____ display of your ideas to our committee. A decision concerning the new 10 _____ will be made in about three weeks.

你可能看過我們今天發表的備忘錄。請不要從公告欄上移除該文件。它說明的是設計工場的一個空缺。我們把文件影印了數份，張貼在總部各處。我們希望這可以激勵一些員工，展現他們的創造力。如果你對這個職位有興趣，請寄給我們的委員會一份你想法的個人化展現。關於此新任命的決定會在三個星期之後做出。

Speed Reading

1　分　秒

2　分　秒

3　分　秒

Day 11 bargain ~ turnover

Vocabulary 🎧 track 21

1. **bargain** *n.[C]* 划算的商品交易
   - That is not a bargain, but we believe in paying a premium to obtain well-made items.
   這不是一個划算的商品，但我們相信付出高價能得到製作精美的東西。

2. **consume** *vt.* 消費；消耗
   - This project has consumed nearly all my time during the past six weeks, and I now wish to spend some time with my family.
   這個專案已經幾乎消耗我過去六個星期的所有時間，我現在希望花點時間陪陪家人。

3. **expire** *vi.* 滿期；到期　◙ end　◙ begin, start
   - The patent will expire in six months, and layoffs will be necessary to compensate for the decreased income.
   這項專利在六個月後將到期，為彌補減少的收入，裁員是必須的。

4. **offer** *n.[C], vt.* 報價；提議；提供　◙ propose, provide
   - We made an offer to Digital Designs, but they rejected it for not being as specific as they would have liked concerning our responsibilities.
   我們提案給Digital Designs公司，但他們拒絕了，表示提案中關於我們的責任方面不如他們想要的那樣精確。

5. **permanent** *adj.* 永久的　◙ lasting　◙ temporary
   - That permanent marker will make for a lasting reminder of what I wish to communicate.
   那個永久的標記可以做為持續的提醒，提醒我想要傳達的事。

6. **substitute** *n.[C]* 代替人；代替的物品 *vt.* 代替　◙ alternate, replace

Chapter 1 商用單字一把抓

● This position will only be as a substitute until our regular employee returns from maternity leave.
這個職位只是代替的，直到我們正職員工從產假返回崗位。

7. **contract** *n.[C]* 合約　　agreement, pact
● We expect to sign a contract for their services sometime in the coming week.
我們期待可以在下週簽好他們提供服務的合約。

8. **transaction** *n.[C]* 交易　　deal
● The transaction was not carried out in a timely manner, and will therefore not be honored.
這交易沒有及時進行，所以將不會被履行。

9. **affordable** *adj.* 負擔得起的
● It is an affordable alternative, and we will be investigating the possibility of using it for our needs.
這個替代方案是負擔得起的，我們將會調查使用這個方案來配合我們需求的可能性。

10. **turnover** *n.[U]* 流動率
● We have not had much turnover in our staff, as we pay them well and honor their achievements.
我們的員工流動率不高，因為我們的薪資合理，並獎勵他們的成就。

Paragraph 🎧 track 22

練習說明：

Step 1　下方有9個單字，請依文意將9個單字填入適當的空格中。

Step 2　播放MP3，確認填入答案是否正確，或可翻至P107-112對答案。

Step 3　請跟著MP3逐句練習，練習完畢，請自己將下列段落念出，並在段落下方的時鐘記錄下時間。

bargain consume affordable permanent
contract substitute transaction offer turnover

We have 1   all the possibilities for making our office comfortable. The 2   furniture we bought was not really 3   , as we have had to replace it much earlier than anticipated. The company that made it has gone bankrupt, as they had such high 4   at their factory that the quality of their products suffered. We are going to sign a 5   with Tainan Furniture to arrange for 6   pieces soon. We 7   them a good deal and expect the 8   to be completed within the week. We will then have quality, 9   furnishings for our offices.

　　我們已經用盡所有的可能性，來讓我們的辦公室舒適。我們之前買的划算家具其實並不是很負擔得起，因為我們必須比預期早很多來替換它（這些家具）。製作這些家具的公司已經破產，因為他們的工廠流動率太高，以致於影響到產品的品質。我們將和台南家具簽約，早日安排代替的配件。我們提供給他們很好的條件，並希望交易可以在本週完成。然後我們將有高品質、永久的辦公設備。

Day 12　background ~ provide

Vocabulary 🎧 track 23

1. **background** *n.[C]* 背景
   ● Her background is in retail management, but we think she has the right skills for our industry.
   她的背景是在零售管理，但我們認為她對於我們的產業有適合的技能。

2. **candidate** *n.[C]* 候選人　📖 nominee, applicant
   ● There are three candidates for the position, and I think it will be difficult to choose between them.
   這個職位目前有三名候選人，我認為從中選出一位很困難。

3. **capacity** *n.[U]* 能力；產能　📖 ability, capability　📕 inability
   ● The sales department must work to increase orders, as we are only running at 65% of capacity.
   業務部必須努力增加訂單，因為我們現在只用了65%的產能而已。

4. **apprentice** *n.[C]* 學徒；見習生；生手　📖 learner, beginner　📕 mentor
   ● In former times, this job would have been taught in the apprentice system.
   在以前，這份工作是透過學徒制來學習的。

5. **include** *vt.* 包括　📖 contain, involve
   ● The display fixtures will be included in the purchase price, but not any of our inventory.
   陳列的固定裝置會包括在購買價格中，但不包括我們的存貨。

6. **compensate** *vt.* 補償；賠償　📖 pay, reward
   ● He expects to be compensated for the work-related injuries he received last month.

他預期因上個月受到的職業災害得到補償。

7. **eligible** *adj.* 有資格的；合適的　圓 qualified, suitable　圆 unsuitable
   ◌ We are eligible for compensation for their violations of fair business practices.
   我們有資格要求賠償，因為他們違反公平的商業慣例。

8. **hire** *vt.* 僱用　圓 employ　圆 fire
   ◌ We expect to hire as many as 75 people in our manufacturing arm in the coming months.
   我們預期接下來幾個月要僱用多達75人在我們的製造部門。

9. **promote** *vt.* 使升遷　圆 degrade
   ◌ He expected to be promoted sooner than he was, but no one above him was moved up, either.
   他預期會比他更快得到升遷，但是在他上面也沒有人得到升遷。

10. **provide** *vt.* 提供　圓 supply, give
    ◌ She does a good job of providing for her family, and her husband is very appreciative of that.
    她在提供照顧她的家庭方面做得很好，而她的丈夫非常地感謝這點。

Paragraph　🎧 track 24

> 練習說明：
>
> Step 1 下方有10個單字，請依文意將10個單字填入適當的空格中。
> Step 2 播放MP3，確認填入答案是否正確，或可翻至P107-112對答案。
> Step 3 請跟著MP3逐句練習，練習完畢，請自己將下列段落念出，並在段落下方的時鐘記錄下時間。

Chapter 1 商用單字一把抓

candidate eligible promote compensate provide
apprentice background hire include capacity

For those employees who are 1　　　　2　　　　 for
3　　　　, we will 4　　　　 training to make the transition
to their new positions easier. We will 5　　　　 those who are
still 6　　　　 and try to 7　　　　 them into a division of
our company in which their skills can shine. The proper candidates will
undergo a 8　　　　 check, 9　　　　 an investigation
of any encounters with the law. We believe we will work at close to
10　　　　 in the coming year, which should provide the opportunity
for advancement for many of our staff.

　　對於有資格獲得升遷的候選職員，我們將會提供訓練，使他們轉換到新職位的過程更容易些。我們將會補償仍是學徒的職員，試著聘請他們進入公司的部門，讓他們的技能可以展現。合適的候選人將進行背景調查，包括是否有任何法律前科的調查。我們相信我們明年會達到產能滿載，這應該可以提供許多職員往前進的機會。

Speed Reading

1　分　秒

2　分　秒

3　分　秒

Day 13 | outage ~ technical

Vocabulary 🎧 track 25

1. **outage** *n.[U]* 停電;停水　回 blackout
   ● The power outage was only part of our problems yesterday, as our tech department was also short-staffed.
   停電只是我們昨天問題的一部分,因為我們的科技部門也人力不足。

2. **compatible** *adj.* 能共處的　反 incompatible
   ● They are not compatible with each other, and we are going to have to separate them in order to finish the project on time.
   他們無法和彼此相處,我們必須把他們分開,以便準時完成專案。

3. **display** *n.[C]* 展覽;展示　回 exhibition, show
   ● The display was not meant to be viewed by the general public; it was for staff only.
   這場展覽並不是要讓一般大眾觀看的;它是員工專屬的。

4. **duplicate** *vt.* 複製
   ● We are duplicating many things in the merger of the two companies and have to eliminate this overlap.
   在這兩家公司的合併當中,我們正在複製許多東西,必須要去除這個重覆部分。

5. **durable** *adj.* 耐用的　回 enduring, sturdy　反 fragile
   ● The production of durable goods increased by ten percentage points last quarter.
   耐用商品的製造在上一季增加了10%。

6. satellite *n.[C]* 衛星
    ○ That is a satellite office; we have our main offices in an industrial park in Kaohsiung.
    那是個衛星辦公室；我們主要的辦公室在高雄一座工業園區裡。

7. software *n.[U]* 軟體   ◻ program
    ○ The software to run this system is some of the most complex we have had experience with.
    執行這個系統的軟體是我們有經驗以來遇到最複雜的一種。

8. laboratory *n.[C]* 實驗室   ◻ lab
    ○ The laboratory is situated at the rear of the building, with its own entrance.
    實驗室位於大樓的後面，有自己的出入口。

9. store *vt.* 儲存   ◻ stock
    ○ We store all the records of the company in our facility in Taichung, with backups at the data center in Hualien.
    我們把公司所有紀錄儲存在台中的辦公室，而備用則是放在花蓮的資料中心。

10. technical *adj.* 技術的；技術性的；專門的   ◻ professional, specialized
    ○ Her technical expertise has become a great asset to our corporation.
    她的技術專業已經變成我們公司的重要資產。

Paragraph 🎧 track 26

練習說明：

Step 1 下方有10個單字，請依文意將10個單字填入適當的空格中。

Step 2 播放MP3，確認填入答案是否正確，或可翻至P107-112對答案。

Step 3 請跟著MP3逐句練習，練習完畢，請自己將下列段落念出，並在段落下方的時鐘記錄下時間。

Chapter 1 商用單字一把抓

software technical satellite laboratory store
display outage compatible durable duplicate

Our 1   ideas are generated by the staff in the
2   3   in Malaysia. That is a 4
operation, which also 5   much of the information needed
on a day-to-day basis by our staff. We always have to keep up on the
latest 6   that they use, so all of our systems can be
7   . An 8   at that location would severely
hinder our ability to function. Therefore, we must make the systems there
as 9   as possible, and also 10   their work in
our backups.

我們的展覽想法是由馬來西亞技術實驗室內的員工所想出來的。那是一個衛星式的運作單位，也儲存了許多員工每天必須使用的資料。我們必須一直把他們使用的軟體保持在最近的狀態，如此我們全部的系統才能相容。那個地點停電會嚴重阻礙我們運行的能力。因此我們必須讓系統盡可能地耐用，也要在備份中複製他們的工作內容。

Speed Reading

1   分   秒

2   分   秒

3   分   秒

Day 14　retrieval ~ outlet

Vocabulary 🎧 track 27

1.　**retrieval** *n.[U]* 取回；取得；取用
　　● The immediate retrieval of customer data is of the highest importance to the ability of our staff to serve them.
　　立刻取得客戶資料是最重要的員工服務能力。

2.　**advanced** *adj.* 先進的；在前面的　回 forward, developed
　　● It is an advanced system, first developed in our aerospace division, and now used by the manufacturing arm.
　　這是先進的系統，首先在我們的航空部門發展，現在是製造部門在使用。

3.　**component** *n.[C]* 成分；零件　回 element, part
　　● The components are manufactured by suppliers from all around Asia, with final assembly at the plant in Thailand.
　　這些零件是由全亞洲各地的供應商製造，最後在泰國的工廠組裝。

4.　**device** *n.[C]* 設備；儀器；裝置　回 instrument, tool
　　● It is a device that makes life in remote areas much less arduous for people assigned there.
　　這個設備可以讓派駐在偏遠地區的人生活輕鬆多了。

5.　**static** *adj.* 靜止的；靜態的 *n.[U]* 雜訊；靜電　回 inactive　反 dynamic
　　● I tried to reach him via the cell phone number he left, but all I got when he answered was static.
　　我嘗試透過他留下的手機號碼找他，但是當他接電話時我只聽到雜訊。

6.　**fuel** *n.[C, U]* 燃料
　　● They are developing an automobile that can run on three different fuels.

他們正在發展一種可以使用三種不同燃料的汽車。

7. innovative *adj.* 創新的　反 traditional
    - He is known as an innovative leader, responsible for much of the progress in the field in the past decade.
    他以身為一位創新的領導者知名，在過去十年中在這個領域負責很多進步發展。

8. troubleshooting *n.[U]* 疑難排除
    - She is the head of the troubleshooting division of our tech arm, responsible for finding solutions to our difficulties.
    她是我們科技部門疑難排除小組的領導者，負責找出我們困難點的解決方法。

9. operate *vt.* 經營；管理　同 manage, conduct
    - We tried to operate everything from the main office, but building satellite facilities allowed us more flexibility.
    我們嘗試從主要辦公室運作一切，但是建立衛星辦公室讓我們有更多彈性。

10. outlet *n.[C]* 出口；（感情，精力等）發洩途徑（或方法）
    - I found that jogging during my lunch break was a good outlet for the stress built up during the morning.
    我發現在午休時間慢跑是很好的宣洩，把早上累積的壓力清除掉。

Paragraph 🎧 track 28

練習說明：

Step 1　下方有10個單字，請依文意將10個單字填入適當的空格中。

Step 2　播放MP3，確認填入答案是否正確，或可翻至P107-112對答案。

Step 3　請跟著MP3逐句練習，練習完畢，請自己將下列段落念出，並在段落下方的時鐘記錄下時間。

retrieval advanced operate innovative device
static troubleshooting outlet fuel component

_1_____ of account information is of the utmost importance. We have to be able to _2_____ at speeds more _3_____ than that of our competitors. Our tech department responded to this need by developing an _4_____ _5_____ that is used in processing our database. This _6_____ was plagued with _7_____ at first, but after initial _8_____ it has proved to be a durable component. Customer service has found it to be a creative _9_____ for advising Good Chemicals, Inc. in the making of their new synthetic _10_____

　　取得客戶資料是最重要的。我們必須要能夠在比競爭者更快的速度之下運作。我們的科技部門回應這個需求，透過發展一項創新的設備，用來處理我們的資料庫。這個零件一開始受到靜電的干擾，但在早期的疑難排解之後，它證明是一個很耐用的零件。客戶服務發現這是一個很有創意的輸出方法，可以提供建議給Good Chemicals公司，在他們新的人造燃料製作方面。

Speed Reading

1 分 秒

2 分 秒

3 分 秒

Day 15 occupy ~ renovate

Vocabulary 🎧 track 29

1. **occupy** *vt.* 佔據；佔用
   - The corporation occupies several floors of skyscrapers in downtown Taipei.
     這家公司使用了台北市中心摩天大樓的好多樓層。

2. **appliance** *n.[C]* 設備；器具   圓 tool, utensil, device
   - We used to have those appliances in the office, but we recently upgraded them and are selling them on Yahoo.
     我們以前在辦公室有那些設備，但我們最近把它們升級，並在奇摩網站上拍賣它們。

3. **mattress** *n.[C]* 床墊
   - The mattress isn't firm enough for my wife, so we are seeking one that provides more support.
     這床墊對我妻子而言不夠穩固，所以我們在尋找一個可以提供更多支撐的床墊。

4. **construction** *n.[U]* 建造   圓 destruction
   - The construction of the new headquarters will begin sometime in the coming year.
     新總部的建造將在明年的某個時候開始。

5. **laundry** *n.[U]* 送洗的衣服；洗好的衣服   圓 wash
   - We did our laundry there when we were in college, but recently it has been turned into an Internet cafe.
     我們在讀大學時都在那裡洗衣服，但最近它被改成一家網咖了。

6. laundromat *n.[C]* 自助洗衣店
    ◉ The laundromat is around the corner from the condominium we currently reside in.
    那家自助洗衣店就在我們剛搬進的公寓轉角。

7. ornament *n.[C]* 裝飾品 回 decoration, adornment
    ◉ He has a fantastic collection of vintage Christmas ornaments.
    他有一項了不起的蒐集，是復古的聖誕節裝飾品。

8. possession *n.[C]* 所有物；所有權 回 ownership
    ◉ We rented that office suite last week, and we will take possession this coming Friday.
    我們上星期租下那間辦公室，在這個星期五會取得所有權。

9. real estate 房地產 回 landed, property
    ◉ The real estate market is on the upswing, following a three-year downturn.
    房地產市場在三年的低潮之後目前在上漲。

10. renovate *vt.* 重建；整修 回 remodel 反 ruin
    ◉ We are going to renovate the old building, as it will be cheaper than leasing a new office complex.
    我們將整修這棟老建物，因為這樣比租一棟新的辦公大樓還便宜。

Paragraph ⏪ track 30

練習說明：

Step 1 下方有10個單字，請依文意將10個單字填入適當的空格中。

Step 2 播放MP3，確認填入答案是否正確，或可翻至P107-112對答案。

Step 3 請跟著MP3逐句練習，練習完畢，請自己將下列段落念出，並在段落下方的時鐘記錄下時間。

renovate laundromat occupy laundry real estate
ornament construction mattress possession appliance

A 1   2   the basement of our building.
We are going to eliminate it when we 3   this year. The
neighbors will have to find a new place to do their 4   ,
but the 5   will be too expensive for that tenant after
6   . We have three possible new tenants. A company selling
Christmas 7   wishes to look at it, but as their business is
only seasonal, they likely won't be able to afford the rent. We may lease to
a 8   and 9   retailer, but they want to take
10   very soon, and we're not sure our timetable will allow that.

　　一家自助洗衣店佔用了我們大樓的地下室。我們今年整修的時候將要把
它去除掉。鄰居們將必須找一個新的地方洗衣服，但是在工程之後，房地產
對那名承租人而言會太貴。我們有三個可能的新承租人。一家販賣聖誕節裝
飾品的公司希望可以看看，但是因為他們的業務只是季節性的，他們很可能
無法負擔房租。我們可能會租給一家床墊及家電零售商，但他們想要早點取
得使用權，而我們不確定時程安排允不允許。

Day 16　rural ~ adapter

Vocabulary 🎧 track 31

1. **rural** *adj.* 鄉村的　同 country　反 urban, city
   ● Tungshiao is a rural area, with a small town and many farms, far away from the cities.
   通宵是一個鄉村地區，有一個小鎮和許多農地，離城市很遠。

2. **suburbs** *n.[P]* 郊區　同 village　反 metropolis
   ● The suburbs of Taipei are expanding further every year, and they are also filling in the open areas between them.
   台北的郊區每年在擴張，它們也填滿郊區之間的開放區域。

3. **landlord** *n.[C]* 地主；房東　同 proprietor　反 renter
   ● My landlord refused to repair my dangerous plumbing, so I moved to this new building.
   我的房東拒絕修繕危險的水管，所以我搬到這棟新的大樓。

4. **balcony** *n.[C]* 陽台　同 porch, veranda, terrace
   ● We have too much junk on our balcony, but there isn't a good location for storage elsewhere.
   我們有太多垃圾在陽台上，但實在沒有其他好地點可以儲存了。

5. **storage** *n.[U]* 儲存
   ● In the US, there are many storage facilities you can rent, but they aren't generally available in Taiwan.
   在美國有很多儲存空間可以租用，但它們在台灣並不普遍。

6. **furnishings** *n.[P]* 室內陳設品
   ● The home furnishings are mostly Swedish, but the appliances were manufactured locally.

家庭室內陳設品大多是瑞典的，但家電設備則是本地製造的。

7. **relocate** *vi.* 重新安置；外派　同 transfer　反 stay
   - I don't want to relocate, as that would upset my family, so I turned down the promotion.
   我不想外派，因為那會使我家人不安，所以我拒絕了升遷。

8. **kitchenware** *n.[U]* 廚房用具
   - As we just moved, we need kitchenware, furnishings, and baking utensils.
   因為我們剛剛搬進來，我們需要廚房用具、室內陳設品和烘焙器具。

9. **burglar** *n.[C]* 闖空門的賊　同 robber, thief
   - We thought it was a burglar, but it was just our roommate tottering around in his drunken sleep.
   我們以為是闖空門的賊，但其實只是我們的室友在喝醉睡意中踉蹌地走。

10. **adapter** *n.[C]* 轉接器
    - You need a 240 volt adapter in order for your Mac to function overseas.
    你需要一個240伏特的轉接器，以便你的Mac電腦能在國外運作。

Paragraph 🎧 track 32

練習說明：

Step 1　下方有10個單字，請依文意將10個單字填入適當的空格中。

Step 2　播放MP3，確認填入答案是否正確，或可翻至P107-112對答案。

Step 3　請跟著MP3逐句練習，練習完畢，請自己將下列段落念出，並在段落下方的時鐘記錄下時間。

relocate suburbs rural adapter burglar
furnishings balcony kitchenware landlord storage

I grew up in the 1 _____ of southern Taipei County, but Dad really wanted to 2 _____ to a 3 _____ area. He was always afraid of 4 _____ in the city, so we had a state-of-the-art alarm system in the house. Dad sent for it all the way to Japan, and we had to get an 5 _____ to make it work on Taiwanese electricity. I'm not sure why he was so paranoid, as our 6 _____ and 7 _____ were nothing special, not silver or anything worth stealing. Dad always thought burglars could come in through the 8 _____ door; I thought that was highly unlikely. Since we owned the house, there wasn't even a 9 _____ to bother us. We kept our really valuable things in 10 _____ in a safe deposit box, so we had little to worry about. That still didn't make Dad feel safe living there, though.

我在台北縣南部的郊區長大，但是我爸爸真的想要重新搬到鄉村地區。他老是害怕城市裡的竊賊，所以我們在房子裡有一套最先進的警報系統。爸爸從日本訂購，而我們必須用一個轉接器讓它在台灣的電流下可以運作。我不確定為什麼他這麼的偏執，因為我們的室內擺設品和廚房器具都沒什麼特別的，不是銀製的、也不是什麼值得偷的東西。爸爸總認為竊賊可能從陽台的門進來，我覺得是不太可能的。因為我們擁有這間房子，甚至沒有房東來打擾我們。我們把真的值錢的東西都收在一個保險箱裡，所以我們沒有什麼好擔心的。然而這還是不能使爸爸覺得住在那裡是安全的。

Speed Reading

1 分 秒

2 分 秒

3 分 秒

Day 17 accelerate ~ customs

Vocabulary 🎧 track 33

1. **accelerate** *vi.* 加速；增加；加快　回 increase, speed　反 decelerate
   - The truck cannot accelerate very quickly, but it has a lot of pulling power for heavy loads.
   這部卡車無法很快地加速，但它有很大的拉力可以承載重物。

2. **cargo** *n.[C]* 貨物　回 load, freight
   - The cargo in the hold is not valuable, but its weight makes it expensive to transport.
   在貨艙裡的貨物價格並不昂貴，但它的重量使得運送費用變得昂貴。

3. **navigate** *vi. vt.* 航行；駕駛　回 sail, steer
   - It is very difficult to navigate around the reefs and sandbars to get into the port.
   在暗礁和沙洲之間航行進入港口是很困難的事。

4. **vehicle** *n.[C]* 交通工具；車輛　回 conveyance, transport
   - He had his first vehicle when he was 15, and he is now collecting and restoring antique trucks.
   他十五歲時擁有第一部車，而他現在蒐集並修復古董卡車。

5. **excursion** *n.[C]* 遠足；短途旅行　回 trip, journey
   - Their excursion turned into a nightmare adventure, lost in a blizzard until the rescuers found them.
   他們的遠足變成一場惡夢探險，在大風雪中迷失直到搜救人員找到他們。

6. **detour** *n.[C]* 繞路　回 bypass
   - The failure of the bridge necessitated a detour of half an hour for all the vehicles on that highway.

橋樑的封閉使得繞路是必要的，那條高速公路的所有車輛都必須繞路半個小時。

7.　accommodation *n.[P]* 住處
　　◉ We tried to find lodgings for the night, but all the accommodations in the district were taken up because of the festival.
　　我們試著找到地方過夜，但這一區所有的住宿都因為節慶而住滿了。

8.　brochure *n.[C]* 小冊子　⊜ pamphlet, booklet
　　◉ The brochure painted a paradise, but in reality it was just another tourist trap.
　　這本小冊子印了一座天堂，但實際上這只是另一個旅客陷阱。

9.　pedestrian *n.[C]* 行人　⊜ walker
　　◉ We used the pedestrian overpass, as the street traffic made crossing at the intersection hazardous.
　　我們使用行人天橋，因為街道上的交通使得從十字路口過馬路是很危險的事。

10.　customs *n.[P]* 海關
　　◉ He tried to smuggle drugs through customs, and now he is locked up in the county jail.
　　他試圖偷渡毒品進海關，而現在他被關在縣立監獄中。

Paragraph　🎧 track 34

練習說明：

Step 1　下方有10個單字，請依文意將10個單字填入適當的空格中。

Step 2　播放MP3，確認填入答案是否正確，或可翻至P107-112對答案。

Step 3　請跟著MP3逐句練習，練習完畢，請自己將下列段落念出，並在段落下方的時鐘記錄下時間。

customs pedestrian accommodation excursion detour
navigate cargo brochure accelerate vehicle

Upon clearing 1   , we took the 2   walkway to the taxicab stand. We 3   away in a shiny, new yellow 4   . But our short drive into the city to our 5   turned into an 6   into the lower reaches of town, as a 7   had blocked the main artery. Our driver had never been in that section before, and he was unable to 8   out of it. We ended up in the port area, which was full of ships unloading their 9   . It was not the sort of place we had meant to spend our vacation; it wasn't the paradise we thought we would see, but it was interesting, anyway. We had certainly never imagined we would end up there when we were reading the 10   !

在過海關後，我們走行人道到計程車招呼站。我們坐上一部閃亮全新的黃色車輛加速離開。但是我們短暫到市區住宿的路程，變成了到城鎮郊外的一趟旅程，因為有一條繞道阻擋了主要幹道。我們的司機以前沒來到那個區域，無法開離。我們最後來到港口區域，那裡充滿了下貨的船隻。那不是我們想要度假的地方，那不是我們以為會看到的天堂，但仍然很有趣。當我們看著小冊子的時候，我們當然不曾想像過我們最後竟會在那裡！

Day 18 exotic ~ cruise

Vocabulary 🎧 track 35

1. **exotic** *adj.* 異國情調的；奇特的　反 ordinary
    - We were promised an exotic and unspoiled island, but it was full of tourists in search of an identical experience.
    我們被承諾一座異國、未受破壞的小島，但這卻充滿了觀光客，尋找相同的旅行經驗。

2. **expedition** *n.[C]* 探險；探險隊　同 exploration
    - The expedition left for points unknown and didn't expect to arrive back at the departure point for several years.
    探險隊前往未知的地點，而且無法預期在數年之後能不能回到出發點。

3. **intersection** *n.[C]* 十字路口　同 crossroad, junction
    - She was waiting for us at the intersection for more than half an hour, but we were held up by the parade through the city.
    她在十字路口等我們超過半個小時，但我們被市區裡的遊行給耽擱了。

4. **itinerary** *n.[C]* 旅程；旅行計劃；旅行記錄
    - The itinerary didn't allow for much sightseeing, so we modified it to include more free time and less movement.
    行程不允許太多的觀光行程，所以我們調整行程來包含更多自由的時間和較少的交通移動。

5. **round trip** 來回票　同 there and back
    - He didn't get a round trip ticket, as he planned to never return from the relocation.
    他沒有買來回票，因為他打算再也不從那邊回來了。

6. freight　n.[U] 貨運；貨物　回 cargo, load
　　○ The freight charge was too high to make economic sense, so we refused the purchase order.
　　貨運費太高了，一點都不經濟，所以我們拒絕了購買訂單。

7. sightseeing　n.[U] 觀光　回 tour
　　○ This is not a trip for sightseeing; we have serious business to conduct before the merger takes effect.
　　這不是一趟觀光旅程；在合併案生效之前，我們有重要的事要處理。

8. valid　adj. 有效的；有根據的；合法的　回 legal　反 invalid
　　○ That is not a valid request; you must submit it in triplicate to each office manager.
　　那不是一個有效的請求；你必須用一式三份的方式呈交給各個辦公室經理。

9. escalator　n.[C] 電扶梯
　　○ The escalator in the MRT station at Taipei Main Station has to have one of the steepest climbs in the nation.
　　台北車站捷運站裡的電扶梯一定是全國最陡的之一。

10. cruise　n.[C] 航遊；（坐船）旅行　回 voyage
　　○ We thought we were going on a pleasure cruise, but it quickly turned into an inescapable sales pitch for his company.
　　我們以為我們將來一趟愉快的郵輪航遊，但很快地變成了無法逃避的推銷他的公司。

Paragraph 🎧 track 36

練習說明：

Step 1 下方有10個單字，請依文意將10個單字填入適當的空格中。

Step 2 播放MP3，確認填入答案是否正確，或可翻至 P107-112對答案。

Step 3 請跟著MP3逐句練習，練習完畢，請自己將下列段落念出，並在段落下方的時鐘記錄下時間。

cruise sightseeing itinerary valid expedition
intersection escalator exotic freight round trip

The 1 _____ pleasure 2 _____ and on-board dinner is an ongoing feature of the company get-together. It's not really a 3 _____ 4 _____, as the 5 _____ is planned ahead of time, but it is an 6 _____ experience nonetheless. It starts from the 7 _____ of Front and Maple, where we take the 8 _____ up to the dock. We don't take on any 9 _____, because we are making a 10 _____; we only need our jackets for the chilly night air. It is always an enjoyable time and makes the employees happier that they work here.

這趟觀光愉悅郵輪旅程和船上晚餐是公司聚會一直以來的特色。這不算是真的探險，因為行程已經事先安排好，然而仍是一個異國的體驗。從Front和Maple的交叉點開始，我們搭乘電扶梯到甲板上。我們沒有帶任何貨物，因為這是一趟來回行程；我們只需要我們的外套，因為晚風很涼。這一直是令人享受的時光，讓員工們感到更開心他們是在這裡工作。

Speed Reading

1 ___ 分 ___ 秒

2 ___ 分 ___ 秒

3 ___ 分 ___ 秒

Day 19 tag ~ diversify

Vocabulary 🎧 track 37

1. **tag** *n.[C]* 標籤；牌子　◙ label, brand
   ○ The tags on those garments show the prices at a full-service store and not an indication of our discounted prices.
   那些衣服上的標籤標示出全面服務商店的價格，並未顯示折扣的價格。

2. **variety** *n.[U]* 多樣化 *[C]* 各種　◙ diversity　◪ uniformity, monotony
   ○ It is a variety store and has many items from different categories of goods.
   這是一間多樣化的商店，有很多不同種類的貨品品項。

3. **garment** *n.[C]* 服裝；（一件）衣服　◙ dress
   ○ Garment makers took all their business to Pakistan and Vietnam long ago, when labor costs rose too quickly in Taiwan.
   服裝製造業者很久之前就把生意移往巴基斯坦和越南，當台灣的勞工成本上升得太快的時候。

4. **menu** *n.[C]* 菜單
   ○ The menu is written in a font that is pleasing to the eye and encourages the diner to enjoy the dining room's atmosphere.
   菜單是用一種賞心悅目的字體書寫，刺激用餐者享受餐廳內的氣氛。

5. **purchase** *n.[C], vt.* 購買　◙ buy　◪ sell
   ○ We need to buy many small items for our home, so we will defer some of the big-ticket purchases until the future.
   我們需要為家裡買一些小東西，所以我們將暫緩一些高價商品的購買。

6. **patron** *n.[C]* 主顧；贊助者　◙ sponsor, client
   ○ The patrons were very satisfied with the selections on the Valentine's

Day menu.

老主顧都非常滿意情人節菜單上的選擇。

7. **delivery** *n.[U]* 遞送　🔲 transmission
   - 🔵 They offer free delivery, which is part of their success in the increasingly competitive local restaurant scene.

   他們提供免費遞送，在日益競爭的本地餐飲盛況中，這是他們成功的一部分。

8. **demand** *n.[C]* 需求；需要　🔲 request
   - 🔵 The demand for our services is expected to increase exponentially as their products become more common in middle class households.

   對於我們服務的需求預計會成倍數成長，因為他們的產品在中產階級家庭中變得更普及了。

9. **drugstore** *n.[C]* 藥局；藥妝店
   - 🔵 We got our medications at the drugstore instead of purchasing them at the hospital pharmacy.

   我們去藥局買藥，而不是去醫院的配藥處買。

10. **diversify** *vt., vi.* 使多樣化；多角經營
    - 🔵 We are going to diversify in the upcoming years, as too much of our capital and company assets are in our traditional field.

    我們在近年內將多角經營，因為太多的資本和公司資產都在傳統產業。

Paragraph 🎧 track 38

練習說明：

Step 1　下方有10個單字，請依文意將10個單字填入適當的空格中。

Step 2　播放MP3，確認填入答案是否正確，或可翻至P107-112對答案。

Step 3　請跟著MP3逐句練習，練習完畢，請自己將下列段落念出，並在段落下方的時鐘記錄下時間。

> drugstore patron demand diversify tag
> purchase menu variety delivery garment

Our 1 _____ 2 _____ are wishing for a more
3 _____ shopping experience. We think the 4 _____
for eating facilities in the neighborhood is increasing, so we will be
introducing a snack bar this week, which we think will complement our
5 _____ and health care offerings. We will offer a quick, set meal
for diners in a hurry to 6 _____ , and also a 7 _____
of 8 _____ selections for those in a more casual frame of mind.
Home 9 _____ will start up in a couple weeks, as soon as we get
all the bugs worked out. For now, watch out for the 10 _____ on
various store products offering 10-25% off on snack bar foods.

我們藥妝店的老主顧希望一個更多元化的購物體驗。我們認為這個社區
內對於飲食店鋪的需求在增加中，所以這個星期我們會引進一個小吃攤，我
們認為會補足我們在服飾及保健的服務提供。我們將會提供快速的套餐給匆
忙的用餐者購買，還有多樣化的菜單選擇給隨性的消費者。外送到家的服務
會在幾個星期後開始，只要我們把一些小地方弄好。現在，請留意各種商店
產品的標籤，有些會提供小吃攤食物10~25%的折扣。

Day 20 digest ~ artificial

Vocabulary 🎧 track 39

1. **digest** *vt.* 消化；領悟；做...的摘要 📖 absorb, dissolve
   - Food is digested in the stomach and intestines, then sent around the body for energy.
   食物在胃腸消化，然後運輸到全身提供能量。

2. **ship** *vt.* 裝運；運送 📖 transport
   - We are going to ship the product next month, so we have to put in a lot of overtime to reach completion.
   我們將在下個月裝運產品，所以我們必須大量加班來完成。

3. **distributor** *n.[C]* 批發商；供應商 📖 wholesaler
   - He has an exclusive agreement with Joe's Jeans to be the distributor for all of Taiwan.
   他和Joe's Jeans取得獨家合約，成為全台灣唯一的批發商。

4. **pushcart** *n.[C]* 手推車
   - There used to be a Thai food pushcart in the courtyard of our building, but he has since moved to the downtown square.
   以前在我們大樓的庭園空地有一台泰國食物的小販推車，但他已經搬到市區廣場了。

5. **fragrant** *adj.* 芳香的 📖 aromatic, perfumed 🔄 stinking
   - The tofu is fragrant and delicious, but many foreigners think it is merely pungent and won't touch it.
   那豆腐又香又好吃，但很多外國人認為它只是味道很刺激，不願意碰它。

6. **request** *n.[C], vt.* 請求；要求 📖 apply, demand
   - We want to request the premium wine for our reception, and we

think we will have finger foods and fresh vegetables for appetizers.
我們想要在招待時用優質的紅酒，而且我們認為我們要有一些小點心和新鮮蔬菜作為開胃菜。

7. **sample** *n.[C]* 樣品；樣本；例子　🔲 example
   🔘 There was a woman dispensing free samples of ice cream at Carrefour, and we decided to take her up on it.
   有個女人在家樂福分發免費的冰淇淋試吃品，我們決定試看看。

8. **wholesale** *adj.* 批發的；整批的；大規模的　🔲 mass　🔲 retail
   🔘 You can't buy small orders at wholesale prices, no matter what those stores advertise; only retail outlets can get true wholesale prices.
   你不能用批發價購買小型訂單，無論那些商店如何廣告；只有零售商才能得到批發價格。

9. **retailer** *n.[C]* 零售商　🔲 wholesaler
   🔘 The wholesaler sells to assorted retailers, and they mark up the price and attempt to interest consumers into making the final purchase.
   批發商賣給各種零售商，他們拉高價格後，試著吸引消費者以完成終端購買。

10. **artificial** *adj.* 人工的；人造的；假的　🔲 fake, unreal　🔲 natural, real
    🔘 That candy isn't healthy for human consumption because it has too many artificial ingredients and sweeteners.
    如果人食用那糖果並不健康，因為它有太多人造的成份和增甜劑。

Paragraph 🎧 track 40

練習說明：

Step 1　下方有10個單字，請依文意將10個單字填入適當的空格中。

Step 2　播放MP3，確認填入答案是否正確，或可翻至P107-112對答案。

Step 3　請跟著MP3逐句練習，練習完畢，請自己將下列段

落念出，並在段落下方的時鐘記錄下時間。

request wholesale retailer distributor fragrant
artificial sample pushcart ship digest

As a 1 _____ of fine foods and cheeses, we are able to 2 _____ unique items from our 3 _____ 4 _____. Because we are reliable customers, she is able to 5 _____ us items that aren't available elsewhere. We specialize in whole, healthy foods, free from 6 _____ ingredients. We have a small army of 7 _____ scattered around the city, and they give out 8 _____ of these unique, 9 _____ specialties. That is one of the best marketing programs we have, as people are able to enjoy our products, 10 _____ them, and come back to purchase more, creating a good amount of business for us.

作為優質食品和起司的零售商，我們能夠向批發的供應商要求特殊的品項。因為我們是可靠的顧客，所以她可以運送其他地方買不到的品項給我們。我們專攻全麥、健康的食品，沒有人工的成份。我們有一組手推車兵團分散市區，發送這些獨特芬芳特產的試吃品。那是我們最好的行銷計畫之一，因為人們可以享受我們的產品、消化它們、然後回來買更多，為我們創造了大量的生意。

Speed Reading

1 分 秒
2 分 秒
3 分 秒

Day 21 defense ~ Fahrenheit

Vocabulary 🎧 track 41

1. **defense** *n.[C]* 守方；防守 *[U]* 防禦　回 protection
   ◎ He is better at playing defense than offense, but he is a good, all-around player who makes considerable contributions to our team.
   他的防守比進攻好，但他是一位優秀、全方位的球員，為我們團隊貢獻很多。

2. **pastime** *n.[C]* 消遣活動；娛樂　回 amusement
   ◎ They say that baseball is the American pastime, but I think basketball, invented in the States, is more appropriate to the pace of these times.
   人們說棒球是美國人的消遣，但我想在美國發明的籃球，對於現在的步調會更合適。

3. **amusing** *adj.* 有趣的；好玩的　回 interesting, entertaining　反 boring
   ◎ Some people find her amusing, but I think she is tedious and never takes people's feelings into account.
   有些人覺得她很有趣，但我覺得她令人乏味，而且從不考慮別人的感受。

4. **celebrity** *n.[C]* 名人　回 somebody, hotshot　反 nobody
   ◎ People dwell on celebrities these days, but eventually they will put them aside and concentrate on more satisfactory pursuits, such as the family.
   人們老是在談論名人，但最終他們會把名人丟掉，專心在更令人滿足的追求上，例如家庭生活。

5. **referee** *n.[C]* 裁判；調停人　回 judge, umpire
   ◎ The referee didn't see the foul, so she chose to commit the same one the next time down the floor.
   裁判沒看到犯規，所以她選擇下一次在地板上重施故計。

6. **scenario** *n.[C]* 情節；局面；方案　◎ plot
   ◎ That scenario is so far-fetched that not even a Hollywood producer would give it a second look.
   那情節如此牽強，沒有一個好萊塢製作人願意再看一眼。

7. **premiere** *n.[C]* 首映；首演　◎ opening
   ◎ The world premiere of the ballet was last night on Broadway, and it got rave notices in many of the morning papers.
   那場芭蕾舞的全球首演在昨晚百老匯登場，在今早的許多報紙得到讚賞的評價。

8. **applaud** *vt. vi.* 鼓掌；贊成　◎ cheer, clap
   ◎ We applauded the performance, giving it a standing ovation for its originality and vision.
   我們為那場表演鼓掌，為它的原創性和視覺效果起立鼓掌。

9. **audition** *n.[C]* 試演；試鏡
   ◎ The audition was in the fall, with production starting last week; we haven't had a moment's rest or recuperation.
   試鏡在秋天，上星期開始製作拍攝；我們沒有時間休息。

10. **Fahrenheit** *n.* 華氏
    ◎ We decided on Celsius as the world standard because it is based on scientific measurements, which Fahrenheit is lacking.
    我們決定以攝氏作為全球標準，因為它是建立在科學測量之上，這點華氏是缺乏的。

Paragraph 🎧 track 42

練習說明：

Step 1 下方有10個單字，請依文意將10個單字填入適當的空格中。

Step 2 播放MP3，確認填入答案是否正確，或可翻至P107-112對答案。

Step 3 請跟著MP3逐句練習，練習完畢，請自己將下列段落念出，並在段落下方的時鐘記錄下時間。

applaud celebrity scenario amusing premiere
Fahrenheit referee defense pastime audition

As a 1 _____, basketball can't be beaten. I'm happy to be playing with a great bunch of guys. I think our teammate Steve is on the way to becoming a 2 _____. That's an 3 _____ 4 _____ since the whole team is contributing to it. This is what happened: It was the 5 _____ game of the season, even though it was still summer. It was 39 Celsius (102 6 _____) outside when we entered the arena. We were glad to be inside. The 7 _____ threw up the ball at midcourt. Our team lost the jump and immediately fell back on 8 _____. Our center blocked the shot, then Marion passed the ball all the way down court to Steve for a slam dunk. The audience went wild 9 _____ him. You would have thought he had passed an 10 _____ for the next Star Wars movie! The game had just started, and he was already the center of attention. It's going to be an exciting season.

作為消遣活動，籃球是無法被打敗的。我很高興和一群很棒的人一起打球。我認為我們的隊員Steve將會成為一位名人。那是一個很好玩的情節，因為整個團隊都加油添醋。以下是故事經過：那是本季的首場比賽，雖然還是夏天。當我們進入賽場時，外面氣溫是攝氏39度（華氏102度）。我們很高興能到室內去。裁判在中線拋球。我們隊沒有跳到球，立刻回防。我們的中鋒擋到了射球，然後Marion傳球傳過球場給Steve灌籃。觀眾瘋狂地為他鼓掌。還以為他已經通過下一部星際大戰電影試鏡呢！比賽才剛開始，而他已經是全場注意的中心。這將會是一次精采的球季。

Day 22 degree ~ trophy

Vocabulary 🎧 track 43

1. **degree** *n.[C]* 度；程度；學位　📖 baccalaureate
   - Her degree is in English, but she avoided graduate school in her subject and instead focused on the law.
   她的學位是英文，但是她在研究所避開了這個學科，反而專注在法律上。

2. **editorial** *n.[C]* 社論；重要評論　📖 critique, commentary
   - It was a guest editorial by a well-known professor of literature that enraged the community.
   這則客座社論是一位知名的文學教授所寫的，激怒了整個社區。

3. **symphony** *n.[C]* 交響樂；交響樂團
   - The symphony may be disbanded for lack of funds to continue rehearsing and performing.
   因為缺乏資金繼續排練和表演，這個交響樂團可能會解散。

4. **rehearsal** *n.[C]* 排練；練習　📖 drill, practice
   - The rehearsal is going to commence in five minutes, so please get to your places and remain attentive.
   排練在五分鐘後將開始，所以請就位並保持注意。

5. **Celsius** *n.* 攝氏
   - Celsius is a scale of temperature developed by a Swedish astronomer and is based on the freezing and boiling points of water.
   攝氏是一個由瑞典天文學家，根據水的冰點和沸點發展出來的溫度量表。

6. **tactic** *n.[C]* 策略；戰略；手法　📖 plan, strategy
   - He has renewed his tactics in order to be more on the offensive and

bring an end to the conflict.
他為了加強攻擊並結束這場衝突，已經更新他的策略。

7. participate *vi.* 參與；參加 ▣ partake, take part
   ◈ It is important that everyone participates in the discussion in order that we may receive input regarding the restructuring.
   重要的是每個人都參與討論，以利我們收到關於重建的投入資訊。

8. periodical *n.[C]* 期刊 ▣ magazine, journal
   ◈ The new periodical will be published quarterly, with the possibility of going monthly if circulation increases.
   這份新期刊將會每季出刊，如果發行量增加有可能改成每月出刊。

9. stadium *n.[C]* 體育場；球場；競技場 ▣ arena
   ◈ The stadium is nearly completed and will be ready for the opening contest of this season.
   這座體育場接近完工，將為本球季的開幕戰準備就序。

10. trophy *n.[C]* 獎品；獎盃 ▣ medal, prize
    ◈ She has trophies dating back four years, featuring accomplishments from all corners of the globe.
    過去四年她有無數的獎盃，記載全球各地的成就。

Paragraph 🎧 track 44

練習說明：

Step 1 下方有10個單字，請依文意將10個單字填入適當的空格中。

Step 2 播放MP3，確認填入答案是否正確，或可翻至P107-112對答案。

Step 3 請跟著MP3逐句練習，練習完畢，請自己將下列段落念出，並在段落下方的時鐘記錄下時間。

editorial participate periodical tactic degree
trophy stadium symphony rehearsal Celsius

Mary Jane has not used her ₁_____ in her field up to this point. In the first part of her career, she worked at a sports ₂_____, ₃_____ in the analysis of ₄_____ and blunders of football teams. She also wrote several guest ₅_____ concerning public finding of the city's new ₆_____, and collected several ₇_____ from community action groups for her work. After that, she went to work for a newspaper, continuing her writing career. Her piece on the efforts of the local ₈_____ to continue was met with praise from the members. She wrote about their efforts to keep going despite funding woes, even to the point of having ₉_____ in a room kept at ten ₁₀_____. She's decided that writing is going to be her focus, and that her career is not going to revolve around the biology that she studied in school.

Mary Jane到目前在她的領域中還沒有用到她的學位。在她職涯一開始，她在一份運動期刊工作，參與足球隊的戰略及失誤分析。她也寫了幾篇關於城市新體育場的公眾資金的客座社論。她得到好幾個獎項，是由社區行動團體表揚她的工作而頒發的。在那之後，她到一家報社工作，繼續她的寫作職涯。她報導關於本地交響樂團的努力經營，此報導獲得了成員的讚美。她報導他們努力維持，不管資金短缺，甚至必須在只有攝氏10度的房間裡排演。她已經決定寫作將是她的重心，她的職涯將不會和她在校所學的生物學有任何關係。

Speed Reading

1	分	秒
2	分	秒
3	分	秒

Day 23 alleviate ~ handicap

Vocabulary 🎧 track 45

1. alleviate *vt.* 減輕；減緩　▣ relieve, mitigate
   ◉ It is important to alleviate the suffering in the area, most importantly by overthrowing the government.
   減輕這個區域的痛苦是重要的，最重要的是藉由把政府推翻。

2. contagious *adj.* 傳染的　▣ infectious
   ◉ He is extremely contagious, so everyone is avoiding him, to keep from becoming sick themselves.
   他現在極具傳染性，所以每個人都避開他，以避免自己生病。

3. emergency *n.[C]* 緊急事件　▣ urgency
   ◉ The flood created an emergency, the likes of which hadn't been seen in Shijr for nearly two decades.
   洪水造成了緊急事件，像是近二十年來不曾在汐止看過的洪水一般。

4. immune *adj.* 免疫的；免於...的
   ◉ He had measles at a young age, and it is believed that he is immune and is not in danger of contracting them again.
   他在年輕時得過麻疹，據信他已經免疫了，再也不會有危險得病。

5. infection *n.[U]* 傳染；感染　▣ contagion
   ◉ The infection overcame his immune system rapidly, despite all the doctor's efforts.
   儘管所有醫生都努力了，感染快速地打敗他的免疫系統。

6. premium *n.[C]* 保險費
   ◉ We have to pay a premium to qualify for the national health insurance, but it isn't much compared to the benefits we receive.

我們必須付一筆保險費才有資格參加全民健保，但和我們得到的好處相比不算什麼。

7. **vital** *adj.* 極為重要的；致命的　圓 essential, important　反 insignificant
   ○ The social networking system we have developed is vital to the success of our employees and will directly benefit the new project.
   我們已經建立的社群網絡系統對於我們員工的成功很重要，且將直接有利於這項新專案。

8. **record** *n.[C]* 記錄
   ○ Let it go down on the permanent record that Missy used every device she could find to save the firm from bankruptcy.
   讓Missy用盡了她能找到的所有辦法來拯救公司免於破產的事，永遠記錄下來。

9. **diagnose** *vt.* 診斷　反 misdiagnose
   ○ He didn't diagnose the illness correctly, but that was to be expected, since it was a new disease that no one had ever encountered before.
   他沒有正確地診斷這個疾病，不過這是可想見的，因為這是一個新疾病，以前從沒有人遇過。

10. **handicap** *n.[C]* 障礙；不利條件　圓 disability
    ○ His handicap has made it difficult to play sports, but it hasn't limited anything else he has ever attempted.
    他的障礙使得他不易從事運動，但這並未限制他嘗試其他的事情。

Paragraph 🎧 track 46

練習說明：

Step 1　下方有10個單字，請依文意將10個單字填入適當的空格中。

Step 2　播放MP3，確認填入答案是否正確，或可翻至P107-112對答案。

Step 3　請跟著MP3逐句練習，練習完畢，請自己將下列段

落念出，並在段落下方的時鐘記錄下時間。

emergency diagnose handicap vital record
contagious immune alleviate infection premium

In the 1 , her 2 proved to be an asset. Although she had been 3 with blindness at an early age, the 4 will show that she was of 5 assistance in 6 suffering for many people. Although many around her were 7 and could have easily infected her, she proved to be 8 to the disease. This freedom from 9 was crucial to the survival of many as the emergency progressed. Governments now pay 10 rates in order to avail themselves of her consulting experience and avoid infection of their citizens.

在這次緊急事件中，她的障礙證明反而是一項資產。雖然她很年輕就被診斷出眼盲，記錄顯示她在減輕許多人的痛苦方面協助很大。雖然她身邊很多人具有傳染性，可能輕易地使她感染，但是她證明她對這疾病是免疫的。隨著這場緊急事件進展，免於受到感染對許多人的存活來說是很重要的。各國政府現在付出高額的費用，為了利用她的諮詢經驗，以及避免他們的公民感染。

Day 24 indemnity ~ stroke

Vocabulary 🎧 track 47

1. **indemnity** *n.[U]* 免罰 *[C]* 賠償金　▣ compensation
   - He has indemnity from prosecution, due to the pardon given to him by the governor.
   他獲得不起訴處份，因為州長給他的特赦。

2. **nutrition** *n.[U]* 營養　▣ nourishment
   - They didn't know much about nutrition in the 19th century, so everyone ate as much meat as they wished, and fiber was not an issue.
   他們在十九世紀時並不太懂營養，所以每個人都吃想吃的肉量，而纖維並不是重點。

3. **pharmacy** *n.[C]* 藥局
   - He has worked continuously at the same pharmacy for 35 years, helping to fulfill the dreams of health for many of the residents of this community.
   他在同一間藥局持續工作35年，幫助這個社區的居民實現健康的夢想。

4. **waive** *vt.* 放棄；擱置　▣ abandon, give up
   - We waived the right to litigate against the organizers in order to enter the race and become part of the massive event.
   我們為了能夠加入比賽並成為這大事件的一部分，放棄對組織者興訟的權利。

5. **collision** *n.[C]* 衝突；碰撞　▣ impact
   - The collision became an integral part of her life, as it left her handicapped and unable to pursue her chosen career.
   這場碰撞變成她的生命中不可缺的一部分，因為留下的是她變成身障，無法追求她選擇的生涯。

6. **purify** *vt.* 使純淨；淨化　　▣ cleanse, clarify　　▨ pollute, corrupt
   ◌ The waste treatment plant does its best to purify the sewage coming onto it before releasing it into the river.
   在把汙水排入河川之前，垃圾處理工廠盡其所能淨化進入廠內的汙水。

7. **investigator** *n.[C]* 調查員；研究者；私人偵探　　▣ researcher
   ◌ The primary investigator was on paid leave, giving me the opportunity to shine in her absence.
   主要的調查員帶薪休假，給了我一個機會在她不在時好好表現。

8. **mandatory** *adj.* 義務的；強制的；命令的　　▣ obligatory　　▨ optional
   ◌ You'll find that the correct footwear is not mandatory, but it will be difficult protecting yourself without it.
   你會發現穿著正確的鞋子並不是強制的，但沒有的話，你並不容易保護自己。

9. **comprehensive** *adj.* 全面的；廣泛的　　▣ inclusive　　▨ exclusive
   ◌ Starting in two years, a comprehensive education will be available to all students through grade 12, thus enabling us to better compete economically with other nations.
   在兩年後，12年全面性的教育將會讓所有學生利用，使我們在經濟上更能與其他國家競爭。

10. **stroke** *n.[C]* 一項工作；一次努力
    ◌ With one brief legislative stroke, he changed the way the Taiwanese would live, study, and conduct national affairs for decades.
    隨著一次簡潔的立法努力，他改變了數十年來台灣人生活、學習、以及處理國家事務的方式。

Paragraph 🎧 track 48

練習說明：

Step 1 下方有10個單字，請依文意將10個單字填入適當的空格中。

Step 2 播放MP3，確認填入答案是否正確，或可翻至 P107-112對答案。

Step 3 請跟著MP3逐句練習，練習完畢，請自己將下列段落念出，並在段落下方的時鐘記錄下時間。

comprehensive pharmacy nutrition purify stroke investigator waive mandatory indemnity collision

He now has 1 _____ from any lawsuits, granted by the president in honor of his contributions to society. In his younger days, he worked in a 2 _____, where he became interested in the health of local residents. He was particularly concerned with their 3 _____, which was generally poor due to low incomes. There was also a lack of knowledge of how to 4 _____ the food and drinking water, which he helped to eliminate through education. His longest-lasting change was developed during a drive home one day, when he observed a 5 _____ on the road ahead of him. While he consulted with the police 6 _____, the officer explained that the driver might not have died, had he been not 7 _____ the opportunity to be held inside the car. This led him to a campaign for 8 _____ seatbelt use in automobiles, leading to the legislation of a 9 _____ seatbelt law 22 years later. With this single 10 _____, the number of lives saved in the country increased every year.

Chapter 1 商用單字一把抓

他現在得到很多法律訴訟的免責，是總統為了紀念他對社會的貢獻而給予他的。在他年輕的時候，他在一家藥局工作，在那裡他對本地居民的健康產生興趣。他尤其關心他們的營養，因為低收入而普遍不好。如何使食物飲水更乾淨的知識是缺乏的，他透過教育的方式協助去除這種無知。他最持久的改變是在他一天開車回家時發展而成的，他看到了前方馬路有一場車禍。當他詢問警方調查員時，警官解釋說，駕駛有可能不會死亡，如果他沒有放棄被留在車子的機會（意指使用安全帶）。這使得他發起活動，主張在汽車內強制使用安全帶，最後在22年後導致全面安全帶的立法。隨著這個努力，這個國家裡被拯救的生命每年都在增加。

Day 25 scrutiny ~ administrative

Vocabulary track 49

1. **scrutiny** *n.[U, C]* 監視；監督
   - He is continually under intense scrutiny from government investigators due to his behavior in the past.
   因為他過去的行為，他正持續受到政府調查員的嚴密監督。

2. **defect** *n.[C]* 缺點；缺陷   同 fault, flaw   反 advantage
   - The defect in the insulation on the space shuttle is what led to the disastrous finish of the mission.
   太空梭上絕緣物的缺陷是導致此任務悲慘失敗的主因。

3. **supervise** *vt.* 監督；管理；指導   同 direct
   - She not only supervises us, she also rolls up her sleeves and helps when we get overloaded.
   她不只管理我們，當我們工作超載的時候，她也捲起袖口幫忙。

4. **system** *n.[C]* 系統   同 scheme
   - It is a good system for detecting malfunctions, but it has been complicated and time-consuming to implement.
   這是個優秀的系統，可以偵測故障，但操作很複雜也很耗時。

5. **executive** *n.[C]* 執行主管；經理   同 CEO, supervisor
   - He is the executive in charge of performing routine checks and notifying middle management of the results.
   他是經理，負責履行常規支票，以及通知中階管理人員結果。

6. **authorize** *vt.* 授權給；批准；允許   同 empower, assign   反 forbid, reject
   - All admittance to the property must be authorized by the technician on duty.

Chapter 1 商用單字一把抓

這塊地產所有進入的行為都必須由當班的技術人員授權。

7. **warning** *n.[C]* 警告　回 caution
　　◉ We gave him a warning and told him that the next infraction would be treated with more severe punishment.
　　我們給他一個警告，並告訴他下次犯規將會受到更嚴厲的處罰。

8. **novice** *n.[C]* 新手　回 newcomer, apparentice　反 expert
　　◉ He came to the firm as a novice mechanic, and now he is an executive in the maintenance division.
　　他來到這家公司一開始是新手機械人員，現在他是維修部門的經理了。

9. **allocate** *vt.* 分派；分配　回 assign
　　◉ We didn't properly allocate our resources, and now we are facing supply-chain delivery problems because of it.
　　我們沒有合適地分配資源，而現在我們因此面臨供應鏈遞送問題。

10. **administrative** *adj.* 管理的；行政的　回 executive
　　◉ It is a purely administrative change; it won't affect day-to-day assembly operations.
　　這完全是管理上的改變；它並不會影響每天的裝組運作。

Paragraph 🎧 track 50

練習說明：

Step 1　下方有10個單字，請依文意將10個單字填入適當的空格中。

Step 2　播放MP3，確認填入答案是否正確，或可翻至P107-112對答案。

Step 3　請跟著MP3逐句練習，練習完畢，請自己將下列段落念出，並在段落下方的時鐘記錄下時間。

novice administrative allocate authorize executive
warning system scrutiny defect supervise

In the beginning, we were all 1 _____ ; we didn't know that what we were trying to do was nearly impossible. We 2 _____ our capital as we saw fit, not according to what some 3 _____ committee 4 _____ . None of us deemed ourselves better than the rest, so there was no 5 _____ in charge. Friends and college associates tried to give us 6 _____ , but we didn't listen. They said our lack of management would lead to product 7 _____ . But our 8 _____ was how we wanted it. We didn't need any more 9 _____ than we had already given ourselves. We simply 10 _____ each other. This friendliness and spirit of accomplishment led to the founding of a great company, and we have a lot to be proud of.

在一開始，我們都是新手；我們不知道我們試著做的事幾乎是不可能的。我們以自己認為合適的方式分配資本，而非依照有些管理委員會所授權的內容。我們沒有一個人認為自己比其他人更優秀，所以並沒有經理執行人負責。朋友和同事試著警告我們，但我們不聽。他們說，我們缺乏管理會導致產品缺陷。但我們的系統就是我們要的樣子。我們不需要任何更多的監督，我們已經自我監督夠了。我們就是監督我們自己。這種友善態度和成就的精神導致一家大公司的成立，而我們有很多值得驕傲的事。

Speed Reading

1 分 秒

2 分 秒

3 分 秒

Day 26　expertise ~ adjust

Vocabulary　🎧 track 51

1. **expertise**　*n.[U]* 專門技術
   🔵 He has great expertise in sales, but he isn't very good at day-to-day office operations.
   他在業務銷售方面有很強的技術，但是他對於每天的辦公室運行就不是很擅長了。

2. **pension**　*n.[C]* 退休金
   🔵 We won't get our pensions until two years after we retire, so we have to maintain our current rate of savings.
   我們退休兩年之後才會拿到退休金，所以我們必須維持目前的存款比例。

3. **recommendation**　*n.[U]* 推薦 *[C]* 推薦信；建議　🔲 reference, advice
   🔵 He was new in town and needed a recommendation for a dentist, so I sent him to Dr. Findlay.
   他剛搬到鎮上，需要人家推薦一名牙醫，所以我請他去看Findlay醫生。

4. **survey**　*n.[C]* 調查；民意調查
   🔵 The high school students were in Shinyi, taking a survey of foreigners and their experiences in Taiwan.
   在信義區的高中生正在進行一項調查，是關於外國人和他們在台灣的經驗。

5. **circumstance**　*n.[P]* 情況；環境　🔲 situation, condition
   🔵 The circumstances were difficult because the company had no prior presence in the region.
   情況很困難，因為這間公司在這個區域並沒有領先的存在感。

6. affect *vt.* 影響　▣ influence
   ● I believe the collapse in the housing industry will affect all sectors of the economy.
   我相信營造業的衰退將會影響經濟所有部分。

7. allow *vt.* 允許　▣ permit, approve　▨ deny, refuse
   ● We will not allow International, Inc to get the better of us in the quest for market supremacy.
   我們將不會允許International公司在追求市場優勢方面贏過我們。

8. ambitious *adj.* 有野心的　▣ aspiring
   ● She has always been ambitious, even to the point of climbing all over her colleagues on her way up the ladder.
   她一直都很有野心，即使是必須踩著她所有同事往階梯上爬。

9. deadline *n.[C]* 截止時間　▣ due date
   ● The deadline in the trade talks passed three days ago, and there is still no word from either side of the negotiations.
   這場貿易談話的截止時間三天前早過了，談判雙方仍究沒有傳出任何消息。

10. adjust *vt.* 調整；改變...以適應
    ● We are going to adjust the prime interest rate downwards to help businesses recover from the previous seven quarters of recession.
    我們將調整主要利率往下，來幫助企業從前七季的不景氣中恢復。

Paragraph　🎧 track 52

練習說明：

Step 1 下方有10個單字，請依文意將10個單字填入適當的空格中。

Step 2 播放MP3，確認填入答案是否正確，或可翻至P107-112對答案。

Step 3 請跟著MP3逐句練習，練習完畢，請自己將下列段落念出，並在段落下方的時鐘記錄下時間。

Chapter 1 商用單字一把抓

expertise ambitious allow recommendation circumstance
survey deadline adjust pension affect

We didn't meet that 1   , but we think it's because the company was too 2 in their ship date. They didn't 3 for 4 that were beyond our control. Our 5 is for them to take a 6 of all employees connected with the effort, and use their 7 to 8 the methods used in future endeavors. The failure of this project will negatively 9 our company, but failure to adjust for the issues brought up by this committee will have more lasting consequences. If we can manage to save our corporation's future, we will all have fewer worries and will have well-funded 10 for our golden years.

  我們沒有趕上截止時間，但我們認為這是因為公司在運送日期方面太有野心了。他們不允許任何無法控制的情況發生。我們的建議是，他們應該做個調查，針對所有和這項努力有關的員工，並利用他們的專業來調整未來努力中所使用的方法。這項專業的失敗將會負面影響我們公司，但是無法配合此委員會提出問題的調整將會有更持續性的後果。如果我們能夠拯救公司的未來，我們將有更少的擔憂，也會在退休之後有資金充裕的退休金。

Day 27 party ~ credit

Vocabulary 🎧 track 53

1. **party** *n.[C]* 派對
   - The party was a raging success; not only did we have a great time, we also got to know the associates at our supplier.
   這場派對非常成功；不只我們玩得很開心，我們也認識了供應商的夥伴。

2. **provision** *n.[U]* 供應；預備 *[C]* 條款 📖 supply, preparation
   - There is a provision in the contract which leads to penalties for not meeting the completion timeline.
   合約中有一項條款，指出沒有達到完成時間的處罰。

3. **apologize** *vi.* 道歉
   - When he apologized in public for the misstep, his media visibility and credibility increased.
   當他當眾為過失道歉時，他的媒體可見度和信賴度都提升了。

4. **competitor** *n.[C]* 競爭者；對手 📖 contestant, opponent
   - They were a great competitor, but they didn't see the direction the market segment was going, and now they face bankruptcy.
   他們曾是很強的競爭者，但他們沒察覺市場部分的方向怎麼走，而現在他們面臨破產。

5. **transit** *n.[U]* 運輸；運送 📖 transportation, carriage
   - The public transit system in Taipei has made for better living and commuting conditions for its residents and for those in its suburbs.
   台北的大眾運輸系統為市民和郊區的居民創造更好的生活及通勤條件。

6. **triumph** *n.[C]* 勝利；成功 📖 victory, conquest 🔄 loss, failure
   - It was a great triumph for the common man, one which still has

relevance to this day.
那是對於人類的一次大勝利，現今仍有影響力。

7. **haggle** *vi.* 討價還價　圓 argue　圖 agree
   ◦ They usually haggle for prices on everything, so they get better prices than I do, as I'm not used to doing that.
   他們通常對每樣東西都會討價還價，所以他們比我得到更好的價格，因為我不習慣殺價。

8. **venue** *n.[C]* 地點　圓 scene
   ◦ It is a great venue for an acoustic show because it's an intimate setting with great acoustics.
   這裡是聽覺表演絕佳的場地，因為這裡配備有精密的音響設備。

9. **payment** *n.[U]* 支付；付款　*[C]* 支付的款項
   ◦ The payment wasn't received in time, so the late fee of 8% will be charged to your account.
   該筆付款沒有及時收到，所以8%的延遲費會向你的帳戶收款。

10. **credit** *n.[U]* 信用；信賴　圓 trust, faith
    ◦ She has a line of credit with that bank that can easily pay off the mortgage on her house and its lot.
    她和那間銀行的信貸額度，可以輕易的付清房屋及土地貸款。

Paragraph 🎧 track 54

練習說明：

Step 1　下方有10個單字，請依文意將10個單字填入適當的空格中。

Step 2　播放MP3，確認填入答案是否正確，或可翻至P107-112對答案。

Step 3　請跟著MP3逐句練習，練習完畢，請自己將下列段落念出，並在段落下方的時鐘記錄下時間。

> triumph payment venue credit transit
> competitor haggle provision party apologize

We've always had really good 1 _____ . This has been a
2 _____ for us, as we've always been motivated to not have
money problems. We started soon after we got married. We bought some
items for our home on time and made the 3 _____ in a timely
manner. We found that the Household Appliances Show at Taoyuan Stadium was a terrific 4 _____ for shopping. We didn't have a car
yet, but it was easily reached via public 5 _____ . We found it
easy to compare products from different companies. When we had made
our decisions, we then spent time 6 _____ with our favorite store
representatives and their 7 _____ . They were all easy to talk to,
and offered us easy terms to buy their wares. It was a big home-outfitting
8 _____ and we loved it. We only had one 9 _____
for any deal: They had to offer free delivery. One of the best dealers
10 _____ that he was not able to do that, so we had to go with our
second choice.

　　我們一直有良好的信用。這對我們來說是種勝利，因為我們一直被鼓勵
不要有金錢問題。我們在結婚之後就開始了。我們為家裡買了一些東西，並
且付款都很及時。我們發現桃園體育館的家電展是個買東西的好地方。我們
還沒有車子，但是那裡很容易利用大眾運輸工具抵達。我們發現比較各家廠
商的產品很容易。當我們做出決定，我們便開始花時間和我們最喜愛的店家
代表及他們的對手討價還價。他們都很好說話，並且提供我們很優惠的條件
購買他們的東西。那是場住家裝潢的派對，我們愛死了。我們對於任何交易
只有一個條件：他們必須免運費。有一個最好的賣家道歉說他無法做到，所
以我們只好去找第二選擇的賣家。

Speed Reading

1   分   秒

2   分   秒

3   分   秒

Day 28 tariff ~ warehouse

Vocabulary 🎧 track 55

1. **tariff** *n.[C]* 關稅　🔄 tax
   ● There are tariffs on most things produced off-shore, which decreases competitiveness and gives an advantage to local manufacturers.
   多數離岸製造的物品都有關稅，可以減低競爭力，並給予本地製造商優勢。

2. **voucher** *n.[C]* 代券　🔄 ticket
   ● We are giving you vouchers instead of a per diem; the vouchers will pay for all meals, excepting alcoholic merchandise.
   我們正提供代券而非每日津貼；代券可以用來支付所有的餐點，除了酒精類產品之外。

3. **consign** *vt.* 把...委託給；託運　🔄 entrust
   ● We consigned the antiques at the dealer, and he will get 40% of the purchase price, excluding taxes.
   我們把這些古董委託給那個業者，他會得到成交價格的40%，不含稅。

4. **dealer** *n.[C]* 業者；交易商　🔄 merchandiser, merchant
   ● He is a dealer of automobiles, specializing in European high-end and boutique models.
   他是汽車的商人，專門是歐洲高端車和精緻的樣式車。

5. **guarantee** *n.[C], vt.* 保證　🔄 pledge, promise　🔁 break
   ● We will guarantee your purchase for the length of ownership of your vehicle, but the warranty may not be transferred.
   我們將會保證您的購買，只要您是車主，但是保證權利可能無法被轉讓。

6. **credible** *adj.* 可靠的；可信的　🔄 conceivable, reliable　🔁 unbelievable
   ● That is a credible theory, and we will pursue it until the evidence

leads us elsewhere.
那是個可靠的推測，我們會追尋直到證據把我們帶到另一個地方。

7. quota *n.[C]* 配額；定額
    ◉ His company has instituted a quota system on sales, and many of their longtime sales force are browsing job sites.　他的公司已經開始業務銷售的配額系統，很多做很久的業務人員在瀏覽求職網站了。

8. surplus *n.[C]* 過剩 圓 excess
    ◉ There was a surplus of commodities this year, as low demand and a bumper crop made for fewer sales than in most recent years.
    今年商品過剩，因為需求減低以及過量盛產使得比往年銷售更少。

9. trademark *n.[C]* 商標 圓 logo, brand
    ◉ Our trademark is the most valuable piece of intellectual property we own, and we go to great lengths to protect it.　我們的商標是我們擁有最有價值的智慧財產，我們會盡一切所能保護它。

10. warehouse *n.[C]* 倉庫 圓 storehouse, depot
    ◉ That has been sitting in our warehouse for so long that its value has depreciated to almost nothing.
    那樣物品在我們的倉庫放太久了，價值已經貶到幾乎等於零了。

Paragraph 🎧 track 56

練習說明：

Step 1 下方有10個單字，請依文意將10個單字填入適當的空格中。

Step 2 播放MP3，確認填入答案是否正確，或可翻至P107-112對答案。

Step 3 請跟著MP3逐句練習，練習完畢，請自己將下列段落念出，並在段落下方的時鐘記錄下時間。

tariff dealer surplus quota warehouse
guarantee voucher trademark consign credible

It's a tough time to be a ₁ _____ . The new ₂ _____ has not made selling our products any easier. We expected low inventories after that legislation, but we are instead stuck with a lot of ₃ _____ stock in our ₄ _____ . There had been a ₅ _____ for foreign goods in place before the tariff was announced, and we assumed that more sales would come our way in the absence of imported competition. We learned, however, that lack of competition was not a ₆ _____ of sales. We are attempting to move more units by giving prospective customers ₇ _____ for discounts, but it appears we are going to have to ₈ _____ much of our present stock to closeout distributors. If things get any worse, we won't have any reason to keep protecting our ₉ _____ . We understand from ₁₀ _____ sources that most people don't see the need to buy by brand name in this market anymore. It is probably past time to try to change our focus and diversify our company.

　　現在當一名交易商很辛苦，新的關稅並未讓我們銷售產品更容易。我們期待在立法後可以減低庫存量，但是我們反而在倉庫裡充滿了大量的剩餘產品。在關稅宣布之前，外國商品有個配額，我們假定在沒有進口的競爭之外，我們可以有更高的銷售量。然而我們學習到，沒有競爭並不保證銷售。我們正透過提供潛在客戶折扣券，試著賣出更多產品，但是看起來我們將必須委託很多現存的產品給出清商。如果事態變得更糟，我們將沒有理由繼續保護我們的商標。我們透過可靠的消息了解到大多數的人再也不認為需要在市場上購買品牌。可能是試著改變我們的焦點的時候，並使公司更多元化。

Speed Reading

1　分　秒

2　分　秒

3　分　秒

Day 29 circulation ~ leaflet

Vocabulary track 57

1. **circulation** *n.[C]* 發行量
   - Magazine circulation has been in steep decline in the last two decades, due to increasing electronic competition.
   雜誌發行量在過去二十年之間劇烈衰退，因為持續增加的電子競爭者。

2. **confidential** *adj.* 秘密的；機密的　同 secret, private　反 public
   - All results are completely confidential and will not be available to anyone outside this drug trial.
   所有的結果都完全保密，此藥檢外的任何人都不會知道。

3. **dictate** *vt.* 口述；要求；指定　同 verbalize
   - In the old days, we dictated any communications we had to a secretary, but now dictation is nearly extinct.
   以前我們口述信件內容給祕書，但現在口述幾乎絕跡了。

4. **translation** *n.[U]* 翻譯　同 interpretation
   - The translation leaves something to be desired, but it makes it possible for non-native speakers to understand the important concepts.
   這份翻譯還可以更好，但是它讓非母語人士可以了解重要的觀念。

5. **campaign** *n.[C]* 活動；競選活動　同 contest
   - Her presidential campaign was mostly self-funded, and the unsuccessful run nearly bankrupted her.
   她的總統競選活動大多是自己提供資金，而失敗的競選幾乎使她破產。

6. **elaborate** *vi.* 詳細說明　反 simplify
   - You need to elaborate, and please use relevant examples, so we can see your side of the problem, too.

你必須詳細說明，並且請使用相關的例子，我們才能看到你那一邊的問題。

7. forward *vt.* 轉交；遞送 圓 deliver
   ◎ The post office forwarded the letter to my current address, but it arrived after the deadline and I lost the chance to gain the position.
   郵局把這封信轉交到我現在的住址，但這在截止日期後才到，我失去了獲得這個職位的機會。

8. compose *vt.* 創作 圓 create
   ◎ You have to compose your speech well in advance of the date you'll give it, so you can eliminate all possible misinterpretations.
   你必須在發表演說之前好好地創作演說的內容，這樣你就能排除所有可能的誤解。

9. notify *vt.* 通知；報告 圓 inform, report 反 conceal, hide
   ◎ In order to avoid restriction of on-duty personnel, you must notify us of any planned leave well in advance.
   為了避免限制當班的人員，你必須通知我們關於任何計劃好的請假。

10. leaflet *n.[C]* 小冊子 圓 brochure, booklet
    ◎ The leaflet gave the hours and dates of operation, also spelling out seasonal and holiday closures.
    這本小冊子提供營業的時間和日期，還有季節性和假日性的歇業。

Paragraph 🎧 track 58

練習說明：

Step 1 下方有10個單字，請依文意將10個單字填入適當的空格中。

Step 2 播放MP3，確認填入答案是否正確，或可翻至P107-112對答案。

Step 3 請跟著MP3逐句練習，練習完畢，請自己將下列段落念出，並在段落下方的時鐘記錄下時間。

compose leaflet elaborate circulation dictate
notify campaign confidential forward translation

I am ___1___ a ___2___ concerning our
___3___ to build youth soccer fields on city land. I need
you to complete the Spanish ___4___ in two days. Please
___5___ me if this is not possible. If it helps, you can
___6___ it to Janie, who has near-fluency in the language. If you
find any necessary changes, please ___7___ your concerns so
you can ___8___ on them. I would like the two of you to keep
the contents of the leaflet ___9___, however, as I don't want any
advance ___10___ of its points. If successful, this campaign will give
local youth an outlet for their athletic pursuits and create a good place to
spend their leisure time.

我正在創作一本小冊子，是關於我們利用市府土地建立青年足球場的活動。我需要你在兩天後完成西班牙文的翻譯。請通知我是否可行。如果有幫助的話，你可以口述給Janie，她的西班牙文很流利。如果你發現任何需要修改的地方，請把你的擔憂轉送出來，這樣你可以詳細說明。我希望你們兩位對於小冊子的內容保密，因為我不希望任何一點內容提前曝光。如果成功的話，這個活動將給本地年輕人一個追求運動的出口，而且創造一個好場所讓他們度過休閒時間。

Speed Reading

1 ___ 分 ___ 秒

2 ___ 分 ___ 秒

3 ___ 分 ___ 秒

Day 30 publicity ~ appendix

Vocabulary 🎧 track 59

1. **publicity** *n.[U]* 名聲；宣傳　回 fame
   - He thinks even negative publicity is good for his visibility, and he likes any opportunity to appear in the media.　他認為即使是負面宣傳對於他的曝光都是好的，他喜歡任何在媒體出現的機會。

2. **circular** *adj.* 公告；通知　回 notice
   - The circular helped form the opinions of many people that a recall was in order for the politician.
   這則公告幫忙形成許多人的意見，罷免那位政客已經就序了。

3. **affirm** *vt.* 堅稱；證實　回 declare, confirm　反 deny
   - I would like to affirm our position on the matter; we believe our player acted in the best interests of the team and our community.
   我想要堅持我們在這件事的立場；我們相信我們的球員是為了團隊和社區的最佳利益而行動。

4. **proofread** *vt.* 校正；校對　回 revise, edit
   - I haven't had time to proofread the bulletin yet, so I won't be circulating it today.　我沒有時間校對公告，所以我今天不會發行它。

5. **postage** *n.[U]* 郵資
   - There isn't enough postage on the package, so the post office rejected it, and I have to get more cash from the ATM.
   這個包裹的郵資不足，所以郵局將它退回，我必須從提款機領更多現金。

6. **actually** *adv.* 真正地　回 truly
   - He actually said that he was in favor of the legislation, and he thinks

he has been greatly misunderstood.
他真的說他比較支持這項立法，他認為他被嚴重誤解了。

7. **tremendous** *adj.* 巨大的；極大的；很棒的　圖 enormous, marvelous
   ● There is a tremendous grassroots movement in favor of saving the building as a historical landmark.
   有一項極大的草根活動，支持保護這棟建物作為歷史地標。

8. **commercial** *n.[C]* 廣告
   ● It isn't a great commercial opportunity, but sometimes I think keeping something I enjoy afloat is just as important as making money.
   這不是個好的廣告機會，但有時候我認為讓我喜歡的東西保持下去，和賺錢一樣重要。

9. **flyer** *n.[C]* 傳單　圖 handbill, leaflet
   ● He composed a flyer to gain support for his neighborhood watch organization.　他作了一份傳單，來獲得他社區守望組織的支持。

10. **appendix** *n.[C]* 附錄；附加物　圖 supplement, attachment
    ● The appendix to the book includes an interview with the author, footnotes made by the editor, and several contemporary critical reviews.
    這本書的附錄包括作者訪問、編者備註、以及幾則當代的評論。

Paragraph 🎧 track 60

練習說明：

Step 1 下方有10個單字，請依文意將10個單字填入適當的空格中。
Step 2 播放MP3，確認填入答案是否正確，或可翻至P107-112對答案。
Step 3 請跟著MP3逐句練習，練習完畢，請自己將下列段落念出，並在段落下方的時鐘記錄下時間。

proofread flyer affirm postage commercial
actually publicity circular appendix tremendous

The 1 _____ generated by the 2 _____ 3 _____ the 4 _____ interest of the local citizenry in the restoration of the city's former 5 _____ district. It was 6 _____ the second attempt by Jim to create enthusiasm for the project, following his written presentation to the city council. I 7 _____ that before it was published, and it was a good piece of work. However, we found that the flyer put his ideas in front of the public more readily. Jim had predicted in the 8 _____ of his work that a 9 _____ would most likely be the best follow-up to the city council testimony. All that was needed was to raise funds for 10 _____ to get it to as many residents as possible, and that was cheerfully given by Kate Humphries, a local business owner.

這份傳單所造成的注意，證實了本地市民極有興趣在恢復這座城市以前的商業區。事實上，這是Jim第二次嘗試，為這個計劃造成熱誠，在他寫了書面的報告給市議會後。我在印刷前校對了那份報告，它寫得很好。然而我們發現，傳單把他想法更快地呈現在大眾面前。Jim在他的作品的附錄已經預視到，一份傳單公報是在市議會證言後最好的後續作法。需要的只是募集郵資來寄出給愈多人愈好，而本地的商人Kate Humphries很樂意地捐獻。

Answer Key

Day 1

1. conference
2. arrangement
3. competition
4. attend
5. cancel
6. agreement
7. assured
8. feedback
9. consequence
10. consider

Day 2

1. Marketing
2. opportunity
3. improve
4. determine
5. assist
6. seminar
7. notify
8. withhold
9. negotiate
10. convince

Day 3

1. pharmacist
2. librarian
3. profession
4. manufactured
5. factory
6. produce
7. employment
8. secretary
9. coordinate
10. operator

Day 4

1. employer
2. employees
3. manipulate
4. attorney
5. assistant
6. architect
7. representative
8. department
9. agricultural
10. transformed

Day 5

1. accounting
2. assets
3. accumulated
4. capital
5. assumed
6. reduce
7. audit
8. aggressive
9. confidence
10. risk

Day 6

1. mortgage
2. invested
3. balanced

4. fluctuate
5. penalty
6. dividend
7. revenue
8. foreign
9. exchange
10. anticipate

Day 7

1. forecast
2. corporation
3. joint venture
4. resolve
5. establish
6. reputation
7. gathering
8. recognition
9. accomplishments
10. evaluate

Day 8

1. prosperity
2. entrepreneurs
3. enhance
4. merit
5. subsidiary
6. adhered to
7. revised
8. reinforced
9. franchise
10. achievement

Day 9

1. situation
2. accommodate
3. strike
4. interrupt
5. prohibit
6. punctually
7. partition
8. calendar
9. directory
10. appointment

Day 10

1. memorandum
2. remove
3. document
4. vacancy
5. workshop
6. Xerox
7. headquarters
8. motivate
9. personalized
10. assignment

Day 11

1. consumed
2. bargain
3. affordable
4. turnover
5. contract
6. substitute
7. offered
8. transaction
9. permanent

Day 12

1. eligible
2. candidates

3. promoting
4. provide
5. compensate
6. apprentices
7. hire
8. background
9. including
10. capacity

Day 13

1. display
2. technical
3. laboratory
4. satellite
5. stores
6. software
7. compatible
8. outage
9. durable
10. duplicate

Day 14

1. Retrieval
2. operate
3. advanced
4. innovative
5. device
6. component
7. static
8. troubleshooting
9. outlet
10. fuel

Day 15

1. laundromat
2. occupies
3. renovate
4. laundry
5. real estate
6. construction
7. ornaments
8. mattress
9. appliance
10. possession

Day 16

1. suburbs
2. relocate
3. rural
4. burglars
5. adapter
6. furnishings
7. kitchenware
8. balcony
9. landlord
10. storage

Day 17

1. customs
2. pedestrian
3. accelerated
4. vehicle
5. accommodations
6. excursion
7. detour
8. navigate
9. cargo
10. brochures

Day 18

1. sightseeing
2. cruise
3. valid
4. expedition
5. itinerary
6. exotic
7. intersection
8. escalator
9. freight
10. round trip

Day 19

1. drugstore
2. patrons
3. diversified
4. demand
5. garment
6. purchase
7. variety
8. menu
9. delivery
10. tags

Day 20

1. retailer
2. request
3. wholesale
4. distributor
5. ship
6. artificial
7. pushcarts
8. samples
9. fragrant
10. digest

Day 21

1. pastime
2. celebrity
3. amusing
4. scenario
5. premiere
6. Fahrenheit
7. referee
8. defense
9. applauding
10. audition

Day 22

1. degree
2. periodical
3. participating
4. tactics
5. editorials
6. stadium
7. trophies
8. symphony
9. rehearsals
10. Celsius

Day 23

1. emergency
2. handicap
3. diagnosed
4. record
5. vital
6. alleviating
7. contagious
8. immune
9. infection
10. premium

Day 24

1. indemnity
2. pharmacy
3. nutrition
4. purify
5. collision
6. investigator
7. waived
8. mandatory
9. comprehensive
10. stroke

Day 25

1. novices
2. allocated
3. administrative
4. authorized
5. executive
6. warnings
7. defects
8. system
9. scrutiny
10. supervised

Day 26

1. deadline
2. ambitious
3. allow
4. circumstances
5. recommendation
6. survey
7. expertise
8. adjust
9. affect
10. pensions

Day 27

1. credit
2. triumph
3. payments
4. venue
5. transit
6. haggling
7. competitors
8. party
9. provision
10. apologized

Day 28

1. dealer
2. tariff
3. surplus
4. warehouses
5. quota
6. guarantee
7. vouchers
8. consign
9. trademark
10. credible

Day 29

1. composing
2. leaflet
3. campaign
4. translation
5. notify
6. dictate
7. forward
8. elaborate
9. confidential
10. circulation

Day 30

1. publicity
2. flyer
3. affirmed
4. tremendous
5. commercial
6. actually
7. proofread
8. appendix
9. circular
10. postage

Chapter 2

閱讀測驗大解密

Part 5　Incomplete Sentences

101. In order to be considered for a _____ , an employee must prove they are an excellent worker. ***
(A) vacation
(B) position
(C) promotion
(D) certificate

中　譯

為了能被考量_____，員工必須證明自己是優秀的人員。
(A) 假期　　　(B) 職位　　　(C) 申遷　　　(D) 證書

解答提示

此題的四個選項和「職場」或多或少都有關係，不過vacation（假期）和 certificate（證書）的關連性較低，所以可以先排除此兩個選項。剩下的兩個選項中，如果選擇position（職位），須注意前面並沒有任何形容詞，會讓句子失去意義，因此必須選擇promotion（升遷）才能完成這個句子。

瑣碎時間看這裡

< 被動語態 >
英文中的被動語態可以表現出「客觀」的語氣，所以在正式書面語言中常使用，特別是商業書信為了避免過於直接、主觀，更是大量使用被動語態。
被動語態：**be + p.p.**
常見用法：**be considered**（被認為是…）、**be seen**（被看成是）、**be thought of**（被想作是）…等。

102. If you have not passed your college entrance exam by August 31st, 2013, your test scores will _____ , and you will not be able to retake the exam this year. *****
(A) expire

(B) retire
(C) expand
(D) include

 中　譯

如果你在2013年8月31日前沒有通過大學入學考試，你的測驗成績將會_____，而且你今年將無法重考。
(A) 到期　　　(B) 退休　　　(C) 擴充　　　(D) 包括

解答提示

介系詞by後面加上時間，通常都表示「期限」的意涵，所以可以朝這個方向解題。加上選項 (B)、(C)、(D) 都和test scores無法形成有意義的組合，所以答案很明顯就是 (A)。

103. Due to inclement weather, the 1:00 p.m. race has been _____. **
　　　(A) finished
　　　(B) awarded
　　　(C) postponed
　　　(D) raced

中　譯

因為險惡的天氣，下午一點鐘的賽跑已經_____了。
(A) 結束　　　(B) 頒獎　　　(C) 延期　　　(D) 比賽

解答提示

此題的重點在於須理解形容詞inclement（天氣險惡的），一旦了解這個字，那麼答案就很明顯是postponed（延期）了。

 瑣碎時間看這裡

<被動語態現在完成式>
「被動語態」加上「現在完成式」的公式如下：
have/has + been + p.p.
been就是be動詞的過去分詞，所以整個公式的分析是：

> have/has + been 　　　　　　　現在完成式
> (be) + p.p. 　　　　　　　　　被動語態
>
> 我們來看看下面的例子就會更清楚囉！
> · The car **is fixed** by the mechanic.
>   → be動詞is改成現在完成式has been
>   → The car **has been fixed** by the mechanic.

104. You should all have received an _____ for this meeting. *
  (A) report
  (B) agenda
  (C) excuse
  (D) reason

中　　譯

你們應該都已經收到這場會議的_____了。
(A) 報告 (B) 議程表 (C) 藉口 (D) 理由

解答提示

此題可以用冠詞來當線索，冠詞是an，所以一定是母音開頭的字，所以可以先把選項 (A) 和 (D) 刪去。然後剩下excuse（藉口）和agenda（議程表），當然只有agenda和meeting是有關係的囉！

 瑣碎時間看這裡

> < 情態助動詞 + 完成式 >
> 常見的情態助動詞加上完成式有以下幾個：
> (1) should + have + p.p.
> (2) must + have + p.p.
> (3) may/might + have + p.p.
> 情態助動詞加上完成式有表示「過去」的意思，從以下兩個例子就可以看出差別囉！
> · You **should** all **receive** an agenda for this meeting.
>   （你們應該都要收到這場會議的議程表。）
>   →表示正要把議程表發送，或即將發送

Chapter 2 閱讀測驗大解密

- You **should** all **have received** an agenda for this meeting.
（你們應該都已經收到這場會議的議程表了。）
→表示早已經把議程表發送出去了

105. Please press 1 to _____ this appointment. *
    (A) affirm
    (B) restate
    (C) confirm
    (D) analyze

中 譯

請按1來_____這個約會。
(A) 聲稱　　　(B) 再聲明　　(C) 確認　　　(D) 分析

解答提示

此題所測驗的是confirm an appointment（確認約定／約會）這個搭配字詞，
嚴格說來，其他的選項都是及物動詞，硬要加上appointment當受詞在文法上
也沒有錯誤，但是語意上並不合適。在準備多益考試的時候，要多多背誦這
一類動詞和名詞的常用搭配。

106. Each Employee of the Month will receive a _____ lunch from the
cafeteria. **
    (A) complimentary
    (B) expensive
    (C) healthy
    (D) costly

中 譯

每月最佳員工將獲得自助餐廳_____午餐。
(A) 贈送的　　(B) 昂貴的　　(C) 健康的　　(D) 貴重的

解答提示

此題測驗的一樣是搭配詞的使用，每月最佳員工獲得的獎品應該是「贈送
的」，所以合理的答案是選項 (A)。其他的選項雖然都是形容詞，但是所造成

的文意並不恰當。

107. This weekend's festival will _____ food, musical entertainment and
activities for the kids. ***
(A) preclude
(B) conclude
(C) include
(D) exclude

中　譯

這個週末的節慶將_____食物、音樂娛樂、和孩子的活動。
(A) 阻止　　　(B) 結束　　　(C) 包括　　　(D) 排除

解答提示

此題的四個選項字尾都相同，是企圖造成干擾的方法，不過如果熟記單字的
意思，其實正確答案是 (C)，include是個很常見的字喔，應該不至於被其他選
項騙到才對呢！

108. The campground _____ cabins for those who would like to stay in
out of the weather. ***
(A) costs
(B) tours
(C) details
(D) provides

中　譯

這個營地_____小屋給想要避避天氣待在室內的人。
(A) 花費　　　(B) 旅行　　　(C) 詳述　　　(D) 提供

解答提示

此題首先可以用字義判斷，只有provide（提供）在這個句子裡，句子才有意
義。此外也可以利用句型 provide sth. for sb. 來作答。

 瑣碎時間看這裡

＜表示人的關係代名詞＞
有時候我們要表達「～的人」，這時候可以用以下方法：
(1) people who
(2) those who
(3) whoever
‧ The campground provides cabins for <u>people who</u> would like to stay in out of the weather.
　= The campground provides cabins for <u>those who</u> would like to stay in out of the weather.
　= The campground provides cabins for <u>whoever</u> would like to stay in out of the weather.

109. There is a very high _____ that your first job out of college will use computer skills. ✳✳✳
(A) likelihood
(B) childhood
(C) personality
(D) employer

中　譯

非常有_____你大學畢業的第一份工作將用到電腦技能。
(A) 可能　　　(B) 童年　　　(C) 人格　　　(D) 雇主

解答提示

此題的答案難度較高，應選 (A)，likelihood（可能性）是從形容詞likely（可能的）而來，是抽象名詞，常見的搭配句型如下：
(1)There is little/much likelihood that S + V（不太可能... / 很有可能...）
(2)The likelihood is that S + V（很可能...）
(3)In all likelihood, S + V（很可能...）

110. I will have to call _____ services to see when they are going to have the computer system repaired. ✳✳✳
(A) advanced

(B) technical
(C) standard
(D) improved

中　譯

我將必須打電話給_____服務部門，看看他們什麼時候要把電腦系統修好。
(A) 先進的　　(B) 技術的　　(C) 標準的　　(D) 改進的

解答提示

修理電腦的工作當然是資訊技術相關的部門，所以答案是選項 (B) technical。
其它像是information（資訊）、technology（科技）、technical（技術的）這
一類的字都是電腦有關的。

 瑣碎時間看這裡

<間接問句>
間接問句（who, when, where, how, what...）也可以視為關係副詞的簡單
化：
· I will have to call technical services to see **when they are going to have the
computer system repaired**.
= I will have to call technical services to see **the time at which** they are
going to have the computer system repaired.

要特別注意使用when的時候，不要和「表示時間的副詞」when搞混，因
為表示時間的副詞when一般不會接未來式。
· Tell me when he comes.
（他來的時候跟我說一聲。）
· Tell me when he is coming.
（跟我說他什麼時候會來。）

111. Are you attending the big art _____ this weekend to benefit the
art museum? **
(A) expense
(B) benefactor
(C) sale
(D) work

中　譯

你要參加這個週末的大型藝術＿＿＿＿＿，替美術館募集經費嗎？
(A) 花費　　　　(B) 捐助人　　(C) 拍賣　　　　(D) 作品

解答提示

句子後面的benefit the art museum（替美術館募集經費）可作為提示，一般就是指拍賣等相關的活動，故選 (C)。

 瑣碎時間看這裡

< 現在進行式表示未來 >
英文中用現在進行式表示未來有以下幾種情況，如果熟悉了用法之後，會發現其實很多句子的功能是重疊的：
(1) 含有動作性的動詞：go, come, leave, arrive…
(2) 計畫中的事件
(3) 帶有意願的句子

以下三個例子我們來看看各含有上述哪些意義？
(A) We are leaving for Japan tomorrow.
　　（我們明天要去日本。）
　　→具有 (1)、(2)、(3)
(B) They are having a barbecue this Saturday.
　　（他們這個星期六要辦烤肉。）
　　→具有 (2)、(3)
(C) Is Amy interviewing the candidate this afternoon?
　　（今天下午Amy要面試應徵者嗎？）
　　→具有 (2)、(3)

112. You should make a ＿＿＿＿＿＿ if you want to eat right away. **
(A) announcement
(B) appointment
(C) plan
(D) reservation

中　譯

如果你想要馬上可以用餐，你應該要＿＿＿＿＿＿。
(A) 宣布　　　(B) 約會　　　(C) 計劃　　　(D) 訂位

解答提示

此題是和餐廳用餐有關係，所以應該選擇make a reservation（預訂；訂位）
這個搭配詞，所以選 (D)。其他的選項也可以和動詞make形成搭配詞，但是
在這個句子中並不恰當。

113. If you buy your _____ online, you can usually save about 30% from
the price at the door. ***
(A) lunch
(B) tickets
(C) photographs
(D) property

中　譯

如果你在網路上購買＿＿＿＿＿＿，你通常可以省下直接買票的30%（打七折）。
(A) 午餐　　　(B) 票券　　　(C) 照片　　　(D) 房地產

解答提示

此題的提示是at the door（在門口），其實就是指到現場買，一般當然是指電
影票或入場券等票券，所以選 (B)。

114. If we have a test done at your lab, will we get the _____ today? **
(A) product
(B) equipment
(C) x-ray
(D) results

中　譯

如果我們在你的實驗室做測試，我們今天能夠得到＿＿＿＿＿＿嗎？
(A) 產品　　　(B) 設備　　　(C) X光　　　(D) 結果

解答提示

相對於test（測試）的就是result（結果；結論），其他的單字雖然多少和lab（實驗）有關係，但是放到句子裡頭語意就會怪怪的唷！

 瑣碎時間看這裡

< have + 物 + p.p. >
這個句型是用來表達「請某人做某件事」，重點是某件事被完成，至於某人是誰則不重要，或是大家心知肚明。

· If we **have a test done** at your lab, will we get the results today?

這個測試不會是we做的，當然是實驗室裡的人員進行的，所以才會用這個句型。

如果真的是we做的測驗，那麼會變成以下的說法：
· If we **do a test** at your lab, will we get the results today?

特別注意在中文翻譯的時候，兩者幾乎沒有差別，都翻成「如果我們在你的實驗室做測試，我們今天能夠得到結果嗎？」但事實上，所要表達的意思是不同的。

我們再來看看一個日常生活的例子：
我想剪頭髮。（當然是設計師來剪，所以重點是「剪頭髮」，而不是誰來剪。）
(1) I want to **have my hair cut**.
(2) I want to **cut my hair**.（→自己剪自己的頭髮）

115. Melissa Ramos, one of our student therapists, invites you to her _____ as an assistant today at 12:30 p.m. ***
(A) house
(B) report
(C) workshop
(D) production

中　譯

Melissa Ramos，我們學生治療師之一，邀請你今天下午12點半到她的＿＿＿＿＿當助理。
(A) 房子　　　　(B) 報告　　　　(C) 研討會　　　(D) 產品

解答提示

這一題可以用assistant（助理）來作為提示，需要助理的場合或情況當然是workshop（研討會）最合適了。

116. Having meaningful relationships is ＿＿＿＿＿ to maintaining your immune system and avoiding depression. ***
(A) critical
(B) valued
(C) required
(D) possible

中　譯

有著有意義的人際關係對於保持免疫系統以及避免憂鬱症很＿＿＿＿＿。
(A) 關鍵的　　(B) 重要的　　　(C) 要求的　　(D) 可能的

解答提示

這一題要注意空格後的介系詞to，可以和它搭配的只有critical，也是最符合句意的選項，故選 (A)。

117. You must take the subway to the Tenth Street station, ＿＿＿＿＿, and hail a taxi from there to Center Park. ***
(A) unload
(B) board
(C) disembark
(D) ride

中　譯

你必須搭地鐵到第十號車站、＿＿＿＿＿、然後從那裡叫計程車到中央公園。
(A) 卸貨　　　(B) 上車　　　(C) 下車　　　(D) 搭乘

解答提示

此題是前往某地的交通方式步驟，一共三個步驟，中間遺失的步驟顯然就是「下車」，才能再叫計程車，所以答案要選 (C)。

118. I have _____ in early childhood education, having been an assistant in a preschool for the past five years. ***
(A) help
(B) practice
(C) experiment
(D) experience

中　　譯

我在早期兒童教育有相關_____，過去五年在幼稚園一直擔任助理工作。
(A) 幫助　　　(B) 練習　　　(C) 實驗　　　(D) 經驗

解答提示

此題是求職時會用到的句子，也是NEW TOEIC常考的範圍。從後半句having been an assistant in a preschool for the past five years即可得知是與工作相關的題目，所以答案就是 (D)。

 瑣碎時間看這裡

< 分詞構句 >
分詞構句是把副詞子句轉化，用來表示「時間」、「原因」、「條件」、「讓步」及「附帶狀況」。
· When I came home, I saw the door opened.
　= When coming home, I saw the door opened.
　（當我回家時，我看到門是打開的。）
· Because he is sick, he didn't come to work today.
　= Being sick, he didn't come to work today.
　（因為生病了，他今天沒來上班。）
要特別注意的地方是，前後兩個子句的主詞應該是同一個人。

119. I'll wave my small Taiwanese flag at the airport, so that you will _____
to pick me out in the crowd. ✱✱✱
(A) appreciate
(B) be able
(C) be unlikely
(D) have

我會在機場揮動小支的台灣國旗，所以你就_____在人群中找到我。
(A) 感謝　　　(B) 能夠　　　(C) 不可能　　　(D) 必須

解答提示

此題可先刪去選項 (A)，因為沒有appreciate to這種搭配詞。剩下三個選項再
以文意判斷，答案即是選項 (B)。

 瑣碎時間看這裡

< so和so that >
以上兩個連接詞雖然很像，但是意思卻有點不同，請看以下例子：
· It is raining, **so** we have to cancel the picnic.
　（下雨了，所以我們必須取消野餐。）
　→表示前面句子所造成的「結果」
· We came early, **so (that)** we could talk to the speaker before the speech.
　（我們提早到，以便我們能在演講前和講者聊一下。）
　→表示前句子所達到的「目的」

因為so that的that可以省略，加上在翻譯時甚至不會有太大的誤解，所以
常常會讓我們搞不清楚：
· We came early, **so (that)** we could talk to the speaker before the speech.
　（誤譯：我們提早到，所以我們能在演講前和講者聊一下。）

重點提醒：so that（以便...）前面的句子通常是含有意志的行為，才能達
到後面句子的目的。

120. I'm sorry, but I think the vase of flowers looks _____ in the corner where it draws attention to the buffet table. ***

(A) terrible

(B) dead

(C) better

(D) unlikely

中　譯

很抱歉，但我覺得這瓶花放在角落看起來_____，可以把大家的注意力吸引到餐桌上。

(A) 可怕的　　(B) 死亡的　　(C) 比較好的　(D) 不可能的

解答提示

句子的後面提到 "draws attention to the buffet table"，所以應該要選擇一個正面的形容詞，選項中只有better（比較好的）是屬於正向的形容詞，答案當然就是 (C) 囉！

121. I _____ for the misunderstanding about the time of the meeting. **

(A) apologize

(B) deny

(C) sorry

(D) forgive

中　譯

我為誤會會議時間而_____。

(A) 道歉　　　(B) 否認　　　(C) 抱歉　　　(D) 原諒

解答提示

因為空格後有介系詞for，而選項 (B) 和 (D) 都是及物動詞，所以可以先刪去。選項 (C) 必須再加上be動詞才能使用，所以答案自然就是 (A) 囉！

122. The Johnson Five will headline this weekend's farm _____ concert at the Canyon Amphitheater, beginning Thursday evening at 7:00 p.m. ****

(A) auction
(B) benefit
(C) equipment
(D) work

中　譯

傑森五人組將是本週末的農場_____演唱會的重頭戲，這個演唱會從星期四晚上七點在峽谷劇場開始。
(A) 拍賣　　　(B) 慈善　　　(C) 設備　　　(D) 工作

解答提示

此題說難不難，主要測驗的是benefit concert（慈善演唱會）這個搭配詞。但如果不知道這個搭配詞，其實也可以發現其他選項根本無法和concert形成搭配，所以答案並不難選。

123. Due to the fire at St. Joseph's downtown therapy center on Saturday, all appointments scheduled there have been _____ to the hospital therapy center until further notice. *****
(A) rescheduled
(B) translated
(C) relocated
(D) cancelled

中　譯

因為聖約瑟夫醫院的市區治療中心星期六的火災，所有原本預定在那裡的約診都已經_____到醫院本部治療中心，直到另外通知。
(A) 重新安排時間　　(B) 轉換　　(C) 重新安置　(D) 取消

解答提示

此題的難度很高，尤其是題目和選項都使用較難的單字。選項 (A) 很容易誤導作答，因為題目中有scheduled，所以自然地會考慮rescheduled，但請注意，這兩個單字都是指和「時間」有關的安排，例如schedule a meeting（安排會議時間）和reschedule a meeting（重新安排會議時間），基本上地點是不變的。但題目中的市區治療中心已經發生火災，地點怎麼可能不變呢！因此不能選這個選項。
選項 (B) 常見的意思是「翻譯」，也有「轉換；轉變」的意思，但是大多是

指本質上的改變，與題目的句子不符合。

選項 (D) 也可能誤導作答，因為題目提到火災，急性子的人就會直接聯想「取消」，但是作答時一定要看清題目、看完題目。

此題答案為 (C)。

124. Unfortunately, the part we need to repair the office security system is on _____, so it will be at least three weeks before it can be fixed.
****

(A) special order
(B) vacation
(C) reliable
(D) backorder

中　譯

不幸的是，我們修理辦公室安全系統所需的零件現在是_____，所以等到系統修好至少要三個星期。

(A) 特別訂單　(B) 假期中　　(C) 可靠的　　(D) 延期交貨

解答提示

首先可以把選項 (B) 和 (C) 刪除，因為這兩個選項很明顯並不搭配此題目。另外選項 (A) 所謂的「特別訂單」意義不明，也可以暫時不考慮。剩下選項 (D) 即是正確的答案。backorder即是「沒有現貨庫存、來日出貨」的訂單。

 瑣碎時間看這裡

< 關係代名詞的受格 >

關係代名詞的受格可見下表：

人	事物
who/whom/that/省略	which/that/省略

雖然有好幾種方式可以用，但是可以發現最常見的就是「省略」關係代名詞。關係代名詞省略之後，有時候會讓句子拆解比較複雜，所以要特別注意。

· Unfortunately, the part **(that)** we need to repair the office security system is on backorder, so it will be at least three weeks before it can be fixed.

125. The company's credit _____ must be strong if they would like to be considered for a construction loan to build additional office space. ****

(A) card
(B) reading
(C) rating
(D) account

中　譯

這間公司的信用_____必須很優良，如果他們想要被（銀行）考慮給予建築貸款來擴充更多的辦公室空間的話。
(A) 卡片　　　(B) 閱讀　　　(C) 評比　　　(D) 帳戶

解答提示

題目中出現了loan（貸款），很快地可以聯想到credit rating（信用評比）。雖然credit card（信用卡）和credit account（信用帳戶）都是正確的搭配字，但是與題意並不符合。

126. With mortgage rates at an all-time low, the CEO would like to move ahead with plans to purchase the _____ Rockwell building. ****

(A) detailed
(B) former
(C) farmer
(D) cheapest

中　譯

抵押利率空前的低，執行長想要執行計畫，買下_____Rockwell大樓。
(A) 詳細的　　　(B) 之前的　　　(C) 農夫　　　(D) 最便宜的

解答提示

選項 (C) 是名詞，所以可以先刪除。選項 (A) 的detailed通常不是用來形容建築物，所以也可以刪去。剩下選項 (B) 和 (D) 中，只有former（之前的）是比較合理的答案，故選 (B)。

127. The graph below_____ the percentage of people age 25 or older

in Boulder City and in the state of Iowa who have earned a bachelor's degree. ****
(A) relates
(B) dictates
(C) compares
(D) transfers

 中　　譯

以下的圖表_____此比例：在巨岩市25歲以上擁有學士學位的人，和在愛荷華州25歲以上擁有學士學位的人。
(A) 敘述　　　　(B) 口述　　　　(C) 比較　　　　(D) 轉換

解答提示

選項 (A) 和 (B) 都是指實際上透過語言的表達，所以不適合用在此句；而選項 (D) 則是意思不符合；故選 (C)。

瑣碎時間看這裡

< 形容詞子句的拆解 >
形容詞子句一般而言會放在所要修飾的名詞之後，但是有時候會因為太長，而被拆解放到後面：
· The graph below compares the percentage of **people age 25 or older** in Boulder City and in the state of Iowa <u>who have earned a bachelor's degree</u>.
→ 形容詞子句who have earned a bachelor's degree修飾的名詞是people age 25 or older，但是中間插入了地點in Boulder City and in the state of Iowa。

128. The insurance industry, accounting, financial planning and child care are the four fields that are expected to have double _____ growth over the next decade. *****
(A) digit
(B) financial
(C) duty
(D) triple

中　譯

保險業、會計業、財務規劃和兒童照顧這四個領域，預期在下個十年會有二_____的成長。
(A) 位數　　　(B) 財務的　　(C) 責任　　　(D) 三倍的

解答提示

這一題的答題線索較少，必須知道double digit（二位數）這個搭配詞才能作答，答案為 (A)。

129. We are looking for a _____ individual with the ability to express thoughts clearly, to manage differing viewpoints, and to collaborate with others. ****
(A) dull
(B) favored
(C) experience
(D) dynamic

中　譯

我們在找一個_____的人，有清楚表達想法的能力，能夠管理不同的觀點以及和別人合作。
(A) 愚笨的　　(B) 受到優惠的　　　(C) 經驗　　　(D) 有活力的

解答提示

因為句子後面的能力描述，所以選項 (C) 容易讓人作答時造成干擾，但是experience一般不會當作形容詞，要用experienced才行，要記清楚哦，答案為 (D)！

 瑣碎時間看這裡

＜對等連接詞and＞
使用對等連接詞and的時候，要特別注意詞性以及結構的對等，如果要連接的是不定詞，那麼最好不要把to省略掉，否則句子看起來會很奇怪：
· We are looking for a dynamic individual with the ability to express thoughts clearly, to manage differing viewpoints, and to collaborate with others.

→ to manage differing viewpoints和 to collaborate with others的to都不要省略。

130. The Network Engineer will be _____ for implementing, supporting, maintaining and troubleshooting the computer system for the company. ＊＊＊＊
(A) responsive
(B) responsible
(C) thoughtful
(D) cared

中　譯

網路工程師將_____執行、支援、維護以及疑難排除公司的電腦系統。
(A) 回應的　　(B) 負責的　　(C) 細心的　　(D) 被在意的

解答提示

此題應注意空格後的介系詞for，然後選擇和它搭配的正確答案 (B)。 "be responsive to" 是「對...回應」的意思。

131. Surely, the most unusual _____ we saw on our trip was the giant ketchup bottle welcoming us to Harting, Illinois, home of the Fabulous Tomatoes Ketchup factory. ＊＊＊＊
(A) animal
(B) attraction
(C) character
(D) attracts

中　譯

當然，我們在旅程中看到最特別的_____是巨大的蕃茄醬瓶子，歡迎我們到伊利諾伊州的Harting ——驚人蕃茄醬工廠的故鄉。
(A) 動物　　(B) 景點　　(C) 人物　　(D) 吸引

解答提示

此題可先將選項 (D) 刪去，因為只有它是動詞。 "we saw on our trip" 是形容

詞子句，空格中的字就是 "the giant ketchup bottle" ，可見應該選擇 (B) 才符合句意。

 瑣碎時間看這裡

< 同位語 >
英文當中的同位語，可以視為是形容詞子句的簡化，例如：
· Mr. Jones, a famous professor, is coming to my college to give a speech.
 = Mr. Jones, who is a famous professor, is coming to my college to give a speech.
 (Jones先生——一位有名的教授——將到我的大學演講。)

另外，有人名的同位語，近年來有省略逗號的趨勢，要特別注意：
· My friend **Jenny** is not going to the movies with us.
(我朋友Jenny沒有要和我們去看電影。)

132. In some cases, headphones are the only way to hear _____ from a portable electronic device. ***
(A) audio
(B) visual
(C) auto
(D) loud

中　譯

在某些情況下，耳機是唯一能聽到可攜式電子設備的_____的方式。
(A) 播音　　　(B) 視頻　　　(C) 汽車　　　(D) 大聲的

解答提示

此題題意很明顯，只是要記得分辨audio和auto的拼字類似，答案為 (A)。

133. Several schools in the area have _____ Science and Technology grants to fund programs which will adequately prepare students for the future. *****
(A) replied to

(B) studied
(C) applied for
(D) implied

中　譯

這個地區的數間學校已經_____了科技補助金來資助計劃，合宜地為學生準備未來。

(A) 回覆　　　(B) 研究　　　(C) 申請　　　(D) 暗指

解答提示

此題的關鍵是，只要看懂grant（補助金），那麼該搭配什麼動詞就很清楚了。其他的選項動都無法和grant搭配，所以答案應該是apply for（申請）。

134. For businesses that design hardware or software products, few decisions have more_____ than the marketing strategy they choose.
　　　 *****

(A) information
(B) competition
(C) interest
(D) impact

中　譯

對於設計硬體或軟體產品的公司來說，和他們選擇的行銷策略相比，很少決定能有更多的_____。

(A) 資訊　　　(B) 競爭　　　(C) 興趣　　　(D) 衝擊

解答提示

這一題難度很高，必須完全看懂題目才行，否則就必須依靠強烈的推理能力才能解題。句子的主題是few decisions（決定），決定會造成什麼樣的結果呢？結果是「資訊／競爭／興趣」？意思都很奇怪，剩下的「衝擊」就是正確答案了，故選 (D)。

Chapter 2　閱讀測驗大解密

 瑣碎時間看這裡

<數量形容詞>
英文中表達數量的形容詞整理如下：

可數名詞	不可數名詞	中文意
many, a lot of	much, a lot of	很多
some, several	some	一些
a few	a little	一點點
few	little	很少
any/no	any/no	任何 / 沒有

其中要注意a little/little以及a few/few的差別，雖然只差了一個不定冠詞a，但是兩者的意思截然不同：

· I have **a few** friends in the new neighborhood.
（我在這個新社區有一些朋友。）
· I have **few** friends in the new neighborhood.
（我在這個新社區幾乎沒有朋友。）

135. Dr. Sinto will be available after the presentation to answer any questions you may have about his _____ to financial integrity. ****
(A) destiny
(B) decline
(C) approach
(D) amount

中　譯

Sinto博士在簡報後會有空，回答各位關於他的財務整合_____的問題。
(A) 命運　　　(B) 下降　　　(C) 方法　　　(D) 總數

解答提示

此題的小技巧是透過搭配的介系詞來解題，destiny後面一般不會接什麼介系詞，decline後面一般接in，amount後面一般接of，而approach則是接to，所以答案可以安心地選 (C)。

136. The plastic on the O-rings must be _____ than 1/2 centimeter thick, in order to pass inspection. ****
(A) no more
(B) about
(C) large
(D) lesser

 中　　譯

O型環上的塑膠必須_____1/2公分厚，才能通過檢驗。
(A) 不超過　　(B) 大約　　　(C) 大的　　　(D) 較少的

解答提示

此題其實是測驗文法，空格後面的than表示是「比較級」的用法，所以選項 (B) 和 (C) 都可以先刪去。至於選項 (D) 雖然是比較級，但是應改為less才對。所以答案就是 (A)。

琐碎時間看這裡

<比較級>
比較級可以分成「優等比較」和「劣等比較」。優等比較就是「更好、更多...」這一類的意思，劣等比較就是「更不好、更少...」這一類的意思。
劣等比較其實比優等比較簡單多了，只要在形容詞或副詞前面加上 less 就可以，不用背什麼變化喔！
· This car runs <u>less fast</u> than that one.
（這輛車跑得沒有比那輛快。）
· This book is <u>less interesting</u> than that one.
（這本書沒有比那本書有趣。）

137. Tickets for the_____ voyage of the new Weekend Onboard program, offered by Sunset Cruise Line have been sold out. ****
(A) beginning
(B) remaining
(C) exciting
(D) inaugural

中　譯

日落遊輪公司所提供全新的週末登船專案_____航行的票券已經賣完了。
(A) 開始的　　　(B) 剩下的　　　(C) 興奮的　　　(D) 開幕的

解答提示

此題可以從形容詞new來推測，所以應該要搭配具有「開始；開幕」等意涵的字才合理，可先刪去選項 (B) 和 (C)。至於beginning一般很少作為形容詞修飾名詞，所以應該選 (D) inaugural最適合。

 瑣碎時間看這裡

< 過去分詞片語 >
被動語態的形容詞子句可以簡化成過去分詞片語，這在書面文章中很常見，因為會顯得比較簡潔有力。省略的方式就是把**關係代名詞**和**be動詞**拿掉就OK囉！
· **Tickets** for the inaugural voyage of the new Weekend Onboard program, (which were) **offered by Sunset Cruise Line** have been sold out.
· Please give me the letter (that was) written by Dr. Peterson.
（ 請給我那封Peterson博士寫的信。 ）

138. An overwhelming _____ of respondents agreed that free delivery is the largest motivator causing them to purchase products online.
****

(A) fraction
(B) addition
(C) majority
(D) minority

中　譯

受訪者中，壓倒性的_____同意，免運費是造就他們線上購買商品的最大動力。
(A) 小部份　　　(B) 附加　　　(C) 多數　　　(D) 少數

 解答提示

overwhelming是「壓倒的；勢不可擋的」，和majority形成搭配詞，就是指「壓倒性多數」。

瑣碎時間看這裡

< 動詞 + 人 + to + V >
這是英文中極常見的句型，很多動詞都可以搭配，這個句型的重點意思是「to + V」的動作是由受詞所作的，請見以下範例：
· My father **allowed me to go** home late this evening.
（我爸爸准我今天晚上晚點回家。）
· The teacher **told everyone to clean** the classroom before leaving school.
（老師叫每個人在離開學校之前把教室打掃乾淨。）
· The violent storm **caused many roads to be closed**.
（暴風雨導致很多路被封閉。）

139. As a _____ of our appreciation for your business, we would like to offer you this complimentary issue of Creative Computing Magazine.
*****
(A) remembrance
(B) token
(C) taken
(D) specialty

中　譯

作為我們感謝貴公司的_____，我們想要免費提供您這一期的Creative Computing雜誌。
(A) 紀念　　　(B) 象徵　　　(C) 拿取　　　(D) 特色

解答提示

答案為 (B)，"as a token of" 是「作為...的象徵」。選項 (C) 是take的過去分詞，和token的拼字類似，特別小心。選項 (A) 的搭配詞應該是 "in remembrance of" 「紀念...」。

140. You can see the full _____ of products we offer on our website, junebugclothing.com. ***

(A) ability

(B) picture

(C) view

(D) range

中　　譯

您可以透過我們的網站junebugclothing.com看到我們所提供的完整商品____
。

(A) 能力　　　　(B) 畫圖　　　　(C) 景觀　　　　(D) 系列

解答提示

full ability 全部的能力；full picture 全貌；full view 全景，以上三個搭配詞都是OK的，但是和此題的句子無法搭配，只有full range「全系列」最符合句意，故選 (D)。

 Part 6　Text Completion

Questions 141-143 refer to the following email:

Thank you for renting with Budget Rental. Details of your rental are as follows:
Pickup Date/Time: June 14th, 2013/10:00 p.m.
Pickup Location: Airport Car Rental Desk
Return Date/Time: June 19th, 2013/10:00 a.m.
Return Location: Airport Car Return Kiosk

中　譯

謝謝您向Budget Rental租車，以下為您的租車詳情：
取車日期／時間：2013年6月14日下午10點
取車地點：機場租車櫃台
還車日期／時間：2013 年6月19日上午10點
還車地點：機場還車亭

Please ------ the vehicle with the same fuel level as you received it. If you do
** **141.** (A) remove
　　　(B) return
　　　(C) drive
　　　(D) park

not, additional fees may apply.

中　譯

請------汽車時，確認和您取車時有相同的汽油量。如果沒有，可能會有額外
的費用。
(A) 移除　　　(B) 歸還　　　(C) 駕駛　　　(D) 停放

解答提示

此題四個選項都是及物動詞，因此必須依靠文意判斷。幸虧文章的前段即是
討論租車情況，例如：rental（租車）、pickup（取車），因此答案就是前文
已經出現過的return（歸還）。

A Loss Damage Waiver is optional. An added daily cost of $26.99 covers your responsibility for damage to our car. Please check with your insurer, as this may duplicate your own car ------.

*** **142.** (A) speed
(B) gas mileage
(C) insurance
(D) color

中　譯

遺失損毀險是可以選擇。每天額外花費$26.99即包括損毀汽車的責任。請與您的保險公司確認，因為這可能和您自己既有的------重覆。
(A) 速度　　　(B) 油錶　　　(C) 保險　　　(D) 顏色

解答提示

此題可以從同一個句子的insurer（保險公司）推測出答案是insurance（保險），其他的選項都是與car合用的搭配詞，但應不致於被誤導。car speed（車速）、car gas mileage（汽車油錶）、car color（汽車顏色）。

We look forward to serving your car rental needs. If you have ------ regarding

****143.** (A) arguments
(B) questions
(C) ailments
(D) issues

this rental, call us at 509-957-1234.

中　譯

我們期待服務您租車的需求。如果您有關於此次租車的------，請來電509-957-1234。
(A) 爭執　　　(B) 問題　　　(C) 病痛　　　(D) 爭論

解答提示

此題相當容易，也是商業書信常見的結尾方式：「如果您有任何問題的話，……。」答案自然是questions（問題）。

The Budget Rental team

Budget Rental團隊

 瑣碎時間看這裡

<千面女郎as>
as看起來是個再不起眼的單字了，但是它卻是一個千面女郎，有好幾個意思，最常見有下列三個。

1. Details of your rental are **as** follows.
   (您租車的細節如下。)
   →這裡的as相當於like，有「像…」的意思。

2. Please check with your insurer, **as** this may duplicate your own car insurance.
   (請跟您的保險公司確認，因為這可能會跟您的車險重覆。)
   →這裡的as等於because（因為）。

3. I saw him **as** I was coming into the building.
   (當我進入建築物時，我看到他。)
   →這裡的as等於when/while（當…）。

Questions 144-146 refer to the following letter:

Financially Relaxed Retirement Plan

Adam LaCross   February 2nd, 2014
677 Adams St
Springdale OR 97777

 中　　譯

財務紓解退休計劃
奧勒崗州Springdale市Adam街677號　2014年2月2日

The personal ------ number (PIN) that Financially Relaxed Retirement has

** **144.** (A) interview
　　(B) identification
　　(C) information
　　(D) identity

on record for you is: 123456.

中　　譯

財務紓解退休計劃中，您紀錄上的個人 ------ 號碼（PIN）是123456。
(A) 面試　　(B) 身分證明　　(C) 資訊　　(D) 身分

解答提示

PIN就是「身分證號碼」，而身分證件的英文是Personal Identification，這是固定用法，identification不能換成identity，正確答案為 (B)。

With this number, you are able to access comprehensive account information and ------ certain transactions.

*** **145.** (A) initiate
　　(B) renew
　　(C) adjust
　　(D) transfer

有這組號碼，您可以取用所有的帳戶資料以及 ------ 部分交易。
(A) 開始　　　(B) 更新　　　(C) 調整　　　(D) 轉換

解答提示

正確答案為 (A)，transaction是「交易」的意思，適合的動詞只有initiate（開始；啟動），準備多益考試背單字時，要多注意互相搭配的名詞和動詞，才能背一個字記更多字！

Two options are available to you:
• Call 1-888-352-1234 (Monday – Friday, 8:30 a.m. to 8:00 p.m. Eastern Time)
• Access your account online www.financiallyrelaxed.org

中　譯

有兩個選項供您選擇：
• 撥打：1-888-352-1234（星期一到星期五，東岸時間早上8:30到晚上8:00）
• 透過網站www.financiallyrelaxed.org使用您的帳戶。

Please take ------ of these convenient tools for accessing and managing your
*** **146.** (A) use
　　　　　(B) interest
　　　　　(C) advantage
　　　　　(D) care

account.

中　譯

請 ------ 這些便利的工具來取用並管理您的帳戶。
(A) 使用　　　(B) 興趣　　　(C) 好處　　　(D) 注意

解答提示

此題測驗的是慣用語take advantage of（使用；利用），advantage是「好處；優點」，字面的解釋是「拿走...的好處、優點」，也就是「使用；利用」的意思囉！所以答案為 (C)。
雖然選項 (A) 是使用的意思，但是並沒有take use of這種用法。

We look forward to working with you.

我們期待與您合作。

 ## 瑣碎時間看這裡

< can vs. be able to >

助動詞can和片語be able to基本上的意思是相同的：
· Jake can play basketball like a professional player.
= Jake is able to play basketball like a professional player.
（Jake能像職業球員一樣打籃球。）

但是be able to還可以和許多情態助動詞搭配，這是助動詞can所無法做到的嗮！以下是be able to和情態助動詞混搭之後的整理：

1. will be able to 將能夠
· She will be able to apply for this position after she finishes the training.
（在她完成訓練之後，她將能夠申請這份職位。）

2. must be able to 一定能夠
· He must be able to come here if he clocks off on time.
（如果他準時打卡下班，他一定能夠來這裡。）

3. may be able to 也許能夠
· We may be able to complete the project because Mike is very good at this field.
（我們也許能夠完成這項專案，因為Mike很擅長這個領域。）

4. should be able to 應該能夠
· They should be able to afford a new house if John gets a raise next month.
（如果John下個月調薪，他們應該能夠買得起新房子。）

Questions 147-149 refer to the following:

Your new bicycle was ------ and tuned in the factory, then partially

*** **147.** (A) riding
(B) assembly
(C) assembled
(D) commuting

disassembled for shipping.

您的新腳踏車在工廠------並調整完成，然後部分拆解以利裝運。
(A) 騎乘　　　(B) 組裝　　　(C) 組裝　　　(D) 通勤

解答提示

此題的動詞都是被動語態，所以只要看哪個選項是被動就沒錯囉！答案為 (C)，另外assembly是assemble的名詞。

You may have purchased the bicycle in its shipping carton, or from a store in fully assembled form. The following instructions will ------ you to prepare

*** **148.** (A) accurately
(B) enable
(C) hinder
(D) preparation

your bicycle for years of enjoyment.

您可能是以裝運紙箱，或是從店面組裝完成旳方式購買此腳踏車。以下的指示使您------整備您的腳踏車，享受好幾年的樂趣。
(A) 正確地　　(B) 能夠　　　(C) 阻礙　　　(D) 準備

解答提示

此題空格前是助動詞will，所以空格內應選擇一個動詞，選項 (A) 和 (D) 可以去刪去。而hinder（阻礙）所搭配的介系詞是from，enable才是接不定詞：enable someone to V，答案為 (B)。

For details on inspections, maintenance and adjustment of any areas, please refer to the relevant section in this manual. If you have questions about how to properly assemble this bicycle, please consult a ------ specialist

****149. (A) stored
(B) standard
(C) quality
(D) qualified

prior to riding it.

中　　譯

關於各方面的檢查、維修、調整等細節，請查詢本手冊中各相關部分。如果您對於如何正確地組裝腳踏車有疑問，請在騎乘之前咨詢------專業人員。
(A) 貯存的　　(B) 標準的　　(C) 品質　　(D) 合格的

解答提示

此題應該找一個可以修飾人的形容詞，選項 (A)、(B)、(C) 都是修飾物品的形容詞，所以答案自然只剩下 (D)。

瑣碎時間看這裡

<祈使句>
英文的祈使句最容易記的方式，就是把主詞省略：
· ~~You~~ Come home early after school.
（你放學後早點回家。）

不過這種記憶方式在遇到be動詞的時候，要記得用be動詞的原形動詞唷：
· ~~You are~~ a good student.
↓
Be
（~~你是~~當個好學生。）

其實省略主詞是標準的形式，但如果想要加強語氣，仍然可以把主詞保留唷！
· You come home early after school!
（你放學後早點回家！）
· You be a good student!
（你當個好學生！）

另外也可以加上助動詞do在動詞前面，一樣有加強語氣的效果：
· **Do** come home early after school!
（放學後早點回家！）

NEW TOEIC 黃金戰鬥力──閱讀篇

Questions 150-152 refer to the following announcement:

Courtesy Information
Regarding Your County Property Tax

中　譯

善意訊息
關於您的縣屬財產稅

Our ------ indicate you or your agent has designated a mortgage company to
150. (A) recordings
(B) papers
(C) thoughts
(D) records

have responsibility for the payment of taxes on this parcel.

中　譯

我們的------顯示您或您的代理人已經委任一家抵押貸款公司,有責支付此土地的稅金。
(A) 錄音　　(B) 文件　　(C) 想法　　(D) 記錄

解答提示

這封信函是由稅務機關寄出,所以在選擇用字的時候,選擇records會比papers更為恰當,故選 (D)。另外recordings雖然也是record的名詞,但是一般指的是「錄音;錄影」。

If this is incorrect, you must pay your taxes prior to the due date to avoid late fees. Under New York State Law, it is the taxpayer's responsibility to ensure property taxes are paid.

中　譯

如果此委任有誤,您必須在截止日期前繳納稅金以避免滯納金的產生。在新的紐約州法之下,納稅義務人有責任確保財產稅已繳納。

Chapter 2　閱讀測驗大解密

150

Please go to yourcounty.org/treasurer for additional information regarding the property taxes for this ------.

*** **151.** (A) parcel
(B) partial
(C) sectional
(D) acreage

 中　　譯

請利用網站yourcounty.org或咨詢財務人員，取得此------的財產稅相關的額外資訊。

(A) 土地　　　(B) 部分的　　　(C) 部分的　　　(D) 英畝數

解答提示

此題的答案在前面的文字即出現過了，parcel一般指包裹，也有「土地」的意思，故選 (A)。

If a mortgage company is not paying your taxes, if you would like a tax ------

*** **152.** (A) reported
(B) statement
(C) stating
(D) information

mailed to you or if you have other questions, please call our office at (02) 2361-5514.

中　　譯

如果沒有抵押貸款公司替您繳納稅金，如果您想要郵寄的稅金------，或如果您有其他的問題，請撥打至辦公室 (02)2361-5514。

(A) 被報告的　　　(B) 表單　　　(C) 敘述　　　(D) 資訊

解答提示

此題空格應選入名詞，所以可以先把選項 (A) 和 (C) 刪去。接著要注意到空格前面有不定冠詞a，所以要選入可數名詞，不能選擇information，正確答案 (B) statement就出來囉！

瑣碎時間看這裡

< **that**名詞子句 >

that名詞子句可以當作主詞（以同位語的方式出現）以及受詞，但是以作為受詞最常見，而且還常常省略that，所以在閱讀的時候要特別注意。

主詞：The fact <u>that he is my cousin</u> really surprised me.
（他是我表哥這件事還真的讓我嚇到了。）

受詞：I didn't know <u>(that) you were coming too</u>.
（我不知道你也要來。）

有時候我們還會看到兩個that在一起，千萬不要吃驚唷：

· Peter told me (that) that girl was beautiful.
（Peter告訴我那個女孩子很漂亮。）

→第一個that是名詞子句，而第二個that是指示形容詞。

Part 7　Reading Comprehension

*Single Passage

Questions 153 through 155 refer to the following article:

Groundbreaking Ceremony Attracts Crowd

Staff, friends and administrators of Deacon Hill Hospital were in attendance Friday for the groundbreaking ceremony of their new hospital. CEO Brian Olson gave a short address highlighting his appreciation for the community support given to this building project. He stated that "building a new hospital has long been a need in this community. We are so appreciative for the support of our community in this endeavor."

The building project has been in the works for over a year, already. Funds have been raised, plans have been completed and the contractors have been hired to begin construction on May 1st of this year. Country Builders will be the general contractor for the project. They expect the new hospital will be ready to accept patients by June 15th of next year.

中　譯

破土典禮吸引人潮

迪肯丘醫院的員工、友人和管理階層在星期五時，皆出席了他們新醫院的破土典禮。執行長布萊恩歐森發表簡短的演講，強調他的感謝，對於社區支持這個建築計劃。他說：「蓋一間新醫院長期以來是這個社區的需求。我們非常感謝我們的社區支持這個努力。」

此項建築計劃已經運作超過一年。資金已募集、設計圖已完成、已僱請承包商在今年5月1日動工。「鄉村建築工」將是此計劃的主要承包商。他們預計新的醫院會在明年的6月15日前準備接受病患。

153. What was Friday's ceremony celebrating? **
  (A) The hospital's 50th anniversary.
  (B) Groundbreaking for the new hospital.
  (C) The arrival of the new CEO.
  (D) The 100th baby born this year.

中　譯

星期五的典禮是為了慶祝什麼？
(A) 醫院的五十週年慶。
(B) 新醫院的破土。
(C) 新的執行長就任。
(D) 今年第一百位新生兒。

解答提示

此題在文章的標題即可找到解答，答案為 (B)，重點是必須看懂單字groundbreaking（破土），ground 指的是「地面」；break 就是指「破、破壞」，所以這個單字很好記哦！

154. What did the CEO praise the community for in his address? ***
  (A) The community's safety record.
  (B) The community's ability to find the emergency room.
  (C) The community support of the building project.
  (D) The new community swimming pool.

中　譯

執行長在演講中因為什麼而稱讚社區？
(A) 社區的安全紀錄。
(B) 社區發現急診室的能力。
(C) 社區對建築計劃的支持。
(D) 新的社區游泳池。

解答提示

此題可以輕易地在文章中找到，應選 (C)，加上其他選項的重點字safety

record、emergency room、swimming pool都未出現在文章中，因此應可快速地答題。

155. According to the article, what happened during the first year of the building project? ***
(A) Fundraising and building plans were completed.
(B) Construction began ahead of schedule.
(C) A new CEO was hired.
(D) The old hospital was demolished.

中　譯

根據文章，建築計劃的第一年有什麼事發生？
(A) 資金募集且設計圖完成。
(B) 建築工程比預定時間提早開始。
(C) 聘請新的執行長。
(D) 舊的醫院被拆除。

解答提示

此題的答案是選項 (A)，(B) 選項與 (C) 選項使用文章中的單字construction（建築）、CEO（執行長）、hire（僱請）來干擾答題，只要注意文章即可克服這些干擾。

 瑣碎時間看這裡

< 現在完成式表示 [已經] >
現在完成式可以表示某個動作或狀態已經開始，但動作還沒有結束、或狀態仍維持，例如：

1. The building project **has been** in the works for over a year, already.
　→已經開始動工，而且狀態是持續的，沒有結束。
2. Funds **have been raised**, plans **have been completed** and the contractors **have been hired** to begin construction on May 1st of this year.
　→資金已經被募集，而且仍在募集中。
　→設計圖已經完成，而且維持在完成的狀態。
　→承包商已經被僱請，而且一直在僱請的狀態之下。

Questions 156 and 157 refer to the following announcement:

Long River Watershed
Residents and Interested Individuals

The Department of Ecology invites you to a meeting on improving water quality in the Long River. Previously, we have focused on temperature and bacteria. Currently we are focusing on nutrients in the river.

Learn how you can be a part of improving the Long River!

When: Thursday, June 27th, 2013
    6:00 p.m.
Where: Elroy Elementary School
    3115 School Road
    in Elroy

For more information on current water quality in the watershed:
www.eco.va.gov/programs/watershed

中　　譯

致隆河水域居民及利害關係人

生態部門邀請您參與會議，主題是提升隆河的水質。先前我們已經專注在溫度和細菌。現在我們要專注在河水中的營養物質。

來了解您如何成為改善隆河的一分子！
時間：2013年6月27日星期四下午六點
地點：Elroy市學校路3115號Elroy小學

關於現在水域的水質狀況，更多訊息請見：www.eco.va.gov/programs/watershed

156. What are residents invited to in this announcement? ***
    (A) A meeting about new curriculum at the elementary school.
    (B) A meeting about the quality of water in the Long River.
    (C) A party celebrating a resident's birthday.
    (D) A meeting about improved boat safety.

中　　譯

在這則公告當中，居名們受邀到什麼場合？
(A) 關於小學新課程的會議。
(B) 關於隆河水質的會議。
(C) 慶祝一位居民生日的派對。
(D) 關於提升船舶安全的會議。

解答提示

此題使用和公告中一樣的字彙quality of water = water quality，所以答案很明顯是 (B)。

157. How are readers instructed to get more information about water quality? ***
    (A) Call the Department of Ecology.
    (B) Visit the river daily to check the water quality.
    (C) Go to the Department of Ecology's website.
    (D) Call the elementary school.

中　　譯

為了獲得更多關於水質的資訊，讀者被指示該怎麼做？
(A) 致電給生態部門。
(B) 每天到河邊檢查水質。
(C) 上生態部門的網站。
(D) 致電給小學。

解答提示

公告的下方有出現網址，很明顯地就是要請讀者上網去，放心選 (C) 就沒錯囉！

瑣碎時間看這裡

< 分詞作形容詞 >

分詞可分成現在分詞和過去分詞兩種，現在分詞通常具有「主動」、「進行」的含義，而過去分詞則具有「被動」的意涵。

· Maria is kind of a **dancing** queen.

（Maria可說是舞后。）

· Nobody can save the **dying** man.

（沒有人能救那個快死去的人。）

· Who threw the **broken** glass?

（誰把破掉的杯子丟掉了？）

另外有一類動詞是帶有情緒性的含義，而這種動詞的現在分詞和過去分詞用法也比較特殊，例如：interest（使感興趣）、excite（使興奮）、satisfy（使滿意）...等。這一類的現在分詞可以形容「人或事物給人的感覺」，而過去分詞則通常只形容「人本身的感受」。

· He is an interesting person.

（他是個有趣的人。）

→ 令周圍的人覺得他很風趣

· This is an interesting book.

（這是本有趣的書。）

→ 令人覺得有趣

· I am interested in what you're saying.

（我對你說的事有興趣。）

→ "I" 本身有興趣

Questions 158 and 160 refer to the following article:

Troubleshooting your new digital camera
You want your new camera to capture many special moments in your life. Don't miss a moment because your camera needs a few simple fixes!

Fuzzy spots on your pictures
Occasionally dust builds up or your fingerprint leaves a smudge on your lens. Breathe across the lens and wipe it with a soft, microfiber cloth. This will remove most marks. For stubborn spots, purchase a lens cleaning solution.

Battery Life
In the beginning, your camera batteries will last several hours before needing to be recharged. Over time a battery wears out. Eventually, it will only give you a few pictures. In this case, simply install a new battery. If you see a white flaky material on the old battery, the battery was likely leaking. The residual acid will need to be wiped off the contacts using a brush and fine sandpaper.

中　譯

疑難排解您的新數位相機
你想要您的新相機捕捉許多生活中特別的時刻。別錯過任何一個時刻，因為您的相機需要一些簡單的修理。

相片上有模糊的小點
有時候灰塵會累積，或者您的指紋會在鏡頭上留下汙跡。輕吹鏡頭並用柔軟的超微細纖維布擦拭。這可以去除多數的汙點。針對頑強的汙點，請購買鏡頭清潔溶劑。

電池壽命
一開始您的相機電池在需要再充電之前，將可維持數個小時。隨著時間過去，電池會疲乏。最終只能拍幾張照片而已。在此情況下，只需安裝新的電池即可。如果您看到白色片狀的物質在舊電池上，這顆電池很可能在滲漏。

在接點上殘留的酸性物質必須擦去，可使用刷子與細砂紙。

158. Where would you read this article? **

　　(A) In an advertisement for digital cameras.

　　(B) On the back of your camera.

　　(C) In the manual for your digital camera.

　　(D) In the newspaper.

中　　譯

你會在哪裡讀到這篇文章？

(A) 在數位相機的廣告中。

(B) 在相機的背面。

(C) 在數位相機的操作手冊中。

(D) 在報紙上。

解答提示

此篇文章討論的是如何排除數位相機的一些疑難雜症，這些資訊都是寫在操作手冊中的，所以答案要選 (C)，manual即是操作手冊的意思。

159. How does the manufacturer recommend removing smudges from your lens? ***

　　(A) Wash the camera in soap and water.

　　(B) Breathe on the lens and wipe it with a soft cloth.

　　(C) Buy a replacement lens.

　　(D) Scrub the lens with an abrasive cloth.

中　　譯

製造商建議如何清除鏡頭上的汙點？

(A) 用肥皂和清水清洗相機。

(B) 輕吹鏡頭，並用軟布擦拭。

(C) 購買取代用的鏡頭。

(D) 用粗磨質地的布擦刷鏡頭。

解答提示

正確答案為 (B) 選項，使用和文章相似的字彙組合，例如breathe, lens, wipe, soft clothe等，所以答案其實並不難判斷。

160. What is the white flaky material on an old battery? **

    (A) Dried milk that was spilled on the camera.

    (B) Residue left over from the production of the camera.

    (C) Dust that has accumulated.

    (D) Battery acid that leaked out.

中　　譯

舊電池上的白色片狀物是什麼？

(A) 灑在相機上乾掉的牛奶。

(B) 相機製造過程中殘留的物質。

(C) 累積的灰塵。

(D) 滲漏出來的電池酸性物質。

解答提示

此題一樣可以在文中找到答案，尤其是看到acid（酸性物質）、leak（滲漏）
這兩個關鍵字，就可以毫不猶豫地選擇 (D) 囉！

 瑣碎時間看這裡

<動名詞表示被動>

英文如果要表示被動，通常都會使用過去分詞，但是有幾個動詞很特別
喔，竟然可以用動名詞（形式上和現在分詞一樣）來表示被動！最常見
的有下列幾個：

· The plants **want watering** every day.

  = The plants **want to be watered** every day.

  （那些植物需要每天澆水。）

· The car **needs washing** because it's really dusty.

  = The car **needs to be washed** because it's really dusty.

  （車子需要洗了，因為真的很多灰塵。）

· Our roof **requires repairing** after the typhoon.

  = Our roof **requires to be repaired** after the typhoon.

  （在颱風之後，我們的屋頂需要修理了。）

· They **deserved punishing**, for they cheated in the exam.

  = They **deserved to be punished**, for they cheated in the exam.

  （他們應該受到懲罰，因為他們在考試中作弊。）

Questions 161 through 163 refer to the following advertisement:

White Beach, Maine
Oceanfront fun
Our unique white sand beach offers 1½ miles in which to build sand castles and fly kites.

Inland Boardwalk
Kids love the free carrousel rides, the Ferris wheel, and especially the haunted beach house. Adults enjoy our 50 boutiques, antique shops and restaurants.

Sand Castle for the Night
Just steps from the beach, the **White House Inn** offers free cookies for the kids. Adults can indulge in free wine and cheese every evening. Rooms with two queen beds start at $200 per night.

The **Hotel Maine** offers shuttle service to the beach. They provide beach chairs, towels, a free breakfast and a heated outdoor pool. Rooms with two double beds start at $220 per night.

中　　譯

白色沙灘，緬因州
海灘之樂
我們獨特的白色沙灘提供一英哩半的部分推沙堡及放風箏。

海濱步道
孩子們喜歡自由自在的旋轉木馬、摩天輪，特別是海邊的鬼屋。成人可享受我們50間的精品店、古董店和餐廳。

過夜的沙堡
離海灘僅幾步之遙，「**白屋客棧**」提供孩子免費的餅乾。成人每晚可以享受免費的紅酒和起士。一間兩張皇后床的房間每晚起價200美金。

緬因旅館提供到海灘的接駁服務。他們提供海灘椅、浴巾、免費早餐及室內溫水游泳池。雙床的房間每晚起價220美金。

161. Where might you read this advertisement? **

    (A) In the sports section of the newspaper.

    (B) In a company memo.

    (C) In a travel magazine.

    (D) At the beach in Maine.

中　譯

你可能在哪裡讀到這則廣告？

(A) 在報紙的體育版。

(B) 在公司的備忘錄裡。

(C) 在旅遊雜誌中。

(D) 在緬因州的海灘。

解答提示

這一題的內容是很輕鬆的軟性題材，介紹緬因州的海灘休憩，所以答案可以很快地聯想到旅遊雜誌，正確答案為 (C)。

162. What is unique about this beach? **

    (A) It is an inland beach.

    (B) It features white sand.

    (C) Kids can build sand castles.

    (D) Adults will enjoy their stay as much as the kids.

中　譯

這個海灘特別的地方是什麼？

(A) 這是一座內陸海灘。

(B) 特色是白色沙子。

(C) 孩子們可以堆沙堡。

(D) 成人將和孩子一樣地享受停留的時光。

Chapter 2 閱讀測驗大解密

廣告的第一個句子就提到 "unique white sand beach" ，所以答案選 (B)。另外廣告提到的inland boardwalk，是美國海邊常見，有一排各式各樣的商店，商店前面則是用木板鋪在地面上，形成一條走道。這條走道（boardwalk）通常是從玩水的海灘，往裡面（inland）走 ，所以才會叫做inland boardwalk。而選項 (A) 的inland beach則是指內陸的海灘，是完全不同的。

163. What does the White House Inn offer that the Hotel Maine does not?
****

(A) White linens for the beds.
(B) A tour of the White house.
(C) Wine and cheese for the adults.
(D) Complimentary breakfast.

中　　譯

白屋客棧提供了什麼東西，是緬因旅館沒有提供的？
(A) 白色床單。
(B) 白宮之旅。
(C) 給成人的紅酒和起士。
(D) 免費的早餐。

解答提示

這一題只要把兩間旅店所提供的物品仔細對照，就可以得到答案囉！答案為 (C)；選項 (A) 和 (B) 都是廣告內容沒有的，可以先刪去。選項 (D) 則是緬因旅館有提供，而白屋客棧沒有的。complimentary *adj.* 免費的

瑣碎時間看這裡

<動詞的省略>
「英文是一個動詞的語言」，意思是英文的核心正是動詞，每一個英文句子一定要有動詞。但是英文又有一個習慣，那就是不重覆已經出現的字，所以變成動詞有時候又會省略。

最常見的動詞省略方式，就是只留下助動詞：

· What does the White House Inn offer that the Hotel Maine **does not (offer)**?
· I like the movie as much as he **does (=likes it)**.
（我喜歡這部電影的程度和他一樣。）
→肯定句則是用助動詞取代。

另外還有更徹底的省略，就是把整個動詞和受詞都省略掉：

· Mike bought some flowers for his girlfriend, and John **(bought some flowers)** for his.
（Mike買了花給他的女朋友，而John也是。）
→第二個his是指示代名詞（ = his girlfriend）

→這個句子因為bought some flowers是完全一樣的字組，所以整個省略掉。造成後半部 "and John for his." 看起來似乎沒有動詞，沒頭沒尾的。這一類的句子雖然並不常見，但是只要一出現，立馬就打敗許多人，所以要特別注意英文中省略的習慣。

Questions 164 through 166 refer to the following article:

Take our Sunday Investment Section Survey
And enter to win a NT$2,000 Visa Gift Card

Like every good business, we want to know if our products are meeting your needs. With so many people going online for their financial information, we are wondering if we should continue providing this service in print. Answer two questions to help us decide to Continue or Not Continue.

Name_____ Phone_____

Email_____

Q_1: How often do you read the investment section?
- ☐ Every Week.
- ☐ 2-3 times a month.
- ☐ Seldom/Never.

Q_2: I'd be willing to subscribe to this product for:
- ☐ NT$3,600 a year.
- ☐ NT$1,200 a year.
- ☐ If I have to pay, I'll just look online.

Contest Rules

Must be at least 18 years of age to participate. Void where prohibited. Limit one entry per email address or phone number. Survey must be submitted by Sunday, November 10th, 2013.

Prize is not redeemable for cash. Prize winner is responsible for any additional expense incurred in accepting the prize. The winner will be randomly selected, from all entries, on November 15th, 2013. They will be notified by email or phone, and their name may be used in e-marketing announcements. Odds of winning are based on total number of entries and must be claimed within 10 days.

中　　譯

參與我們的「週日投資版」問卷
登錄贏得2,000元的Visa儲值卡

就像每一個優良的企業，我們想要知道我們的產品是否滿足您的需求。隨著許多人上網獲得財經資訊，我們考慮是否應該繼續提供此項書面服務。回答兩則問題幫助我們決定該繼續或不再繼續。

姓名_____　電話_____

Email_____

問題一：您多久看一次投資版？

　　　　□ 每週。

　　　　□ 一個月2到3次。

　　　　□ 很少／從不。

問題二：我願意訂購此產品，如果訂價是：

　　　　□ 一年3,600元。

　　　　□ 一年1,200元。

　　　　□ 如果要付費，我就會在網路看看。

抽獎規則

參加者須年滿18歲以上。禁止地區無效。每個email信箱或電話號碼僅限登錄一次。問卷須在2013年11月10日星期日前送出。

獎品不得兌現。得獎者自負任何接受此獎品之額外費用。2013年11月15日將從所有登錄者中隨機選出得獎者。得獎者將以email或電話通知，得獎者姓名可能用在電子行銷的公告中。獲獎機率取決於登錄者總數，並且必須在10日內領取獎品。

164. Where would you read this announcement? **

　　　(A) On a newspaper website.

　　　(B) In the investment section of the newspaper.

　　　(C) On the front page of a newspaper.

　　　(D) In a store advertisement.

中　　譯

你可能在哪裡讀到這則公告？

(A) 在報紙的網站。

(B) 在報紙的投資版。

(C) 在報紙的首頁。
(D) 在商店廣告中。

解答提示

公告的內容是關於某份報紙星期日的投資版，所以最合適的答案是 (B)。另外報紙的首頁通常不會有類似的問卷調查，在作答的時候，要挑選最合適的答案。

165. What is the newspaper trying to decide? ****
  (A) If they should continue to provide financial information in their print edition.
  (B) If they should give away NT$2,000 to the winner.
  (C) If they should discontinue printing the paper on Sundays.
  (D) If they should include more advertisements.

中　譯

這份報紙正試著決定什麼事情？
(A) 他們是否應該繼續在印刷版本內提供財經資訊。
(B) 他們是否應該送出2,000元給得獎者。
(C) 他們是否應該在星期日停止出刊。
(D) 他們是否應該包含更多廣告。

解答提示

公告的前言即透露出問卷的目的，答案選 (A)。至於 (B) 選項提到了2,000元，這是報紙決定要送的獎品，並不是要讀者替他們決定的事情。而 (D) 選項提到的更多廣告（more advertisements），在公告中根本沒有，作答時完全不用考慮。

166. How will the winner of the NT$2,000 be selected? ***
  (A) The first entry received will win.
  (B) The entry with the correct answer will win.
  (C) The winner will be randomly selected.
  (D) The person who reads the investment section most often will win.

中　　譯

2,000元的得獎者將如何選出？
(A) 最先登錄者將贏得。
(B) 有正確答案的登錄者將贏得。
(C) 得獎者將隨機選出。
(D) 最常閱讀投資版的人將贏得。

解答提示

這一題可以在Contest Rules中找到答案，另外也可以運用一些日常生活常識，一般的抽獎當然是隨機抽出的囉！正確答案為 (C)，不過重點是必須要看懂 randomly *adv*. 隨機地。

 瑣碎時間看這裡

< 名詞子句**that**和**if** >
這兩種名詞子句都可以作為動詞的受詞，但是意義卻大不同！
· We want to know **if** our products are meeting your needs.
（我們想要知道我們的產品是否達到您的需求。）
· We want to know **that** our products are meeting your needs.
（我們想要知道我們的產品達到您的需求。）
→我們知道我們的產品有達到您的需求，但我們想要從您口中說出來。

從上面的例子可以看出來，if子句所傳達的意思是「不確定」，甚至可以說是帶有疑問的味道。而that子句則是傳達肯定的事實。我們再多看一個例子加強一下：
· I have no idea **if** he is coming.
（我不知道他有沒有要來。）
· I have no idea **that** he is coming.
（我不知道他要來耶。）

Questions 167 through 169 refer to the following announcement:

Power Interruption Notice

To provide for new customers and to improve the reliability of electrical service, we will be working on the electric service in your area. To ensure the safety of residents and employees, your electrical service will be turned off during the following times:

Thursday September 9th, 2013 10:00 p.m. – 12:00 a.m.
Friday September 10th, 2013   10:00 p.m. – 12:00 a.m.

Area(s) affected: All properties on Cedar Road and Blue Quail Drive in Elroy
Work Order: # 456-321

We will make every effort to restore power in a timely manner. Service may be restored faster than expected. There is also the possibility of unforeseen circumstances that extend the interruption. We apologize for this inconvenience. If you have questions or concerns, please call our toll free number 0800-321-4567.

Inland Power
A division of Inland Electric Corporation
inlandpower.net

中　譯

電力中斷通知

為了提供服務給新的顧客，並提升電力服務的可靠，我們將在您的區域內針對電力服務施工。為確保住戶及員工的安全，您的電力服務將在以下時段內中斷：

2013年9月9日星期四晚上10點到凌晨12點
2013年9月10日星期五晚上10點到凌晨12點

受影響區域：Elroy的Cedar路和Blue Quail大道上所有房屋
工程編號：456-321

我們將努力及時恢復電力。服務恢復可能比預期更快。也可能有無法預知的

情況造成中斷延長。我們為此不便向您致歉。如果您有任何問題或疑慮，請撥打免付費電話0800-321-4567。

內陸電力廠
內陸電力公司分公司
inlandpower.net

167. What is this postcard announcing? ***
    (A) A meeting to discuss the electricity needs in the area.
    (B) That the company has no power to change things.
    (C) That there will be several new electric customers this year.
    (D) That electricity to the area will be turned off temporarily.

【中　譯】

這張郵寄卡片公告什麼事？
(A) 討論此區域的電力需求的會議。
(B) 公司沒有能力改變事情。
(C) 今年將有幾位新的電力客戶。
(D) 此區域的電力將暫時中斷。

【解答提示】

這一題只要看懂標題就可以作答了！interrupt　*vt.* 中斷，就等於片語動詞turn off，選項 (D) 準沒錯！

168. How many hours is the power scheduled to be off each night? *
    (A) 24 hours.
    (B) All day.
    (C) 2 hours.
    (D) 12 hours.

【中　譯】

每一晚電力預計會中斷幾個小時？
(A) 24小時。
(B) 全日。
(C) 2個小時。
(D) 12個小時。

解答提示

這一題稍微算一下就OK囉，從晚上10點到凌晨12點，也就是2個小時，答案為 (C)。

169. What could make the power outage last longer than planned? **

(A) If too many customers complain.
(B) Unforeseen circumstances.
(C) If workers don't show up for work.
(D) New homes built in the area.

中　　譯

什麼事情可能會使得電子中斷比預期更久？
(A) 如果有太多客戶抱怨。
(B) 無法預知的情況。
(C) 如果工人沒有上工。
(D) 此區域所蓋的新房子。

解答提示

這一題的答案是選項 (B) unforeseen circumstances（無法預知的情況），其實公告內容中就可以找到這兩個字，所以可以大膽地作答。不過這一題的題目有點難度，因為刻意使用和內容不一樣的同義字來干擾，例如power outage就等於power interruption，last longer than planned（比預計中更久）就等於extend the interruption（延長中斷），老話一句，準備多益一定要熟讀同義字喔！

 瑣碎時間看這裡

<各種表示未來的時態>
英文中有好幾種表示未來的時態，以下是重點小整理：

未來 簡單 式1	最常見的未來式，用來表達對未來事件的預測或假設。 · She will carry the bag for you. （她將會替你拿袋子。）
未來 簡單 式2	常見的未來式，用來表達一個計劃好的行動，或是合理的未來結果。 · We are going to fly to Japan this summer. （我們今年夏天要飛去日本。）

現在簡單式	常用來表達固定的未來事件，例如交通工具的時刻表。 · The train <u>leaves</u> at 7 p.m. （這班火車晚上七點出發。）
現在進行式	表達短期內計劃好的行動。 · I <u>am going</u> to a party tonight. （我今晚要去參加一場派對。）
未來進行式	表達幾乎可以肯定一定會發生的事。 · They <u>will be playing</u> basketball on Sunday afternoon. （他們星期日下午將要打籃球。）

雖然有這些方式可以表達未來的事件，但其實它們之間的差別並不大，甚至混用也不會造成誤解，可是語感上還是有些許差別：

· We <u>will be working</u> on the electric service in your area.

→電力公司要進行維修是肯定的事，所以在公告通知中使用未來進行式，表達肯定的語感。

Questions 170 and 171 refer to the following advertisement:

SAVE 66%

YES! Send me two years (20 issues) of YOU CAN BE HEALTHY for only $30. I SAVE 66% off the newsstand price! I can also access the online edition for the length of my subscription for FREE.

Name:_____

Address:_____ Apt. No:_____

City:_____ State:_____ Zip:_____

Email:_____

To order faster, go to www.youcanbehealthy.com/save66
☐ I prefer to subscribe for 1 year (10 issues) for just $20
☐ Payment enclosed
☐ Bill me later

Plus sales tax where applicable. YOU CAN BE HEALTHY is published 10 times a year and may also publish occasional extra issues. Offer good in U.S. only. Your first issue will mail 4-8 weeks from receipt of order.

NOW SALE!

中　　譯

大省66%

是的！寄給我兩年（20期）的「你會健康」，只需30元。和書報攤相比，我可以節省66%！我也可以在訂閱期間免費取得線上版本。

姓名：_____

地址：_____ 公寓號碼：_____

城市：_____ 州：_____ 郵遞區號：_____

Email：_____

更快速地訂閱，請上 www.youcanbehealthy.com/save66
☐ 我比較想要訂閱一年份（10期），20元。
☐ 隨函附上支票。
☐ 稍後付款。

可適用地區會有外加的銷售稅。「你會健康」雜誌一年發行10次，並可能偶爾有額外的發行本。此優惠提供僅限美國。您將在收到訂購後4到8週內收到第一期訂閱雜誌。

170. How can you read *You Can be Healthy*? *
    (A) In print and online.
    (B) Online only.
    (C) On your Kindle or Tablet only.
    (D) In print only.

中　譯

你可以如何閱讀「你會健康」雜誌？
(A) 紙本和線上。
(B) 只有線上。
(C) 只有在平版閱讀器。
(D) 只有紙本。

解答提示

這張訂購單的前言有提到，訂購兩年的雜誌還可以獲得免費線上閱讀的權限，可見是紙本和線上兩種媒介都有，所以選 (A)。

171. What might be added to your purchase price? **
    (A) The cost for an additional year.
    (B) The cost of shipping.
    (C) Sales tax.
    (D) An administrative fee.

中　譯

你購買的金額還有可能外加什麼？
(A) 額外訂閱一年的費用。
(B) 寄送費用。
(C) 銷售稅。
(D) 行政處理費。

解答提示

內容中有一句 "Plus sales tax where applicable." 指的就是如果訂閱人所在的州政府規定須課銷售稅的話，訂閱人必須自付，所以選 (C)。

 瑣碎時間看這裡

< percent的用法 >
percent是我們常見的英文，甚至受到日語影響的台語，在日常生活中也常常說「幾趴？」但是在英文中真正的用法是什麼呢？以下做個小整理：

1. 數字 + percent of
· Only 40 percent of people voted in the election.
（只有40%的人在選舉中投票。）
· Many poor families spend about 80 to 90 percent of their income on food.
（許多貧窮的家庭花費收入的80~90%在食物上。）
· It is often said that we use only 10 percent of our brain.
（人們常說我們只使用了大腦的10%。）

2. by + 數字 + percent
· Interest rates are expected to rise by one percent.
（利率預計會上升1%。）
· My salary will decrease by two percent next year.
（我的薪水明年會減少2%。）

Questions 172 through 174 refer to the following advertisement:

IS IT TIME TO EXAMINE WHAT YOUR PORTFOLIO IS MISSING?

It's time to take stock!
Market volatility has caused some investors to ignore equities, potentially putting their long-term financial goals at risk. If you are one of those investors, it may be time for you to reconsider equities.

It starts by speaking with a financial advisor.
Frankly Reliable Investments
Gain knowledge from our perspective

You should carefully consider a fund's investment goals, risks, and expenses before investing. You'll find this information in the fund's prospectus, which you can obtain from your financial advisor.
All investments involve risk, including possible loss of principal. Stock prices fluctuate, sometimes rapidly, due to factors affecting individual companies or industries and general market conditions.
Frankly Reliable Investments, Inc. One Reliable Parkway, San Rosa CA 99999

 中　譯

到了檢視你的投資組合少了什麼的時候了嗎？

盤點的時候到了！
市場的易變已經使得一些投資者忽略資產配置，可能將他們的長期財務目標置於危險當中。如果您是這些投資者之一，也許是時候您重新考慮資產配置。

開始和理財專員談一談吧。
Frankly Reliable投資公司
從我們的觀點獲得知識

您應該謹慎考慮基金投資的目標、風險以及投資前的成本。您可以在基金投資計劃書中找到這些資訊，計劃書可從您的理財專員取得。

所有投資皆具有風險，包括本金可能損失。股票價格波動，有時因個別公司或產業的因素，又或整體市場的情況而劇烈變動。

Frankly Reliable投資公司　One Reliable Parkway, 聖羅沙 加州 CA99999

172. What might happen when investors ignore equities? ***
　　　(A) Their financial advisor might get mad at them.
　　　(B) Their long-term financial goals might be at risk.
　　　(C) They might lose their vision for the future.
　　　(D) They might overdraw their checking account.

中　譯

當投資者忽略資產配置時，什麼事可能發生？
(A) 他們的理財專員可能會生氣。
(B) 他們的長期財務目標可能會有危機。
(C) 他們可能失去未來的願景。
(D) 他們可能透支自己的支票帳戶。

解答提示

內容提到 "potentially putting their long-term financial goals at risk"，所以答案可以放心地選下去，就是 (B) 沒有錯！

173. Where can you find a fund's investment goals and risks? ***
　　　(A) In the owner's manual.
　　　(B) On the website.
　　　(C) In the fund's prospectus.
　　　(D) Stored on your computer.

中　譯

你可以在哪裡找到基金投資的目標和風險？
(A) 在擁有人的手冊中。
(B) 在網站上。
(C) 在基金投資計劃書。
(D) 存放在你的電腦。

解答提示

內文中也是用prospectus *n.[C]* 計劃書，所以可以很快找到 (C) 為正確答案。在閱讀的時候，可以一邊把特殊的單字做記號，因為這些特別的字都很可能是問題的核心。

174. What risk is mentioned that all investments could face? **
   (A) A difficult relationship with your advisor.
   (B) Identity theft.
   (C) Physical risk to the investor.
   (D) Loss of principal.

中　　譯

有提到所有的投資都可能面臨什麼樣的風險？
(A) 和理財專員的關係不佳。
(B) 身分被盜用。
(C) 投資者生理上的風險。
(D) 本金損失。

解答提示

內容寫到：All investments involve risk, including possible **loss of principal**，因此答案即是選項 (D)。

 瑣碎時間看這裡

< It is time用法 >
(1) It is time + to V
　· It is time to start the game.
　　（現在是時候開始比賽了。）
　· It is time to take a break.
　　（現在是時候休息一會兒了。）
(2) It is time + for + ... + to V
　· It is time for us to leave the office.
　　（現在是時候讓我們離開辦公室了。）

· It is time for you to go.
（你現在是時候去了。）
(3) It is time + for + N
· It is time for breakfast.
（現在是時候吃早餐了。）
· It is time for a break.
（現在是時候休息一會兒了。）
(4) It is time + S + V-ed
· It is time we went home.
（是時候我們該回家了。）
· It is time you made up your mind.
（是時候你要下定決心了。）

(1)~(3) 表達的是做某事的時間到了。而 (4) 更暗示現在才做某事已經有點晚了。要更強調這個意思，可以說 It is high time（現在是非常適當的時候）。

Questions 175 through 177 refer to the following email:

March 5th, 2013
To all full-time staff:

This is to remind you that you must plan ahead for use of your paid time off for vacations this summer. Requests for time off from June 1st through August 31st are due to my office by March 15th. If you turn in a request in a timely manner, I will do everything I can to grant you your requested vacation dates. Please remember that I must take all requests into consideration, leaving enough staff to cover all vacancies.

To aid in this, please list your 1st and 2nd choices for time off, and note if the date is for a specific event you already have plans to attend.

If you choose not to turn in a vacation request at this time, I may be unable to grant you a request turned in at a later date.

Thank you for your cooperation!
Kevin Chan
Human Services

中　譯

2013年3月5日
致所有全職員工：

這封email是提醒您，您必須事先規劃今年夏天的支薪特休。6月1日到8月31日的請假申請必須在3月15日送到我的辦公室。如果您在時間內提出申請，我會盡量同意您申請的休假日期。請記得我必須考量所有的申請，為所有的空缺留下足夠的員工。

為請您協助，請列出您休假的第一選擇和第二選擇，並註明該日期是否有您已計劃好參加的特別事項。

如果您選擇不在此時提出休假申請，我可能無法准予較晚提出的申請。

謝謝合作！
Kevin Chan
人資部

175. What time period does Kevin need time off requests for? **
    (A) The month of March.
    (B) October and November.
    (C) June through August.
    (D) Christmas vacation.

中　譯

Kevin需要休假申請落在什麼時間？
(A) 3月。
(B) 10月和11月。
(C) 6月到8月。
(D) 聖誕假期。

解答提示

內文中提到：from June 1st through August 31st，所以答案當然是 (C) 囉！

176. What must Kevin consider when granting people's requests? ****
    (A) That there will be enough staff on duty at all times.
    (B) Who it was that made the request.
    (C) The rate of pay for those taking time off.
    (D) That Kevin gets his own vacation when he wants it.

中　譯

在批准休假申請時，Kevin必須考量什麼事？
(A) 任何時候都有足夠的員工上班。
(B) 提出申請的人是誰。
(C) 休假人員的薪資。
(D) 當Kevin自己想休假的時候可以休假。

解答提示

這一題的正確答案 (A)，是用換句話說的方式，內文是寫：leaving enough staff

to cover all vacancies（留下足夠的員工來代理所有的空缺），而選項 (A) 則是寫：enough staff on duty at all times（任何時候有足夠的員工上班），兩者意思相同，只是用不同的文字表達。

177. If you do not turn in your request on time, what can happen? ***
    (A) Your co-workers may get mad at you.
    (B) You may not get your vacation at all.
    (C) You may forfeit your seniority at work.
    (D) You may get a poor review at the end of the year.

中　譯

如果你沒有準時提出申請，會發生什麼事？
(A) 你的同事可能會生你的氣。
(B) 你可能無法獲得休假。
(C) 你可能喪失資深的資格。
(D) 你可能在年終得到不好的考核。

解答提示

這題的答案是 (B)。內容寫的是：I may be unable to grant you a request turned in at a later date.，也就是有可能休假申請不會被批准。

🌀 瑣碎時間看這裡

< 授與動詞 >
授與動詞最明顯的特徵就是有兩個受詞，通常直接受詞是物品，而間接受詞則是人。授與動詞的句型如下：
(1) 主詞 + 授與動詞 + 直接受詞 + 介系詞 + 間接受詞
  · Mike gave **some flowers** to <u>his girlfriend</u>.
(2) 主詞 + 授與動詞 + 間接受詞 + 直接受詞
  · Mike gave <u>his girlfriend</u> **some flowers**.

但是如果直接受詞是代名詞的形式，則通常使用 (1) 的句型：
  · Mike gave **them** to <u>his girlfriend</u>.
  · Mike gave his girlfriend them.（X）
  · Please give it to me.
→如果兩個受詞都是代名詞，通常也是使用 (1) 的句型。

Questions 178 through 180 refer to the following article:

ART AT WORK

ART AT WORK

Let ART AT WORK transform your workplace! ART AT WORK can deliver a selection of original fine art created by exceptional regional artists, at a very reasonable cost.

BUSINESS WITH STYLE

The fine original art provided by ART AT WORK offers a pleasing experience that only original art can provide! It demonstrates your support for our leading regional artists and the Arts and Cultural Museum. A three-month rental period allows for flexibility and the opportunity to display a wide variety of artwork.

HOW?

Visit our gallery or call for a free art consultation. We can suggest art suitable for your space. Works of art are rented for three months and installed for free. At the end of the rental period, your art rental can be renewed, rotated for new artwork, returned or purchased. A portion of the rental fee may be applied toward the purchase.

ART AT WORK gallery is located in the Ruth Anderson Gallery at the Arts and Cultural Museum.
CALL Tammy Voigt, Manager: (503) 123-1234

中　　譯

工作中的藝術

工作中的藝術

讓「工作中的藝術」轉變您的工作環境！「工作中的藝術」能夠提供一系列由傑出的地方藝術家所創作的原創藝術品，價格合理。

有風格的商業

「工作中的藝術」所提供的原創藝術品，給予您愉悅的經驗，只有原創藝術

才能提供！這也展現您的支持，對於我們重要的區域藝術家以及美術文化博物館。三個月的租期允許高彈性，和展示廣泛多樣藝術品的機會。

如何利用？
造訪我們的藝廊，或致電詢問免費的藝術咨詢。我們可以為您的空間推薦合適的藝術品。藝術品租借為期三個月，並免費為您擺設。租期結束時，您的藝術品租約可以更新、調動成新的藝術品、歸還或是購買。租約費用的一部分可以折抵為購買價金。

「工作中的藝術」藝廊位於美術文化博物館的Ruth Anderson藝廊中。
來電 (503) 123-1234，請洽經理Tammy Voigt。

178. Who creates the art that you can exhibit at your business? **
 (A) Well-known artists from around the country.
 (B) Students from local schools.
 (C) Regional artists.
 (D) University art students.

中　　譯

你可以在辦公場所展示的藝術品，是誰創作的？
(A) 全國各地知名的藝術家。
(B) 本地的學生。
(C) 區域的藝術家。
(D) 大學美術系學生。

解答提示

內文中提到：created by exceptional **regional artists**，所以答案就是 (C) 選項。

179. How long can a business display the works of art? ****
 (A) They display it until the artist sells it.
 (B) It can only be displayed for the length of time they originally rent it.
 (C) ART AT WORK will remove it when they need it somewhere else.
 (D) For three months, at which time they can choose to renew the
  rental.

Chapter 2 閱讀測驗大解密

中　譯

一家公司可以展示藝術品多久？
(A) 他們可以展示到藝術家賣出作品為止。
(B) 藝術品只能展示的時間是他們原本租借的時間。
(C) 「工作中的藝術」會移除藝術品，當他們需要把它放到別的地方時。
(D) 為期三個月，屆時他們可以選擇更新租約。

解答提示

內容中有寫：Works of art are rented for three months，所以答案是 (D) 選項。
其他選項的回答方式也是關於時間，但是都和內容沒有關係。

180. Who do you contact to ask about a rental? **
  (A) Call the Arts and Cultural Museum.
  (B) Tammy Voigt, the ART AT WORK manager.
  (C) Talk to your supervisor at work.
  (D) Call the city council and see if they know about it.

中　譯

你可以和誰聯絡，詢問租約事項？
(A) 打電話給美術文化博物館。
(B) 「工作中的藝術」經理Tammy Voigt。
(C) 和你職場的上司談。
(D) 打電話給市議會看看他們知道不知道。

解答提示

這一題非常容易，問題是問who，而內容的最後又剛好有署名，所以答案直
接選 (B) 就沒錯了！

瑣碎時間看這裡

< 地點的表示 >
英文當中表示地點最簡單的方式就是使用be動詞：
· That store __is__ next to the bakery.
（那家店在麵包店旁邊。）

但是大家在學習的過程中，應該會發現其實英文還有其他表達地點的方式，尤其是在閱讀的時候，因為單單用一個be動詞感覺實在太弱了！所以就發展出不同的說法，特別以被動語態的表示最多：
(1) be located in/at...
· Our office __is located__ downtown.
（我們的辦公室位在市中心。）
(2) be situated in/at...
· The resort __is situated in__ the mountains so that tourists can take a break from the sizzling summer.
（那個度假勝地位於山裡，所以遊客可以逃離酷熱的夏天。）
(3) lie in/at...
· That town __lies on__ the coast.
（那座小鎮位置面向海岸。）

*Double Passages

Questions 181 through 185 refer to the following letter and coupon:

Dear Community Member,

Whether or not you are a member of Numbers Credit Union, we invite you to participate in our 20K Win! Win! Sweepstakes.

Give and receive. It's the ultimate win, win situation. If you are the winner, you will receive $10,000 for yourself AND $10,000 for your favorite non-profit charity.

To enter, simply drop off the attached coupon at any of our Numbers Credit Union Branches. You do not have to be a member to win.

Good Luck!
Numbers Credit Union

*By entering this contest you give us permission to contact you.
**All entrants must be over 18 years of age.
***For complete rules, see our website NumbersCU.com.

中　　譯

親愛的社區會員，

無論您是否為數字信用社的會員，我們邀請您參與20K雙贏抽獎。

付出並獲得，這是終極的雙贏局面。如果您獲獎，您將會得到$10,000給您自己，還有$10,000給您最喜愛的慈善機構。

參加方式，只要把隨附的票券交給任何一家數字信用社的分店。您不需具會員身分仍可獲獎。

祝好運！

數字信用社

*經由參加此抽獎您同意我們與您聯繫。
**參加者需年滿十八歲。
***完整規則請詳見網站NumbersCU.com。

Numbers Credit Union

Twice the Nice.
With the Numbers $20,000 Win! Win!
You can indulge with confidence.
Bring this coupon to any Numbers branch to enter!

Name:_____

Phone Number:_____

Email:_____

中　　譯

數字合作社

好，還要更好！
參加數字合作社的$20,000雙贏，您可以享受自信。
請攜此票券至任一數字合作社分店。

姓名：_____
電話號碼：_____
電子信箱：_____

181. Who is eligible to enter the sweepstakes? ***
　　(A) Only members of the credit union.
　　(B) Anyone over the age of 18.
　　(C) Only employees of the credit union.
　　(D) Anyone who lives in the area.

中　　譯

誰有資格參加此抽獎？
(A) 只有合作社的會員。
(B) 任何年滿十八歲的人。

(C) 只有合作社的員工。
(D) 任何居住附近的人。

解答提示

此題的問句重點是eligible（有資格的），只要看得懂這個字，就可以輕鬆選對答案，答案為 (B)。

182. Why is this called a win, win situation? ＊＊
  (A) Because two people in the same family will win money.
  (B) Because the credit union will win.
  (C) Because both you and a charity will win $10,000.
  (D) Because two families will win money.

中　　譯

為什麼這稱為雙贏局面？
(A) 因為同一個家庭的兩個人將贏得抽獎。
(B) 因為合作社將會贏。
(C) 因為你和一個慈善機構都將贏得一萬元。
(D) 因為兩個家庭將會贏錢。

解答提示

此題的答案在文章中即寫明，win, win situation是雙贏局面的意思，所以選 (C)。

183. How do you enter this sweepstakes? ＊＊
  (A) Call the credit union.
  (B) Enter online.
  (C) Send the coupon in the mail.
  (D) Drop off the coupon at any Numbers branch.

中　　譯

你要如何參加這項抽獎？
(A) 打電話給合作社。
(B) 線上參加。
(C) 把票券郵寄出去。
(D) 把票券交給任何一家數字分店。

解答提示

此題的答案為 (D)，相關內容可以在文章中可輕易找到，尤其是答案使用了和文章中一樣的片語動詞drop off（在...放下），可以作為答題提示。

184. How will Numbers Credit Union contact you if you are the winner? ****
(A) They will send someone to your house.
(B) You have to be present at the drawing to win.
(C) They will contact you via phone or email.
(D) They have no way to contact you.

中　譯

如果你得獎，數字合作社將如何與你聯繫？
(A) 他們會派人到府。
(B) 你必須現身抽獎現場才能得獎。
(C) 他們會透過電話或電子郵件聯繫你。
(D) 他們無法聯繫你。

解答提示

此題的答案在文章中雖然沒有直接相關的句子描述，但是在票券需留下電話號碼和電子信箱，因此可判斷是透過此兩種方式聯繫。正確答案為 (C)。

185. According to the letter, will the credit union likely contact you about their services? *****
(A) No, you do not give them permission to contact you.
(B) Yes, by entering you give them permission to contact you.
(C) They will only contact you if you ask them to.
(D) No, they won't have contact information for you.

中　譯

根據此信，合作社可能因為他們提供的服務而和你聯繫嗎？
(A) 不，你並未給予他們同意來聯繫你。
(B) 是，透過參加，你給予他們同意來聯繫你。
(C) 如果你要求，他們將會聯繫你。
(D) 不，他們將沒有你的聯繫資料。

解答提示

從內容即可找到By entering this contest you give us permission to contact you. · 用字一模一樣，所以不用客氣選 (B) 就對囉！

 瑣碎時間看這裡

< 連接詞if表示 [假設] >
連接詞if (如果) 的用法其實不難，有時候甚至用中文去想就可以了：
「如果...就...」（ 如果A成立，B就會發生 ）。
1. If you are the winner, you will receive $10,000 for yourself AND $10,000 for your favorite non-profit charity.
2. You can stay here for the weekend if you like.
（ 如果你喜歡，你可以留在這裡過週末。 ）

→注意if子句中的動詞時態是現在式，主要子句中則常用情態助動詞（ will/can/may/should/must... ）、祈使句或現在式。

Questions 186 through 190 refer to the following letter and brochure:

Dear Mrs. Chang,

Thank you for your interest in River's Glory Hotel in Istanbul, Turkey. River's Glory overlooks the Bosphorus River and the palaces of Istanbul's history, in one of the city's liveliest neighborhoods.

What you'll love:
- ❖ Complimentary breakfast highlights Turkey's best honey, cheese and olives
- ❖ Candlelit Spa features a Turkish bath, sauna and steam room
- ❖ Spacious Italian marble bathrooms
- ❖ Cozy window benches to view the scenic river and the lightshow on the bridge
- ❖ A short walk to Istanbul's main street (Kebab's anyone? How about folk music?)
- ❖ A short walk to a ferry to the islands or the subway to the old city

Have we piqued your interest?
- ❖ Corner rooms with a view feature one queen bed
- ❖ Deluxe suites feature one queen bed
- ❖ Garden View rooms feature one queen bed or two twin beds.

Our website lists full amenities and pricing. Quotes listed online are subject to change due to currency conversion. Visit us at Riversglory.com. We think you'll like what you see!

Sincerely,
Ahmet Demir

*Minimum Check-in Age is 18.
**Smoking and pets are not permitted.

中　　譯

親愛的張女士您好，

感謝您對於土耳其伊斯坦堡River's Glory飯店有興趣。River's Glory俯瞰博斯普魯斯河以及伊斯坦堡歷史上的宮殿，位於這座城市最具生氣的社區之一。

您將會愛上：
❖ 免費早餐，特色是土耳其最佳的蜂蜜、起司和橄欖
❖ 燭光spa，特色是土耳其浴、三溫暖和蒸氣室
❖ 寬敞的義大利大理石浴室
❖ 舒適的窗邊長凳，可飽覽風光明媚的河川和橋上的燈光秀
❖ 步行一小段路即抵達伊斯坦堡的主要街道（誰要烤肉串嗎？來點民族音樂如何？）
❖ 步行一小段路即搭乘到小島上的渡輪，或搭乘捷運到舊城區

我們引起您的興趣了嗎？
❖ 有景觀的轉角房是一張皇后尺寸的床
❖ 豪華套房是一張皇后尺寸的床
❖ 花園景觀房是一張皇后尺寸的床，或兩張單人床

我們的網站列出了完整的舒適備品及價格。線上的報價會因為貨幣轉換而有所變動。請造訪我們的網站Riversglory.com。我們認為您會喜歡您所見的！

誠摯地，
Ahmet Demir敬上

*最低入住年齡為18歲。
**禁止吸菸與攜帶寵物。

We would like to offer you
25% off
your first night's lodging!

*When you reserve by June 31st.
**When reserving online or by phone use
 promotional code RVR25.

中　譯

我們想要提供給您第一晚住宿25%的折扣！
*當您在6月31日前訂房。
**線上或電話訂房時使用推廣碼RVR25。

186. Why did Ahmet write this letter to Mrs. Chang? **
　　(A) He heard about her online and was interested.
　　(B) She expressed interest in staying at the hotel.
　　(C) She won a drawing for a free stay at River's Glory.
　　(D) Her business wants to lead a conference there.

中　譯

為什麼Ahmet要寫這封信給張女士？
(A) 他在線上聽過她，而對她感到興趣。
(B) 她表達了住宿這間飯店的興趣。
(C) 她贏得抽獎，得到River's Glory飯店的免費住宿。
(D) 她的公司要在那裡舉辦會議。

解答提示

這一題可以在信件的最一開始找到答案：Thank you for your interest...，會這麼寫一定是表示對方已經先表達對飯店有興趣，所以飯店這方才會回信。所以選 (B)。

187. According to the letter, what might the hotel serve for breakfast? ****
　　(A) Cold cereal with fresh fruit and a glass of juice.
　　(B) Pancakes with fresh maple syrup, sausage and peaches.
　　(C) Toast with honey, a Mediterranean spread with olives, and various sliced cheeses.
　　(D) Noodles with sautéed vegetables, juice and a banana.

中　譯

根據信件，飯店的早餐可能會提供什麼？
(A) 冷的麥片、新鮮水果和一杯果汁。
(B) 鬆餅搭配新鮮楓糖、臘腸和水蜜桃。
(C) 蜂蜜土司、地中海式烤餅加橄欖以及各樣切片起司。
(D) 麵條佐香炒蔬菜、果汁和一根香蕉。

解答提示

看到題目問早餐，就要趕快回到信件中關於早餐的部分：Complimentary breakfast highlights Turkey's best **honey**, **cheese** and **olives**，所以最合適的答案是 (C)。

188. What things of interest are within a short walking distance from the hotel? ****
(A) Main Street, the ferry and the subway.
(B) Markets, businesses and a carnival.
(C) A history museum.
(D) The national palaces.

中　譯

什麼景點是在飯店的短程步行距離內？
(A) 主要街道、渡輪和捷運。
(B) 市集、商店和狂歡節。
(C) 一間歷史博物館。
(D) 國家宮殿。

解答提示

這一題可以利用題目中的walking distance，回去內容尋找類似的用字，可以找到：
(1) **A short walk** to Istanbul's main street (2) **A short walk** to a ferry to the islands or the subway to the old city，這樣就知道正確答案是 (A) 囉！

189. If anyone in Mrs. Chang's family smokes, what will they want to make note of? ***
(A) Cigarettes may cost more to purchase in Turkey.
(B) River's Glory has very few smoking rooms.
(C) It will be difficult to travel with cigarettes in your baggage.
(D) River's Glory is a non-smoking hotel.

中　譯

如果張女士的家庭成員有人抽菸，他們會想要特別注意什麼事？
(A) 在土耳其，香菸可能比較貴。
(B) River's Glory的吸菸房很少。
(C) 在行李中攜帶香菸旅行是困難的。
(D) River's Glory是禁菸飯店。

解答提示

信件的最後有特別寫到：Smoking and pets are **not permitted**，所以就是 (D) 禁菸飯店。

190. What must Mrs. Chang do to take advantage of the 25% coupon she received? ***
(A) Reserve the hotel for a weekend conference.
(B) Make a reservation by June 31st.
(C) Make a reservation for at least three people.
(D) Make her reservation online.

中　譯

張女士要利用收到的優惠券25%折扣，她必須做什麼事？
(A) 為週末的會議而訂飯店。
(B) 在6月31日前訂房。
(C) 為至少三個人訂房。
(D) 在線上訂房。

解答提示

回答這一題就要回到折扣券本身，其中的條件是："When you reserve by June 31st. When reserving online or by phone use promotional code RVR25."
選項中符合的只有選項 (B)，選項 (D) 是不完全正確的，因為張女士也可以用電話訂房而享受優惠價格。

瑣碎時間看這裡

<英文最高級>
英文最高級常見的句型如下：
(1) ... the 最高級 + 介系詞 + 地點 / 範圍
(2) ... the 最高級 + of/among + 人
‧ The Nile River is the longest river in the world.
（尼羅河是世界上最長的河流。）
‧ Peter is the tallest child in his family.
（Peter是他家最高的小孩。）
‧ Joe is the oldest boy among us.
（Joe是我們之間年紀最大的男孩。）
‧ Nicky is the prettiest girl of them.
（Nicky是她們裡面最漂亮的女生。）

一般來說，最高級搭配上範圍，目的是讓聽話的人更清楚了解。不過如果對方已經知道談話的內容是什麼，其實不加上範圍也是OK的！

Questions 191 through 195 refer to the advertisement:

YOU MAY BE THE LUCKY WINNER!

It may be you who drives away in a new car this weekend! Take a test drive during our NEW CAR EXTRAVAGANZA and walk away with a prize!

We are locating the extravaganza at the corner of Northport Highway and Division Road, for easy access from anywhere in the city. We'll have hundreds of makes and models available to test drive. Even if you aren't the winner of the NEW CAR, you will walk away with a prize. Everyone who stops by can reach into the GAS CARD EXTRAVAGANZA box and pull out a winner. You are guaranteed to walk away with a valuable gas card!

New Car Extravaganza
Newport Motors
Saturday, July 13th, 2014   Sunday July 14th, 2014
8:00 a.m. to 9:00 p.m.   8:00 a.m. to 9:00 p.m.

*Gas cards range in value in value from $5 to $500
**No test drive necessary to win

中　譯

你可能是幸運得主！

本週末開著新車離開的可能就是你！在我們的新車大展中試駕，並帶著獎品回家！

為了在城市中任何地方都可以輕鬆來到，我們把此大展設定在Northport公路和Division路的轉角。我們將準備上百款品牌和型號供試駕。即使您不是「新車」的得獎者，您一樣可以帶著獎品回家。任何路過的人都可以伸到「加油卡大放送」的箱子試試手氣。保證您一定可以帶著已儲值的加油卡離開！

新車大展
Newport汽車公司
2014年7月13日星期六　　2014年7月14日星期日
上午8點~晚上9點　　　　上午8點~晚上9點

*加油卡金額從5元到500元。
**不需試駕即可抽獎。

Bring this card in with the attached key to WIN A NEW CAR!
Try the key in the lock box of our prize vehicle. If your key opens the box, you are the new owner of the car. Drive away in style!

One key mailed out is guaranteed to open the lock box

中　　譯

帶上這張卡片和隨附的鑰匙來贏得新車！
把鑰匙插入獎品汽車的鎖盒中。如果您的鑰匙開啟盒子，您就是汽車的新主人。有型地開車吧！

保證寄出的鑰匙中定有一把可開啟鎖盒。

191. What is the point of this advertisement? *****
    (A) To give a car away to someone who really needs it.
    (B) To help families with the rising cost of gas, by giving them gas cards.
    (C) To attract customers who will possibly buy a new vehicle while they are there.
    (D) To sell cars at the lowest price of the year.

中　　譯

這則廣告的重點是什麼？
(A) 送一部車給真的需要的人。
(B) 幫助家庭度過上漲的油價，送他們加油卡。
(C) 吸引到場時有可能會買新車的顧客。
(D) 以今年度最低價銷售汽車。

解答提示

此類的汽車展當然是為了吸引消費者囉！所以答案選 (C) 一定沒錯。而選項 (A)（送車）和 (B)（送加油卡）都是廣告中提到的活動，但並不是這個廣告最主要的重點。

192. If you don't take a test drive, can you still get a gas card? ***

    (A) Yes, if you give a small donation.

    (B) Yes, anyone who stops by can get one.

    (C) No, they are only available for those who test drive a vehicle.

    (D) No, the gas card is only for the winner of the car.

中　　譯

如果你沒有試駕，你還是可以得到加油卡嗎？
(A) 是的，如果你稍微捐一點錢的話。
(B) 是的，任何路過的人都可以得到。
(C) 不行，加油卡只給有試駕的人。
(D) 不行，加油卡只給新車得主。

解答提示

廣告內容即提及：**Everyone who stops by** can reach into the GAS CARD EXTRAVAGANZA box and pull out a winner.，正確答案是 (B)。

193. How do you know if you're the winner of the car? ***

    (A) When you reach into the box and pull out the card that says WINNER.

    (B) There will be a drawing on Sunday and they will call the winner.

    (C) If the key you received in the mail opens the lock box, you are the winner.

    (D) If you are the 100th customer to bring in the key, you win.

中　　譯

你如何知道自己是不是汽車得主？
(A) 你把手伸進盒子裡，然後抽出卡片上片寫著：「恭喜中獎」。
(B) 星期日會舉辦抽獎，他們會公布得獎者。
(C) 如果你在郵件收到的鑰匙打開了鎖盒，你就是得獎者。
(D) 如果你是第一百名把鑰匙帶來的人，你就贏了。

解答提示

廣告附上的小說明寫：If your key opens the box, you are the new owner of the

car. · 所以答案是 (C)。選項 (A) 所描述的情況是在抽加油卡。

194. How likely is it that you will win a $500 gas card? ***
    (A) Everyone will pull out one worth $500.
    (B) You should assume that most of the cards are for $5.
    (C) You are guaranteed at least $100.
    (D) Only the winner of the car gets $500.

中　譯

你得到500元加油卡的可能性高嗎？
(A) 每個人都會抽到等值500元的加油卡。
(B) 你應該假設大多數的卡是5元的加油卡。
(C) 保證你至少會抽到100元的加油卡。
(D) 只有汽車得主得到500元的加油卡。

解答提示

這一題的題目本身較有難度，How likely is it...?是問某種情況的可能性有多高，我們必須用常理邏輯判斷一下。每個路過的人都能抽加油卡，而加油卡的金額從5元到500元不等，當然多數的加油卡的金額會是5元，否則主辦單位不是賠大了嗎？所以最合適的答案應該是 (B)。

195. Is someone guaranteed to win the car? *****
    (A) The only guarantee is that there is a box full of gas cards.
    (B) There are never any guarantees in life.
    (C) The advertisement didn't say anything about a guarantee.
    (D) The winning key was mailed out, but there's no guarantee that person will attend.

中　譯

保證有人會贏得汽車嗎？
(A) 唯一保證的是盒子有滿滿的加油卡。
(B) 人生中沒有什麼保證。
(C) 這則廣告沒有提到任何保證。
(D) 中獎的鑰匙已寄出，但不保證收到鑰匙的人一定會出現。

解答提示

廣告的小說明寫：One key mailed out is guaranteed to open the lock box. · 也就是保證主辦單位所寄發的鑰匙當中，一定有一把可以打開鎖盒得到汽車大獎。但是，主辦單位無法保證那個人一定會出席新車大展來試手氣。所以正確答案是 (D)。

🌀 瑣碎時間看這裡

< even if/even though >
因為這兩個連接詞通常都翻譯成「即使」，所以有時候會誤會它們是一樣的，但是它們是截然不同的喔！
· (Even) if he comes, I won't let him in.
（即使 / 如果他來，我也不會讓他進來。）
· (Even) though he came, I didn't let him in.
（即使 / 雖然他來了，我也不讓他進來。）

大家可以注意到，如果這兩個句子把even去掉，句意是不會改變的喔！所以even可以視為是用來加強語氣的副詞，實際上沒有了even也OK。
所以看到even if和even though的時候，只要在腦海中自動把even刪掉，肯定就不會弄錯囉！

Questions 196 through 200 refer to the following letter:

Dear athlete,

We are so glad you ran the Blooming 10K last year. Lilacs are in bloom along the race course again this year, and we look forward to seeing you again.

Special events along the course include live music, high school cheerleaders to motivate you, graffiti alley created by local elementary school students, and this year's Lilac Princesses lining the final mile in full princess dress.

Costumes are encouraged for teams. Please register your team as soon as possible. Water stations and medical tents will be placed along the race course. This year features heightened security for all racers and volunteers. Please return the enclosed registration form by April 10th.

If you cannot run this year, but would like to volunteer, please call Ron at 504-231-3131. We need people to monitor streets, water stations, medical tents, parking lots, and check-in tables.

中　譯

親愛的運動員，

我們很高興您去年參加了Blooming 10公里路跑。路跑路線沿路的紫丁香花今年又盛開了，我們期待再次看到您的參與。

沿路上的特別活動包括：現場音樂、激勵您的高中啦啦隊表演、當地小學生創作的塗鴉小徑，以及今年度的紫丁香小姐參賽者，會穿著完整的公主裝，在最後一英哩沿路迎接您。

團體成員建議穿著團體服裝。請盡早為您的團體登記。給水站和醫療帳篷會沿路設置。今年特別為所有跑者和志工加強安全措施。請在4月10日前回覆隨函的登記卡。

如果您今年無法參與路跑，但願意擔任志工，請撥打504-231-3131與Ron聯繫。我們需要志工監看街道、給水站、醫療帳篷、停車場和報到櫃台。

Chapter 2 閱讀測驗大解密

Blooming 10K

Name:_____

Address:_____

Email:_____

Age:_____ 10k time (for starting placement)_____

T-shirt Size:

Youth___S___M___L   Adult___S___M___L___XL

Registration Fee: $15 Due by April 10th

____ Check Enclosed   ____Charge my credit card # _____

*Please fill out one registration form per person.

**Families and business can pay for all registrations in one payment.

中　　譯

Blooming 10公里路跑

姓名：_____

住址：_____

Email:_____

年齡：_____10公里最佳成績（供起跑點安排用）_____

T恤尺寸：

未成年人____ S____ M____ L____ 　成年人____ S____ M____ L____ XL

登記費用：15元　4月10日前完成繳費

_____ 隨附支票 _____ 信用卡支付，卡號_____

*請一人使用一張登記表格。

**家庭或企業可以為所有的登證進行一次繳費。

196. Why would someone receive this letter? **

(A) Because they have already registered for this year's race.

(B) Everyone in the community received this mailing.

(C) Because they ran the race last year.

(D) They asked to be put on the mailing list.

中　　譯

為什麼有人會收到這封信？

(A) 因為他們已經登記今年的路跑。

(B) 社區裡每個人都收到這封信。

(C) 因為他們去年有參加路跑。

(D) 他們要求把名字放在郵寄清單中。

解答提示

信件的一開始就寫著：We are so glad you **ran** the Blooming 10K **last year**.，可見是因為收信人去年就參加過了，所以今年主辦單位再發信詢問他們參加的意願。所以答案選 (C)。

197. How are elementary students helping with the race? ***
    (A) Cheering people on.
    (B) Creating graffiti art to encourage runners on the course.
    (C) Running the race with their parents.
    (D) Handing out water bottles.

中　　譯

小學生如何在這次路跑提供協助？
(A) 替人們加油。
(B) 在路線上創作塗鴉藝術鼓勵跑者。
(C) 和他們的父母親一起路跑。
(D) 傳遞水瓶。

解答提示

這一題要聯想一下，信件內容是：graffiti alley created by local elementary school students，而小學生創作這些塗鴉正是為了激勵（encourage）跑者，所以應該選 (B)。

198. If you are a nurse, what would be a good volunteer position for you? **
    (A) Directing traffic.
    (B) Becoming a Lilac Princess.
    (C) Checking people in as they arrive.
    (D) Working in a medical tent.

中　　譯

如果你是一名護士，擔任哪種志工對你最合適？
(A) 指揮交通。
(B) 變成紫丁香公主。
(C) 人們抵達時替他們報到。

(D) 在醫療帳篷裡工作。

解答提示

這一題很容易，護士（nurse）當然是要從事和醫療（medical）相關的工作任務囉，所以選 (D)！

199. Why do the race organizers need to know your 10K time? ****
    (A) To see if you qualify to run.
    (B) To see if you are faster than last year.
    (C) To place you in the appropriate starting position.
    (D) To predict who will win this year.

中 譯

為什麼路跑主辦單位需要知道你的10公里成績？
(A) 看看你是否符合資格參加路跑。
(B) 看看你是否跑得比去年快。
(C) 為了把你放在合適的起跑位置。
(D) 來預測今年誰會贏。

解答提示

報名表格中有寫：for starting placement，而選項 (C) 則是換句話說，一樣都是使用place這個字，所以選 (C)。place *vt.* 將...放置在...；placement *n.[C]* 人員配置。

200. How can families pay for the race? ***
    (A) Fill out separate registrations, but pay together.
    (B) Write a separate check for each person.
    (C) Families must pay with credit card.
    (D) Each person must pay a separate registration fee.

中 譯

家庭可以如何為這場路跑繳費？
(A) 分別填寫登記表格，但一起繳費。
(B) 每個人分別寫一張支票。
(C) 家庭必須以信用卡繳費。

(D) 每個人必須各自付登記費。

解答提示

報名登記表格上有註明：Please fill out one registration form per person. Families and business can pay for all registrations in one payment.，也就是每一個人都必須填寫獨自的表格，但是像家庭或公司企業這種團體的繳費可以一起繳，所以這題答案選 (A)。

瑣碎時間看這裡

<花費>
英文中有四個動詞cost, pay, spend, take都有「花費（時間／金錢）」的意思，常讓很多人頭痛，我們來好好看看這四個動詞的真面目！

(1) cost
主詞一定是「物品」，或是虛主詞搭配不定詞用來表示「一件事」，也只用在「金錢」方面的花費。
· **The book** cost me two hundred dollars.　（這本書花了我兩百元。）
· It cost me three thousand dollars **to have my car fixed**.
（修我的車花了花三千元。）

(2) pay
就是「付錢」的意思，所以主詞一定是「人」，受詞一定是「錢／金額數量」，然後才是用介系詞for表示買的東西。
· I paid **one hundred thousand dollars** for the new smart phone.
（我花了一萬塊買新的智慧型手機。）

(3) spend
可以用在花費「時間或金錢」，主詞一定是「人」，後面可以接動名詞。
· My father spent **one hour** cleaning the house.
（我父親花了一小時清掃房子。）

(4) take
take是用在花費「時間」，句型有三種，我們看一下以下的例句說明：
· It took me one hour to wash the car.　（我花了一小時洗車。）
= Washing the car took me one hour.
= I took one hour to wash the car.

Chapter 3
模擬實戰
演練教室

READING TEST

In the Reading test, you will read a variety of texts and answer several different types of reading comprehension questions. The entire Reading test will last 75 minutes. There are three parts, and directions are given for each part. You are encouraged to answer as many questions as possible within the time allowed.

You must mark your answers on the separate answer sheet. Do not write your answers in the test book.

Part 5

Directions: A word or phrase is missing in each of the sentences below. Four answer choices are given below each sentence. Select the best answer to complete the sentence. Then mark the letter (A), (B), (C), or (D) on your answer sheet.

101. Commuters are _____ to carpool or ride the bus, to cut down on pollution in the city.
(A) demanded
(B) wanted
(C) encouraged
(D) caring

102. VW _____ cars in several countries around the world.
(A) sales
(B) manufactures
(C) creates
(D) finances

103. Please use the side _____ today, due to construction in front of the building.
(A) entrance
(B) walk

(C) entering

(D) window

104. When will the interviews for regional manager be _____ ?
    (A) talking
    (B) photographed
    (C) taken
    (D) completed

105. For store hours and _____, please press 1.
    (A) times
    (B) places
    (C) location
    (D) marketing

106. The house features four bedrooms, plus one room completely wired for an at-home _____.
    (A) storage
    (B) office
    (C) cooking
    (D) facility

107. What will be the main topic of _____ at the forum?
    (A) meeting
    (B) arguments
    (C) discussion
    (D) talking

108. High _____ and low atmospheric pressure are generating extreme high tides this week.
    (A) winds
    (B) blowing
    (C) buildings
    (D) rivers

Go on to the next page.

109. While you're on a long flight, staying well _____ may stave off jet lag and keep you energized.
(A) water
(B) hydrated
(C) cleaned
(D) sanitized

110. Dr. Thomas is taking new patients, but there's a two month wait for a new patient _____.
(A) appointment
(B) survey
(C) appointed
(D) schedule

111. Martin Cinemas is the only _____ in town that is hosting the midnight premiere.
(A) store
(B) movie
(C) show
(D) theater

112. The concert for tonight has been _____ because the lead singer became sick very suddenly.
(A) scheduled
(B) cancelled
(C) sold out
(D) relocated

113. I always forget to empty my water bottle before I go through _____ security.
(A) airplane
(B) flight
(C) airport
(D) flying

Chapter 3　模擬實戰演練教室

114. They will be installing natural gas pipeline in our _____ this summer.
 (A) neighboring
 (B) housing
 (C) residential
 (D) neighborhood

115. Ortega's Resort is now closed for the season, but we appreciate your _ and hope to see you again next summer!
 (A) patronage
 (B) visiting
 (C) swimming
 (D) businesses

116. Do you know the square _____ of the new building?
 (A) area
 (B) footage
 (C) root
 (D) shape

117. They're scheduled to pour _____ for the foundation next week.
 (A) water
 (B) certainly
 (C) safely
 (D) cement

118. Most mortgage companies require _____ of home insurance before they finalize your loan.
 (A) statement
 (B) proof
 (C) satisfaction
 (D) money

119. Auto manufacturers are planning models that brake for other cars, and even bicycles, if the drivers _____ to do so themselves.

Go on to the next page.

(A) don't
(B) stop
(C) fail
(D) break

120. We are looking for an _____ person to lead the company into the future.
(A) social
(B) interesting
(C) innovative
(D) smart

121. If we want to renew the contract, this paperwork must be completed before July 19th, when our current contract _____.
(A) expires
(B) renews
(C) revises
(D) expands

122. They were unable to _____ a satisfactory salary for the new superintendent, so he has turned down the job.
(A) decide
(B) budget
(C) negotiate
(D) finance

123. Local _____ are campaigning for stronger laws protecting factory workers.
(A) politics
(B) legalism
(C) politicians
(D) policies

124. The plant _____ must be someone who is honest, organized and hardworking.

(A) assembly
(B) manager
(C) employees
(D) employer

125. The board meeting is the third Thursday of every month, in the _____ room.
(A) meets
(B) conference
(C) reservation
(D) conferred

126. The facilities committee is looking at the possibility of _____ office space next year.
(A) added
(B) addendum
(C) increased
(D) increasing

127. Jane Frost called this morning, and would like you to _____ her call as soon as possible.
(A) return
(B) returns
(C) replace
(D) collect

128. If you have _____ this message during business hours, I am either away from my desk or am helping another customer.
(A) heard
(B) returned
(C) written
(D) received

129. Only two of the jobs I have _____ for require me to mail in my resume, instead of posting it online.

Go on to the next page.

(A) requests
(B) applied
(C) responded
(D) application

130. You'll have to pay most of this bill yourself because you have not met your _____ for the year, yet.
(A) deduction
(B) plan
(C) deductible
(D) money

131. We would like to put a large _____ on the house, so we don't have to borrow very much.
(A) down-payment
(B) promise
(C) payment
(D) amount

132. For an international _____, you should arrive at the airport at least two hours prior to boarding.
(A) trip
(B) vacation
(C) flight
(D) destination

133. Doctor Griffin would like you to _____ a follow-up appointment in two weeks.
(A) offer
(B) schedule
(C) bring
(D) plan

Chapter 3 模擬實戰演練教室

134. Carnation Cruise Line is now _____ a two-week cruise to the islands, with daily stops for local sightseeing.
(A) building
(B) floating
(C) offering
(D) shipping

135. It's a traveling _____, and it will only be at our museum until the end of the month.
(A) history
(B) exhibit
(C) station
(D) tour

136. The _____ of the year will receive an all expenses paid trip for two to Hawaii.
(A) salesperson
(B) winner
(C) people
(D) outstanding

137. You can change the date of your reservation, but there is a $50 processing _____ for doing so.
(A) account
(B) amount
(C) bill
(D) fee

138. We are developing a new medication that will have the same _____ without the side-effects.
(A) amount
(B) price
(C) benefit
(D) activity

Go on to the next page.

139. I like to meet my _____ at a coffee shop, because we can stay and talk as long as we need to, without feeling rushed.
(A) friendly
(B) clients
(C) neighbors
(D) families

140. We don't have any window seats available for that flight, but we can offer you an _____ seat near the front of the plane.
(A) aisle
(B) adjustable
(C) first-class
(D) other

Part 6

Directions: Read the texts on the following pages. A word or phrase is missing in some of the sentences. Four answer choices are given below each of these sentences. Select the best answer to complete the text. Then mark the letter (A), (B), (C), or (D) on your answer sheet.

Questions 141-143 refer to the following email:

Tablets For You

Thank you for ------ your new tablet with us!

      141. (A) requesting
           (B) listing
           (C) purchasing
           (D) researching

Wondering how you can use your new tablet on a Wi-Fi connection?

Most tablets include access to several Web services. This includes webmail, video-streaming, and online storage. Here is a small ------ of what you'll be

      142. (A) idea
           (B) sample
           (C) vision
           (D) indication

able to do with your new tablet, using a Wi-Fi connection.

- ✓ Send and receive email.
- ✓ Browse the web.
- ✓ Receive news and weather updates.
- ✓ Locate nearby attractions.
- ✓ Upload and download documents, files and images.
- ✓ Stream movies and music.
- ✓ Download apps.
- ✓ Videochat.

Go on to the next page.

✓ Play games with ------ players.

143. (A) one
(B) personal
(C) multiple
(D) numbered

Need more ideas? <u>TabletsForYou.com</u>

Questions 144-146 refer to the following proposal:

Proposal
Andrew's
Heating and Air Conditioning
1390 E Trent Blvd
Sioux Valley, WA 99220
TEL: (509) 922-1212   FAX: (509) 922-1313

<u>PROPOSAL SUBMITTED TO:</u>
Paul Raj and Kaia Kumar

<u>JOB:</u>
1503 Burrows Rd
Valley View WA

<u>PHONE:</u>
272-3434

<u>DATE:</u>
October 11th, 2013

<u>WE HEREBY SUBMIT SPECIFICATIONS AND ESTIMATES FOR:</u>
Provide and install:
• New Energetics electric furnace with 15K heat strip and indoor coil.
• New Energetics 3 ton, 15 seer heat pump.
• Pad and pump ups.
• Install refrigeration lines from ------ furnace to outdoor heat pump.

144. (A) indoor
(B) refrigerator
(C) outlining
(D) outstanding

- Complete duct system with heat runs in every room.
- Return air in bedrooms and living room.
- Return air in basement walls and in upstairs walls where possible.
- Rigid round pipe in basement.
- Ceiling diffusers and volume dampers in basement.

❖ Owner to remove all sheetrock and insulation in area of ductwork and pipe.

❖ Andrew's to supply all finish registers.

❖ Line voltage to be completed by a ------ electrician.

145. (A) knowlegable
(B) licensed
(C) good
(D) excellent

❖ Andrew's to provide permit and 5 year warranty on all parts and labor.

Labor/Material	7900.00
Tax	583.20
Total	8423.20

Electric Company Rebates: $400
Federal Tax Credit: 30% or $1500 maximum

Payment to be made as follows: 25% down and total due upon completion
All material is ------ to be as specified. All work to be completed in a

146. (A) planned
(B) thought
(C) guaranteed
(D) hoped

workmanlike manner according to standard practices. Any alteration from the above specifications, involving extra cost will only be executed upon written order and will be an extra charge over and above the estimate. Our

Go on to the next page.

workers are fully covered by workman's compensation insurance in case of injury.

Note: This proposal may be withdrawn by Andrew's if not accepted within 30 days. All accounts are subject to 18% A.P.R. if payment is not received by due date.

Questions 147-149 refer to the following notice:

Escrow: Taxes and Insurance Statement

Why do I get this statement?
This statement is known as an Annual Escrow Account Disclosure Statement. You receive this statement because you have an escrow ------.

147. (A) accounting
(B) amount
(C) account
(D) bank

Escrow is a special account your bank provides for you to pay your property taxes and/or insurance. With an escrow account, part of each monthly ------

148. (A) housing
(B) mortgage
(C) rent
(D) utility

payment you make goes into your escrow account. When your taxes and/or insurance premiums are due, we pay those bills for you with the money set aside in your escrow account.

Once a year, your bank is required by law to review your account. This statement includes the results of that review. It includes a history of the tax and insurance activity on your account this year and the activity ------ for

149. (A) planning
(B) requiring

(C) thought
(D) expected

the next year. Please see the attached report for the details of your account review.

Questions 150-152 refer to the following article:

The current Deer Lake Volunteer Ambulance building was first built in 2005. James Rice painted the organization's name on the fascia of the building at that time. Lately, the lettering has become quite ------.

150. (A) bright
(B) unwritten
(C) faded
(D) unseen

On July 20th, 2013 James was at the annual Deer Lake Airport Fly-in. He approached the DLVA ambulance volunteers there and asked if he could repaint the sign for them sometime. He offered to paint for free, if the ambulance Corps would supply the ------.

151. (A) coloring
(B) paint
(C) building
(D) painting

Ramie Schliner, Operations Officer, accepted James' generous offer.

The crews reporting for duty at 6:00 a.m. the following day, found James on a ladder already busy painting. James says he believes in the concept of paying it forward. He felt it was a perfect way to ------ his gratitude for the

152. (A) thank
(B) say
(C) showing
(D) express

work the Ambulance crews do for our community.

Go on to the next page.

Part 7

Directions: In this part you will read a selection of texts, such as magazine and newspaper articles, letters, and advertisements. Each text is followed by several questions. Select the best answer for each question and mark the letter (A), (B), (C), or (D) on your answer sheet.

Questions 153 through 155 refer to the following article:

Annual Concert in the Park

Join the River City Symphony over Memorial Day weekend for its annual Concert in the Park. This year's concert is sponsored by River City Bank. Edward Prau will conduct his orchestra in a mix of classical music, show tunes and patriotic marches. Bring a picnic dinner, blankets, and chairs and enjoy a music-filled evening under the stars. The whole family will enjoy this concert by our favorite orchestra!

When: May 29th, 2014
      7:00 p.m. ~ 8:30 p.m.

Where: Riverfront Park, at 29th St and Grand Avenue

Cost: FREE

Phone: 503-222-1212

Website: www.rivercitysymphony.org

153. How often does the River City Symphony perform this concert?
    (A) Monthly during the summer.
    (B) Every Sunday evening.
    (C) Once a year on Memorial Day Weekend.
    (D) As often as patrons request it.

154. What kind of music will the orchestra play?
  (A) Classic rock music.
  (B) Ballet classics.
  (C) A mix of hymns and spirituals.
  (D) Show tunes and patriotic marches.

155. Why would this be a good family event?
  (A) It's good for kids to learn stringed instruments.
  (B) Because the music is great and it's free.
  (C) Kids love to play at the park.
  (D) You don't have to cook dinner for your family.

Questions 156 through 158 refer to the following letter:

Dear Ron,

I have read several travel brochures from your area and all of them mention the great hiking in the region. I found your hiking club listed online and wonder if you could give me some more specific information. My family will be there from July 7th~ July 18th. We would love to hike as many trails as possible in that time. My family consists of myself, my husband and our three kids, ages 10~14. I would appreciate any information you could give me about trails suitable for family hikes. We have done a lot of hiking, but nothing overly strenuous. We love trails with a view, but are not prepared for overnight backpacking on this trip. Day trips of 4-7 hours are perfect. Thank you so much for your time!

You can reach me at:
email: evag@email.com
Phone: 502-111-4343
Address: Eva Garber
         2507 N. Wilson Rd
         Ann Arbor WY 99006

Go on to the next page.

156. Why has Eva written this letter?
  (A) She is trying to decide where her family should go for vacation.
  (B) She wants to know about things to do in the area.
  (C) She is looking for information about specific trails to hike.
  (D) She wants to go hiking with Ron while they are in town.

157. What kind of hiking does the family want to do on this trip?
  (A) Some day trips and some overnights.
  (B) Day trips only.
  (C) Overnight backpacking.
  (D) Hiking along the ocean.

158. How can Ron best get in touch with Eva?
  (A) Look up her contact information online.
  (B) She would prefer a phone call.
  (C) He can choose to email, call or mail information to her.
  (D) He only has an email address for her.

Questions 159 and 160 refer to the following letter:

Overland Tours
New York City, NY

Mr. and Mrs. Adams,

We regret to inform you that the bus tour that you have scheduled for March 15th – 22nd has been cancelled. There are simply not enough people registered. Normally, at that time of year, our tours fill to capacity. We aren't sure what has caused the lack of interest in this tour. We know this is a disappointment for both of you. We have enjoyed having you on our tours in the past, and hope you will tour with us again in the future. We encourage you to transfer your deposit to a future tour. If you would rather have a full refund, you are welcome to do that as well. Please call our office at your earliest convenience to let us know what you would like to do.

Paul Ramos
Overland Tours Customer Service
1-888-222-3232

159. Why has this tour been cancelled?
(A) The weather will be stormy that week.
(B) Nobody knows why it had to be cancelled.
(C) They could not find a tour guide.
(D) Not enough people signed up for the tour.

160. How do you know the Adams have traveled with this company before?
(A) The letter states that Overland tours has enjoyed having them before.
(B) Mr. and Mrs. Adams have enjoyed many trips with Overland Tours.
(C) Overland Tours is located in the city where they live.
(D) Mrs. Adams' father owns Overland Tours.

Questions 161 through 163 refer to the following advertisement:

Grand Opening!
You have watched the construction of the new Hotel Ritz for over a year.
Finally, we invite you to a Grand Opening Gala!
Saturday, October 22nd
Sunday, October 23rd

Dinner served in the Ritz Banquet Hall from 5:00 p.m. to 8:00 p.m.

Dancing begins in the Grand Ballroom at 9:00 p.m.

Enjoy dinner, wander our grounds along the river, tour our rooms and suites. Dance the night away.

Special Room rates for Saturday and Sunday nights!

Go on to the next page.

Place your reservation today for dinner or for the complete overnight experience!

1-888-131-2222
www.hotelritz.com

161. How long did the construction of the new hotel take?
(A) About six months.
(B) Several years.
(C) Over one year.
(D) A long time.

162. What is the October Gala celebrating?
(A) Octoberfest Weekend.
(B) The grand opening of the hotel.
(C) Special room rates.
(D) That construction is finally completed.

163. Do Gala guests have to stay overnight?
(A) Yes. If they make a reservation, they must spend Saturday night at the hotel.
(B) Not at this time, but they must make a reservation for a future stay.
(C) No, but they will definitely wish they did.
(D) They can choose dinner only, or they can spend the night there.

Questions 164 through 166 refer to the following email:

To: Elizabeth James
From: Jordan Kennedy
Date: December 5th
Subject: Order

Dear Elizabeth,

Thank you for returning my call today. It was good to talk with you. This email is to confirm the details of your order. Please review this email and let me know if there are any errors. As I mentioned on the phone, if you need to make any additions to the order, December 23rd is the final day to make revisions. The books will go into print on January 4th. They will be available for pick-up on January 17th. Good luck preparing for the conference. I appreciate working with you!

Title	Order #	Quantity	Cost	Total
Communication in the Workplace	650912	150	$15.99	$2398.50

Jordan Kennedy
Post Printing

164. What is the purpose of this email?
   (A) To confirm Elizabeth's order for books for the conference.
   (B) To see if Elizabeth has any changes in mind for the book.
   (C) To cancel the book order Elizabeth placed earlier.
   (D) Jordan wanted to ask Elizabeth to write the book herself.

165. How did Jordan get the information that he is confirming?
   (A) He asked his boss to give it to him.
   (B) He received a letter from Elizabeth with all the details.
   (C) He spoke with Elizabeth on the phone earlier that day.
   (D) Jordan talked with Elizabeth's boss yesterday.

166. How many people are they planning to have at the conference?
   (A) Over 2000.
   (B) Around 150, since that is the number of books they ordered.
   (C) Elizabeth has no idea how many people will come.
   (D) Elizabeth told Jordan they'll have 40-50 people.

Go on to the next page.

Chapter 3 模擬實戰演練教室

Questions 167 through 169 refer to the following article:

Controversy over Wolves likely to Continue

Both sides agree that wolves are majestic creatures. Both sides agree that wolves are a threat to farmers and ranchers in the west. At a town meeting in Dakota last night, that's where the similarities stopped.

Ranchers and friends of ranchers suggested the government issue a kill order for the wolves. They want to protect their livelihood. Too many livestock are killed by hungry wolves each year, at a cost of up to $800 per animal.

Local tourism officials believe the ranchers must upgrade their fencing and other protective measures. Wolf tourism is big business in this state. Nearby state and national park lands offer camera laden tourists daily views of the great creatures in action.

The meeting ended at an impasse, with emotions running high. Local officials agreed to work closely with state officials to study the issue further.

---

167. Where might you read this article?
(A) In the newspaper.
(B) In a magazine article.
(C) In an office memo.
(D) On a billboard.

168. What do the ranchers believe the government should do?
(A) Pay the ranchers for their dead livestock.
(B) There is nothing they can do.
(C) Kill off some of the wolves.
(D) Relocate the wolves.

169. What brings wolf lovers to nearby park lands?
(A) A zoo where wolves live.
(B) The opportunity to photograph the wolves in the wild.
(C) They want to listen to the controversy.
(D) They come to pet the wolves.

Questions 170 through 172 refer to the following notice:

Job Fair
All upcoming graduates are encouraged to attend!
The fair will feature employers in the business, health and technical fields.

How can this help you?
- Hand out your resume in person.
- Reach multiple employers in a short time.
- Make personal contacts with possible employers.
- Increase your confidence for interview situations.

Date: Friday, April 2nd
Location: Mead Hall
Wellesley University
Time: 9:00 a.m.- 3:00 p.m.
Cost to attend: FREE

Also featuring **Resume Writing Sessions** throughout the day.

---

170. Where might this notice be posted?
(A) In a local restaurant.
(B) On a college campus.
(C) In the local hospital.
(D) At the high school.

171. Who will want to attend this job fair?
(A) Teachers and classroom assistants.
(B) People unhappy with their job.
(C) People graduating this year.
(D) Those just starting college this year.

172. How could a graduate benefit from attending?
(A) Have a great free lunch.
(B) Be hired that day.
(C) Find out if they will graduate on time.
(D) Meet possible employers in person. **Go on to the next page.**

Questions 173 through 175 refer to the following article:

Hughes Electric Building Completed

Hughes Electric has completed construction of its newest facility on Electric Avenue. This building will house all of the trucks Hughes uses locally. The $3 million project is a 10,000 square foot building, allowing space for maintenance and repair of Hughes vehicles. The compressed natural gas trucks will also be housed there.

The project was so costly due to special ventilation systems needed where natural gas vehicles are repaired. General contractor Tom Vance commented that the project was completed ahead of schedule and therefore actually cost less than projected.

---

173. What does the article announce?
(A) Completion of the new Hughes building.
(B) Hughes plan for future growth.
(C) Electric use in the city.
(D) The use of compressed natural gas.

174. What will the new building be used for?
(A) Office space.
(B) Storage of excess building materials.
(C) Apartments for Hughes workers.
(D) Maintenance and repair of vehicles.

175. Why was the project so costly?
(A) It ran over budget.
(B) It was completed two months late.
(C) Special ventilation systems were required.
(D) Hughes did not budget well for the building.

Questions 176 and 177 refer to the following email:

Dear Martha,

As part of our ongoing efforts to best serve our members, we are upgrading all of our computer systems. Due to this effort, all of our online services will be unavailable from June 29th until July 1st, 2013. This includes:
- Knowledgeable Surveys
- The Knowledgeable Members Website and Rewards Center (knowledgeablemembers.com)

Also, our Knowledgeable Surveys Support Department (1-800-333-2323, and support@knowledgeablemembers.com) will be closed from June 30th to July 1st, 2013.

We apologize for any inconvenience this may cause you. If you have questions about this closure—or anything else related to your knowledgeable surveys participation—please contact our office.
- 1-800-333-5555
- support@knowledgeablemembers.com

We look forward to hearing from you!

Sincerely,

The Knowledgeable Surveys Support Team

176. Why will all the Knowledgeable Surveys systems be unavailable?
(A) It will be too hot to work.
(B) They are updating the entire system.
(C) They will be closed for the 4th of July holiday.
(D) They are trying to serve people better.

177. Why does the Support Team apologize for this closure?
(A) It's rude to close for so many days.
(B) They think no one will want to be a customer any more.
(C) The closure will be inconvenient for their members.
(D) They wish they didn't have to close.

Go on to the next page.

Questions 178 through 180 refer to the following announcement:

Digital Media Sales Executive

Are you looking for a rewarding career in the local media industry?

Are you a person who:
- Generates new business?
- Builds positive relationships with customers?
- Efficiently records and maintains customer and order information?
- Demonstrates critical thinking and troubleshooting?

Then, we may have the perfect full-time sales position for you! The person in this position will generate advertising revenue by marketing our extensive print, online and mobile products and services.

Bring with you a proven ability to meet and exceed sales goals in a highly competitive industry. A college degree or equivalent experience is required. Experience in media sales is highly desired, but not required.

Apply in person at Artful Media, 1000 Lignon Ave., or email don@artfulmedia.com with your resume and cover letter.

---

178. Where would you find this ad?
- (A) In a television advertisement.
- (B) In the employment section of the newspaper.
- (C) On the radio.
- (D) In a local tourism guide.

179. What type of job is being advertised?
- (A) Sales.
- (B) Reporting.
- (C) Accounting.
- (D) Administration.

180. If you email about the job, what should you include?
    (A) A picture of yourself.
    (B) Your qualifications.
    (C) Your resume and cover letter.
    (D) Your desired wage.

Go on to the next page.

Questions 181 through 185 refer to the following advertisement and coupons:

Take a friend to Breakfast!

Introducing our new Sour Cream Blueberry Pancakes
Blueberries are in season for a few short months.
Take advantage of their flavor today!

We start with organic whole grain flour, add farm fresh eggs, organic whole milk and blueberries brought fresh to our door every morning!
Add some scrambled eggs, pork sausage and fresh squeezed orange juice and you have yourself a breakfast fit for a king.

Who could ask for a healthier start to the day?
Bring a friend and get your day off to a great start!

Farm Fresh Kitchen
We grow it. You love it!
See you in the morning.

Don't Forget!
Breakfast is on us!

2 FREE Sour Cream Blueberry Pancakes
Expires August 31st, 2014

Not valid with any other offer, discount or coupon.
Limit one coupon per person, per visit.

Don't Forget to Bring a Friend!

2 FREE Sour Cream Blueberry Pancakes
Expires August 31ˢᵗ, 2014

Not valid with any other offer, discount or coupon.
Limit one coupon per person, per visit.

181. What could you buy with your free pancakes?
(A) Pork sausage and juice.
(B) Butter and syrup.
(C) Soup and a salad.
(D) Toast and cocoa.

182. How often does the restaurant receive their blueberries?
(A) Nightly.
(B) Once a month.
(C) Once a week.
(D) Every morning.

183. What can you infer from this ad?
(A) That blueberry pancakes are the owner's favorite.
(B) That most of the food served in the restaurant is grown on the farm.
(C) The restaurant offers strawberry pancakes during strawberry season.
(D) They serve blueberries year-round.

Go on to the next page.

184. Why are there two coupons offered?
   (A) Because there was extra room on the page.
   (B) So you'll come twice.
   (C) One for you, one for a friend.
   (D) So you can use two coupons and get four pancakes.

185. Why would Farm Fresh Kitchen offer this coupon during the summer only?
   (A) That's when blueberries are in season.
   (B) People like to eat pancakes on hot days.
   (C) The restaurant wants to increase sales during the summer.
   (D) The owner loves summer.

Questions 186 through 190 refer to the following press release and email:

To: Saachi Jayaraman
From: Daksha Nayar
Date: May 5th
Subject: Press Release

Dear Saachi,

Here is a sample of what I would like the press release to say. Does it seem appropriate for our Indian audience? Please let me know if you think there should be any changes before it goes to the newspaper. I am so excited for this venture! I know you will be a great manager for our India location. I look forward to seeing you in a couple of weeks to get the store set up! I will send you my flight details next week. Thank you so much!

Sincerely,

Daksha

MUMBAI, India May 10th – U.S. based Blue Skink Jewelry, has announced it will be opening a small store in Mumbai to create and market its unique jewelry designs. The owner and creator of Blue Skink Jewelry is originally from India and wanted to expand her business to her homeland. Designs created in India will blend traditional Indian design with a contemporary style. Stones used in production will come from locations in India. The store is expected to be in operation in early June, with a grand opening scheduled for June 30th.

Go on to the next page.

Chapter 3 模擬實戰演練教室

186. Why is Blue Skink Jewelry opening a location in India?
  (A) It is cheap to make the jewelry in India.
  (B) The owner is from India and wants to market her jewelry there.
  (C) Saachi likes the jewelry so much, so she wanted it to come to India.
  (D) The store will open in early June.

187. What will the jewelry made in India look like?
  (A) It will be made with stones from America.
  (B) It will look like American jewelry.
  (C) It will have a mix of traditional Indian and contemporary designs.
  (D) It will be shaped like its namesake, the blue skink.

188. Who will help Saachi set up the store in India?
  (A) Daksha will fly there to set up the store in a few weeks.
  (B) Saachi has found several of her Indian relatives to help her.
  (C) It will be difficult to get it set up in time.
  (D) Daksha is looking for people to help her.

189. How does Daksha plan to run the store in India when she lives in the U.S.?
  (A) She will visit India every two weeks to make sure things are running smoothly.
  (B) She has hired Sacchi to manage the store in India..
  (C) She will email the store every day to let them know what to do.
  (D) She doesn't have a plan for the India store, yet.

190. Why does Daksha send this email?
  (A) To let Saachi know her travel plans.
  (B) To find out if the store is still on schedule for its June opening.
  (C) To say that the press release has some errors in it.
  (D) To ask Saachi to preview the press release before it goes to print.

Questions 191 through 195 refer to the following letter and survey:

May 23rd, 2013

Dear Mr. Vans,

Our records show that you were treated recently at Two Waters Hospital. We would appreciate it if you would take a few minutes of your time to fill out the attached survey. Your feedback and the feedback of other customers helps us improve our medical services and our personal service.

Be assured that your privacy is of great importance to us. Your name and reason for hospitalization are completely confidential. All comments are anonymous. We thank you for helping us offer the best service to our patients.

Sincerely,

Paul Jonas
Patient Satisfaction Coordinator
Two Waters Hospital

Two Waters Hospital
Patient Satisfaction Survey

We would like to know what you think about your experience at our facility. Your responses are directly responsible for improving our services. All responses will be kept confidential and anonymous. Thank you for your time.

Age: 51

Sex:
 M   X
 F____

Race/Ethnicity: ____Asian
____Pacific Islander
____Black/African American
____American Indian/Alaska Native
 X White (not Hispanic or Latino)
____Hispanic or Latino

Go on to the next page.

Chapter 3 模擬實戰演練教室

	Excellent	Good	Average	Poor
Waiting:				
Wait time to register	X			
Wait time to be admitted		X		
Time it took for Dr. to see you		X		
Physicians:				
Listens to you	X			
Takes enough time with you		X		
Explains things clearly	X			
Provides appropriate treatment	X			
Nurses and Medical Assistants:				
Friendly and helpful			X	
Answer your questions		X		
Facility:				
Ease of finding your way around		X		
Neat and clean	X			
Allows for privacy	X			

Did you have any negative experiences during this stay?

There was an issue with the bathroom needing cleaning. I told a nurse and no one came to clean it until the next morning. I don't know if the nurse forgot to tell someone about it, or not.

What do you like best about our hospital?

The doctor let me ask as many questions as I wanted and explained things a couple of times, if I needed more explanation.

Are there any improvements you would suggest?

Make sure that nurses pass along patients' requests to the correct people. And have better follow up.

THANK YOU FOR COMPLETING OUR SURVEY!

191. Why did Mr. Vans receive this survey?
    (A) He asked if he could assess the hospital.
    (B) He was recently treated at the hospital.
    (C) Mr. Vans had some complaints about the hospital staff.
    (D) Two Rivers sends annual surveys to the community.

192. What race is Mr. Vans?
    (A) White.
    (B) Asian.
    (C) He didn't say.
    (D) American.

193. What was the only thing Mr. Vans marked down to "average" on his survey?
    (A) The food service.
    (B) The comfort level of his bed.
    (C) The time the Dr. spent with him.
    (D) The nurses being friendly and helpful.

194. What does Mr. Vans like best about the hospital?
    (A) The ease of finding where he needs to go.
    (B) That the doctor explained things thoroughly.
    (C) The look of the hospital from the street.
    (D) That he was admitted quickly.

195. What was a complaint Mr. Vans had?
    (A) The food was tasteless.
    (B) His wife could not stay after visiting hours were over.
    (C) There was no response to the request he made to one of the nurses.
    (D) He still felt sick after leaving the hospital.

Go on to the next page.

Questions 196 through 200 refer to the following letter and order form:

Dear Valued Customer,

Your order # 2363654 has been received and will be processed soon. If you experience any problems or have questions, please call our customer support at 501-444-2230. Thanks!

Please note: This confirmation is not a guarantee that all items will be available for shipping. You will receive an email after your order has shipped that will include an invoice for shipped items. Please note that your account will not be charged until your order is packed and ready to leave our warehouse.

Regards,
Whole Foods Inc.

Order Number: 2363654
Ships by: Truck Route B2 - Leaves 07/23/13

Sold To:
Garden Market
333 6th Ave E
Springdale OR 90000

Ship To:
Garden Market
333 6th Ave E
Springdale OR 90000
Phone: 501-276-7676

Billing: Invoice upon Shipping

Items

Code	Product Name	Size	Qty	Price	Total
PA302	Lasagna, Whole Wheat	12 x 12 ozs	5	$31.60	$158.00
PA269	Spaghetti, Whole Wheat	12 x 16 ozs	5	$26.80	$134.00
SE021	Bulk Poppy Seeds	5 lbs.	1	$12.50	$12.50
BP079	Organic Cornstarch	6 x 6 ozs.	3	$14.60	$43.80
DF132	Cranberries, Dried	1 lb.	10	$5.35	$53.50
GY426	Green Chiles, Diced	24 x 4 ozs.	1	$19.50	$19.50
DP042	Yogurt, Plain Nonfat, Organ	16 ozs.	10	$1.75	$17.50
QP063	Fresh Produce Celery, Organ	1 Bunch	10	$2.50	$25.00
Sub Total: $463.80					
Estimated Total: $463.80					

Chapter 3 模擬實戰演練教室

196. Why was this letter sent?
  (A) To let Garden Market know that Whole Foods has received its order.
  (B) To let Garden Market know that some products were not available for shipping.
  (C) To announce the monthly sale prices.
  (D) The newsletter is sent once a month.

197. How is this order being billed?
  (A) The credit card was charged when the order was placed.
  (B) Garden Market will received an invoice to be paid at a later date.
  (C) The delivery driver should receive Cash On Delivery.
  (D) The order will be free because of credits from last month's order.

198. Why is the total listed as an *Estimated* Total?
  (A) The office worker may have incorrectly added the total.
  (B) Garden Market might decide to add some things to its order.
  (C) The total may change if some items are not available when the order is shipped.
  (D) The date is wrong on the order.

Go on to the next page.

199. According to the order form, how many types of pasta did the market order?
(A) They did not order pasta this month.
(B) Two—lasagna and spaghetti.
(C) They ordered organic pasta.
(D) The pasta will be back-ordered.

200. When can Garden market expect delivery?
(A) They plan to pick up the order in person.
(B) Anytime during the month of July.
(C) On July 23rd.
(D) Sometime after the July 23rd shipment date.

Chapter 4
實戰演練
答案與詳解

Answer Key

101. ~ 105.　C B A D C
106. ~ 110.　B C A B A
111. ~ 115.　D B C D A
116. ~ 120.　B D B C C
121. ~ 125.　A C C B B
126. ~ 130.　D A D B C
131. ~ 135.　A C B C B
136. ~ 140.　A D C B A
141. ~ 145.　C B C A B
146. ~ 150.　C C B D C
151. ~ 155.　B D C D B
156. ~ 160.　C B C D A
161. ~ 165.　C B D A C
166. ~ 170.　B A C B B
171. ~ 175.　C D A D C
176. ~ 180.　B C B A C
181. ~ 185.　A D B C A
186. ~ 190.　B C A B D
191. ~ 195.　B A D B C
196. ~ 200.　A B C B D

Part 5

101. Commuters are _____ to carpool or ride the bus, to cut down on pollution in the city. ***
(A) demanded
(B) wanted
(C) encouraged
(D) caring

中　　譯

通勤的人被_____共乘或是搭乘公車，以減低城市中的汙染。
(A) 要求　　　　(B) 希望　　　　(C) 鼓勵　　　　(D) 關心

解答提示

這一題的選項 (A)、(B)、(C) 都是符合文法的選項，所以就必須從文意去判斷。選項 (A) 和 (B) 的語氣都太過強勢，而且和現實生活根本不符合，所以選項 (C) 是較好的答案。

102. VW _____ cars in several countries around the world. **
    (A) sales
    (B) manufactures
    (C) creates
    (D) finances

中　　譯

福斯汽車在世界上好幾個國家_____汽車。
(A) 銷售　　　(B) 製造　　　(C) 創造　　　(D) 提供資金給

解答提示

選項 (A) 是名詞，不符合空格位置的文法，所以可以先刪除。接下來就要靠文意來判斷答案，create（創造）的受詞如果是cars，意思會和「發明汽車」相似，但是福斯汽車公司並不是發明汽車的人呀，所以選項 (C) 也不對。而選項 (D) 的finance意思是「提供資金給...」，文意也不對，提供資金給汽車做什麼呢？受詞應該是某間公司或某個人才對，所以應該選 (B)。

103. Please use the side _____ today, due to construction in front of the building. ***
    (A) entrance
    (B) walk
    (C) entering
    (D) window

中　譯

今天請使用側邊的＿＿＿＿，因為大樓的正前面在施工。
(A) 入口　　　(B) 人行道　　(C) 進入　　　(D) 窗戶

解答提示

這一題只要配合後半句就很好解題了，看到後半句的building（大樓）就直接聯想entrance（入口）就對了！選項 (B) 和 (D) 都不符合句意，而選項 (C) 則是動名詞，文法不符合；所以要選 (A)。

104. When will the interviews for regional manager be ＿＿＿＿? **
　　　　(A) talking
　　　　(B) photographed
　　　　(C) taken
　　　　(D) completed

中　譯

針對區域經理的面試何時會＿＿＿＿？
(A) 說話　　　(B) 拍照　　　(C) 拿取　　　(D) 完成

解答提示

這一題的主詞是the interviews for regional manager，所以不可以選擇主動的talking，而其他的選項 (B) 和 (C) 文意都不符合，只有 (D) 是最合適的選項。

105. For store hours and ＿＿＿＿, please press 1. *
　　　　(A) times
　　　　(B) places
　　　　(C) location
　　　　(D) marketing

中　譯

關於商店營業時間和＿＿＿＿，請按1。
(A) 次數
(B) 地方

(C) 地點
(D) 行銷

解答提示

store是名詞轉化作為形容詞，所以要找出哪一個選項可以和store形成搭配詞，只有 "store location"（商店地點）能形成搭配詞，而且符合句意，所以選 (C)。

106. The house features four bedrooms, plus one room completely wired
for an at-home _____. ***
(A) storage
(B) office
(C) cooking
(D) facility

中　譯

這間房子的特色，有四間臥室，加上一間房間完整接線適合家庭_____使用。
(A) 儲存　　　(B) 辦公室　　(C) 料理　　　(D) 設備

解答提示

wired是指「接線；裝線」，也就是把一些辦公室設備需要的線路先接好，所以答案就是 (B) 選項。

107. What will be the main topic of _____ at the forum? **
(A) meeting
(B) arguments
(C) discussion
(D) talking

中　譯

在論壇中，_____的主要主題將是什麼？
(A) 會議　　　(B) 爭論　　　(C) 討論　　　(D) 說話

解答提示

在論壇中當然是要討論（discussion），所以答案是 (C)。

108. High _____ and low atmospheric pressure are generating extreme high tides this week. *****
(A) winds
(B) blowing
(C) buildings
(D) rivers

中　譯

強_____和低氣壓本週將造成極大的海浪。
(A) 風　　　(B) 刮風　　　(C) 大樓　　　(D) 河流

解答提示

和形容詞high可以形成搭配詞的只有winds和buildings，從句意看來要選和天氣有關的字，所以答案是 (A) winds。

109. While you're on a long flight, staying well _____ may stave off jet lag and keep you energized. ***
(A) water
(B) hydrated
(C) cleaned
(D) sanitized

中　譯

當你長途飛行時，保持_____可以避免時差，並保持活力。
(A) 水　　　　　(B) 含水的　　　(C) 清潔的　　　(D) 消毒的

解答提示

stay在這裡是連綴動詞，後面要接形容詞，所以可以先排除選項 (A)。接著再用句意判斷，「保持水分」是比較合理的意思，所以答案選 (B)。

110. Dr. Thomas is taking new patients, but there's a two month wait for a new patient _____. ****
(A) appointment
(B) survey
(C) appointed
(D) schedule

中　　譯

Thomas醫生有收新的病人，但是新的病患_____要等上兩個月。
(A) 約見　　　(B) 調查　　　(C) 指定的　　　(D) 時刻表

解答提示

appointment在日常生活中，最常見的意思就是醫生和病人的「約診」，如果看到醫病相關的題目，選 (A) appointment準沒錯！

111. Martin Cinemas is the only _____ in town that is hosting the midnight premiere. **
(A) store
(B) movie
(C) show
(D) theater

中　　譯

Martin影城是鎮上唯一的_____，有午夜場的首映。
(A) 商店　　　(B) 電影　　　(C) 放映　　　(D) 戲院

解答提示

這一題考的是同義字，cinema就是「電影院；戲院」的意思，所以答案要選同義字 (D) theater。

112. The concert for tonight has been _____ because the lead singer became sick very suddenly. ***
(A) scheduled
(B) cancelled

(C) sold out

(D) relocated

中　　譯

今晚的演唱會已經被_____，因為主要歌手突然生病了。
(A) 排定時間　　　(B) 取消　　　　(C) 賣光　　　(D) 改地點

解答提示

這一題四個選項填入前半句都可以，但是必須配合後面的句子，因為歌手生病，所以演唱會當然是被「取消」，答案要選 (B)。

113. I always forget to empty my water bottle before I go through _____ security. **

(A) airplane

(B) flight

(C) airport

(D) flying

中　　譯

在經過_____安檢前，我總是忘記把水瓶清空。
(A) 飛機　　　(B) 航班　　　(C) 機場　　　(D) 飛行

解答提示

這一題除了要知道搭配詞之外，再加上一點點生活常識就可以輕鬆答題了。和security（安檢）形成較合適的搭配詞應該是airport security（機場安檢），答案為 (C)。

114. They will be installing natural gas pipeline in our _____ this summer. **

(A) neighboring

(B) housing

(C) residential

(D) neighborhood

中　譯

他們將在今年夏天在我們的＿＿＿＿安裝天然瓦斯管線。
(A) 鄰近的　　　　(B) 房屋　　　(C) 住宅的　　　(D) 社區

解答提示

這一題在空格應該填入名詞，所以可以先把選項 (A) 和 (C) 刪去。剩下選項 (B) 和 (D)，用文意判斷即可知道答案是 (D)。

115. Ortega's Resort is now closed for the season, but we appreciate your __ and hope to see you again next summer! ***
　　(A) patronage
　　(B) visiting
　　(C) swimming
　　(D) businesses

中　譯

Ortega's度假中心現在因季節關閉，但是我們感謝您的＿＿＿＿，並希望明年夏天能再見到您。
(A) 光顧　　　　(B) 拜訪　　　(C) 游泳　　　　(D) 生意

解答提示

這一題的選項 (A) 和 (B) 會造成答題時的困擾，visiting是動名詞，如果所有格要接動名詞的話，用法比較特別，一般很少使用，所以選擇原本就是名詞的patronage比較合適，正確答案為 (A)。

116. Do you know the square ＿＿＿＿＿＿ of the new building? ****
　　(A) area
　　(B) footage
　　(C) root
　　(D) shape

中　譯

你知道這棟新大樓的平方＿＿＿＿（面積）嗎？
(A) 區域　　　　(B) 英呎長度　　　(C) 根部　　　(D) 形狀

解答提示

這一題的難度頗高，square後面要接長度的單位，所以答案只能選 (B)。

117. They're scheduled to pour _____ for the foundation next week. **
   (A) water
   (B) certainly
   (C) safely
   (D) cement

中　譯

他們預計下個星期要倒_____打地基。
(A) 水　　　　(B) 當然　　　(C) 安全地　　(D) 水泥

解答提示

空格應該要填入名詞，所以可以先把選項 (B) 和 (C) 刪去。foundation是「地基」的意思，所以合適的答案是 (D) cement。

118. Most mortgage companies require _____ of home insurance before they finalize your loan. **
   (A) statement
   (B) proof
   (C) satisfaction
   (D) money

中　譯

在完成借款之前，大多數的抵押公司要求房屋保險的_____。
(A) 對帳單　　(B) 證明　　　(C) 滿意　　　(D) 金錢

解答提示

這一題需要一些財務金融的知識，拿房屋抵押貸款時，通常必須確認房屋保險，所以要提出證明，答案選 (B)。

119. Auto manufacturers are planning models that brake for other cars, and even bicycles, if the drivers _____ to do so themselves. ***
(A) don't
(B) stop
(C) fail
(D) break

中　譯

汽車製造商正在設計汽車款式，它們可以感應其他車輛甚至腳踏車而自動煞車，如果駕駛自己_____煞車的話。
(A) 不要　　　(B) 停止　　　(C) 沒有　　　(D) 打破

解答提示

fail to加上原形動詞，意思是「沒有；不能；忘記（做某事）」的意思。選項 (A) 不符合文法，而選項 (B) 和 (D) 則是不符合文意；所以選 (C)。

120. We are looking for an _____ person to lead the company into the future. ****
(A) social
(B) interesting
(C) innovative
(D) smart

中　譯

我們正在尋找_____人，可以帶領公司迎向未來。
(A) 社交的　　(B) 有趣的　　(C) 創新的　　(D) 聰明的

解答提示

這一題要配合句意選擇答案，和後半部的「迎向未來」最搭配的形容詞應該是 (C) innovative（創新的）。

121. If we want to renew the contract, this paperwork must be completed before July 19th, when our current contract _____. **
(A) expires

(B) renews
(C) revises
(D) expands

中　譯

如果我們想要更新合約，文件必須在7月19日前完成，也就是我們現在的合約_____前。
(A) 到期　　　(B) 更新　　　(C) 修訂　　　(D) 擴大

解答提示

before July 19th和when our current contract expires是同位語，所以依照句意選 (A) 最合適。

122. They were unable to _____ a satisfactory salary for the new superintendent, so he has turned down the job. ****
(A) decide
(B) budget
(C) negotiate
(D) finance

中　譯

他們無法_____一份滿意的薪資給新的主管，所以他拒絕了這份工作。
(A) 決定　　　(B) 編預算　　(C) 談成　　　(D) 提供資金

解答提示

薪資是雙方協調溝通談妥的，所以合適的答案要選 (C) negotiate。

123. Local _____ are campaigning for stronger laws protecting factory workers. ***
(A) politics
(B) legalism
(C) politicians
(D) policies

中　　譯

本地的＿＿＿＿正提倡更強力的法律來保護工廠工人。
(A) 政治　　　　(B) 守法主義　　　(C) 政治家　　　(D) 政策

解答提示

這個句子的動詞是campaign（從事活動；提倡），所以主詞選人就沒錯了！
答案選 (C)。

124. The plant ＿＿＿＿＿＿ must be someone who is honest, organized and hardworking. **
(A) assembly
(B) manager
(C) employees
(D) employer

中　　譯

工廠＿＿＿＿＿必須是誠實、有組織、努力工作的人。
(A) 裝配　　　(B) 經理　　　(C) 員工　　　(D) 雇主

解答提示

這一題可以選 (B) 或 (C)，但是必須選擇單數的名詞，所以只能選 (B)。

125. The board meeting is the third Thursday of every month, in the ＿＿＿＿＿＿ room. *
(A) meets
(B) conference
(C) reservation
(D) conferred

中　　譯

董事會召開是在每個月的第三個星期四，在＿＿＿＿＿室。
(A) 會面　　　(B) 會議　　　(C) 保留　　　(D) 協商

解答提示

這一個唯一可以形成搭配詞的只有conference room，而且也符合句意，所以選 (B)。

126. The facilities committee is looking at the possibility of _____ office space next year. ***
(A) added
(B) addendum
(C) increased
(D) increasing

中　　譯

設備委員會正在檢視明年_____辦公空間的可能性。
(A) 附加的　　　(B) 追加　　　(C) 增加的　　　(D) 增加

解答提示

這一題在介系詞of後面只能填入動名詞或名詞，選項 (B) 雖然是名詞，但是語意不符合，所以只能選 (D)。

127. Jane Frost called this morning, and would like you to _____ her call as soon as possible. **
(A) return
(B) returns
(C) replace
(D) collect

中　　譯

Jane Frost今天早上打過電話，並且希望你盡快_____她電話。
(A) 回覆　　　(B) 回覆　　　(C) 取代　　　(D) 收集

解答提示

這一題在to後面要接原形動詞，所以選項 (B) 可以不用考慮。而用文意判斷，只有選項 (A) 才合句意。

128. If you have _____ this message during business hours, I am either away from my desk or am helping another customer. ✱✱✱
(A) heard
(B) returned
(C) written
(D) received

中　譯

如果你在營業時間_____這個留言，我不是不在辦公室，就是在幫忙其他顧客。
(A) 聽到　　　(B) 回覆　　　(C) 書寫　　　(D) 收到

解答提示

這一題用文意判斷可以選 (A) 或是 (D)，但是這個句子是主動的表現，所以選擇 (D) received會比較合適。

129. Only two of the jobs I have _____ for require me to mail in my resume, instead of posting it online. ✱✱✱
(A) requests
(B) applied
(C) responded
(D) application

中　譯

我已經_____的工作中，只有兩份工作要求我郵寄履歷表，而非刊登到網路上。
(A) 要求　　　(B) 申請　　　(C) 回應　　　(D) 申請

解答提示

選項 (D) 是名詞，所以不能選，而只有apply可以和for形成搭配詞，所以答案自然是 (B)。

130. You'll have to pay most of this bill yourself because you have not met your _____ for the year, yet. ✱✱✱✱

(A) deduction
(B) plan
(C) deductible
(D) money

中　譯

你將必須自己支付這筆帳單的一大部分，因為你還沒達到今年的_____。
(A) 扣除　　(B) 計畫　　　(C) 可扣除額　　　(D) 金錢

解答提示

這題難度很高，deductible是「可扣除額」的意思，選項 (A) 只是單純指「扣除的金額」，較合適的用法應該是選項 (C)。

131. We would like to put a large _____ on the house, so we don't have to borrow very much. ***
(A) down-payment
(B) promise
(C) payment
(D) amount

中　譯

我們想要在這棟房子付大筆的_____，這樣我們就不必借太多錢。
(A) 頭期款　　(B) 承諾　　　(C) 款項　　　(D) 數量

解答提示

這一題可以從題目的後半句得知答案，不過還是要知道down-payment是「頭期款」的意思唷，所以這題答案選 (A)！

132. For an international _____, you should arrive at the airport at least two hours prior to boarding. **
(A) trip
(B) vacation
(C) flight
(D) destination

Chapter 4 實戰演練答案與詳解

針對國際_____，你應該在登機前至少2小時抵達機場。
(A) 旅程　　　　(B) 假期　　　　(C) 航班　　　　(D) 目的地

解答提示

這一題的答案非常明顯，應該選 (C)，international flight是「國際航班」，
domestic flight則是「國內航班」。

133. Doctor Griffin would like you to _____ a follow-up appointment in
two weeks. **
(A) offer
(B) schedule
(C) bring
(D) plan

中　　譯

Griffin醫生希望你針對兩週後的複診_____。
(A) 提供　　　　(B) 預訂時間　　(C) 帶來　　　　(D) 計畫

解答提示

題目中的受詞是appointment（約見），可以搭配的動詞只有schedule和
plan，但是schedule的意思較明確，所以 (B) 是比較合適的答案。

134. Carnation Cruise Line is now _____ a two-week cruise to the islands,
with daily stops for local sightseeing. **
(A) building
(B) floating
(C) offering
(D) shipping

中　　譯

康乃馨輪船公司現在正_____一個遊輪行，為期兩週到各個島嶼，每天停留
進行當地觀光。
(A) 建造　　　　(B) 飄浮　　　　(C) 提供　　　　(D) 運送

解答提示

cruise是「遊輪；遊輪行程」的意思，輪船公司當然是提供（offer）行程囉！所以答案選 (C)，這一題要注意ship當動詞用的時候，指的是「運送；裝運」。

135. It's a traveling _____, and it will only be at our museum until the end of the month. ***
(A) history
(B) exhibit
(C) station
(D) tour

中　　譯

這是個旅遊_____，只在我們的博物館到月底。
(A) 歷史　　　　(B) 展覽　　　　(C) 車站　　　　(D) 旅行團

解答提示

這一題看到museum這麼明顯的提示，就知道答案該選 (B) exhibit囉！其他traveling history、traveling station、traveling tour都是很奇怪的搭配詞，也是不用考慮的。

136. The _____ of the year will receive an all expenses paid trip for two to Hawaii. **
(A) salesperson
(B) winner
(C) people
(D) outstanding

中　　譯

年度_____將獲得全程免費的夏威夷兩人行。
(A) 業務員　　　(B) 贏家　　　　(C) 人們　　　　(D) 傑出的

解答提示

這一格應該填入名詞，可以先把 (D) 刪去。剩下的選項中只有 "salesperson of

the year" 才是合理的搭配詞，所以選 (A)。

137. You can change the date of your reservation, but there is a $50 processing _____ for doing so. ✱✱
(A) account
(B) amount
(C) bill
(D) fee

中　譯

你可以更改訂位的日期，但是這麼做有五十元的處理_____。
(A) 帳戶　　　(B) 數量　　　(C) 帳單　　　(D) 費用

解答提示

"processing fee"（處理費）是很常見的搭配詞，尤其是fee這個字要熟記，常常出現在和費用相關的英文當中，這題答案選 (D)。

138. We are developing a new medication that will have the same _____ without the side-effects. ✱✱✱
(A) amount
(B) price
(C) benefit
(D) activity

中　譯

我們正在發展一項新的藥品，將有相同的_____，卻沒有副作用。
(A) 數量　　　(B) 價格　　　(C) 益處　　　(D) 活動

解答提示

可以從side effects反推，推測出答案應該是有相反意思的benefit，故選 (C)。

139. I like to meet my _____ at a coffee shop, because we can stay and talk as long as we need to, without feeling rushed. ✱✱✱

(A) friendly
(B) clients
(C) neighbors
(D) families

中　譯

我喜歡在咖啡店和＿＿＿＿見面，因為我們可以依照需求，停留並交談多久都可以，不用感到匆忙。
(A) 友善的　　　(B) 客戶　　　　(C) 鄰居　　　　(D) 家庭

解答提示

空格要填入名詞，所以先把選項 (A) 刪除。剩下的3個選項雖然似乎都可以，但是我們必須選擇一個最合適的選項，「客戶」在這裡是比較合宜的答案，所以選 (B)。

140. We don't have any window seats available for that flight, but we can offer you an ＿＿＿＿ seat near the front of the plane. **
(A) aisle
(B) adjustable
(C) first-class
(D) other

中　譯

那班飛機我們沒有任何窗邊座位了，但是我們可以提供您靠近機身前面的一個＿＿＿＿座位。
(A) 走道　　　(B) 可調整的　　(C) 頭等的　　　(D) 其他的

解答提示

選項 (D) 不合文法，可以先刪去。至於選項 (B) 和 (C) 都和生活經驗不符合，一般搭乘飛機，常見的兩種走道是window seat（靠窗座位）和aisle seat（走道座位）。所以應該選 (A)。

Part 6　Text Completion

Questions 141-143 refer to the following email:

Tablets For You
Thank you for ------ your new tablet with us!
　　　　141. (A) requesting
　　　　　　(B) listing
　　　　　　(C) purchasing
　　　　　　(D) researching

 中　　譯

您的平板電腦！
謝謝您向我們------您的新平板電腦！
(A) 要求
(B) 列表
(C) 購買
(D) 研究

解答提示

這是一封來自廠商的email，所以當然選擇 (C) purchasing最合適囉！

Wondering how you can use your new tablet on a Wi-Fi connection?

中　　譯

不知道如何使用您的新平板電腦連上Wi-Fi嗎？

Most tablets include access to several Web services. This includes webmail,
video-streaming, and online storage. Here is a small ------ of what you'll be
　　　　　　　　　　　　　　　　　****142.** (A) idea
　　　　　　　　　　　　　　　　　　　(B) sample
　　　　　　　　　　　　　　　　　　　(C) vision
　　　　　　　　　　　　　　　　　　　(D) indication

able to do with your new tablet, using a Wi-Fi connection.

Chapter 4 實戰演練答案與詳解

中　譯

多數的平板電腦包括取用多種網路服務的功能。包括電子郵件、視訊串流、以及網路儲存。這裡有個小------，說明您將可以透過您的新平板電腦連接Wi-Fi所進行的功能。
(A) 想法
(B) 範本
(C) 視覺
(D) 指示

解答提示

這一題配合下面的功能清單就可以知道空格內應該填入 (B) sample（範本；範例）最合適。

　✓ Send and receive email.
　✓ Browse the web.
　✓ Receive news and weather updates.
　✓ Locate nearby attractions.
　✓ Upload and download documents, files and images.
　✓ Stream movies and music.
　✓ Download apps.
　✓ Videochat.
　✓ Play games with ------ players.
　　　　　****143.** (A) one
　　　　　　　(B) personal
　　　　　　　(C) multiple
　　　　　　　(D) numbered

中　譯

✓ 收發電子郵件。
✓ 瀏覽網路。
✓ 接收新聞和氣象更新。
✓ 定位附近景點。
✓ 上傳及下載文件、檔案、影像。
✓ 串流電影和音樂。
✓ 下載應用程式。

✓ 視訊通話。
✓ 和------玩遊戲。
(A) 一種
(B) 個人的
(C) 多人享有（或參加）的
(D) 計算的

解答提示

空格後的名詞是複數players，所以選項 (A) 不能選。而其他三個選項只有
multiple players（多個玩家）這個搭配詞才是正確的，所以選 (C)。

Need more ideas? TabletsForYou.com

 中　譯

需要更多想法嗎？請上TabletsForYou.com。

Questions 144-146 refer to the following proposal:

Proposal
Andrew's
Heating and Air Conditioning
1390 E Trent Blvd
Sioux Valley, WA 99220
TEL: (509) 922-1212　　FAX: (509) 922-1313

 中　譯

提案
Andrew's暖氣及空調公司
99220華盛頓州蘇族谷Trent東大道1390號
電話：(509) 922-1212　　傳真：(509) 922-1313

PROPOSAL SUBMITTED TO:　　　　　　JOB:
Paul Raj and Kaia Kumar　　　　　　1503 Burrows Rd
　　　　　　　　　　　　　　　　　Valley View WA

提案對象：
Paul Raj與Kaia Kumar

工作地點：
華盛頓州谷景市Burrows路1503號

PHONE:
272-3434

DATE:
October 11th, 2013

中　　譯

電話號碼：
272-3434

日期：
2013年10月11日

WE HEREBY SUBMIT SPECIFICATIONS AND ESTIMATES FOR:

Provide and install:

- New Energetics electric furnace with 15K heat strip and indoor coil.
- New Energetics 3 ton, 15 seer heat pump.
- Pad and pump ups.
- Install refrigeration lines from ------ furnace to outdoor heat pump.

****144. (A) indoor
　　　 (B) refrigerator
　　　 (C) outlining
　　　 (D) outstanding

中　　譯

我們在此提出各項明細及估價：
提供並安裝：

- 新的省電暖爐，配備15K電熱燈管與室內配線。
- 新的省電熱泵，規格3噸，季節能源效率比15。
- 護墊與打氣機。
- 從------暖爐安裝冷卻管線到室外的熱泵。

(A) 室內的
(B) 冰箱
(C) 大綱
(D) 傑出的

解答提示

空格要填入形容詞，所以可以把選項 (B) 和 (C) 先刪去。剩下的只有 (A) indoor 比較適合修飾furnace。

- Complete duct system with heat runs in every room.
- Return air in bedrooms and living room.
- Return air in basement walls and in upstairs walls where possible.
- Rigid round pipe in basement.
- Ceiling diffusers and volume dampers in basement.

中　譯

• 完整的導管系統，暖氣可以到每個房間。
• 回送臥室和客廳的空氣。
• 回送地下室牆內和樓上牆內可能的空氣。
• 地下室堅固的圓管。
• 天花板散佈器及地下室消音器。

❖ Owner to remove all sheetrock and insulation in area of ductwork and pipe.
❖ Andrew's to supply all finish registers.
❖ Line voltage to be completed by a ------ electrician.

　　　　　*****145. (A) knowlegable
　　　　　　　　　(B) licensed
　　　　　　　　　(C) good
　　　　　　　　　(D) excellent

中　譯

❖ 屋主須移除管線施工區域內的所有石膏板與絕緣材料。
❖ Andrew's公司提供所有通風調節系統。
❖ 線路電壓須由------電氣技師完工。
(A) 有知識的
(B) 有執照的
(C) 優良的
(D) 絕佳的

解答提示

這裡的主題是關於暖氣施工，雖然其他形容詞都可以修飾electrician，但是比較合適的形容詞應該選 (B) licensed。

❖ Andrew's to provide permit and 5 year warranty on all parts and labor.

 中　　譯

❖ Andrew's公司提供許可證，以及所有零件和施工的5年保證。

Labor/Material	7900.00
Tax	583.20
Total	8423.20

 中　　譯

施工／材料	7900.00
稅金	583.20
總價	8423.20

Electric Company Rebates: $400
Federal Tax Credit: 30% or $1500 maximum

中　　譯

電力公司折扣：$400
聯邦稅扣抵：30% 或最高$1500

Payment to be made as follows: 25% down and total due upon completion
All material is ------ to be as specified. All work to be completed in a

**** **146.** (A) planned
　　　　(B) thought
　　　　(C) guaranteed
　　　　(D) hoped

workmanlike manner according to standard practices. Any alteration from the above specifications, involving extra cost will only be executed upon written order and will be an extra charge over and above the estimate. Our workers are fully covered by workman's compensation insurance in case of injury.

中　譯

應付費用如下：25%訂金，完工結算總價
所有材料------與說明相同。所有工程根據標準作業以精工方式完成。任何不同於上述明細的修改，包括額外成本，僅以書面訂單執行，並將在估價上額外收費。萬一受傷，貴公司員工受到勞工補償保險全部保障。
(A) 計畫
(B) 思考
(C) 保證
(D) 希望

解答提示

因為這個內容是施工明細的報價，所以選擇 (C) guaranteed會比較合適。

Note: This proposal may be withdrawn by Andrew's if not accepted within 30 days. All accounts are subject to 18% A.P.R. if payment is not received by due date.

中　譯

備註：此提議若在30天內未被接受，Andrew's公司可以撤回。如果付款未在到期日收到，所有的帳戶都將負擔18%的年利率。

Questions 147-149 refer to the following notice:

Escrow: Taxes and Insurance Statement

中　譯

託管：稅務及保險對帳單

Why do I get this statement?
This statement is known as an Annual Escrow Account Disclosure Statement. You receive this statement because you have an escrow ------.

** **147.** (A) accounting
(B) amount
(C) account
(D) bank

中　譯

為什麼我會收到這份對帳單？
此份對帳單又稱年度託管帳戶公開對帳單。您收到此份對帳單是因為您有一個託管------。
(A) 會計
(B) 數量
(C) 帳戶
(D) 銀行

解答提示

這一題簡直是送分題唷！escrow account指的是「托管帳戶」，在房屋買賣中，貸款銀行為確保買方能及時支付稅款和房屋保險的保險金，常常要求買方設立一個托管帳戶，所以選 (C)。

Escrow is a special account your bank provides for you to pay your property taxes and/or insurance. With an escrow account, part of each monthly ------

*** **148.** (A) housing
(B) mortgage
(C) rent
(D) utility

payment you make goes into your escrow account. When your taxes and/or insurance premiums are due, we pay those bills for you with the money set aside in your escrow account.

中　譯

託管是一種特別的帳戶，銀行提供給您支付房屋稅和／或保險。有託管帳戶，您繳交的每個月------金額一部分會到託管帳戶。當您的稅款和／或保費到期時，敝行會使用您的託管帳戶中儲存的金錢為您繳交。
(A) 房屋
(B) 貸款
(C) 房租
(D) 水電費

解答提示

這一題如果對於escrow account有概念的話，就知道是用來支付房屋的稅金和保險費，是從每個月的繳的貸款金額提撥的，所以選 (B)。

Once a year, your bank is required by law to review your account. This statement includes the results of that review. It includes a history of the tax and insurance activity on your account this year and the activity ------ for

**** **149.** (A) planning
(B) requiring
(C) thought
(D) expected

the next year. Please see the attached report for the details of your account review.

中　譯

每年一次，您的銀行依據法律要求會檢視您的帳戶。此份對帳單包括檢視結果。包括今年帳戶的稅務與保險活動記錄，以及明年------的活動。請查看附件的報告，了解您帳戶檢視的各項細節。
(A) 計畫
(B) 要求
(C) 思考
(D) 預計

解答提示

這一題應該填入一個過去分詞表示被動語態，而選項 (C) 是不及物動詞，所以不合文法，只能選 (D)。

Questions 150-152 refer to the following article:

The current Deer Lake Volunteer Ambulance building was first built in 2005. James Rice painted the organization's name on the fascia of the building at that time. Lately, the lettering has become quite ------.

*****150.** (A) bright
(B) unwritten
(C) faded
(D) unseen

中　　譯

現今的Deer Lake義消大樓首建於2005年。James Rice當時把該組織的名稱粉刷在招牌上。最近，字跡已經變得相當------。
(A) 明亮
(B) 未寫
(C) 褪色
(D) 未見

解答提示

字跡通常都是被慢慢不見，所以答案要選 (C) faded。如果選unseen是指字跡完全不見，這樣太誇張囉！

On July 20th, 2013 James was at the annual Deer Lake Airport Fly-in. He approached the DLVA ambulance volunteers there and asked if he could repaint the sign for them sometime. He offered to paint for free, if the ambulance Corps would supply the ------.

****151.** (A) coloring
(B) paint
(C) building

(D) painting

在2013年6月20日，James出席每年的Deer Lake機場飛行聚會。他走近義消大樓的義消員，詢問他是否可以找一天替他們重新刷上招牌。他提議免費粉刷，如果消防隊願意提供------。
(A) 上色
(B) 油漆
(C) 大樓
(D) 圖畫

解答提示

粉刷需要使用的當然是油漆，所以答案很明顯是 (B)。注意paint的動名詞就變成「圖畫」了，完全不適合用在這裡唷！

Ramie Schliner, Operations Officer, accepted James' generous offer.

營運經理Ramie Schliner接受了James大方的提議。

The crews reporting for duty at 6:00 a.m. the following day, found James on a ladder already busy painting. James says he believes in the concept of paying it forward. He felt it was a perfect way to ------ his gratitude for the

****152. (A) thank
(B) say
(C) showing
(D) express

work the Ambulance crews do for our community.

中　譯

隔天早上六點鐘，隊員報到上工，發現James已經在梯子上忙碌的粉刷。James表示他相信「把愛傳出去」的信念。他覺得這是個完成的方式，來------他的感謝，對於消防隊員為社區所做的事。

(A) 謝謝
(B) 說出
(C) 表示
(D) 表達

解答提示

空格內必須填入原形動詞，所以可以把showing先刪除。另外gratitude（謝意；感謝）這個字通常搭配的動詞是express，而不是say，所以選 (D)。

Part 7　Reading Comprehension

Questions 153 through 155 refer to the following article:

Annual Concert in the Park

Join the River City Symphony over Memorial Day weekend for its annual Concert in the Park. This year's concert is sponsored by River City Bank. Edward Prau will conduct his orchestra in a mix of classical music, show tunes and patriotic marches. Bring a picnic dinner, blankets, and chairs and enjoy a music-filled evening under the stars. The whole family will enjoy this concert by our favorite orchestra!

When: May 29th, 2014
　　　 7:00 p.m. ~ 8:30 p.m.

Where: Riverfront Park, at 29th St and Grand Avenue

Cost: FREE

Phone: 503-222-1212

Website: www.rivercitysymphony.org

中　譯

公園年度音樂會

在陣亡將士紀念日的週末，來參加River市交響樂會，在公園舉行的一年一度音樂會。今年的音樂會由River市銀行贊助。Edward Prau將指揮他的管弦樂團，混合了古典樂、表演名曲，以及愛國進行曲。帶份野餐晚餐、毯子以及椅子，在星光下享受充滿音樂的夜晚。全家人都將享受這場我們最愛管弦樂團的音樂會。

時間：2014年5月29日
　　　 晚上7:30 ~ 8:30

地點：河濱公園，29街和格蘭大道交叉

NEW TOEIC 黃金戰鬥力——閱讀篇

費用：免費

電話：503-222-1212

網站：www.rivercitysymphony.org

153. How often does the River City Symphony perform this concert? ****
(A) Monthly during the summer.
(B) Every Sunday evening.
(C) Once a year on Memorial Day Weekend.
(D) As often as patrons request it.

中　　譯

River市交響樂會多久表演這場音樂會一次？
(A) 夏季每個月一次。
(B) 每個星期日晚上。
(C) 在每年的陣亡將士紀念日週末表演一次。
(D) 只要有贊助者要求就會表演。

解答提示

這一題可說是非常容易也有難度喔！重點就是annual這個字，annual是「一年一次；年度」的意思，所以只要看得懂這個字，答案就很明顯囉！這題的答案是 (C)。

154. What kind of music will the orchestra play? ***
(A) Classic rock music.
(B) Ballet classics.
(C) A mix of hymns and spirituals.
(D) Show tunes and patriotic marches.

中　　譯

管弦樂團將演奏什麼樣的音樂？
(A) 經典的搖滾樂。
(B) 芭蕾經典曲目。
(C) 混合詩歌和靈魂樂。

(D) 表演名曲和愛國進行曲。

解答提示

這一題從內容即可找到答案，管弦樂團將表演三種音樂類型：classical music, show tunes and patriotic marches，注意不要被選項 (A) 誤導囉！正確答案應為 (D)。

155. Why would this be a good family event? **
　　(A) It's good for kids to learn stringed instruments.
　　(B) Because the music is great and it's free.
　　(C) Kids love to play at the park.
　　(D) You don't have to cook dinner for your family.

中　　譯

為什麼這會是個很棒的家庭活動？
(A) 小孩子學習弦樂器很好。
(B) 因為音樂很棒，而且是免費的。
(C) 小孩子喜歡在公園玩。
(D) 你不需要替家人煮晚餐。

解答提示

這一題在內容中找不到，必須透過一些推測和判斷。選項 (A) 和 (C) 所敘述的內容雖然都是正確的，但是和內容並沒有關係。而選項 (D) 則是錯誤的，所以應該選 (B)。

Questions 156 through 158 refer to the following letter:

Dear Ron,

I have read several travel brochures from your area and all of them mention the great hiking in the region. I found your hiking club listed online and wonder if you could give me some more specific information. My family will be there from July 7th~ July 18th. We would love to hike as many trails as possible in that time. My family consists of myself, my husband and our three kids, ages 10 ~ 14. I would appreciate any information you could give me about trails suitable for family hikes. We have done a lot of hiking, but nothing overly strenuous. We love trails with a view, but are not prepared for overnight backpacking on this trip. Day trips of 4-7 hours are perfect. Thank you so much for your time!

You can reach me at:
email: evag@email.com
Phone: 502-111-4343
Address: Eva Garber
2507 N. Wilson Rd
Ann Arbor WY 99006

親愛的Ron，
我已經閱讀過一些旅遊手冊介紹您的所在地區，都有提到這個地區很棒的健行活動。我在網路上找到您的健行俱樂部，不曉得您是否可以給我一些更多具體的資訊。我和家人將在7月7日～18日在那裡。我們想要在那期間盡可能地多走幾條健行路線。我的家庭包括我自己、我丈夫和我們三個小孩，小孩年齡是10歲到14歲。我非常感謝您能提供適合家庭健行的路線相關資訊。我們曾健行很多次，但是並不是很激烈的型態。我們喜歡有景觀的路線，但我們在這趟行程並不準備要健行過夜。每天4~7小時就很完美了。謝謝您撥時間協助！

我的聯絡方式：
email: evag@email.com
電話：502-111-4343

地址：Eva Garber
　　　99006懷俄明州安娜堡市北Wilson路2507號

156. Why has Eva written this letter? ***
　　(A) She is trying to decide where her family should go for vacation.
　　(B) She wants to know about things to do in the area.
　　(C) She is looking for information about specific trails to hike.
　　(D) She wants to go hiking with Ron while they are in town.

中　　譯

為什麼Eva要寫這封信？
(A) 她正試著決定她的家人要去哪裡度假。
(B) 她想要知道在那個區域有什麼事可以做。
(C) 她正在找具體健行路線的資訊。
(D) 當他們在鎮上的時候，她想要和Ron去健行。

解答提示

這一題在信件內容即可找到答案，Eva是在為了她們一家人健行尋找具體的資訊，所以應該選 (C)。

157. What kind of hiking does the family want to do on this trip? ***
　　(A) Some day trips and some overnights.
　　(B) Day trips only.
　　(C) Overnight backpacking.
　　(D) Hiking along the ocean.

中　　譯

在這次旅程中，這家人想要進行什麼樣的健行活動？
(A) 有一些單日的健行，有一些過夜的。
(B) 只有單日的健行。
(C) 過夜的背包健行。
(D) 沿著海邊健行。

解答提示

在信件的最後Eva有說，他們並不準備要過夜，所以答案是 (B) 選項。

158. How can Ron best get in touch with Eva? **

    (A) Look up her contact information online.

    (B) She would prefer a phone call.

    (C) He can choose to email, call or mail information to her.

    (D) He only has an email address for her.

中　譯

Ron如何和Eva取得聯繫？

(A) 在網路上查詢她的聯絡方式。

(B) 她比較喜歡接到電話。

(C) 他可以寄email、打電話，或郵寄資料給她。

(D) 他只有她的email信箱。

解答提示

在信件最後Eva留下了email信箱、電話號碼以及地址，所以Ron可以透過這三種方式來和她聯繫，所以應該選 (C)。

Chapter 4 實戰演練答案與詳解

Questions 159 and 160 refer to the following letter:

Overland Tours
New York City, NY

Mr. and Mrs. Adams,

We regret to inform you that the bus tour that you have scheduled for March 15th – 22nd has been cancelled. There are simply not enough people registered. Normally, at that time of year, our tours fill to capacity. We aren't sure what has caused the lack of interest in this tour. We know this is a disappointment for both of you. We have enjoyed having you on our tours in the past, and hope you will tour with us again in the future. We encourage you to transfer your deposit to a future tour. If you would rather have a full refund, you are welcome to do that as well. Please call our office at your earliest convenience to let us know what you would like to do.

Paul Ramos
Overland Tours Customer Service
1-888-222-3232

越陸旅行社
紐約市，紐約州

亞當斯先生和亞當斯太太，

我們很遺憾通知您，您預訂的3月15~22日巴士旅程已經取消。登記參加的人數不足。通常每年那個時候，我們的行程都會報名額滿。我們不確定是什麼造成大家對這個行程不感興趣。我們了解這讓兩位非常失望。我們很榮幸過去的旅程都有兩位參與，也希望您在未來能再參加我們的旅程。我們建議您把訂金轉到未來的行程。如果您寧願全額退費，我們也歡迎您這麼做。如果方便，請您盡早致電我們的辦公室，讓我們知道您決定如何處理。

Paul Ramos
越陸旅行社客戶服務部
1-888-222-3232

159. Why has this tour been cancelled? **
    (A) The weather will be stormy that week.
    (B) Nobody knows why it had to be cancelled.
    (C) They could not find a tour guide.
    (D) Not enough people signed up for the tour.

為什麼這個行程會取消？
(A) 那個星期的天氣將有暴風雨。
(B) 沒有人知道為什麼會被取消。
(C) 他們找不到導遊。
(D) 報名參加行程的人數不足。

解答提示

信件內容是There are simply not enough people registered.，register和sign up是同義字，所以答案選 (D)。

160. How do you know the Adams have traveled with this company before? **
    (A) The letter states that Overland tours has enjoyed having them before.
    (B) Mr. and Mrs. Adams have enjoyed many trips with Overland Tours.
    (C) Overland Tours is located in the city where they live.
    (D) Mrs. Adams' father owns Overland Tours.

中　　譯

如何得知亞當斯一家人以前曾經和這家公司旅行？
(A) 信件說到跨陸旅行社以前曾有榮幸有他們作為客戶。
(B) 亞當斯夫婦曾經和跨陸旅行社享受過許多旅程。
(C) 跨陸旅行社位於他們所居住的城市。
(D) 亞當斯太太的父親是跨陸旅行社的老闆。

解答提示

這一題的答案在We have enjoyed having you on our tours in the past.，信件中就有提到這點，所以答案是 (A) 選項。

Questions 161 through 163 refer to the following advertisement:

Grand Opening!
You have watched the construction of the new Hotel Ritz for over a year.
Finally, we invite you to a Grand Opening Gala!

Saturday, October 22nd
Sunday, October 23rd

Dinner served in the Ritz Banquet Hall from 5:00 p.m. to 8:00 p.m.

Dancing begins in the Grand Ballroom at 9:00 p.m.

Enjoy dinner, wander our grounds along the river, tour our rooms and suites. Dance the night away.

Special Room rates for Saturday and Sunday nights!

Place your reservation today for dinner or for the complete overnight experience!

1-888-131-2222
www.hotelritz.com

盛大開幕！

您已經看著麗池飯店的建設超過一年了。
終於，我們邀請您來參與盛大開幕慶祝！

10月22日星期六
10月23日星期日

晚餐在麗池飯店宴席廳提供，從下午5點至晚上8點

舞會在大舞廳，晚上9點開始

享用晚餐、漫步在河畔區域、參觀我們的房間及套房。整夜跳舞吧。

星期六日晚上特別房價！

今天就預定晚餐或完整的過夜體驗！

電話：1-888-131-2222
網站：www.hotelritz.com

161. How long did the construction of the new hotel take? *
   (A) About six months.
   (B) Several years.
   (C) Over one year.
   (D) A long time.

中　　譯

這間新飯店的建造花了多久？
(A) 大約六個月。
(B) 好幾年。
(C) 超過一年。
(D) 很久。

解答提示

廣告的一開始即寫明「超過一年」，答案是 (C) 選項。

162. What is the October Gala celebrating? **
   (A) Octoberfest Weekend.
   (B) The grand opening of the hotel.
   (C) Special room rates.
   (D) That construction is finally completed.

中　　譯

十月的盛會是要慶祝什麼？
(A) 十月啤酒節週末。
(B) 飯店的盛大開幕。
(C) 特別房價。
(D) 建造工程終於完成。

解答提示

Octoberfest是德國幕尼黑知名的啤酒節，和這個廣告一點關係也沒有。而特別房價和工程完成也不是廣告的重點，重點是飯店即將盛大開幕，所以選(B)。

163. Do Gala guests have to stay overnight? ***
  (A) Yes. If they make a reservation, they must spend Saturday night at the hotel.
  (B) Not at this time, but they must make a reservation for a future stay.
  (C) No, but they will definitely wish they did.
  (D) They can choose dinner only, or they can spend the night there.

中　　譯

盛會的賓客一定要在飯店過夜嗎？
(A) 是的，如果他們預約的話，他們必須星期六晚上待在飯店過夜。
(B) 這次不用，但是他們必須預約一次未來的住房。
(C) 不用，但他們當然會這麼希望。
(D) 他們可以選擇只用晚餐，或者他們也可以在那裡過夜。

解答提示

廣告內容的最後有說明，可以預訂晚餐，或是預訂一整晚完整的體驗，包括住房，意思就是他們可以選擇，答案應該選 (D)。

Questions 164 through 166 refer to the following email:

To: Elizabeth James
From: Jordan Kennedy
Date: December 5th
Subject: Order

Dear Elizabeth,

Thank you for returning my call today. It was good to talk with you. This email is to confirm the details of your order. Please review this email and let me know if there are any errors. As I mentioned on the phone, if you need to make any additions to the order, December 23rd is the final day to make revisions. The books will go into print on January 4th. They will be available for pick-up on January 17th. Good luck preparing for the conference. I appreciate working with you!

Title	Order #	Quantity	Cost	Total
Communication in the Workplace	650912	150	$15.99	$2398.50

Jordan Kennedy
Post Printing

中　譯

寄給：Elizabeth James
來自：Jordan Kennedy
日期：12月5日
主旨：訂單

親愛的Elizabeth，
謝謝你今天回覆我的電話，與您談話非常愉快。這封電子郵件是要確認您的訂單細節，請檢視郵件，並讓我知道是否有任何錯誤。如同我在電話中提到

的，如果您需要在訂單中增加任何品項，12月23日是最後修改的日期。這些書將在1月4日付印，會在1月17日備妥交貨。祝您準備會議順利，感謝能和您一起合作。

名稱	編號#	數量	單價	總價
職場溝通	650912	150	$15.99	$2398.50

Jordan Kennedy
Post印刷公司

164. What is the purpose of this email? ***
    (A) To confirm Elizabeth's order for books for the conference.
    (B) To see if Elizabeth has any changes in mind for the book.
    (C) To cancel the book order Elizabeth placed earlier.
    (D) Jordan wanted to ask Elizabeth to write the book herself.

 中　譯

這封email的用意是什麼？
(A) 確認Elizabeth會議用書的訂單。
(B) 確認Elizabeth是否心裡對於書籍有任何變更的想法。
(C) 取消Elizabeth稍早下訂的書籍訂單。
(D) Jordan想要求Elizabeth自己寫書。

解答提示

信件內容就有提到：This email is to confirm the details of your order.，只要回頭去找關鍵字confirm就很快可以找到答案囉！所以這答案應為 (A)。

165. How did Jordan get the information that he is confirming? ****
    (A) He asked his boss to give it to him.
    (B) He received a letter from Elizabeth with all the details.
    (C) He spoke with Elizabeth on the phone earlier that day.
    (D) Jordan talked with Elizabeth's boss yesterday.

中　譯

Jordan確認的資料是從哪裡得到的？

(A) 他請他的老闆提供給他的。
(B) 他從Elizabeth那裡收到信，寫明了所有細節。
(C) 他和Elizabeth在當天稍早講過電話。
(D) Jordan昨天和Elizabeth的老闆講過話。

解答提示

這一題的答案就在信件的第一句話：Thank you for returning my call today. It was good to talk with you.，可見他們是先在電話中談過訂單之後，Jordan再寫email作為正式的確認，所以正確答案應為 (C)。

166. How many people are they planning to have at the conference? ****
　　(A) Over 2000.
　　(B) Around 150, since that is the number of books they ordered.
　　(C) Elizabeth has no idea how many people will come.
　　(D) Elizabeth told Jordan they'll have 40-50 people.

中　　譯

他們計畫有多少人參與會議？
(A) 超過兩千人。
(B) 大約150人，因為那是訂購的書籍數量。
(C) Elizabeth不知道有多少人會來。
(D) Elizabeth告訴Jordan會有40~50人。

解答提示

這一題在信件的內容當中完全沒有提到，但是只需要找到相同的數字，就可以立刻破解了！訂單細節中的數量是150，而選項 (B) 正好有一模一樣的數字，也確實就是正確答案。

Questions 167 through 169 refer to the following article:

Controversy over Wolves likely to Continue

Both sides agree that wolves are majestic creatures. Both sides agree that wolves are a threat to farmers and ranchers in the west. At a town meeting in Dakota last night, that's where the similarities stopped.

Ranchers and friends of ranchers suggested the government issue a kill order for the wolves. They want to protect their livelihood. Too many livestock are killed by hungry wolves each year, at a cost of up to $800 per animal.

Local tourism officials believe the ranchers must upgrade their fencing and other protective measures. Wolf tourism is big business in this state. Nearby state and national park lands offer camera laden tourists daily views of the great creatures in action.

The meeting ended at an impasse, with emotions running high. Local officials agreed to work closely with state officials to study the issue further.

關於狼的爭論可能持續

兩邊同意狼是崇偉的生物。兩邊同意狼對西部的農夫和農牧場主人是個威脅。昨夜在達科他州的一場市鎮會議，那就是雙方相似點中止之處。

農牧場主人和其朋友建議，政府公布對狼的屠殺命令。他們想要保護自己的生計。每年有太多的家畜死於飢餓狼群的口中，每頭動物損失達800美金。

當地旅遊官員相信，農牧場主人必須提升柵欄防護以及其他保護措施。狼群觀光在本州是很重大的生意。鄰近的州立和國立國家公園每天提供這些美妙生物活動的景象，給帶著照相機的觀光客。

這場會議以僵局結束，情緒都很高漲。當地官員同意和州政府官員密切合作，進一步研究此議題。

167. Where might you read this article? ***
(A) In the newspaper.
(B) In a magazine article.
(C) In an office memo.
(D) On a billboard.

中　譯

你可能在哪裡讀到這篇文章？
(A) 在報紙中。
(B) 在雜誌文章中。
(C) 在辦公室備忘錄。
(D) 在公告欄。

解答提示

這一篇文章的標題省略了冠詞和be動詞，是標準新聞標題的作法，所以答案是選項 (A)。

168. What do the ranchers believe the government should do? ****
(A) Pay the ranchers for their dead livestock.
(B) There is nothing they can do.
(C) Kill off some of the wolves.
(D) Relocate the wolves.

中　譯

農牧場主人相信政府應該做什麼？
(A) 補償農牧場主人死掉的家畜。
(B) 他們無能為力。
(C) 宰殺一些狼群。
(D) 將狼群移到別的地方。

解答提示

報導內容寫到：Ranchers and friends of ranchers suggested the government issue a kill order for the wolves.，也就是他們希望透過宰殺的方式讓狼群的數量減少，所以正確答案是 (C)。

169. What brings wolf lovers to nearby park lands? ***
    (A) A zoo where wolves live.
    (B) The opportunity to photograph the wolves in the wild.
    (C) They want to listen to the controversy.
    (D) They come to pet the wolves.

中 譯

什麼因素把狼的愛好者帶到鄰近的公園地？
(A) 一座有狼的動物園。
(B) 拍攝野生狼群的機會。
(C) 他們想要聽聽這個爭議。
(D) 他們來撫摸狼群。

解答提示

報導最後有提到：camera laden tourists，就是帶著相機的觀光客，可見有很多觀光客是抱著拍攝狼群的目的前來的，所以正確答案是 (B)。

Chapter 4 實戰演練答案與詳解

Questions 170 through 172 refer to the following notice:

Job Fair
All upcoming graduates are encouraged to attend!
The fair will feature employers in the business, health and technical fields.

How can this help you?
- Hand out your resume in person.
- Reach multiple employers in a short time.
- Make personal contacts with possible employers.
- Increase your confidence for interview situations.

Date: Friday, April 2nd
Location: Mead Hall
Wellesley University
Time: 9:00 a.m.- 3:00 p.m.
Cost to attend: FREE

Also featuring **Resume Writing Sessions** throughout the day.

工作博覽會
所有即將畢業的畢業生都歡迎參加！
這場博覽會主要有商界、保健醫療、和技術業界的僱主。

這能如何幫助你？
- 親自交出你的履歷表。
- 在短時間內與多位僱主接洽。
- 和潛在的僱主親身接觸。
- 提升你的信心面對面試情況。

日期：4月2日星期五
地點：綠草堂　Wellesley大學
時間：上午9點到下午3點
參加費用：免費

全天同時有**履歷表教寫課程**。

170. Where might this notice be posted? **
(A) In a local restaurant.
(B) On a college campus.
(C) In the local hospital.
(D) At the high school.

中　譯

這則公告可能貼在哪裡？
(A) 在當地一家餐廳。
(B) 在大學校園裡。
(C) 在當地一家醫院。
(D) 在一所高中。

解答提示

公告裡的地點就寫明了Wellesleey University，university在許多情況下和college是同義字，所以答案選 (B)。

171. Who will want to attend this job fair? ***
(A) Teachers and classroom assistants.
(B) People unhappy with their job.
(C) People graduating this year.
(D) Those just starting college this year.

中　譯

誰會想要參加這場工作博覽會？
(A) 教師和課堂助理。
(B) 對工作不滿意的人。
(C) 今年要畢業的人。
(D) 今年剛讀大學的人。

解答提示

公告一開始就說明歡迎畢業生參加，所以答案是 (C)。其實這一題用生活常識判斷也可以回答哦！

172. How could a graduate benefit from attending? ****
    (A) Have a great free lunch.
    (B) Be hired that day.
    (C) Find out if they will graduate on time.
    (D) Meet possible employers in person.

中　　譯

畢業生可以從參加博覽會得到什麼好處？
(A) 得到免費午餐。
(B) 當天被雇用。
(C) 得知他們是否能準時畢業。
(D) 親自和可能（成為他們老闆）的僱主們會面。

解答提示

公告中總共有四個好處，其中之一就是可以面對面和僱主談話，所以答案是
(D)。

Questions 173 through 175 refer to the following article:

Hughes Electric Building Completed

Hughes Electric has completed construction of its newest facility on Electric Avenue. This building will house all of the trucks Hughes uses locally. The $3 million project is a 10,000 square foot building, allowing space for maintenance and repair of Hughes vehicles. The compressed natural gas trucks will also be housed there.

The project was so costly due to special ventilation systems needed where natural gas vehicles are repaired. General contractor Tom Vance commented that the project was completed ahead of schedule and therefore actually cost less than projected.

Hughes電氣公司大樓完工

Hughes電氣公司已經完成在Electric大道上最新的設備建築。這棟建物將停放Hughes公司使用的所有本地卡車。這項3百萬的工程是一棟1萬平方英呎的大樓,提供空間給Hughes公司的車輛維修。壓縮的天然氣卡車也將停放在此。

此工程非常昂貴,因為天然氣車輛修理時需要特殊的通風系統。整承包商Tom Vance評論說,這項工程提前時程完成,因此其實比預計的花費更少。

173. What does the article announce? **

(A) Completion of the new Hughes building.
(B) Hughes plan for future growth.
(C) Electric use in the city.
(D) The use of compressed natural gas.

這篇文章宣布什麼事?

(A) 新的Hughes公司大樓完工。
(B) Hughes公司對於未來成長的計畫。
(C) 城市中的電力使用。
(D) 壓縮天然氣的使用。

解答提示

標題即說明了是Hughes公司的大樓完工，所以答案很明顯是 (A)。complete是動詞，completion是名詞。

174. What will the new building be used for? ***
    (A) Office space.
    (B) Storage of excess building materials.
    (C) Apartments for Hughes workers.
    (D) Maintenance and repair of vehicles.

中　　譯

這棟新大樓的用途是什麼？
(A) 辦公室空間。
(B) 儲存過多的建築材料。
(C) Hughes公司員工的公寓。
(D) 車輛的維修。

解答提示

公告的內容提到：allowing space for maintenance and repair of Hughes vehicles，所以只要看到選項 (D) 有相同的單字maintenance和repair，就可以大膽地選囉！

175. Why was the project so costly? *****
    (A) It ran over budget.
    (B) It was completed two months late.
    (C) Special ventilation systems were required.
    (D) Hughes did not budget well for the building.

中　譯

為什麼這項工程如此昂貴？
(A) 超出預算。
(B) 晚了兩個月完工。
(C) 需要特殊的通風系統。
(D) Hughes公司並未替這棟大樓做出良好預算。

解答提示

這一題的ventilation system（通風系統）算是比較難的單字，正好可以作為答題的線索，看到選項 (C) 出現一模一樣的字，就肯定是答案囉！

Questions 176 and 177 refer to the following email:

Dear Martha,

As part of our ongoing efforts to best serve our members, we are upgrading all of our computer systems. Due to this effort, all of our online services will be unavailable from June 29th until July 1st, 2013. This includes:
- Knowledgeable Surveys
- The Knowledgeable Members Website and Rewards Center (knowledgeablemembers.com)

Also, our Knowledgeable Surveys Support Department (1-800-333-2323, and support@knowledgeablemembers.com) will be closed from June 30th to July 1st, 2013.

We apologize for any inconvenience this may cause you. If you have questions about this closure—or anything else related to your knowledgeable surveys participation—please contact our office.
- 1-800-333-5555
- support@knowledgeablemembers.com.

We look forward to hearing from you!

Sincerely,

The Knowledgeable Surveys Support Team

 中　譯

親愛的Martha，

我們目前正努力做到服務會員的最佳品質，其中一部分是，我們正在升級所有的電腦系統。為了這個努力，我們全部的線上服務從2013年6月29日到7月1日將無法使用。
- 知識問卷
- 知識會員網站與回饋中心 (knowledgeablemembers.com)

同時，我們的知識問卷支援部門（1-800-333-2323, and support@ knowledgeablemembers.com）將在2013年6月30日到7月1日關閉。

我們為造成您的不方便而感到抱歉。如果您對於這項關閉有任何疑問，或其他任何事關於您在知識問卷的參與，請聯絡我們的辦公室。

- 1-800-333-5555
- support@knowledgeablemembers.com

我們期待能聽到你的消息！

敬上，

知識問卷支援團隊

176. Why will all the Knowledgeable Surveys systems be unavailable? ****
　　(A) It will be too hot to work.
　　(B) They are updating the entire system.
　　(C) They will be closed for the 4th of July holiday.
　　(D) They are trying to serve people better.

中　　譯

為什麼知識問卷的所有系統都將不能用？
(A) 過熱而無法工作。
(B) 他們在升級整個系統。
(C) 他們將在美國國慶日假期關閉。
(D) 他們試著更好地服務人們。

解答提示

email的內容即提到：we are upgrading all of our computer systems，看到關鍵字upgrade就幾乎可以肯定答案是 (B) 囉！

177. Why does the Support Team apologize for this closure? ****
　　(A) It's rude to close for so many days.
　　(B) They think no one will want to be a customer any more.
　　(C) The closure will be inconvenient for their members.
　　(D) They wish they didn't have to close.

Chapter 4 實戰演練答案與詳解

中　譯

為什麼支援團隊為了這項關閉道歉？
(A) 關閉這麼多天很沒有禮貌。
(B) 他們認為再也沒有人想成為客戶了。
(C) 這項關閉將對他們的會員造成不便。
(D) 他們希望他們不用關閉。

解答提示

email的最後寫：We apologize for any inconvenience this may cause you. ，意思就是為了造成的不方便而致歉，所以答案是 (C) 選項。

Questions 178 through 180 refer to the following announcement:

Digital Media Sales Executive

Are you looking for a rewarding career in the local media industry?

Are you a person who:
- Generates new business?
- Builds positive relationships with customers?
- Efficiently records and maintains customer and order information?
- Demonstrates critical thinking and troubleshooting?

Then, we may have the perfect full-time sales position for you! The person in this position will generate advertising revenue by marketing our extensive print, online and mobile products and services.

Bring with you a proven ability to meet and exceed sales goals in a highly competitive industry. A college degree or equivalent experience is required. Experience in media sales is highly desired, but not required.

Apply in person at Artful Media, 1000 Lignon Ave., or email don@artfulmedia.com with your resume and cover letter.

數位媒體銷售業務主管

你正在本地的媒體產業尋找一個良好報酬的職涯嗎？

你是這樣的人嗎？
- 開發新客戶？
- 與客戶建立正面關係？
- 有效率地記錄並維護客戶和訂單資料？
- 展示出批判性思考與問題解決能力？

那麼，我們也許有個絕佳的全職銷售職位可以給你！此職位將透過行銷公司的大量印刷品、線上與行動產品和服務，來創造廣告收入。

Chapter 4 實戰演練答案與詳解

請帶來你證明你可以在高度競爭的產業中達到並超過銷售目標的能力。大學學歷或同等經驗是必須的。我們非常需要媒體經驗，但並非必須。

親洽Artful媒體公司，Lignon大道1000號，或email你的履歷表和求職信到 don@artfulmedia.com。

178. Where would you find this ad? ***
    (A) In a television advertisement.
    (B) In the employment section of the newspaper.
    (C) On the radio.
    (D) In a local tourism guide.

中　譯

你可能在哪裡發現這則廣告？
(A) 在電視廣告中。
(B) 在報紙的求職版。
(C) 在廣播中。
(D) 在本地的旅遊導覽書中。

解答提示

這則廣告是求職廣告，所以最有可能出現的地方就是報紙的求職版，所以答案選 (B)。

179. What type of job is being advertised? **
    (A) Sales.
    (B) Reporting.
    (C) Accounting.
    (D) Administration.

中　　譯

廣告的是什麼樣的工作？
(A) 銷售。
(B) 報導。
(C) 會計。
(D) 行政管理。

解答提示

這一題的答案就在廣告標題，所以正確答案應該是 (A)！

180. If you email about the job, what should you include? **
  (A) A picture of yourself.
  (B) Your qualifications.
  (C) Your resume and cover letter.
  (D) Your desired wage.

中　　譯

如果你用email接洽這份工作，你應該附件什麼？
(A) 一張你個人的照片。
(B) 你的各項資格證書。
(C) 你的履歷表和求職信。
(D) 你的理想薪資。

解答提示

廣告的最後說明可以親自到公司，或是用email把履歷表和求職信寄過去，所以答案應為 (C)。

Questions 181 through 185 refer to the following advertisement and coupons:

Take a friend to Breakfast!

Introducing our new Sour Cream Blueberry Pancakes
Blueberries are in season for a few short months.
Take advantage of their flavor today!

We start with organic whole grain flour, add farm fresh eggs, organic whole milk and blueberries brought fresh to our door every morning!
Add some scrambled eggs, pork sausage and fresh squeezed orange juice and you have yourself a breakfast fit for a king.

Who could ask for a healthier start to the day?
Bring a friend and get your day off to a great start!

Farm Fresh Kitchen
We grow it. You love it!
See you in the morning.

Don't Forget!
Breakfast is on us!

2 FREE Sour Cream Blueberry Pancakes
Expires August 31th, 2014

Not valid with any other offer, discount or coupon. Limit one coupon per person, per visit.

Don't Forget to Bring a Friend!

2 FREE Sour Cream Blueberry Pancakes
Expires August 31th, 2014

Not valid with any other offer, discount
or coupon. Limit one coupon per person,
per visit.

中　譯

帶朋友吃早餐！

隆重介紹本店全新酸奶藍莓鬆餅
藍莓在這短短幾個月當中盛產
今天就好好嘗嘗它們的味道！

我們用有機穀粉、加上農場新鮮雞蛋、有機全脂牛奶以及藍莓，
都是每天早上新鮮送到店舖！
加上一些炒蛋、豬肉香腸，以及新鮮現榨柳橙汁，
您將得到一份國王的早餐。

誰能要求一天更健康的開始呢？
帶個朋友來，用最棒的開始迎接您的一天！

新鮮農場廚房
我們種，您愛瘋！
早上見。

上：
別忘記！
早餐算我們的！

2份免費酸奶藍莓鬆餅
2014年8月31日到期

不可與其他方案、折扣、或優惠券併用。一人一次限用一張。

下：
別忘記帶朋友來！

2份免費酸奶藍莓鬆餅
2014年8月31日到期
不可與其他方案、折扣、或優惠券併用。一人一次限用一張。

181. What could you buy with your free pancakes? ***
(A) Pork sausage and juice.
(B) Butter and syrup.
(C) Soup and a salad.
(D) Toast and cocoa.

中　譯

你得到免費鬆餅，你還可以一起買什麼東西？
(A) 豬肉香腸和果汁。
(B) 奶油和糖漿。
(C) 湯和沙拉。
(D) 吐司和可可亞。

解答提示

這一題可以在廣告內容找到，店家建議可以搭配炒蛋、豬肉香腸以及新鮮現榨柳橙汁，所以答案是 (A)。

182. How often does the restaurant receive their blueberries? **
(A) Nightly.
(B) Once a month.
(C) Once a week.
(D) Every morning.

中　譯

這家餐廳多久一次會收到藍莓？
(A) 每天晚上。

(B) 每個月一次。
(C) 每個星期一次。
(D) 每天早上。

解答提示

廣告內容寫：brought fresh to our door every morning（每天早上新鮮送到我們門口），所以答案就是 (D) 囉！

183. What can you infer from this ad? *****
  (A) That blueberry pancakes are the owner's favorite.
  (B) That most of the food served in the restaurant is grown on the farm.
  (C) The restaurant offers strawberry pancakes during strawberry season.
  (D) They serve blueberries year-round.

中　　譯

從這則廣告可以推論出什麼？
(A) 藍莓鬆餅是店家的最愛。
(B) 這家餐廳提供的食物大多數是在農場種植的。
(C) 這家餐廳在草莓盛產期提供草莓鬆餅。
(D) 他們全年都提供藍莓。

解答提示

廣告內容除了提到brought fresh to our door every morning（每天早上新鮮送到我們門口），還有標語We grow it. You love it!（我們種，您愛瘋！），可以推測這家餐廳可能有自己的農場，食材都是自己種的，所以答案選 (B)。

184. Why are there two coupons offered? ***
  (A) Because there was extra room on the page.
  (B) So you'll come twice.
  (C) One for you, one for a friend.
  (D) So you can use two coupons and get four pancakes.

Chapter 4 實戰演練答案與詳解

中　譯

為什麼提供兩張優惠券？
(A) 因為頁面還有多餘的空間。
(B) 這樣顧客就會來兩次。
(C) 一張給你，一張給朋友用。
(D) 這樣可以用兩張優惠券，得到四份鬆餅。

解答提示

優惠券上有寫明「一人一次限用一張」，所以是一個人用一張，答案是 (C)。

185. Why would Farm Fresh Kitchen offer this coupon during the summer only? *****
(A) That's when blueberries are in season.
(B) People like to eat pancakes on hot days.
(C) The restaurant wants to increase sales during the summer.
(D) The owner loves summer.

中　譯

為什麼新鮮農場廚房只在夏季提供這張優惠券？
(A) 這是藍莓盛產的季節。
(B) 人們喜歡在熱天吃鬆餅。
(C) 這家餐廳想要在夏季增加銷售。
(D) 店主喜歡夏天。

解答提示

廣告傳單的一開始即說明目前是藍莓盛產的季節，所以特別推出這項優惠，答案應該是 (A)。

Questions 186 through 190 refer to the following press release and email:

To: Saachi Jayaraman
From: Daksha Nayar
Date: May 5th
Subject: Press Release

Dear Saachi,

Here is a sample of what I would like the press release to say. Does it seem appropriate for our Indian audience? Please let me know if you think there should be any changes before it goes to the newspaper. I am so excited for this venture! I know you will be a great manager for our India location. I look forward to seeing you in a couple of weeks to get the store set up! I will send you my flight details next week. Thank you so much!

Sincerely,

Daksha

中　譯

致：Saachi Jayaraman
來自：Daksha Nayar
日期：5月5日
主旨：新聞稿
親愛的Saachi，
這裡是範本，是我希望在新聞稿裡說的。對於印度籍的讀者來說是否合適呢？如果您認為在送到報社前應該做些改變，請讓我知道。對於這個事業我很興奮！我知道您將是印度地區一位很棒的經理。我期待在幾個星期後與您見面，把店舖開立完成！下個星期我會把我的航班細節寄給您。非常謝謝您！

誠摯地，

Daksha

MUMBAI, India May 10th – U.S. based Blue Skink Jewelry, has announced it will be opening a small store in Mumbai to create and market its unique jewelry designs. The owner and creator of Blue Skink Jewelry is originally from India and wanted to expand her business to her homeland. Designs created in India will blend traditional Indian design with a contemporary style. Stones used in production will come from locations in India. The store is expected to be in operation in early June, with a grand opening scheduled for June 30th.

孟買，印度，5月10日──以美國為基地的Blue Skink珠寶公司已經宣布將在孟買開設小型店舖，以創造並行銷其獨特的珠寶設計。Blue Skink珠寶公司的所有人暨創始人來自印度，想要擴展她的事業回故鄉。在印度創造的設計將融合傳統印度設計以及當代風格。製作使用的寶石將來自印度各地。其店舖預計在六月初開始營業，盛大開幕式則預計在6月30日。

186. Why is Blue Skink Jewelry opening a location in India? **
(A) It is cheap to make the jewelry in India.
(B) The owner is from India and wants to market her jewelry there.
(C) Saachi likes the jewelry so much, so she wanted it to come to India.
(D) The store will open in early June.

中　譯

為什麼Blue Skink珠寶公司要在印度設點？
(A) 在印度製作珠寶很便宜。
(B) 所有人來自印度，並想要在那裡行銷她的珠寶。
(C) Saachi非常喜歡該珠寶，因此想要它到印度來。
(D) 店舖將在六月初開幕。

解答提示

這一題必須從新聞稿中找到答案，雖然選項 (D) 在新聞稿中也有提到，但是並非本題的答案，答案應該是 (B) 選項才對。

187. What will the jewelry made in India look like? ***
(A) It will be made with stones from America.

(B) It will look like American jewelry.

(C) It will have a mix of traditional Indian and contemporary designs.

(D) It will be shaped like its namesake, the blue skink.

中 譯

在印度製作的珠寶會是什麼樣子？

(A) 將使用來自美國的寶石製作。

(B) 看起來像美國的珠寶。

(C) 將會混合傳統印度設計和當代設計。

(D) 形狀會和珠寶公司的名字一樣，像隻藍色蜥蜴。

解答提示

這一題一樣要在新聞稿中找出答案：Designs created in India will blend traditional Indian design with a contemporary style.。mix和blend是同義字，所以答案選 (C) 就沒錯了！

188. Who will help Saachi set up the store in India? ****

　　(A) Daksha will fly there to set up the store in a few weeks.

　　(B) Saachi has found several of her Indian relatives to help her.

　　(C) It will be difficult to get it set up in time.

　　(D) Daksha is looking for people to help her.

中 譯

誰將幫助Saachi設立印度的店舖？

(A) Daksha將在幾個星期後飛到那裡開設店舖。

(B) Saachi已經找到幾個印度親戚來幫忙她。

(C) 及時設立店舖將會很困難。

(D) Daksha正在找人幫忙她。

解答提示

這一題要從信件內容找答案：I look forward to seeing you in a couple of weeks to get the store set up!，可見Daksha要親自飛到印度，和Saachi一起把店舖設立完成，所以答案選 (A)。

189. How does Daksha plan to run the store in India when she lives in the U.S.? *****

(A) She will visit India every two weeks to make sure things are running smoothly.

(B) She has hired Sacchi to manage the store in India.

(C) She will email the store every day to let them know what to do.

(D) She doesn't have a plan for the India store, yet.

中　譯

當Daksha住在美國時，她計畫如何經營印度的店舖？
(A) 她將會每隔兩個星期造訪印度，以確認事情都很順利。
(B) 她已經聘請Sacchi來管理印度的店舖。
(C) 她將會每天email給店舖，讓他們知道該做什麼事。
(D) 她目前對於印度店舖還沒有計畫。

解答提示

這一題有點難度，必須讀完信件之後做出合理的推理。Daksha在信件中指出，Sacchi將會是優秀的經理，可見Daksha聘請Sacchi來替她管理店舖，所以應選 (B)。

190. Why does Daksha send this email? ****

(A) To let Saachi know her travel plans.

(B) To find out if the store is still on schedule for its June opening.

(C) To say that the press release has some errors in it.

(D) To ask Saachi to preview the press release before it goes to print.

中　譯

為什麼Daksha要寄這封email？
(A) 讓Saachi知道她的旅遊計畫。
(B) 要知道店舖是否照著時程在六月開幕。
(C) 說明新聞稿中有些錯誤。
(D) 要求Saachi在付印之前預視新聞稿內容。

解答提示

這一題在信件的一開始，Daksha就指出來了。雖然選項 (A) 和 (B) 都和整個信件的內容有關，但是都不是這封信最主要的目的。英文書信一開始一定會把開門見山把目的明顯寫出來，所以這一類的問題只要在最開頭尋找答案就沒錯囉，答案應該是 (D)！

Questions 191 through 195 refer to the following letter and survey:

May 23rd, 2013

Dear Mr. Vans,

Our records show that you were treated recently at Two Waters Hospital. We would appreciate it if you would take a few minutes of your time to fill out the attached survey. Your feedback and the feedback of other customers helps us improve our medical services and our personal service.

Be assured that your privacy is of great importance to us. Your name and reason for hospitalization are completely confidential. All comments are anonymous. We thank you for helping us offer the best service to our patients.

Sincerely,

Paul Jonas
Patient Satisfaction Coordinator
Two Waters Hospital

2013年5月23日

親愛的Vans先生,

我們的紀錄顯示,您最近在Two Waters醫院接受治療。如果您願意花幾分鐘填寫附上的問卷,我們會非常感謝。您的回饋和其他顧客的回饋可以幫助我們提升醫療服務以及個人服務。請放心您的隱私對我們來說非常重要,您的姓名與住院原因完全保密。所有的評論都是匿名的。我們感謝您幫助我們來提供病人最好的服務。

敬上,

Paul Jonas
病患滿意協調人
Two Waters醫院

Two Waters Hospital
Patient Satisfaction Survey

We would like to know what you think about your experience at our facility. Your responses are directly responsible for improving our services. All responses will be kept confidential and anonymous. Thank you for your time.

Age: 51   **Race/Ethnicity:** ___Asian
___Pacific Islander
Sex: ___Black/African American
M X ___American Indian/Alaska Native
F ___ X White (not Hispanic or Latino)
___Hispanic or Latino

	Excellent	Good	Average	Poor
Waiting:				
Wait time to register	X			
Wait time to be admitted		X		
Time it took for Dr. to see you		X		
Physicians:				
Listens to you	X			
Takes enough time with you		X		
Explains things clearly	X			
Provides appropriate treatment	X			
Nurses and Medical Assistants:				
Friendly and helpful			X	
Answer your questions		X		
Facility:				
Ease of finding your way around		X		
Neat and clean	X			
Allows for privacy	X			

Did you have any negative experiences during this stay?

There was an issue with the bathroom needing cleaning. I told a nurse and no one came to clean it until the next morning. I don't know if the nurse forgot to tell someone about it, or not.

What do you like best about our hospital?

The doctor let me ask as many questions as I wanted and explained things a couple of times, if I needed more explanation.

Are there any improvements you would suggest?

Make sure that nurses pass along patients' requests to the correct people. And have better follow up.

THANK YOU FOR COMPLETING OUR SURVEY!

Two Waters醫院
病患滿意度調查

我們想要知道您在敝醫院就醫經驗的想法，您的回覆是我們提供服務的直接原因。所有的回覆都將保密且匿名。感謝您的時間。

年齡：51　　　　　　　　種族：_____亞洲人
性別：男__X__　　　　　　　　　_____太平洋島國人
　　　女_____　　　　　　　　　_____黑人／非裔美國人
　　　　　　　　　　　　　　　　_____印地安人／阿拉斯加原民
　　　　　　　　　　　　　__X__白種人（非拉丁民族）
　　　　　　　　　　　　　　　　_____拉丁民族

	極佳	好	普通	不佳
候診：				
等待時間掛號	X			
等待時間看診		X		
看診的時間		X		
醫師：				
傾聽您的敘述	X			

看診時間足夠		X		
清楚解釋	X			
提供合適的治療	X			
護士及醫療助理人員：				
友善且有幫助			X	
回答您的提問		X		
設備：				
容易找到方向指引		X		
整齊清潔	X			
保有隱私感	X			

在留院期間，您是否有任何負面的經驗？
有件事是關於廁所需要清潔。我告訴一位護士，直到隔天早上都沒有人來清潔。我不知道那位護士是不是忘了告訴相關人員。

關於我們的醫院，您最喜歡什麼部分？
醫生讓我盡情地問許多問題，而且如果我需要更多解釋，他會解釋事情好幾次。

有建議任何我們能進步的地方嗎？
請確保護士能把病患的要求傳達給正確的人，並且要跟進。

感謝您完成問卷！

191. Why did Mr. Vans receive this survey? **
    (A) He asked if he could assess the hospital.
    (B) He was recently treated at the hospital.
    (C) Mr. Vans had some complaints about the hospital staff.
    (D) Two Rivers sends annual surveys to the community.

 中　譯

為什麼Vans先生收到這份問卷？
(A) 他問說他是否可以評估這家醫院。
(B) 他最近在這家醫院接受治療。
(C) Vans先生對醫院員工有一些抱怨。
(D) Two Rivers醫院每年會寄這份問卷給社區成員。

解答提示

信件的一開始即說明：Our records show that you were treated recently at Two Waters Hospital.，也是因為這樣他才會收到問卷，所以選 (B)。

192. What race is Mr. Vans? *
  (A) White.
  (B) Asian.
  (C) He didn't say.
  (D) American.

中　譯

Vans先生的種族是什麼？
(A) 白種人。
(B) 亞洲人。
(C) 他沒有說。
(D) 美國人。

解答提示

這一題直接看問卷就可以知道答案是 (A)。

193. What was the only thing Mr. Vans marked down to "average" on his survey? ***
  (A) The food service.
  (B) The comfort level of his bed.
  (C) The time the Dr. spent with him.
  (D) The nurses being friendly and helpful.

中　譯

Vans先生在問卷唯一評分「普通」的是什麼？
(A) 飲食服務。
(B) 病床的舒適度。
(C) 醫生的看診時間。
(D) 護士的友善和有助程度。

解答提示

這一題也是可以直接從問卷中作答，答案是 (D)。

194. What does Mr. Vans like best about the hospital? ***
  (A) The ease of finding where he needs to go.
  (B) That the doctor explained things thoroughly.
  (C) The look of the hospital from the street.
  (D) That he was admitted quickly.

中　譯

Vans先生最喜歡這家醫院什麼部分？
(A) 他很容易可以找到方向指引。
(B) 醫生仔細地解釋。
(C) 醫院從街道上看起來的樣子。
(D) 他很快地就可以看診。

解答提示

這一題從問卷後的問題可以找到，Vans先生很滿意醫生的解釋態度，所以選 (B)。

195. What was a complaint Mr. Vans had? *****
  (A) The food was tasteless.
  (B) His wife could not stay after visiting hours were over.
  (C) There was no response to the request he made to one of the
     nurses.
  (D) He still felt sick after leaving the hospital.

中　譯

Vans先生的抱怨是什麼？
(A) 食物沒有味道。
(B) 在探視病人時間結束後，他的妻子無法過夜。
(C) 他對護士提出的要求沒有得到回應。
(D) 在出院後他仍然感到不舒服。

解答提示

從問卷後的問題可以知道，Vans先生對於護士的回應不是很滿意，故選 (C)。

Questions 196 through 200 refer to the following letter and order form:

Dear Valued Customer,

Your order # 2363654 has been received and will be processed soon. If you experience any problems or have questions, please call our customer support at 501-444-2230. Thanks!

Please note: This confirmation is not a guarantee that all items will be available for shipping. You will receive an email after your order has shipped that will include an invoice for shipped items. Please note that your account will not be charged until your order is packed and ready to leave our warehouse.

Regards,
Whole Foods Inc.

親愛的重要顧客：

您的訂單編號# 2363654已經收到，我們將盡快處理。如果您遇到任何問題或有任何疑問，請撥打我們的顧客支持專線501-444-2230。謝謝！

請注意：此確認信並非保證所有訂購品項皆有貨可以配送。在您的訂單配送後，您將收到email，內有配送品項的商業發票。請注意您的帳戶不會被索取費用，一直到您的訂單包裝完成，並準備離開倉庫。

向您致意，
Whole Foods公司

Order Number: 2363654
Ships by: Truck Route B2 - Leaves 07/23/13

Sold To:
Garden Market
333 6th Ave E

Springdale OR 90000

Ship To:
Garden Market
333 6th Ave E
Springdale OR 90000
Phone: 501-276-7676

Billing: Invoice upon Shipping

Items

Code	Product Name	Size	Qty	Price	Total
PA302	Lasagna, Whole Wheat	12 x 12 ozs	5	$31.60	$158.00
PA269	Spaghetti, Whole Wheat	12 x 16 ozs	5	$26.80	$134.00
SE021	Bulk Poppy Seeds	5 lbs.	1	$12.50	$12.50
BP079	Organic Cornstarch	6 x 6 ozs.	3	$14.60	$43.80
DF132	Cranberries, Dried	1 lb.	10	$5.35	$53.50
GY426	Green Chiles, Diced	24 x 4 ozs.	1	$19.50	$19.50
DP042	Yogurt, Plain Nonfat, Organ	16 ozs.	10	$1.75	$17.50
QP063	Fresh Produce Celery, Organ	1 Bunch	10	$2.50	$25.00

Sub Total: $463.80

Estimated Total: $463.80

中　譯

訂單號碼：2363654
配送資料：卡車路線B2 - 2013年7月23日配送

買家地址：
Garden Market
90000奧勒崗州斯普林戴爾市東區第六大道333號

配送地址：
Garden Market
90000奧勒崗州斯普林戴爾市東區第六大道333號
電話：501-276-7676

付款方式：配送時付款開立商業發票

品項

貨號	產品名稱	尺寸	數量	單價	總價
PA302	千層麵，全麥	12 x 12盎司	5	$31.60	$158.00
PA269	義大利麵，全麥	12 x 16盎司	5	$26.80	$134.00
SE021	罌粟籽	5磅	1	$12.50	$12.50
BP079	有機玉米澱粉	6 x 6盎司	3	$14.60	$43.80
DF132	小紅莓，乾燥	1 lb.	10	$5.35	$53.50
GY426	綠辣椒，乾燥	24 x 4盎司	1	$19.50	$19.50
DP042	有機原味脫脂優格	16盎司	10	$1.75	$17.50
QP063	有機新鮮生蔬 - 芹菜	1束	10	$2.50	$25.00
小計: $463.80					
預估總價: $463.80					

196. Why was this letter sent? ***

(A) To let Garden Market know that Whole Foods has received its order.

(B) To let Garden Market know that some products were not available for shipping.

(C) To announce the monthly sale prices.

(D) The newsletter is sent once a month.

中　譯

這封信為什麼寄發？
(A) 讓Garden Market公司知道Whole Foods公司已經收到訂單。
(B) 讓Garden Market公司知道有些產品缺貨無法配送。
(C) 公告每個月的銷售價格。
(D) 這則通訊報每個月發送一次。

解答提示

從信件的第一段就可以知道，這是一封訂單的確認信，所以答案選 (A)。

197. How is this order being billed? ***

(A) The credit card was charged when the order was placed.

(B) Garden Market will received an invoice to be paid at a later date.

(C) The delivery driver should receive Cash On Delivery.

(D) The order will be free because of credits from last month's order.

中　譯

這筆訂單將如何付款？

(A) 下訂單時，已經用信用卡付款。

(B) Garden Market公司將收到商業發票，稍後付款。

(C) 運送司機應該在遞送時收取現金。

(D) 此訂單免費，因為上個月訂單累積的點數。

解答提示

注意信件的第二段：Please note that your account will not be charged until your order is packed and ready to leave our warehouse. ，意思即是稍後付款即可，所以選 (B)。

198. Why is the total listed as an Estimated Total? *****

(A) The office worker may have incorrectly added the total.

(B) Garden Market might decide to add some things to its order.

(C) The total may change if some items are not available when the order is shipped.

(D) The date is wrong on the order.

中　譯

為什麼總價被標作「預估總價」？

(A) 辦公室人員可能錯誤地加總。

(B) Garden Market公司可能決定增加部分商品到訂單中。

(C) 總價可能變動，如果某些品項在訂單裝送時缺貨。

(D) 訂單中的日期錯誤。

解答提示

內容的第二段註明 "This confirmation is not a guarantee that all items will be available for shipping." ，可見並不一定所有訂購的商品都會有貨，所以目前的總價只是預估而已，所以選 (C)。

199. According to the order form, how many types of pasta did the market order? ***
(A) They did not order pasta this month.
(B) Two—lasagna and spaghetti.
(C) They ordered organic pasta.
(D) The pasta will be back-ordered.

中　譯

根據訂購單，這家公司訂購了幾種義大利麵食？
(A) 他們這個月沒有訂購義大利麵食。
(B) 兩種──千層麵和義大利麵。
(C) 他們訂購了有機義大利麵食。
(D) 義大利麵食將是未交貨訂單。

解答提示

從訂購清單就可以知道答案，只不過義大利麵食的字彙常常讓人搞不清楚，pasta是義大利麵食的泛稱，而lasagna則是千層麵，spaghetti是一般常見的義大利麵，所以選 (B)。

200. When can Garden market expect delivery? ***
(A) They plan to pick up the order in person.
(B) Anytime during the month of July.
(C) On July 23rd.
(D) Sometime after the July 23rd shipment date.

中　譯

Garden Market公司什麼時候可以預計收到？
(A) 他們計畫親自去取貨。
(B) 7月的任何時間。
(C) 在7月23日。
(D) 在7月23日配送日之後。

解答提示

這一題很明顯唷，既然配送日是7月23日，那當然是在配送日之後才會收到囉！所以正確答案是 (D)。

附錄一　動詞時態表格

	現在	過去	未來
簡單	{am/is/are {V-es	V-ed	<u>will/be going to</u> + VR
進行	<u>am/is/are</u> + V-ing	<u>was/were</u> + V-ing	will be + V-ing
完成	<u>have/has</u> + p.p.	had + p.p.	will have + p.p.
完成進行	<u>have/has</u> + been + V-ing	had + been + V-ing	will have + been + V-ing

* 關於常見的動詞，在附錄二有動詞三態及中文意。

附錄二 實用動詞三態表

原形	過去式	過去分詞	中文意
A			
abandon	abandoned	abandoned	拋棄；遺棄
abbreviate	abbreviated	abbreviated	縮寫；簡寫
abide	abode	abode	忍受；容忍
abolish	abolished	abolished	廢除；廢止
abound	abounded	abounded	大量存在
absorb	absorbed	absorbed	吸收
abuse	abused	abused	濫用；虐待
accelerate	accelerated	accelerated	加速；增快；加快
accept	accepted	accepted	接受
access	accessed	accessed	接近；進入
accommodate	accommodated	accommodated	通融；給…方便；提供住宿
accompany	accompanied	accompanied	陪伴
accomplish	accomplished	accomplished	完成
accord	accorded	accorded	與…一致
account	accounted	accounted	解釋；說明
accumulate	accumulated	accumulated	累積
accuse	accused	accused	控告
accustom	accustomed	accustomed	使適應
ache	ached	ached	疼痛
acknowledge	acknowledged	acknowledged	承認
acquaint	acquainted	acquainted	使認識
acquire	acquired	acquired	得到；取得
act	acted	acted	演戲；行動
add	added	added	增加；加入

addict	addicted	addicted	上癮
address	addressed	addressed	稱呼；處理
adhere	adhered	adhered	堅持；堅守
adjust	adjusted	adjusted	調整；改變...以適應
administer	administered	administered	管理；掌管
admire	admired	admired	崇拜；敬愛
admit	admitted	admitted	承認
adopt	adopted	adopted	領養
adore	adored	adored	喜愛
advance	advanced	advanced	前進
advertise	advertised	advertised	做廣告
advise	advised	advised	建議
advocate	advocated	advocated	提倡；主張
affect	affected	affected	影響
affirm	affirmed	affirmed	堅稱；證實
afford	afforded	afforded	買得起
age	aged	aged	變老
agree	agreed	agreed	同意
aid	aided	aided	幫助
aim	aimed	aimed	以...為目標
alarm	alarmed	alarmed	使驚慌不安
alert	alerted	alerted	提醒
alienate	alienated	alienated	使疏離
alleviate	alleviated	alleviated	減輕；減緩
allocate	allocated	allocated	分派；分配
allow	allowed	allowed	允許
alter	altered	altered	改變
alternate	alternated	alternated	替換

amaze	amazed	amazed	使驚訝
ambush	ambushed	ambushed	埋伏
amount	amounted	amounted	合計；共計
amplify	amplified	amplified	放大
amuse	amused	amused	娛樂
analyze	analyzed	analyzed	分析
anchor	anchored	anchored	下錨
animate	animated	animated	使具有生氣
announce	announced	announced	宣布
annoy	annoyed	annoyed	惹惱
answer	answered	answered	回答
anticipate	anticipated	anticipated	預期；預測
apologize	apologized	apologized	道歉
appeal	appealed	appealed	上訴
appear	appeared	appeared	出現
applaud	applauded	applauded	鼓掌；贊成
apply	applied	applied	申請
appoint	appointed	appointed	指派
appreciate	appreciated	appreciated	感謝
approach	approached	approached	接近
approve	approved	approved	同意
argue	argued	argued	爭論
arise	arose	arisen	昇起；起床
arm	armed	armed	配備武裝
armor	armored	armored	配備裝甲
arouse	aroused	aroused	喚起
arrange	arranged	arranged	安排
arrest	arrested	arrested	逮捕
arrive	arrived	arrived	抵達

articulate	articulated	articulated	清晰地發音
ascend	ascended	ascended	登高；上升
ask	asked	asked	詢問
assassinate	assassinated	assassinated	暗殺
assault	assaulted	assaulted	攻擊
assemble	assembled	assembled	集合
assert	asserted	asserted	斷言；聲稱
assess	assessed	assessed	評估
assign	assigned	assigned	分配；指派
assist	assisted	assisted	協助；幫助
associate	associated	associated	聯想
assume	assumed	assumed	假設；假定
assure	assured	assured	保證；確保
astonish	astonished	astonished	使驚訝
attach	attached	attached	附屬
attack	attacked	attacked	攻擊
attain	attained	attained	達到；獲得
attempt	attempted	attempted	嘗試
attend	attended	attended	參加；出席
attract	attracted	attracted	吸引
auction	auctioned	auctioned	拍賣
authorize	authorized	authorized	授權給；批准；允許
autograph	autographed	autographed	簽名
avoid	avoided	avoided	避免
await	awaited	awaited	等待
awake	awoke	awaken	叫醒
award	awarded	awarded	頒獎
awe	awed	awed	使驚訝

B			
back	backed	backed	支持
bake	baked	baked	烤
balance	balanced	balanced	平衡
ban	banned	banned	禁止
bandage	bandaged	bandaged	上繃帶
bang	banged	banged	砰砰作響
bankrupt	bankrupted	bankrupted	破產
bar	barred	barred	禁止
barbecue	barbecued	barbecued	烤肉
bargain	bargained	bargained	協議
bark	barked	barked	吠叫
base	based	based	以...為基礎
bathe	bathed	bathed	沐浴
batter	battered	battered	打；擊
battle	battled	battled	作戰
be	was/were	been	be動詞
bear	bore	born	生產
bear	bore	borne	忍受；承受
beat	beat	beaten	打
beautify	beautified	beautified	美化
beckon	beckoned	beckoned	招手示意
become	became	become	變成
beg	begged	begged	乞求
begin	began	begun	開始
behave	behaved	behaved	行為舉止
believe	believed	believed	相信
belong	belonged	belonged	屬於
bend	bent	bent	彎腰

benefit	benefited	benefited	得利；獲利
besiege	besieged	besieged	圍攻
bet	bet	bet	打賭
betray	betrayed	betrayed	背叛
bias	biased	biased	有偏見
bid	bad	bidden	出價
bind	bound	bound	捆綁
bite	bit	bitten	咬
blame	blamed	blamed	責怪
blast	blasted	blasted	爆炸
blaze	blazed	blazed	燃燒
bleach	bleached	bleached	漂白
bleed	bled	bled	流血
blend	blended	blended	混合
bless	blessed	blessed	祝福
blind	blinded	blinded	使眼盲
blink	blinked	blinked	眨眼
block	blocked	blocked	阻擋
bloom	bloomed	bloomed	開花
blot	blotted	blotted	弄髒
blow	blew	blown	吹
blunder	blundered	blundered	犯錯
blur	blurred	blurred	使模糊
blush	blushed	blushed	臉紅
boast	boasted	boasted	吹噓
boil	boiled	boiled	煮
bomb	bombed	bombed	炮擊
bombard	bombarded	bombarded	轟炸
boom	boomed	boomed	發出隆隆聲

boost	boosted	boosted	支持
border	bordered	bordered	與...為鄰
bore	bored	bored	使厭倦
borrow	borrowed	borrowed	借入
bother	bothered	bothered	打擾
bounce	bounced	bounced	跳
bound	bounded	bounded	跳躍
bow	bowed	bowed	鞠躬
boycott	boycotted	boycotted	杯葛
brace	braced	braced	支撐；加固
braid	braided	braided	綁辮子
brake	braked	braked	踩煞車
branch	branched	branched	分支；分歧
brand	branded	branded	烙印
break	broke	broken	打破
breathe	breathed	breathed	呼吸
breed	bred	bred	生產
brew	brewed	brewed	釀酒
bribe	bribed	bribed	賄賂
bring	brought	brought	帶來
broadcast	broadcast	broadcast	廣播
broaden	broadened	broadened	使變寬；加寬
broil	broiled	broiled	烤
brood	brooded	brooded	孵蛋
browse	browsed	browsed	瀏覽
bruise	bruised	bruised	淤血
brush	brushed	brushed	刷洗
buckle	buckled	buckled	扣住
bug	bugged	bugged	煩擾

build	built	built	建立
bulge	bulged	bulged	膨漲
bully	bullied	bullied	欺負
bump	bumped	bumped	衝撞
burden	burdened	burdened	負擔
burn	burned	burned	燃燒
burst	burst	burst	爆炸
bury	buried	buried	埋葬
buy	bought	bought	買
C			
calculate	calculated	calculated	計算；估計
call	called	called	喊叫；打電話
calm	calmed	calmed	平靜；鎮定
camp	camped	camped	露營
campaign	campaigned	campaigned	參加競選
cancel	canceled	canceled	取消
capture	captured	captured	捕獲；俘虜
care	cared	cared	在乎；關心
caress	caressed	caressed	輕撫
carry	carried	carried	帶著
carve	carved	carved	雕刻
cast	cast	cast	投擲
catch	caught	caught	抓到；捕捉
cater	catered	catered	提供飲食
cause	caused	caused	造成
caution	cautioned	cautioned	警告
cease	ceased	ceased	停止
celebrate	celebrated	celebrated	慶祝
cement	cemented	cemented	加強；鞏固

center	centered	centered	以...為中心
certificate	certificated	certificated	認證
certify	certified	certified	確認
chain	chained	chained	用鍊子鍊住
challenge	challenged	challenged	挑戰
chance	chanced	chanced	碰巧
change	changed	changed	改變
channel	channeled	channeled	輸送；傳送
chant	chanted	chanted	歌頌
characterize	characterized	characterized	以...為特色
charge	charged	charged	索費；控告
charm	charmed	charmed	吸引
chase	chased	chased	追趕；追逐
chat	chatted	chatted	聊天
chatter	chattered	chattered	嘮叨
cheat	cheated	cheated	作弊
check	checked	checked	檢查
cheer	cheered	cheered	歡呼
cherish	cherished	cherished	珍惜
chew	chewed	chewed	咀嚼
chill	chilled	chilled	變冷
chirp	chirped	chirped	啾啾叫（鳥）
choke	choked	choked	窒息
choose	chose	chosen	選擇
chop	chopped	chopped	砍
chuckle	chuckled	chuckled	咯咯地笑
circle	circled	circled	環繞
circulate	circulated	circulated	循環
cite	cited	cited	引用

civilize	civilized	civilized	使文明化
claim	claimed	claimed	宣稱
clamp	clamped	clamped	鋏住；鎮壓
clap	clapped	clapped	拍手鼓掌
clarify	clarified	clarified	澄清；闡明
clash	clashed	clashed	發生衝突
clasp	clasped	clasped	緊抱；緊握
classify	classified	classified	分類
clean	cleaned	cleaned	清理
cleanse	cleansed	cleansed	清洗
clear	cleared	cleared	清除
clench	clenched	clenched	緊抓
click	clicked	clicked	發出咔嗒聲
climb	climbed	climbed	爬
cling	clung	clung	黏住；緊握
clip	clipped	clipped	夾住
clone	cloned	cloned	複製
close	closed	closed	關上
clothe	clothed	clothed	使穿衣
club	clubbed	clubbed	用棍棒打
cluster	clustered	clustered	聚集
coach	coached	coached	當教練
cocoon	cocooned	cocooned	緊緊包住
coil	coiled	coiled	盤繞
coin	coined	coined	鑄造
coincide	coincided	coincided	同時發生
collapse	collapsed	collapsed	倒塌
collect	collected	collected	收集
collide	collided	collided	碰撞

color	colored	colored	上色；著色
comb	combed	combed	梳（髮）
combat	combated	combated	戰鬥
combine	combined	combined	合併
come	came	come	來
comfort	comforted	comforted	安慰；安撫
command	commanded	commanded	命令
commemorate	commemorated	commemorated	慶祝；紀念
commence	commenced	commenced	開始
comment	commented	commented	評論
commission	commissioned	commissioned	委任；委託
commit	committed	committed	犯罪；做錯
communicate	communicated	communicated	溝通
commute	commuted	commuted	通勤
compare	compared	compared	比較
compel	compelled	compelled	強迫
compensate	compensated	compensated	補償；賠償
compete	competed	competed	競爭
compile	compiled	compiled	匯編
complain	complained	complained	抱怨
complement	complemented	complemented	補充；補足
complete	completed	completed	完成
complicate	complicated	complicated	使複雜
compliment	complimented	complimented	讚美
compose	composed	composed	創作
compound	compounded	compounded	增加；加重
comprehend	comprehended	comprehended	了解
comprise	comprised	comprised	組成
compromise	compromised	compromised	妥協；和解

compute	computed	computed	計算
computerize	computerized	computerized	使電腦化
conceal	concealed	concealed	隱藏
concede	conceded	conceded	讓步
conceive	conceived	conceived	設想；想出
concentrate	concentrated	concentrated	集中
concern	concerned	concerned	關係到；擔心
conclude	concluded	concluded	總結
condemn	condemned	condemned	責備；責難
condense	condensed	condensed	壓縮；濃縮
conduct	conducted	conducted	引導；實施
confer	conferred	conferred	授予；給予
confess	confessed	confessed	告解；坦白
confine	confined	confined	限制
confirm	confirmed	confirmed	確認；確定
conflict	conflicted	conflicted	衝突
conform	conformed	conformed	遵守
confront	confronted	confronted	面臨；遭遇
confuse	confused	confused	使困惑
congratulate	congratulated	congratulated	恭喜
connect	connected	connected	連結；有關係
conquer	conquered	conquered	征服
consent	consented	consented	同意
conserve	conserved	conserved	保存
consider	considered	considered	考慮；考量
consign	consigned	consigned	把...委託給；託運
consist	consisted	consisted	組成
console	consoled	consoled	安慰；安撫

constitute	constituted	constituted	組成
construct	constructed	constructed	建造
consult	consulted	consulted	咨詢
consume	consumed	consumed	消費；消耗
contact	contacted	contacted	接觸；連絡
contain	contained	contained	包含；包括
contaminate	contaminated	contaminated	汙染
contemplate	contemplated	contemplated	考慮；深思
contend	contended	contended	競爭
contest	contested	contested	競賽
continue	continued	continued	繼續
contract	contracted	contracted	簽約
contradict	contradicted	contradicted	與...矛盾
contrast	contrasted	contrasted	使對比
contribute	contributed	contributed	貢獻；捐款
control	controlled	controlled	控制
converse	conversed	conversed	談話
convert	converted	converted	轉換；轉變
convey	conveyed	conveyed	傳達；傳送
convict	convicted	convicted	判有罪
convince	convinced	convinced	說服
cook	cooked	cooked	煮；料理
cool	cooled	cooled	使變涼
cooperate	cooperated	cooperated	合作
coordinate	coordinated	coordinated	協調
cope	coped	coped	處理；應付
copy	copied	copied	拷貝
correct	corrected	corrected	改錯；更正
correspond	corresponded	corresponded	符合；一致

corrupt	corrupted	corrupted	使敗壞；使貪腐
cost	cost	cost	花費
cough	coughed	coughed	咳嗽
counsel	counseled	counseled	提議；勸告
count	counted	counted	計算
court	courted	courted	追求
cover	covered	covered	覆蓋
covet	coveted	coveted	貪圖；渴望
crack	cracked	cracked	使爆裂
cradle	cradled	cradled	撫育
cram	crammed	crammed	塞進；塞滿
cramp	cramped	cramped	夾緊；控制
crash	crashed	crashed	碰撞；墜下
crawl	crawled	crawled	爬
creak	creaked	creaked	發出咯吱聲
create	created	created	創造
credit	credited	credited	相信；稱讚
creep	crept	crept	爬行
cripple	crippled	crippled	使殘廢
criticize	criticized	criticized	批評
crop	cropped	cropped	播種
cross	crossed	crossed	穿越；越過
crouch	crouched	crouched	蹲伏
crowd	crowded	crowded	擠滿
crown	crowned	crowned	為...加冕
cruise	cruised	cruised	巡航
crumble	crumbled	crumbled	粉碎；破碎
crunch	crunched	crunched	嘎吱地咬
crush	crushed	crushed	壓碎

343

cry	cried	cried	哭泣
cue	cued	cued	暗示
cultivate	cultivated	cultivated	耕作；種植
curb	curbed	curbed	控制
cure	cured	cured	治療
curl	curled	curled	使捲曲
curse	cursed	cursed	咀咒
cushion	cushioned	cushioned	緩和衝擊
cut	cut	cut	剪；切；割；砍
cycle	cycled	cycled	循環
D			
damage	damaged	damaged	破壞
damn	damned	damned	咒罵
damp	damped	damped	使潮溼
dance	danced	danced	跳舞
dare	dared	dared	膽敢
dart	darted	darted	猛衝；狂奔
dash	dashed	dashed	破滅；粉碎
date	dated	dated	約會
dazzle	dazzled	dazzled	使眼花；使目眩
deafen	deafened	deafened	使聽不見
deal	dealt	dealt	處理；應付
debate	debated	debated	爭論
decay	decayed	decayed	腐爛；腐壞
deceive	deceived	deceived	欺騙
decide	decided	decided	決定
declare	declared	declared	宣布
decline	declined	declined	拒絕
decorate	decorated	decorated	裝飾

decrease	decreased	decreased	減少
dedicate	dedicated	dedicated	以...奉獻
deem	deemed	deemed	認為
deepen	deepened	deepened	使變深
defeat	defeated	defeated	擊敗
defect	defected	defected	變節
defend	defended	defended	防衛；保護
define	defined	defined	定義
degrade	degraded	degraded	使降級
delay	delayed	delayed	延誤
delegate	delegated	delegated	委派...為代表
delight	delighted	delighted	使高興
deliver	delivered	delivered	投遞；傳送
demand	demanded	demanded	要求
demonstrate	demonstrated	demonstrated	展示
denounce	denounced	denounced	指責
deny	denied	denied	否認
depart	departed	departed	離開；出發
depend	depended	depended	依賴；依靠
depict	depicted	depicted	描繪；描寫
deposit	deposited	deposited	放下；存錢
depress	depressed	depressed	使憂鬱
deprive	deprived	deprived	奪去；剝奪
derive	derived	derived	取得；得到
descend	descended	descended	下來；下降
describe	described	described	描述
deserve	deserved	deserved	值得
design	designed	designed	設計
designate	designated	designated	指定；指派

desire	desired	desired	想要
despair	despaired	despaired	絕望；失去信心
despise	despised	despised	輕視；看不起
destroy	destroyed	destroyed	摧毀
detach	detached	detached	分開；分離
detain	detained	detained	留住；扣留
detect	detected	detected	發現；查覺
deter	deterred	deterred	使斷念
deteriorate	deteriorated	deteriorated	惡化
determine	determined	determined	決定
devalue	devalued	devalued	降低價值
develop	developed	developed	發展
devise	devised	devised	設計；發明
devote	devoted	devoted	將...奉獻
devour	devoured	devoured	狼吞虎嚥地吃
diagnose	diagnosed	diagnosed	診斷
dial	dialed	dialed	播（電話）
dictate	dictated	dictated	口述；要求；指定
die	died	died	死亡
differ	differed	differed	不同；有差異
differentiate	differentiated	differentiated	使有差異
dig	dug	dug	挖
digest	digested	digested	消化；領悟；做...的摘要
diminish	diminished	diminished	減少；變小
dine	dined	dined	吃晚餐
dip	dipped	dipped	浸泡
direct	directed	directed	指揮；管理；主持
disable	disabled	disabled	使失去能力

disadvantage	disadvantaged	disadvantaged	使處於不利地位
disagree	disagreed	disagreed	不同意
disappear	disappeared	disappeared	消失
disappoint	disappointed	disappointed	使失望
disapprove	disapproved	disapproved	不同意
discard	discarded	discarded	丟棄
discharge	discharged	discharged	排出；允許...離開
discipline	disciplined	disciplined	訓練
disclose	disclosed	disclosed	揭發；洩露
disconnect	disconnected	disconnected	使失去連絡
discount	discounted	discounted	折扣
discourage	discouraged	discouraged	使洩氣
discover	discovered	discovered	發現
discriminate	discriminated	discriminated	區別；分別；歧視
discuss	discussed	discussed	討論
disgrace	disgraced	disgraced	使丟臉
disguise	disguised	disguised	偽裝
disgust	disgusted	disgusted	使作嘔；使厭惡
dislike	disliked	disliked	不喜歡
dismantle	dismantled	dismantled	拆開；解體
dismay	dismayed	dismayed	使氣餒；使喪氣
dismiss	dismissed	dismissed	解散；讓...離開
dispatch	dispatched	dispatched	派遣
dispense	dispensed	dispensed	分配；分發
disperse	dispersed	dispersed	驅散；解散
displace	displaced	displaced	取代；迫使離開
display	displayed	displayed	陳列；展出
displease	displeased	displeased	使不高興
dispose	disposed	disposed	配置；佈置

NEW TOEIC 黃金戰鬥力──閱讀篇

dispute	disputed	disputed	爭論；爭執
disregard	disregarded	disregarded	不理會；不顧
dissolve	dissolved	dissolved	分解；溶解
dissuade	dissuaded	dissuaded	勸阻
distinguish	distinguished	distinguished	區別；識別
distort	distorted	distorted	扭曲；曲解
distract	distracted	distracted	轉移；分散
distress	distressed	distressed	使悲痛；使傷心
distribute	distributed	distributed	分發；分配
distrust	distrusted	distrusted	不信任；懷疑
disturb	disturbed	disturbed	妨礙；打擾
dive	dived	dived	跳水；潛水
diversify	diversified	diversified	使多樣化；多角經營
divert	diverted	diverted	使轉向；使分心
divide	divided	divided	劃分；分裂
divorce	divorced	divorced	離婚
do	did	done	做
dock	docked	docked	使靠碼頭
document	documented	documented	用文件證明
dodge	dodged	dodged	閃躲；躲開
dominate	dominated	dominated	支配；統治
donate	donated	donated	捐獻；捐贈
doom	doomed	doomed	注定；命定
dot	dotted	dotted	在...上打點
double	doubled	doubled	加倍
doubt	doubted	doubted	懷疑；不相信
download	downloaded	downloaded	下載
doze	dozed	dozed	打瞌睡；打盹

draft	drafted	drafted	起草；設計
drag	dragged	dragged	拖拉；拖著行進
drain	drained	drained	排出；使流出
drape	draped	draped	覆蓋；垂掛
draw	drew	drawn	畫；拖；拉；取出
dread	dreaded	dreaded	害怕；擔心
dream	dreamed	dreamed	做夢；夢想
dress	dressed	dressed	穿衣；打扮
drift	drifted	drifted	漂流；漂泊
drill	drilled	drilled	鑽孔；訓練
drink	drank	drunk	飲；喝
drip	dripped	dripped	滴下；漏下
drive	drove	driven	開車；駕駛
drizzle	drizzled	drizzled	下毛毛雨
drop	dropped	dropped	滴下；丟下
drown	drowned	drowned	淹死；淹沒
dry	dried	dried	弄乾；變乾
duck	ducked	ducked	低下身子
dump	dumped	dumped	傾倒；拋棄
duplicate	duplicated	duplicated	複製
dwarf	dwarfed	dwarfed	使矮小
dwell	dwelled	dwelled	居住；生活
dye	dyed	dyed	染色
E			
earn	earned	earned	賺得；掙得
ease	eased	eased	減輕；緩和
eat	ate	eaten	吃
ebb	ebbed	ebbed	退潮
echo	echoed	echoed	發出回聲

eclipse	eclipsed	eclipsed	使失色；（日月）蝕
edit	edited	edited	編輯；校訂
educate	educated	educated	教育；訓練
effect	effected	effected	造成；完成
elaborate	elaborated	elaborated	詳細說明
elect	elected	elected	選舉；推選
elevate	elevated	elevated	舉起；抬起
eliminate	eliminated	eliminated	排除；消除
email	emailed	emailed	寄發電子郵件
embark	embarked	embarked	上船／飛機；著手
embarrass	embarrassed	embarrassed	使窘；使不好意思
embrace	embraced	embraced	擁抱；包括
emerge	emerged	emerged	浮現；出現
emigrate	emigrated	emigrated	移居國外
emphasize	emphasized	emphasized	強調；著重
employ	employed	employed	雇用；使用
empty	emptied	emptied	使成為空的；清空
enable	enabled	enabled	使能夠；賦予能力
enact	enacted	enacted	制定；頒布
enclose	enclosed	enclosed	圍住；圈起
encounter	encountered	encountered	遭遇；遇到
encourage	encouraged	encouraged	鼓勵；慫恿
end	ended	ended	結束；終止
endanger	endangered	endangered	危及；使受到危險
endeavor	endeavored	endeavored	努力；力圖

endure	endured	endured	忍受；忍耐
enforce	enforced	enforced	實施；執行
engage	engaged	engaged	吸引；佔用
enhance	enhanced	enhanced	提高；增加；提升
enjoy	enjoyed	enjoyed	享受；喜愛
enlarge	enlarged	enlarged	擴大；放大
enlighten	enlightened	enlightened	啟發；教育
enrich	enriched	enriched	使富裕；使豐富
enroll	enrolled	enrolled	登記；使進入
ensure	ensured	ensured	保證；擔保
enter	entered	entered	進入；加入
entertain	entertained	entertained	使歡樂；娛樂
entitle	entitled	entitled	給予權力資格
envy	envied	envied	妒忌；羨慕
equal	equaled	equaled	等於；比得上
equate	equated	equated	使相等
equip	equipped	equipped	裝備；配備
erase	erased	erased	擦掉；消除
erect	erected	erected	豎立；建立
erode	eroded	eroded	腐蝕；侵蝕
erupt	erupted	erupted	噴出；爆發
escalate	escalated	escalated	使逐步上升
escape	escaped	escaped	逃跑；逃脫
escort	escorted	escorted	護送；陪同
establish	established	established	建立
esteem	esteemed	esteemed	尊重；尊敬
estimate	estimated	estimated	估計；估量
evacuate	evacuated	evacuated	撤空；撤離

evaluate	evaluated	evaluated	評估
evolve	evolved	evolved	形成；發展
exaggerate	exaggerated	exaggerated	誇張；誇大
examine	examined	examined	檢查；審查
exceed	exceeded	exceeded	超過；勝過
excel	excelled	excelled	優於；勝過
exchange	exchanged	exchanged	交換；調換
excite	excited	excited	刺激；使興奮
exclaim	exclaimed	exclaimed	呼喊；驚叫
exclude	excluded	excluded	把…排除在外
excuse	excused	excused	原諒
execute	executed	executed	實施；執行
exercise	exercised	exercised	鍛煉；運動
exert	exerted	exerted	用力；運用
exhaust	exhausted	exhausted	用完；耗盡
exhibit	exhibited	exhibited	展示；陳列
exile	exiled	exiled	流放；放逐
exist	existed	existed	存在
exit	exited	exited	出去；退去
expand	expanded	expanded	展開；擴大
expect	expected	expected	預計；期待
expel	expelled	expelled	驅逐；趕走
experience	experienced	experienced	經歷；感受
experiment	experimented	experimented	實驗；試驗
expire	expired	expired	滿期；到期
explain	explained	explained	解釋；說明
explode	exploded	exploded	使爆炸；使爆發
exploit	exploited	exploited	剝削
explore	explored	explored	探測；探究

export	exported	exported	輸出;出口
expose	exposed	exposed	使暴露;揭發
express	expressed	expressed	表達;陳述
extend	extended	extended	延長;擴大
extract	extracted	extracted	抽出;提取
F			
face	faced	faced	面臨;面對
facilitate	facilitated	facilitated	促進;幫助
fade	faded	faded	凋謝;枯萎
fail	failed	failed	失敗;不及格
faint	fainted	fainted	昏倒
fake	faked	faked	假裝;佯裝
fall	fell	fallen	落下;跌落
falter	faltered	faltered	蹣跚;搖晃
fancy	fancied	fancied	想像;喜好
fascinate	fascinated	fascinated	迷住;吸引
fasten	fastened	fastened	紮牢;繫緊
fault	faulted	faulted	挑毛病;找缺點
favor	favored	favored	支持;偏好
fax	faxed	faxed	傳真
fear	feared	feared	害怕;恐懼
feature	featured	featured	以...為特色
feed	fed	fed	餵食
feel	felt	felt	摸;感覺
fence	fenced	fenced	防護;保衛
fetch	fetched	fetched	去拿來
fiddle	fiddled	fiddled	浪費時間
fight	fought	fought	打架;吵架;戰鬥
figure	figured	figured	計算;認為

file	filed	filed	歸檔；提出
fill	filled	filled	裝滿；填滿
film	filmed	filmed	把...拍成電影
filter	filtered	filtered	過濾
finance	financed	financed	提供資金給
find	found	found	建立；建造
fine	fined	fined	罰款
finish	finished	finished	結束；完成
fire	fired	fired	開火；解雇
fish	fished	fished	捕魚；釣魚
fit	fitted	fitted	適合；合身
fix	fixed	fixed	固定；修理
flame	flamed	flamed	燃燒；閃耀
flap	flapped	flapped	拍打；拍擊
flare	flared	flared	燃燒；閃耀
flash	flashed	flashed	閃爍；閃光
flatter	flattered	flattered	諂媚；使高興
flavor	flavored	flavored	給...調味
flaw	flawed	flawed	使破裂；使有缺陷
flee	fled	fled	逃走；逃跑
flick	flicked	flicked	輕彈
flicker	flickered	flickered	閃爍；擺動
fling	flung	flung	丟扔；拋擲
flip	flipped	flipped	輕拋；輕彈
float	floated	floated	漂浮；浮起
flock	flocked	flocked	聚集；成群
flood	flooded	flooded	淹沒；泛濫
flourish	flourished	flourished	茂盛；興旺

flow	flowed	flowed	流動
fluctuate	fluctuated	fluctuated	波動；變動
flunk	flunked	flunked	不及格
flush	flushed	flushed	用水沖洗；臉紅
flutter	fluttered	fluttered	振翼；拍翅
fly	flew	flown	飛；飛行
foam	foamed	foamed	起泡沫
focus	focused	focused	聚焦；集中
fold	folded	folded	摺疊；對摺
follow	followed	followed	跟隨
fool	fooled	fooled	愚弄；欺騙
forbid	forbade	forbidden	禁止；阻止
force	forced	forced	強迫；迫使
forecast	forecast	forecast	預測
foresee	foresaw	foreseen	預見；預言
forget	forgot	forgotten	忘記
forgive	forgave	forgiven	原諒；寬恕
form	formed	formed	形成；成立
formulate	formulated	formulated	使公式化；規劃
forsake	forsook	forsaken	拋棄；革除
fortify	fortified	fortified	增加；加強
forward	forwarded	forwarded	轉交；遞送
foster	fostered	fostered	養育；培養
found	founded	founded	建立；建造
fracture	fractured	fractured	破裂；斷裂
fragment	fragmented	fragmented	使成為碎片
frame	framed	framed	裝框；構造
free	freed	freed	使自由；釋放
freeze	froze	frozen	結冰；凝固

附錄二 實用動詞三態表

frequent	frequented	frequented	常去；常到(地方)
fret	fretted	fretted	使苦惱；使煩躁
frighten	frightened	frightened	使驚恐；使害怕
front	fronted	fronted	朝向
frost	frosted	frosted	結霜
frown	frowned	frowned	皺眉；表示不滿
frustrate	frustrated	frustrated	挫敗；使感到灰心
fry	fried	fried	油煎；油炸
fuel	fueled	fueled	供給燃料；刺激
fulfill	fulfilled	fulfilled	履行；實現
fume	fumed	fumed	冒煙；發怒
function	functioned	functioned	運行；起作用
fund	funded	funded	提供資金給
furnish	furnished	furnished	裝備；供應
fuse	fused	fused	接上保險絲
fuss	fussed	fussed	大驚小怪
G			
gain	gained	gained	得到；獲得
gallop	galloped	galloped	奔馳；飛跑
gamble	gambled	gambled	賭博；打賭
gasp	gasped	gasped	倒抽一口氣；喘氣
gather	gathered	gathered	蒐集
gaze	gazed	gazed	凝視；注視
gear	geared	geared	搭上齒輪
generalize	generalized	generalized	泛論；歸納
generate	generated	generated	產生；造成
get	got	gotten	得到；獲得
giggle	giggled	giggled	咯咯地笑

give	gave	given	送給；給與
glance	glanced	glanced	看一下；掃視
glare	glared	glared	怒目注視
gleam	gleamed	gleamed	發微光；閃爍
glide	glided	glided	滑動；滑行
glimpse	glimpsed	glimpsed	看一眼；瞥見
glisten	glistened	glistened	閃耀；發光
glitter	glittered	glittered	閃閃發亮；閃耀
gloom	gloomed	gloomed	變陰暗；變不高興
glory	gloried	gloried	驕傲；自豪
glow	glowed	glowed	發光；發熱
glue	glued	glued	膠合；黏牢
gnaw	gnawed	gnawed	咬；啃
go	went	gone	去；離去
gobble	gobbled	gobbled	狼吞虎嚥
gorge	gorged	gorged	狼吞虎嚥
gossip	gossiped	gossiped	閒聊；八卦
govern	governed	governed	統治；管理
grab	grabbed	grabbed	抓取；奪得
grade	graded	graded	分等級；分類
graduate	graduated	graduated	畢業
grant	granted	granted	同意；准予
grasp	grasped	grasped	抓牢；握緊
graze	grazed	grazed	吃草；放牧
grease	greased	greased	塗油脂在...
greet	greeted	greeted	問候；迎接
grieve	grieved	grieved	悲傷；哀悼
grill	grilled	grilled	烤；烤問

357

grin	grinned	grinned	露齒而笑
grind	ground	ground	磨碎；碾碎
grip	gripped	gripped	緊握；夾住
groan	groaned	groaned	呻吟；呻吟地說
grope	groped	groped	觸摸；摸索
gross	grossed	grossed	獲得⋯收入
ground	grounded	grounded	使擱淺
grow	grew	grown	成長；種植
growl	growled	growled	嗥叫；咆哮
grumble	grumbled	grumbled	抱怨；發牢騷
guarantee	guaranteed	guaranteed	保證
guard	guarded	guarded	保衛；守衛
guess	guessed	guessed	猜測；推測
guide	guided	guided	帶領；引導
gulp	gulped	gulped	狼吞虎嚥地吃喝
gun	gunned	gunned	用槍射擊
H			
hack	hacked	hacked	砍劈；開闢
haggle	haggled	hagglee	討價還價
hail	hailed	hailed	為⋯歡呼；喝采
halt	halted	halted	停止；終止
hand	handed	handed	面交；傳遞
handicap	handicapped	handicapped	妨礙；使不利
handle	handled	handled	操作；處理
hang	hung	hung	把⋯掛起來
hang	hanged	hanged	吊死
happen	happened	happened	發生；碰巧
harass	harassed	harassed	使煩惱；煩擾
harden	hardened	hardened	使變硬；使堅強

harm	harmed	harmed	傷害;損害
harness	harnessed	harnessed	治理;利用
harvest	harvested	harvested	收割;收獲
hasten	hastened	hastened	催促;加快速度
hatch	hatched	hatched	孵出;策劃
hate	hated	hated	討厭;怨恨
haul	hauled	hauled	拖拉;搬運
haunt	haunted	haunted	常出沒在 (鬼魂)
have	had	had	有;擁有
head	headed	headed	作為領袖
heal	healed	healed	治療;痊癒
heap	heaped	heaped	堆積;裝滿
hear	heard	heard	聽見;聽到
heat	heated	heated	加熱;使變暖
hedge	hedged	hedged	閃避問題
heed	heeded	heeded	留心;注意
heel	heeled	heeled	裝鞋跟;緊跟著
heighten	heightened	heightened	加高;增高
help	helped	helped	幫助;促進
herald	heralded	heralded	宣佈;通報
herd	herded	herded	放牧;把...趕到一起
hesitate	hesitated	hesitated	猶豫;躊躇
hide	hid	hidden	隱藏;躲藏
highlight	highlighted	highlighted	照亮;強調
hijack	hijacked	hijacked	劫機
hike	hiked	hiked	遠足;健行
hint	hinted	hinted	暗示;示意
hire	hired	hired	雇用

hiss	hissed	hissed	發出嘶嘶聲
hit	hit	hit	打擊；碰撞
hold	held	held	握著；抓住
honk	honked	honked	鳴喇叭
honor	honored	honored	使增光；尊敬
hook	hooked	hooked	鈎住
hop	hopped	hopped	跳過；躍過
hope	hoped	hoped	希望；盼望
horrify	horrified	horrified	使恐懼；使害怕
hospitalize	hospitalized	hospitalized	使住院治療
host	hosted	hosted	作主人；主辦
house	housed	housed	給...房子住
hover	hovered	hovered	徘徊；猶豫
howl	howled	howled	大叫；吼叫
hug	hugged	hugged	緊抱；擁抱
hum	hummed	hummed	發嗡嗡聲
humiliate	humiliated	humiliated	羞辱；使丟臉
hunt	hunted	hunted	打獵；獵捕
hurdle	hurdled	hurdled	克服困難
hurl	hurled	hurled	猛力投擲
hurry	hurried	hurried	使趕緊；催促
hurt	hurt	hurt	使受傷；疼痛
hush	hushed	hushed	使沉默；使安靜
I			
identify	identified	identified	識別；鑑定
idle	idled	idled	無所事事；閒晃
ignore	ignored	ignored	不理會；忽視
illuminate	illuminated	illuminated	照亮；啟發
illustrate	illustrated	illustrated	說明；加插圖

imagine	imagined	imagined	想像；猜想
imitate	imitated	imitated	模仿；仿效
immigrate	immigrated	immigrated	遷移；遷入
impact	impacted	impacted	壓緊；擠壓
implement	implemented	implemented	實施；執行
imply	implied	implied	暗指；意味著
import	imported	imported	進口；輸入
impose	imposed	imposed	把...強加；徵稅
impress	impressed	impressed	給...印象； 使銘記
imprison	imprisoned	imprisoned	監禁；關押
improve	improved	improved	改進
incline	inclined	inclined	傾斜；有...傾向
include	included	included	包括
increase	increased	increased	增加；增多
indicate	indicated	indicated	指示；指出
induce	induced	induced	引誘；引起
indulge	indulged	indulged	沉迷於
industrialize	industrialized	industrialized	使工業化
infect	infected	infected	傳染；感染
infer	inferred	inferred	推斷；推論
influence	influenced	influenced	影響；感化
inform	informed	informed	通知；告知
inhabit	inhabited	inhabited	居住於
inherit	inherited	inherited	繼承
initiate	initiated	initiated	開始；創始
inject	injected	injected	注射；插話
injure	injured	injured	傷害；損害
inquire	inquired	inquired	詢問；訊問

附錄二　實用動詞三態表

insert	inserted	inserted	插入；嵌入
insist	insisted	insisted	堅持；堅決主張
inspire	inspired	inspired	鼓舞；激勵
install	installed	installed	安裝；安置
institute	instituted	instituted	創立；開始
instruct	instructed	instructed	指示；命令
insult	insulted	insulted	侮辱；羞辱
insure	insured	insured	投保；接受保險
integrate	integrated	integrated	使結合；使合併
intend	intended	intended	想要；打算
intensify	intensified	intensified	加強；增強
interact	interacted	interacted	互相作用；互動
interest	interested	interested	使產生興趣
interfere	interfered	interfered	妨礙；衝突
interpret	interpreted	interpreted	口譯；翻譯
interrupt	interrupted	interrupted	打斷
intervene	intervened	intervened	介入；干涉
interview	interviewed	interviewed	訪問；面試
intimidate	intimidated	intimidated	威嚇；脅迫
introduce	introduced	introduced	介紹；引見
intrude	intruded	intruded	侵入；闖入
invade	invaded	invaded	侵入；侵略
invent	invented	invented	發明；創造
invest	invested	invested	投資
investigate	investigated	investigated	調查；研究
invite	invited	invited	邀請；招待
involve	involved	involved	連累；牽涉
iron	ironed	ironed	熨衣；燙平
irritate	irritated	irritated	使惱怒；使煩躁

isolate	isolated	isolated	使孤立；使脫離
issue	issued	issued	發行；發佈
itch	itched	itched	使發癢
J			
jam	jammed	jammed	塞進；擠進
jaywalk	jaywalked	jaywalked	不守交通規則過馬路
jeer	jeered	jeered	嘲笑；嘲弄
jog	jogged	jogged	慢跑
join	joined	joined	連結；使結合
joke	joked	joked	開玩笑
judge	judged	judged	審判；評斷
justify	justified	justified	證明...是正當的
K			
keep	kept	kept	保持；持有
kick	kicked	kicked	踢
kidnap	kidnapped	kidnapped	綁架
kill	killed	killed	殺死；殺害
kindle	kindled	kindled	點燃；燃起
kiss	kissed	kissed	親吻；接吻
kneel	knelt	knelt	跪下
knit	knitted	knitted	編織；使接合
knock	knocked	knocked	相撞；碰擊
knot	knotted	knotted	打結
know	knew	known	知道；認識
L			
label	labeled	labeled	貼標籤
labor	labored	labored	勞動；工作
lace	laced	laced	穿帶子於

附錄一 實用動詞三態表

lack	lacked	lacked	缺少；缺乏
lag	lagged	lagged	走得慢；落後
lame	lamed	lamed	使跛腳
lament	lamented	lamented	哀悼；悲痛
land	landed	landed	使登陸；使降落
landscape	landscaped	landscaped	造園；造景
last	lasted	lasted	持續
laugh	laughed	laughed	笑；大笑
launch	launched	launched	發射；發動
lay	laid	laid	放置；擱著
lead	led	led	領導；引領
leak	leaked	leaked	漏水；洩漏
lean	leaned	leaned	傾斜；傾身
leap	leapt	leapt	跳躍；跳
learn	learned	learned	學習；學得
leave	left	left	離開；留下
lecture	lectured	lectured	講課；授課
lend	lent	lent	借出
lengthen	lengthened	lengthened	加長；增長
lessen	lessened	lessened	減少；減低
let	let	let	讓
liberate	liberated	liberated	使自由；解放
license	licensed	licensed	許可；准許
lick	licked	licked	舔
lie	lied	lied	說謊
lie	lay	lain	躺下；躺著
lift	lifted	lifted	舉起；抬起
light	lit	lit	點燃；點亮
lighten	lightened	lightened	變亮；發亮

like	liked	liked	喜歡
limit	limited	limited	限制；限定
line	lined	lined	排隊
linger	lingered	lingered	徘徊；逗留
link	linked	linked	連接；結合
list	listed	listed	編表；列舉
listen	listened	listened	聽見；聽到
litter	littered	littered	亂丟垃圾
live	lived	lived	生活；活著
load	loaded	loaded	裝；裝載
loan	loaned	loaned	借出
locate	located	located	位於…；確定…的位置
lock	locked	locked	鎖住；鎖上
log	logged	logged	記錄；伐木
look	looked	looked	看
loosen	loosened	loosened	鬆開；解開
lose	lost	lost	失去；輸
love	loved	loved	愛；喜歡
lower	lowered	lowered	放下；降低
lure	lured	lured	引誘；誘惑
M			
magnify	magnified	magnified	放大；擴大
mail	mailed	mailed	郵寄
maintain	maintained	maintained	保持；維持
major	majored	majored	主修
make	made	made	做；製造
manage	managed	managed	管理；經營
manifest	manifested	manifested	表明；顯示

manipulate	manipulated	manipulated	利用；操縱(市場的漲落等)
manufacture	manufactured	manufactured	製造
mar	marred	marred	毀損；損傷
march	marched	marched	行軍；前進
mark	marked	marked	作記號；標示
market	marketed	marketed	銷售
marry	married	married	結婚；嫁娶
marvel	marveled	marveled	對...感到驚異
mash	mashed	mashed	壓碎；壓壞
massacre	massacred	massacred	屠殺；殘殺
massage	massaged	massaged	給...按摩
master	mastered	mastered	控制；精通
match	matched	matched	相配；適合
mate	mated	mated	使配對
matter	mattered	mattered	有關係；要緊
mean	meant	meant	意指
measure	measured	measured	測量；計量
mediate	mediated	mediated	居中調停
meditate	meditated	meditated	沉思；深思
meet	met	met	遇見；碰面
mellow	mellowed	mellowed	成熟；使成熟
melt	melted	melted	融化；融解
memorize	memorized	memorized	記憶；記住
menace	menaced	menaced	威脅；恐嚇
mend	mended	mended	修理；修補
mention	mentioned	mentioned	提及；提到
merchandise	merchandised	merchandised	買賣；經營
merge	merged	merged	使合併

mess	messed	messed	弄髒；弄亂
migrate	migrated	migrated	遷移；移居
mimic	mimicked	mimicked	模仿；學...的樣子
mind	minded	minded	注意；介意
mingle	mingled	mingled	使混合
minimize	minimized	minimized	使減到最少
mirror	mirrored	mirrored	反映；反射
mislead	misled	misled	把...帶錯方向
miss	missed	missed	未擊中；未得到
mistake	mistook	mistaken	弄錯；誤解
misunderstand	misunderstood	misunderstood	誤會；曲解
mix	mixed	mixed	使混和；攪和
moan	moaned	moaned	呻吟；嗚咽
mobilize	mobilized	mobilized	動員；調動
mock	mocked	mocked	嘲弄；嘲笑
modernize	modernized	modernized	使現代化
modify	modified	modified	更改；修改
mold	molded	molded	鑄造；塑造
monitor	monitored	monitored	監控；監聽
mop	mopped	mopped	用拖把拖洗
motion	motioned	motioned	向...打手勢
motivate	motivated	motivated	刺激；激發
mount	mounted	mounted	登上；爬上
mourn	mourned	mourned	哀痛；哀悼
move	moved	moved	使移動；搬動
mow	mowed	mowed	除草
multiply	multiplied	multiplied	使相乘
mumble	mumbled	mumbled	含糊地說

附錄二 實用動詞三態表

murder	murdered	murdered	謀殺；兇殺
murmur	murmured	murmured	發出輕柔持續的聲音
mute	muted	muted	消除（聲音）
mutter	muttered	muttered	低聲嘀咕
N			
nag	nagged	nagged	使煩惱
nail	nailed	nailed	將...釘牢；使固定
name	named	named	給...取名
nap	napped	napped	打盹；小睡
narrate	narrated	narrated	講述；敘述
narrow	narrowed	narrowed	使變窄
navigate	navigated	navigated	航行；駕駛
near	neared	neared	靠近；接近
need	needed	needed	需要
neglect	neglected	neglected	忽視；忽略
negotiate	negotiated	negotiated	談判；協商
nest	nested	nested	築巢；巢居
net	netted	netted	用網捕
nibble	nibbled	nibbled	一點點地咬
nickname	nicknamed	nicknamed	給...起綽號
nod	nodded	nodded	點頭
nominate	nominated	nominated	提名；任命
note	noted	noted	注意；注目
notice	noticed	noticed	注意；通知
notify	notified	notified	通知；報告
nourish	nourished	nourished	養育；滋養
nurture	nurtured	nurtured	養育；培育

O

obey	obeyed	obeyed	服從;聽從
object	objected	objected	反對
oblige	obliged	obliged	使不得不;迫使
obscure	obscured	obscured	使變暗;遮掩
obtain	obtained	obtained	得到;獲得
occasion	occasioned	occasioned	引起;惹起
occupy	occupied	occupied	佔據;佔用
occur	occurred	occurred	發生
offend	offended	offended	冒犯;觸怒
offer	offered	offered	給予;提供
oil	oiled	oiled	在...塗油
omit	omitted	omitted	遺漏;省略
open	opened	opened	開;打開
operate	operated	operated	經營;管理
oppose	opposed	opposed	反對;反抗
oppress	oppressed	oppressed	壓迫;壓制
orbit	orbited	orbited	環繞(天體等)的軌道運行
order	ordered	ordered	命令;指揮
organize	organized	organized	組織;安排
originate	originated	originated	發源;來自
ornament	ornamented	ornamented	裝飾;美化
outdo	outdid	outdone	勝過;超越
outfit	outfitted	outfitted	裝備;配備
outline	outlined	outlined	概述;略述
outnumber	outnumbered	outnumbered	數量上超過
overcome	overcame	overcome	戰勝;克服
overdo	overdid	overdone	把...做得過分

overeat	overate	overeaten	吃得過飽
overflow	overflowed	overflowed	泛濫
overhear	overheard	overheard	偶然聽到
overlap	overlapped	overlapped	與...部分重疊
overlook	overlooked	overlooked	眺望；俯瞰
oversleep	overslept	overslept	睡過頭
overtake	overtook	overtaken	追上；趕上
overthrow	overthrew	overthrown	打倒；推翻
overturn	overturned	overturned	使翻轉；使倒下
overwhelm	overwhelmed	overwhelmed	戰勝；征服
owe	owed	owed	欠（債）
own	owned	owned	有；擁有
P			
pack	packed	packed	裝（箱）捆紮；包裝
package	packaged	packaged	把...打包；包裝
pad	padded	padded	填塞；襯填
paddle	paddled	paddled	用槳划
pain	pained	pained	使煩惱；使痛苦
paint	painted	painted	油漆；繪畫
pair	paired	paired	使成對
panic	panicked	panicked	使恐慌
parachute	parachuted	parachuted	跳傘
parade	paraded	paraded	在...遊行
parallel	paralleled	paralleled	使成平行
paralyze	paralyzed	paralyzed	使麻痺；使癱瘓
parcel	parceled	parceled	分配；捆紮
pardon	pardoned	pardoned	原諒；饒恕
park	parked	parked	停放車輛

part	parted	parted	使分開；分手
participate	participated	participated	參與；參加
pass	passed	passed	前進；通過
paste	pasted	pasted	用漿糊黏貼
pat	patted	patted	輕拍；輕打
patch	patched	patched	補綴；修補
patent	patented	patented	給予...專利權
patrol	patrolled	patrolled	巡邏；巡查
pause	paused	paused	中斷；暫停
pave	paved	paved	鋪；築
pay	paid	paid	支付；償還
peak	peaked	peaked	達到高峰
peck	pecked	pecked	啄食
pedal	pedaled	pedaled	踩踏板
peddle	peddled	peddled	叫賣；兜售
peek	peeked	peeked	偷看；窺視
peel	peeled	peeled	削去...的皮
peep	peeped	peeped	偷看
peer	peered	peered	凝視；盯著看
peg	pegged	pegged	用木釘釘牢
penetrate	penetrated	penetrated	穿過；刺入
perceive	perceived	perceived	察覺；感知
perch	perched	perched	棲息
perfect	perfected	perfected	使完美；做完
perform	performed	performed	履行；執行
peril	periled	periled	使有危險
perish	perished	perished	消滅；死去
permit	permitted	permitted	允許；許可
persevere	persevered	persevered	堅持不懈

371

persist	persisted	persisted	堅持；固執
personalize	personalized	personalized	使個人化
persuade	persuaded	persuaded	說服；勸服
pet	petted	petted	鍾愛；寵愛
phone	phoned	phoned	打電話給...
photograph	photographed	photographed	為...拍照
pick	picked	picked	挑選；選擇
picnic	picnicked	picnicked	郊遊；野餐
picture	pictured	pictured	想像；描繪
pierce	pierced	pierced	刺穿；刺破
pile	piled	piled	堆積；累積
pin	pinned	pinned	別住；釘住
pinch	pinched	pinched	捏；擰
pioneer	pioneered	pioneered	開闢；倡導
pirate	pirated	pirated	掠奪；非法翻印
piss	pissed	pissed	小便；撒尿
pitch	pitched	pitched	搭帳篷；紮營
pity	pitied	pitied	憐憫；同情
place	placed	placed	放置；安置
plan	planned	planned	計劃；打算
plant	planted	planted	栽種；播種
play	played	played	玩耍；遊戲
plead	pleaded	pleaded	辯護；答辯
please	pleased	pleased	使高興；使喜歡
pledge	pledged	pledged	保證；誓言
plot	plotted	plotted	密謀；策劃
plow	plowed	plowed	犁地；耕地
pluck	plucked	plucked	採；摘
plug	plugged	plugged	把...塞住；堵塞

plunge	plunged	plunged	使投入；將...插入
poach	poached	poached	偷獵
point	pointed	pointed	指出；指明
poison	poisoned	poisoned	使中毒；毒死
poke	poked	poked	戳；捅
polish	polished	polished	磨光；擦亮
pollute	polluted	polluted	污染；弄髒
ponder	pondered	pondered	仔細考慮；衡量
pop	popped	popped	發出砰的響聲
populate	populated	populated	居住於
portion	portioned	portioned	分配
portray	portrayed	portrayed	畫；描寫
pose	posed	posed	擺姿勢
position	positioned	positioned	把...放在適當位置
possess	possessed	possessed	擁有；持有
post	posted	posted	郵寄；投寄
postpone	postponed	postponed	使延期；延遲
pound	pounded	pounded	搗碎
pour	poured	poured	倒；灌
practice	practiced	practiced	實行；實施
praise	praised	praised	讚美；表揚
pray	prayed	prayed	祈禱；祈求
preach	preached	preached	講道；說教
precede	preceded	preceded	處在...之前
predict	predicted	predicted	預言；預料
prefer	preferred	preferred	寧可；寧願
prejudice	prejudiced	prejudiced	使抱偏見
prepare	prepared	prepared	準備

prescribe	prescribed	prescribed	規定；指定；開藥方
present	presented	presented	贈送；呈獻
preserve	preserved	preserved	保存；保藏
preside	presided	presided	主持；指揮
press	pressed	pressed	按；壓
pressure	pressured	pressured	迫使
presume	presumed	presumed	擅自；冒昧
pretend	pretended	pretended	佯裝；假裝
prevail	prevailed	prevailed	勝過；戰勝
prevent	prevented	prevented	防止；預防
preview	previewed	previewed	預看
prey	preyed	preyed	捕食
price	priced	priced	給...定價
prick	pricked	pricked	刺穿；扎穿
pride	prided	prided	使得意
print	printed	printed	印；印刷
privilege	privileged	privileged	給予...特權
prize	prized	prized	重視；珍視
proceed	proceeded	proceeded	繼續進行
process	processed	processed	加工
produce	produced	produced	生產
profit	profited	profited	有益於
progress	progressed	progressed	前進；進行
prohibit	prohibited	prohibited	禁止
project	projected	projected	計劃；企劃
prolong	prolonged	prolonged	延長；拉長
promise	promised	promised	允諾；答應
promote	promoted	promoted	使升遷

prompt	prompted	prompted	促使；激勵
pronounce	pronounced	pronounced	發...的音
proofread	proofread	proofread	校正；校對
prop	propped	propped	支撐
propel	propelled	propelled	推進
proportion	proportioned	proportioned	使成比例
propose	proposed	proposed	提議；建議
prosecute	prosecuted	prosecuted	起訴；告發
prospect	prospected	prospected	勘探；勘察
prosper	prospered	prospered	繁榮；昌盛
protect	protected	protected	保護；防護
protest	protested	protested	抗議；反對
prove	proved	proven	證明；證實
provide	provided	provided	提供
provoke	provoked	provoked	挑釁；煽動
prowl	prowled	prowled	四處覓食
prune	pruned	pruned	修剪；修整
publicize	publicized	publicized	宣傳；公佈
publish	published	published	出版；發行
puff	puffed	puffed	一陣陣地吹
pull	pulled	pulled	拉；拖
pulse	pulsed	pulsed	搏動；跳動
pump	pumped	pumped	用唧筒抽
punch	punched	punched	用拳猛擊
punish	punished	punished	懲罰；處罰
purchase	purchased	purchased	購買
purify	purified	purified	使純淨；淨化
pursue	pursued	pursued	追趕；追蹤
push	pushed	pushed	推動；推進

附錄二 實用動詞三態表

put	put	put	放；擺
puzzle	puzzled	puzzled	使迷惑；使為難
Q			
quack	quacked	quacked	呱呱叫
quake	quaked	quaked	顫抖；哆嗦
qualify	qualified	qualified	使合格
quarrel	quarreled	quarreled	爭吵；不和
quench	quenched	quenched	壓制；抑制
query	queried	queried	質問；詢問
question	questioned	questioned	詢問；訊問
quit	quit	quit	離開；退出
quiver	quivered	quivered	顫抖；發抖
quote	quoted	quoted	引用；引述
R			
race	raced	raced	參加競賽
radiate	radiated	radiated	散發；輻射
rage	raged	raged	發怒；怒斥
raid	raided	raided	襲擊
rain	rained	rained	下雨；降雨
raise	raised	raised	舉起；抬起
rally	rallied	rallied	集合；重整
range	ranged	ranged	排列；將...排成行
rank	ranked	ranked	排列；把...排成行
rate	rated	rated	對...估價；對...評價
rattle	rattled	rattled	使發出咯咯聲
ravage	ravaged	ravaged	使荒蕪；毀滅
reach	reached	reached	抵達；到達
react	reacted	reacted	作出反應；反應

read	read	read	閱讀；朗讀
realize	realized	realized	領悟；了解
reap	reaped	reaped	收割
reason	reasoned	reasoned	推論；推理
rebel	rebelled	rebelled	造反；反叛
recall	recalled	recalled	回想；回憶
receive	received	received	收到；接到
recite	recited	recited	背誦；朗誦
reckon	reckoned	reckoned	計算；數
recognize	recognized	recognized	認出；識別
recommend	recommended	recommended	推薦；介紹
reconcile	reconciled	reconciled	使和解；使和好
record	recorded	recorded	記載；記錄
recover	recovered	recovered	恢復； 使恢復原狀
recruit	recruited	recruited	徵募（新兵）； 吸收
recur	recurred	recurred	再發生；復發
recycle	recycled	recycled	使再循環； 再利用
reduce	reduced	reduced	減少
refer	referred	referred	把...歸因（於）
refine	refined	refined	提煉；精鍊
reflect	reflected	reflected	反射；照出
reform	reformed	reformed	改革；革新
refresh	refreshed	refreshed	使清新；使清涼
refund	refunded	refunded	退還；歸還
refuse	refused	refused	拒絕；拒受
refute	refuted	refuted	駁斥；反駁
regard	regarded	regarded	注重；注意

register	registered	registered	登記；註冊
regret	regretted	regretted	懊悔；遺憾
regulate	regulated	regulated	管理；控制
rehearse	rehearsed	rehearsed	排練；排演
reign	reigned	reigned	支配；統治
reinforce	reinforced	reinforced	加強；補充；補強
reject	rejected	rejected	拒絕；抵制
rejoice	rejoiced	rejoiced	欣喜,；高興
relate	related	related	敘述；使有聯繫
relax	relaxed	relaxed	使鬆懈；放鬆
relay	relayed	relayed	轉達；轉播
release	released	released	釋放；解放
relieve	relieved	relieved	緩和；減輕
relish	relished	relished	喜愛；愛好
relocate	relocated	relocated	重新安置；外派
rely	relied	relied	依靠；依賴
remain	remained	remained	剩下；餘留
remark	remarked	remarked	談到；評論
remedy	remedied	remedied	醫治；治療
remember	remembered	remembered	記得；想起
remind	reminded	reminded	提醒；使想起
remove	removed	removed	移除
render	rendered	rendered	使得；使成為
renew	renewed	renewed	使更新；使復原
renovate	renovated	renovated	重建；整修
rent	rented	rented	租用；租入
repair	repaired	repaired	修理；修補
repay	repaid	repaid	償還；報答

repeat	repeated	repeated	重複；重做
replace	replaced	replaced	取代
reply	replied	replied	回答；答覆
report	reported	reported	報告；報導
represent	represented	represented	描繪；表現
repress	repressed	repressed	抑制；壓制
reproduce	reproduced	reproduced	繁殖；複製
request	requested	requested	請求；要求
require	required	required	需要
rescue	rescued	rescued	援救；營救
research	researched	researched	研究；探究
resemble	resembled	resembled	像；類似
resent	resented	resented	憤慨；怨恨
reserve	reserved	reserved	儲備；保存
reside	resided	resided	住；居住
resign	resigned	resigned	放棄；辭去
resist	resisted	resisted	抵抗；反抗
resolve	resolved	resolved	解決；消除
respect	respected	respected	敬重；尊敬
respond	responded	responded	作答；回答
rest	rested	rested	休息；睡
restore	restored	restored	恢復
restrain	restrained	restrained	抑制；遏制
restrict	restricted	restricted	限制；限定
result	resulted	resulted	發生；產生
resume	resumed	resumed	重新開始；繼續
retail	retailed	retailed	以零售方式
retaliate	retaliated	retaliated	報復；回敬
retire	retired	retired	使退休；退休

附錄二 實用動詞三態表

retort	retorted	retorted	反擊;就...進行報復
retreat	retreated	retreated	撤退;退卻
retrieve	retrieved	retrieved	重新得到;收回
return	returned	returned	返回;歸還
reveal	revealed	revealed	展現;顯露出
revenge	revenged	revenged	替...報仇
reverse	reversed	reversed	顛倒;翻轉
review	reviewed	reviewed	再檢查;重新探討
revise	revised	revised	修改;修正
revive	revived	revived	甦醒;復甦
revolt	revolted	revolted	反叛;起義
revolve	revolved	revolved	旋轉;自轉
reward	rewarded	rewarded	報答;報償
rhyme	rhymed	rhymed	押韻
rid	rid	rid	使免除;使擺脫
ride	rode	ridden	騎馬;乘車
ridicule	ridiculed	ridiculed	嘲笑;揶揄
ring	rang	rung	鈴響
riot	rioted	rioted	暴亂;聚眾鬧事
rip	ripped	ripped	撕;扯
ripple	rippled	rippled	起漣漪
rise	rose	risen	上升;升起
risk	risked	risked	冒...的風險
rival	rivaled	rivaled	與...競爭
roam	roamed	roamed	漫步;漫遊
roar	roared	roared	吼叫;呼嘯
roast	roasted	roasted	烤;炙
rob	robbed	robbed	搶劫;劫掠

rock	rocked	rocked	搖動；使搖晃
rocket	rocketed	rocketed	向前急衝
roll	rolled	rolled	滾動；打滾
rot	rotted	rotted	腐爛；腐壞
rotate	rotated	rotated	旋轉；轉動
round	rounded	rounded	使變圓；環繞…而行
row	rowed	rowed	划（船）
rub	rubbed	rubbed	擦；磨擦
ruin	ruined	ruined	毀滅；崩潰
rule	ruled	ruled	統治；管轄
rumble	rumbled	rumbled	隆隆地響
rumor	rumored	rumored	謠傳；傳說
run	ran	run	跑；奔
rush	rushed	rushed	衝；奔
rust	rusted	rusted	生鏽
rustle	rustled	rustled	沙沙作響
S			
sacrifice	sacrificed	sacrificed	犧牲；獻出
saddle	saddled	saddled	使負擔；強加
safeguard	safeguarded	safeguarded	保護；防衛
sail	sailed	sailed	航行
salute	saluted	saluted	向...行禮
sample	sampled	sampled	品嚐；體驗
sanction	sanctioned	sanctioned	認可；批准
satisfy	satisfied	satisfied	使滿意；使高興
save	saved	saved	救；挽救
say	said	said	說；講
scan	scanned	scanned	細看；審視

scar	scarred	scarred	在...留下疤痕
scare	scared	scared	驚嚇；使恐懼
scatter	scattered	scattered	使消散；使分散
scent	scented	scented	嗅出；聞到
scold	scolded	scolded	罵；責罵
scoop	scooped	scooped	用勺舀；用鏟子鏟
score	scored	scored	得分
scorn	scorned	scorned	輕蔑；藐視
scout	scouted	scouted	偵察；搜索
scramble	scrambled	scrambled	爬行；攀爬
scrap	scrapped	scrapped	廢棄
scrape	scraped	scraped	刮；擦
scratch	scratched	scratched	抓；搔
scream	screamed	screamed	尖叫
screen	screened	screened	掩蔽；遮護
screw	screwed	screwed	旋；擰
scrub	scrubbed	scrubbed	用力擦洗；揉
seal	sealed	sealed	密封
search	searched	searched	搜查；搜尋
seat	seated	seated	使就座
section	sectioned	sectioned	把...分成段
secure	secured	secured	把...弄牢；關緊
seduce	seduced	seduced	誘惑；引誘
see	saw	seen	看見；看到
seek	sought	sought	尋找；探索
seem	seemed	seemed	看來好像；似乎
segment	segmented	segmented	分割；切割
select	selected	selected	選擇；挑選

sell	sold	sold	賣；銷售
send	sent	sent	發送；寄
sense	sensed	sensed	感覺到；意識到
sentence	sentenced	sentenced	宣判；判決
separate	separated	separated	分隔；分割
serve	served	served	為...服務
set	set	set	放置
settle	settled	settled	安放；安頓
sew	sewed	sewn	縫合；縫上
shade	shaded	shaded	遮蔽；蔽蔭
shadow	shadowed	shadowed	遮蔽；使變暗
shake	shook	shaken	搖動；震動
shame	shamed	shamed	使感到羞恥
shampoo	shampooed	shampooed	洗頭髮
shape	shaped	shaped	使成形；塑造
share	shared	shared	分享；分擔
sharpen	sharpened	sharpened	削尖
shatter	shattered	shattered	粉碎；砸碎
shave	shaved	shaved	剃去...上的毛髮
shed	shed	shed	流出；流下
shelter	sheltered	sheltered	掩蔽；遮蔽
shield	shielded	shielded	保護；保衛
shift	shifted	shifted	轉移；移動
shine	shone	shone	發光；照耀
ship	shipped	shipped	裝運；運送
shiver	shivered	shivered	發抖；打顫
shock	shocked	shocked	使震動；使震盪
shoot	shot	shot	發射；放射
shop	shopped	shopped	購物

附錄二　實用動詞三態表

shoplift	shoplifted	shoplifted	順手牽羊
shorten	shortened	shortened	使變短；縮短
shoulder	shouldered	shouldered	擔負；承擔
shout	shouted	shouted	呼喊；喊叫
shove	shoved	shoved	推；撞
shovel	shoveled	shoveled	鏟起；用鐵鍬挖
show	showed	shown	顯示；露出
shred	shredded	shredded	切成條狀；切絲
shriek	shrieked	shrieked	尖叫；喊叫
shrink	shrank	shrunk	收縮；縮短
shrug	shrugged	shrugged	聳肩
shudder	shuddered	shuddered	發抖；戰慄
shun	shunned	shunned	躲開；避開
shut	shut	shut	關上；閉上
shutter	shuttered	shuttered	為...裝百葉窗
shuttle	shuttled	shuttled	短程來回運送
sigh	sighed	sighed	嘆氣；嘆息
sight	sighted	sighted	看見；發現
sign	signed	signed	簽名
signal	signaled	signaled	發信號；打信號
signify	signified	signified	表示；表明
silence	silenced	silenced	使沈默；使啞口無言
simmer	simmered	simmered	煨；燉
simplify	simplified	simplified	簡化；精簡
sin	sinned	sinned	犯罪
sing	sang	sung	唱；唱歌
sink	sank	sunk	下沈
sip	sipped	sipped	啜飲

sit	sat	sat	坐下；坐著
skate	skated	skated	滑冰；溜冰
sketch	sketched	sketched	寫生；速寫
ski	skied	skied	滑雪
skim	skimmed	skimmed	瀏覽；略讀
skip	skipped	skipped	略過；漏掉
skirt	skirted	skirted	繞開；避開
slam	slammed	slammed	猛扔；猛推
slap	slapped	slapped	摑耳光；用手掌打
slash	slashed	slashed	砍擊；砍傷
slaughter	slaughtered	slaughtered	屠宰
slave	slaved	slaved	奴隸般工作；苦幹
slay	slew	slain	殺死；殺害
sled	sledded	sledded	乘雪橇
sledge	sledged	sledged	乘雪橇
sleep	slept	slept	睡；睡覺
sleigh	sleighed	sleighed	乘雪橇
slice	sliced	sliced	把...切成薄片
slide	slid	slid	滑；滑動
slip	slipped	slipped	滑動；滑行
slow	slowed	slowed	使慢；放慢
slump	slumped	slumped	倒下；陷落
smack	smacked	smacked	稍帶特定味道
smash	smashed	smashed	粉碎；打碎
smell	smelled	smelled	嗅；聞
smile	smiled	smiled	微笑
smoke	smoked	smoked	抽菸
smooth	smoothed	smoothed	使光滑；使平滑

smother	smothered	smothered	使窒息；使透不過氣來
smuggle	smuggled	smuggled	走私；非法私運
snap	snapped	snapped	猛咬；突然折斷
snare	snared	snared	捕捉
snarl	snarled	snarled	吠；嗥
snatch	snatched	snatched	奪走；奪得
sneak	sneaked	sneaked	偷偷地走；溜
sneer	sneered	sneered	輕蔑地笑；冷笑
sneeze	sneezed	sneezed	打噴嚏
sniff	sniffed	sniffed	嗅；聞
snore	snored	snored	打鼾
snort	snorted	snorted	噴鼻息；輕蔑或憤怒地哼
snow	snowed	snowed	下雪
soak	soaked	soaked	浸泡；浸漬
soar	soared	soared	往上飛舞；升騰
sob	sobbed	sobbed	嗚咽；啜泣
sober	sobered	sobered	使醒酒；使清醒
socialize	socialized	socialized	參與社交
soften	softened	softened	使變柔軟
soil	soiled	soiled	弄髒
solve	solved	solved	解決；解釋
soothe	soothed	soothed	安慰；撫慰
sort	sorted	sorted	把...分類
sound	sounded	sounded	聽起來
sow	sowed	sowed	播種
span	spanned	spanned	橫跨；跨越
spare	spared	spared	分出；騰出
spark	sparked	sparked	發動；點燃

sparkle	sparkled	sparkled	發火花;閃耀
speak	spoke	spoken	說話;講話
specialize	specialized	specialized	專攻;專門從事
specify	specified	specified	具體指定
speculate	speculated	speculated	沈思;推測
speed	sped	sped	迅速前進;快行
spell	spelled	spelled	用字母拼;拼寫
spend	spent	spent	花錢;花費
spill	spilled	spilled	使溢出;使濺出
spin	spun	spun	紡;旋轉
spiral	spiraled	spiraled	成螺旋形
spit	spit	spit	吐口水
splash	splashed	splashed	濺;潑
split	split	split	劈開;切開
spoil	spoiled	spoiled	損壞;糟蹋
sponge	sponged	sponged	(用海綿或濕布)擦拭;吸取
sponsor	sponsored	sponsored	發起;主辦
spot	spotted	spotted	使沾上污點;弄髒
sprain	sprained	sprained	扭傷
sprawl	sprawled	sprawled	伸開四肢躺
spray	sprayed	sprayed	噴灑;噴塗
spread	spread	spread	使伸展;使延伸
spring	sprang	sprung	跳;躍
sprinkle	sprinkled	sprinkled	灑;噴淋
sprint	sprinted	sprinted	奮力而跑;衝刺
spur	spurred	spurred	鞭策;鼓勵
squash	squashed	squashed	壓扁;壓碎;擠壓

NEW TOEIC 黃金戰鬥力——閱讀篇

附錄二 實用動詞三態表

squat	squatted	squatted	蹲踞;蹲下
squeeze	squeezed	squeezed	榨;擠
stab	stabbed	stabbed	刺;戳;刺入
stabilize	stabilized	stabilized	使穩定;使穩固
stack	stacked	stacked	堆放
staff	staffed	staffed	給...配備人力
stagger	staggered	staggered	搖搖晃晃;蹣跚而行
stain	stained	stained	沾污;染污
stake	staked	staked	把...押下打賭;拿...冒險
stalk	stalked	stalked	偷偷靠近
stall	stalled	stalled	使陷入泥潭;使動彈不得
stammer	stammered	stammered	口吃;結結巴巴地說話
stamp	stamped	stamped	貼郵票於;跺腳
stand	stood	stood	站立;站著
staple	stapled	stapled	用訂書針釘
stare	stared	stared	盯;凝視
start	started	started	開始
starve	starved	starved	挨餓;餓死
state	stated	stated	陳述;聲明
station	stationed	stationed	駐紮;部署
stay	stayed	stayed	停留;留下
steady	steadied	steadied	使穩固;使穩定
steal	stole	stolen	偷;竊取
steam	steamed	steamed	蒸煮
steel	steeled	steeled	使堅強;使下決心

steer	steered	steered	掌船舵；駕駛
stem	stemmed	stemmed	起源於
stew	stewed	stewed	（用文火）煮；燉；燜
stick	stuck	stuck	黏貼；張貼；伸出
stimulate	stimulated	stimulated	刺激；激勵
sting	stung	stung	刺；螫；叮
stink	stank	stunk	發惡臭
stir	stirred	stirred	攪拌；攪動
stitch	stitched	stitched	縫紉；編結
stock	stocked	stocked	庫存；貯存
stoop	stooped	stooped	屈身；彎腰
stop	stopped	stopped	停止；中止
store	stored	stored	儲存
straighten	straightened	straightened	把...弄直；使挺直
strain	strained	strained	拉緊；拖緊
strand	stranded	stranded	使擱淺
strangle	strangled	strangled	扼死；勒死
strap	strapped	strapped	用帶捆綁
stray	strayed	strayed	迷路；走失
strengthen	strengthened	strengthened	加強；增強
stress	stressed	stressed	強調；著重
stretch	stretched	stretched	伸直；伸出
stride	strode	stridden	邁大步走
strike	struck	stricken	打,擊,攻擊
string	strung	strung	（用線，繩）縛；紮；掛
strip	stripped	stripped	剝去；剝光

strive	strived	strived	努力；苦幹
stroke	stroked	stroked	打；擊；敲
stroll	strolled	strolled	散步；溜達
structure	structured	structured	構造；組織；建造
struggle	struggled	struggled	奮鬥；鬥爭
study	studied	studied	學習；研究
stuff	stuffed	stuffed	裝；填；塞
stumble	stumbled	stumbled	絆腳；絆倒
stump	stumped	stumped	砍去...的樹幹
stun	stunned	stunned	把...打昏；使昏迷
stunt	stunted	stunted	阻礙...的發育
stutter	stuttered	stuttered	結結巴巴地說話
submit	submitted	submitted	使服從；使屈服
subscribe	subscribed	subscribed	認捐；捐助
substitute	substituted	substituted	用...代替；代替
subtract	subtracted	subtracted	減去；去掉
succeed	succeeded	succeeded	成功；辦妥
suck	sucked	sucked	吸；吮
suffer	suffered	suffered	遭受；經歷
suffocate	suffocated	suffocated	使窒息；把...悶死
suggest	suggested	suggested	建議；提議
suit	suited	suited	適合；中...的意
sum	summed	summed	計算...的總和
summarize	summarized	summarized	總結；概述；概括
summon	summoned	summoned	召喚；傳喚
supervise	supervised	supervised	監督；管理；指導

supplement	supplemented	supplemented	增補；補充
supply	supplied	supplied	供給；供應
support	supported	supported	支撐；支托
suppose	supposed	supposed	猜想；以為
suppress	suppressed	suppressed	鎮壓；平定
surf	surfed	surfed	衝浪
surface	surfaced	surfaced	浮出水面；顯露
surge	surged	surged	洶湧；奔騰
surpass	surpassed	surpassed	勝過；優於
surprise	surprised	surprised	使吃驚；使感到意外
surrender	surrendered	surrendered	使投降；使自首
surround	surrounded	surrounded	圍繞；圈住
survey	surveyed	surveyed	檢視；調查
survive	survived	survived	在...之後仍然生存；從...中逃生
suspect	suspected	suspected	察覺；不信任
suspend	suspended	suspended	懸掛
sustain	sustained	sustained	支撐；承受；維持
swallow	swallowed	swallowed	吞下；嚥下
swamp	swamped	swamped	使陷入困境
swap	swapped	swapped	交換；以...作交換
swarm	swarmed	swarmed	擠滿
sway	swayed	swayed	搖動；搖擺
swear	swore	sworn	發誓；宣誓
sweat	sweated	sweated	出汗
sweep	swept	swept	清掃；打掃
swell	swelled	swollen	腫起；腫脹

附錄二 實用動詞三態表

swim	swam	swum	游泳
swing	swung	swung	搖擺；擺動
switch	switched	switched	打開或關掉開關；改變
symbolize	symbolized	symbolized	象徵
sympathize	sympathized	sympathized	同情；憐憫
T			
tack	tacked	tacked	用平頭釘釘
tackle	tackled	tackled	著手對付
tag	tagged	tagged	給...加標籤
tail	tailed	tailed	尾隨；盯梢
take	took	taken	拿；取
talk	talked	talked	講話；談話
tame	tamed	tamed	馴化；馴養
tan	tanned	tanned	使曬成棕褐色
tangle	tangled	tangled	使糾結；使糾纏
tap	tapped	tapped	輕拍；輕叩
tape	taped	taped	用膠布把...黏牢；用錄音帶為...錄音(或影)
tar	tarred	tarred	用焦油覆蓋
target	targeted	targeted	把...作為目標
taste	tasted	tasted	嚐；嚐到
taunt	taunted	taunted	辱罵；嘲笑
teach	taught	taught	教；講授；訓練
tear	tore	torn	撕開；撕裂
tease	teased	teased	戲弄；逗弄
telegraph	telegraphed	telegraphed	打電報給
telephone	telephoned	telephoned	打電話給
tell	told	told	告訴；講述

tempt	tempted	tempted	引誘；誘惑
tend	tended	tended	走向；趨向
terminate	terminated	terminated	使停止；使結束
terrify	terrified	terrified	使害怕；使恐怖
test	tested	tested	試驗；檢驗
thank	thanked	thanked	感謝
think	thought	thought	想；思索
thread	threaded	threaded	通過；穿過
threaten	threatened	threatened	威脅；恐嚇
thrill	thrilled	thrilled	使興奮；使緊張
thrive	thrived	thrived	興旺；繁榮
throb	throbbed	throbbed	跳動；悸動
throng	thronged	thronged	擠滿；湧入
throw	threw	thrown	投；擲；拋；扔
thrust	thrust	thrust	用力推
tickle	tickled	tickled	使發癢
tidy	tidied	tidied	收拾；整理
tie	tied	tied	繫；拴；捆；紮
tighten	tightened	tightened	使變緊；使繃緊
tilt	tilted	tilted	使傾斜；使翹起
time	timed	timed	測定...的時間
tiptoe	tiptoed	tiptoed	踮起腳走
tire	tired	tired	使疲倦
title	titled	titled	加標題於
toast	toasted	toasted	祝酒；敬酒
toil	toiled	toiled	苦幹
tolerate	tolerated	tolerated	忍受；容忍
top	topped	topped	高於；超過；勝過

附錄二 實用動詞三態表

topple	toppled	toppled	使倒塌；推翻；顛覆
torment	tormented	tormented	使痛苦；折磨
torture	tortured	tortured	拷打；拷問
toss	tossed	tossed	拋；扔；投
touch	touched	touched	接觸；碰到
tour	toured	toured	旅行；旅遊
tow	towed	towed	拖；拉；牽引
toy	toyed	toyed	玩弄；戲耍
trace	traced	traced	跟蹤；追蹤
track	tracked	tracked	跟蹤；追蹤
trade	traded	traded	交換；做買賣
trail	trailed	trailed	拖曳；跟蹤
tramp	tramped	tramped	腳步沈重地行走
trample	trampled	trampled	踐踏；蹂躪
transfer	transferred	transferred	搬；轉換；調動
transform	transformed	transformed	使改變；使轉變
transit	transited	transited	通過；運送
translate	translated	translated	翻譯；轉譯
transmit	transmitted	transmitted	傳送；傳達
transplant	transplanted	transplanted	移植；移種
transport	transported	transported	運送；運輸
trap	trapped	trapped	設陷阱；設圈套
travel	traveled	traveled	旅行；旅遊
tread	trod	trodden	踩；踏
treasure	treasured	treasured	珍愛；珍視
treat	treated	treated	對待；請客
trek	trekked	trekked	艱苦跋涉；緩慢地行進
tremble	trembled	trembled	發抖；震顫

附錄二 實用動詞三態表

trespass	trespassed	trespassed	擅自進入
trick	tricked	tricked	哄騙
trifle	trifled	trifled	閒混；浪費時間
trigger	triggered	triggered	扣扳機
trim	trimmed	trimmed	修剪；修整
trip	tripped	tripped	絆倒
triple	tripled	tripled	增至三倍
triumph	triumphed	triumphed	獲得勝利
trot	trotted	trotted	小跑；快步
trouble	troubled	troubled	使煩惱；使憂慮
trumpet	trumpeted	trumpeted	大聲宣告
trust	trusted	trusted	信任；信賴
try	tried	tried	試圖；努力
tuck	tucked	tucked	把...塞進；把...藏入
tug	tugged	tugged	用力拉（或拖）
tumble	tumbled	tumbled	跌倒；滾下；墜落
tune	tuned	tuned	使協調；使一致
tunnel	tunneled	tunneled	挖掘隧道
turn	turned	turned	使轉動；使旋轉
tutor	tutored	tutored	當家庭教師
twinkle	twinkled	twinkled	閃爍；閃耀
twist	twisted	twisted	扭轉；扭彎；旋轉
type	typed	typed	打字
U			
uncover	uncovered	uncovered	揭開...的蓋子
underestimate	underestimated	underestimated	低估
undergo	underwent	undergone	經歷；經受
underline	underlined	underlined	在...的下面劃線

附錄二　實用動詞三態表

undermine	undermined	undermined	暗中破壞；逐漸損害
understand	understood	understood	理解；懂
undertake	undertook	undertaken	試圖；著手做
undo	undid	undone	解開；打開
unfold	unfolded	unfolded	展開；攤開
unify	unified	unified	統一；聯合
unite	united	united	使聯合；統一
unlock	unlocked	unlocked	開...的鎖
unpack	unpacked	unpacked	打開包裹
update	updated	updated	使現代化；更新
upgrade	upgraded	upgraded	升級
uphold	upheld	upheld	舉起；高舉
upload	uploaded	uploaded	上傳
upset	upset	upset	弄翻；打翻
urge	urged	urged	催促；力勸
use	used	used	用；使用
usher	ushered	ushered	引領；招待
utilize	utilized	utilized	利用
utter	uttered	uttered	說；講；表達
V			
vacation	vacationed	vacationed	度假
vacuum	vacuumed	vacuumed	用吸塵器清掃
value	valued	valued	估價；重視
vary	varied	varied	變更；修改
veil	veiled	veiled	掩飾；遮蓋
vend	vended	vended	出售；販賣
venture	ventured	ventured	使冒險
verge	verged	verged	接近；瀕臨

veto	vetoed	vetoed	否決
vibrate	vibrated	vibrated	顫動；振動
victimize	victimized	victimized	使犧牲；使痛苦
view	viewed	viewed	觀看；查看
violate	violated	violated	違犯；違背
visit	visited	visited	參觀；拜訪
visualize	visualized	visualized	使形象化；想像
voice	voiced	voiced	表達；說出
volunteer	volunteered	volunteered	自願
vomit	vomited	vomited	嘔吐
vote	voted	voted	投票
vow	vowed	vowed	發誓要
W			
wade	waded	waded	涉水而行
wag	wagged	wagged	搖擺；搖動
wail	wailed	wailed	慟哭；嚎啕
wait	waited	waited	等待
waive	waived	waived	放棄；擱置
wake	waked	waken	醒來；醒著
waken	wakened	wakened	醒來；睡醒
walk	walked	walked	走；散步
wander	wandered	wandered	漫遊；閒逛
want	wanted	wanted	想要
warm	warmed	warmed	使暖和
warn	warned	warned	警告；告誡
wash	washed	washed	洗；洗滌
waste	wasted	wasted	浪費；濫用
watch	watched	watched	觀看；注視
water	watered	watered	給...澆水；灌溉

wave	waved	waved	對...揮
wax	waxed	waxed	給...上蠟
weaken	weakened	weakened	削弱；減弱
wear	wore	worn	穿著；戴著
weave	weaved	weaved	織；編
wed	wedded	wedded	娶嫁；與...結婚
weep	wept	wept	哭泣；流淚
weigh	weighed	weighed	稱...的重量
welcome	welcomed	welcomed	歡迎
wet	wetted	wetted	打濕；弄濕
wheel	wheeled	wheeled	突然轉變方向；轉彎
whine	whined	whined	嘀咕；發牢騷
whip	whipped	whipped	鞭笞；抽打
whirl	whirled	whirled	旋轉；迴旋
whisk	whisked	whisked	拂；輕抹
whisper	whispered	whispered	低語；耳語
whistle	whistled	whistled	吹口哨；鳴笛
wholesale	wholesaled	wholesaled	批發
widen	widened	widened	放寬；加寬
win	won	won	在...中獲勝
wind	wound	wound	轉動（把手）
wink	winked	winked	眨眼
wipe	wiped	wiped	擦乾；擦淨
wire	wired	wired	用電報發送
wish	wished	wished	想要；希望
withdraw	withdrew	withdrawn	抽回；拉開
wither	withered	withered	枯萎；乾枯
withhold	withheld	withheld	抑制；保留

withstand	withstood	withstood	抵擋；反抗
witness	witnessed	witnessed	目擊
wonder	wondered	wondered	納悶；想知道
woo	wooed	wooed	向...求愛
work	worked	worked	工作；勞動
worry	worried	worried	使擔心；使發愁
worship	worshiped	worshiped	崇拜；敬仰
wound	wounded	wounded	受傷
wrap	wrapped	wrapped	包裹
wreck	wrecked	wrecked	使失事；使遇難
wrench	wrenched	wrenched	猛扭；猛擰
wrestle	wrestled	wrestled	摔角
wring	wrung	wrung	絞；擰
wrinkle	wrinkled	wrinkled	使起皺紋
write	wrote	written	寫下；書寫
wrong	wronged	wronged	冤枉；委屈
X			
Xerox	Xeroxed	Xeroxed	複印
X-ray	X-rayed	X-rayed	用X光線檢查
Y			
yawn	yawned	yawned	打呵欠
yearn	yearned	yearned	思念；渴望
yell	yelled	yelled	叫喊；吼叫
yield	yielded	yielded	出產；結出
Z			
zip	zipped	zipped	拉開（扣上）拉鍊
zoom	zoomed	zoomed	發出嗡嗡聲；上升

附錄三 Word List

A

- □ accelerate
- □ accommodate
- □ accommodation
- □ accomplishment
- □ accounting
- □ accumulate
- □ achievement
- □ actually
- □ adapter
- □ adhere to
- □ adjust
- □ administrative
- □ advanc
- □ affect
- □ affirm
- □ affordable
- □ aggressive
- □ agreement
- □ agricultural
- □ alleviate
- □ allocate
- □ allow
- □ ambitious
- □ amusing
- □ anticipate
- □ apologize
- □ appendix
- □ applaud
- □ appliance
- □ appointment
- □ apprentice

- □ architect
- □ arrangement
- □ artificial
- □ asset
- □ assignment
- □ assist
- □ assistant
- □ assume
- □ assure
- □ attend
- □ attorney
- □ audit
- □ audition
- □ authorize

B

- □ background
- □ balance
- □ balcony
- □ bargain
- □ brochure
- □ burglar

C

- □ calculate
- □ calendar
- □ campaign
- □ cancel
- □ candidate
- □ capacity
- □ capital

- cargo
- celebrity
- Celsius
- circular
- circulation
- circumstance
- collision
- commercial
- compatible
- compensate
- competition
- competitor
- component
- compose
- comprehensive
- conference
- confidence
- confidential
- consequence
- consider
- consign
- construction
- consume
- contagious
- contract
- convince
- coordinate
- corporation
- credible
- credit
- cruise
- customs

D

- deadline
- dealer

- defect
- defense
- degree
- delivery
- demand
- department
- determine
- detour
- device
- diagnose
- dictate
- digest
- directory
- display
- distributor
- diversify
- dividend
- document
- drugstore
- duplicate
- durable

E

- editorial
- elaborate
- eligible
- emergency
- employee
- employer
- employment
- enhance
- entrepreneur
- escalator
- establish
- evaluate
- excursion

☐ executive
☐ exotic
☐ expedition
☐ expertise
☐ expire

F

☐ factory
☐ Fahrenheit
☐ feedback
☐ fluctuate
☐ flyer
☐ forecast
☐ foreign exchange
☐ forward
☐ fragrant
☐ franchise
☐ freight
☐ fuel
☐ furnishings

G

☐ garment
☐ gather
☐ guarantee

H

☐ haggle
☐ handicap
☐ headquarters
☐ hire

I

☐ immune
☐ improve

☐ include
☐ indemnity
☐ infection
☐ innovative
☐ interrupt
☐ intersection
☐ invest
☐ investigator
☐ itinerary

J

☐ joint venture

K

☐ kitchenware

L

☐ laboratory
☐ landlord
☐ laundromat
☐ laundry
☐ leaflet
☐ librarian

M

☐ mandatory
☐ manipulate
☐ manufacture
☐ marketing
☐ mattress
☐ memorandum
☐ menu
☐ merit
☐ mortgage
☐ motivate

附錄三 Word List

N
- navigate
- negotiate
- notify
- novice
- nutrition

O
- occupy
- offer
- operate
- operator
- opportunity
- ornament
- outage
- outlet

P
- participate
- partition
- party
- pastime
- patron
- payment
- pedestrian
- penalty
- pension
- periodical
- permanent
- personalize
- pharmacist
- pharmacy
- possession
- postage
- premiere

- premium
- produce
- profession
- prohibit
- promote
- proofread
- prosperity
- provide
- provision
- publicity
- punctual
- purchase
- purify
- pushcart

Q
- quota

R
- real estate
- recognition
- recommendation
- record
- reduce
- referee
- rehearsal
- reinforce
- relocate
- remove
- renovate
- representative
- reputation
- request
- resolve
- retailer

□ retrieval
□ revenue
□ revise
□ risk
□ round trip
□ rural

S

□ sample
□ satellite
□ scenario
□ scrutiny
□ secretary
□ seminar
□ ship
□ sightseeing
□ situation
□ software
□ stadium
□ static
□ storage
□ store
□ strike
□ stroke
□ subsidiary
□ substitute
□ suburbs
□ supervise
□ surplus
□ survey
□ symphony
□ system

T

□ tactic

□ tag
□ tariff
□ technical
□ trademark
□ transaction
□ transform
□ transit
□ translation
□ tremendous
□ triumph
□ trophy
□ troubleshooting
□ turnover

V

□ vacancy
□ valid
□ variety
□ vehicle
□ venue
□ vital
□ voucher

W

□ waive
□ warehouse
□ warning
□ wholesale
□ withhold
□ workshop

X

□ Xerox

♥ 新多益 001

NEW TOEIC 黃金戰鬥力—閱讀篇
Tactics for NEW TOEIC Reading Test
—— 一個月掌握商用必備單字及考試技巧，目標990

作　　者 / 徐維克＆麥禾陽光編輯部
總 編 輯 / Estelle Chen
特約編輯 / 林怡璇
外籍顧問 / Mark Venekamp & Melanie Allen
封面設計 / 陳小KING
內頁構成 / 麥禾陽光文化出版社
圖片出處 / www.dreamstime.com
印　　製 / 世和印製企業有限公司
出　　版 / 麥禾陽光文化出版社
總 經 銷 / 易可數位行銷股份有限公司
地　　址 / 231 新北市新店區寶橋路 235 巷 6 弄 3 號 5 樓
電　　話 / (02) 8911-0825
傳　　真 / (02) 8911-0801
初　　版 / 2013 年 11 月
定　　價 / 新台幣 399 元

國家圖書館出版品預行編目 (CIP) 資料

NEW TOEIC 黃金戰鬥力—閱讀篇 / 徐維克＆麥禾
　陽光編輯部著.
　初版. -- 新北市：麥禾陽光文化, 2013.11
　面；　　公分
　ISBN 978-986-89735-3-4（平裝附光碟片）

　1. 多益測驗

805.1895　　　　　　　　　　　　　102020302

麥禾陽光 Sun&Wheat

一個溫暖、高質感、充滿趣味的閱讀環境，
帶給讀者一個全然不同的學習感受。

麥禾陽光 Sun&Wheat

一個溫暖、高質感、充滿趣味的閱讀環境，
帶給讀者一個全然不同的學習感受。